Praise for *Born of Persuasion*

"An intrepid heroine falling for two different men; a plot brimming with secrets, scandal, and suspense; and a richly atmospheric setting are the key ingredients in the first novel in Dotta's Price of Privilege trilogy. Readers who miss Victoria Holt will swoon with delight upon discovering this retro-gothic winner."

BOOKLIST

"With crossover appeal for mainstream historical romance fans of Victoria Holt, Dotta's debut novel will have readers demanding book two immediately."

LIBRARY JOURNAL

"I was delighted, enthralled, and utterly captivated by the way Jessica Dotta cleverly mixed a cast of Austen-like characters into a creative Charlotte-Brontë-meets-Victoria-Holt setting. . . . With twists, turns, and a hopeful ending that leaves so very much to be resolved, *Born of Persuasion* will no doubt make my list of top favorite debuts this year."

SERENA CHASE
USA Today

"Dotta's new series . . . has something for all fans of this time period: romance, family secrets, overbearing guardians, and even a little laughter. The characters are well-rounded and the author's research on the setting shines through."

ROMANTIC TIMES

"The best Christian fiction I've read in a very long time. . . . [It] perfectly blends mystery, drama, heartbreak, and romance with just a touch of sermonizing. I believe this book could be in the running for one of my favorite Christian books of the decade."

RADIANT LIT

"Absolutely entertaining and brilliantly written, with lovable flawed characters. Jane Austen fans will love this instant classic that dropped me into all the richness of the Victorian era. I highly recommend this book for a great read and a book club pick."

THE SUSPENSE ZONE

"*Born of Persuasion* is the sort of book in which readers of historical fiction long to lose themselves: rich with period detail and full of intrigue and deception. Fans of Philippa Gregory and Sarah Dunant will fall in love with this arresting story."

TASHA ALEXANDER
New York Times bestselling author

"With a voice you'll love, Jessica Dotta paints a vivid portrait in words, drawing her readers through an unexpected maze of plot twists. *Born of Persuasion* is a story of betrayal and perseverance, rich with unforgettable characters."

CINDY WOODSMALL
New York Times bestselling author of *The Winnowing Season*

"A fascinating cast of characters and breathless twists and turns make this story anything but predictable. Mystery and romance, sins of the past and fears of the future all combine for a page-turning experience."

LIZ CURTIS HIGGS
New York Times bestselling author of *Mine is the Night*

"*Born of Persuasion* is among the best novels I've ever read. This allegory is beautifully developed and the story descriptive, suspenseful, and absolutely captivating. Not since *Jane Eyre* have I wanted to reread a story again and again."

GINA HOLMES

bestselling author of *Crossing Oceans*

"Filled with romantic twists, social intrigue, and beautiful writing, Dotta's *Born of Persuasion* is an alluring debut that will leave fans of Victorian fiction clamoring for more."

TOSCA LEE

New York Times bestselling author

"Jessica Dotta is this generation's Jane Austen but with a twenty-first-century voice, and *Born of Persuasion* is a riveting saga that will keep you turning page after page."

ANE MULLIGAN

President of *Novel Rocket*

❖⦑ MARK OF DISTINCTION ⦒❖

MARK

of

Distinction

Tyndale House Publishers, Inc., Carol Stream, Illinois

JESSICA
DOTTA

From one Sissee to another With Love, Marianne 6/5/16

Visit Tyndale online at www.tyndale.com.

Visit Jessica Dotta's website at www.jessicadotta.com.

The author is represented by Chip MacGregor of MacGregor Literary Inc., 2373 NW 185th Avenue, Suite 165, Hillsboro, OR 97124.

Scripture quotations are taken from the *Holy Bible*, King James Version.

"Can a Maid That Is Well Bred," by Martin Peerson, is quoted in chapter 16.

Mark of Distinction is a work of fiction. Where real people, events, establishments, organizations, or locales appear, they are used fictitiously. All other elements of the novel are drawn from the author's imagination.

Library of Congress Cataloging-in-Publication Data

Dotta, Jessica.
   Mark of Distinction / Jessica Dotta.
      pages cm.—(Price of Privilege Trilogy ; 2)
    ISBN 978-1-4143-7556-4 (sc)
1. Heiresses—Fiction. 2. Upper class—England—London—Fiction. 3. London (England)—History—19th century—Fiction. 4. Christian fiction. I. Title.
   PS3604.O87M37 2014
   813'.6—dc23   2013050943

Printed in the United States of America

20   19   18   17   16   15   14
7   6   5   4   3   2   1

For my grandmother:

Mildred Frances Rohrer

One

THE EIGHT MONTHS following my arrival at Maplecroft have been called one of the greatest cozenages of our age. My father and I have endured endless speculation as to the number of hours poured into its plan and execution.

Truth comprised of bare facts is rarely more flattering than legend. In reality, our sham was little more than a mad-dash scramble of one improvisation after another. Events kept unfolding, forcing us to take new action, making it impossible to steer from collision.

I am an old woman now. Ancient some days. I had no idea my story would cause such an uproar. When I first penned it, my only intent was to address the rumors of how the entire affair started. I was weary of hearing how *I* seduced Mr. Macy. As if *I*, or anyone, could. The very idea is laughable. Long life has its advantages. Your perception grows clearer, even if your sight dims. How much better I now understand the shock Lady Foxmore must have felt during our presentation. Her pretension was unequalled. Yet there I stood, a pale, scrawny girl in rags, chosen by one of the most illustrious men in her circle to be wed to him. It is no wonder she thought it a grand jest. How could she, or anyone who knew Macy intimately, have guessed just how resolute he was upon marrying me?

Since my story's publication, I have been accused of besmirching the innocent by fabricating events to gain public sympathy. Some have pointed out that I unfairly suggest Mr. Macy is responsible for Churchill's murder. They remind me that it is a documented fact that the culprit, an unstable man, was apprehended—and that it's nothing more than coincidence Churchill's death occurred on the same day Mr. Macy collected me.

Others state that if I were truly innocent, then how is it that my story escalated to treason and then ended so tragically?

It is this last challenge that causes me unrest. I cannot recount the mornings I've stood before my window, debating whether it is best to allow the matter to rest or to persevere and tell the tale in its entirety. I've wrestled with my conscience, wondering what good revealing all would do. Shall I so easily expose the sins of my father? Like Ham, shall I peel back the tent flap that covers his nakedness to the world? Will it bring back the dead?

It was only this morning, as I turned to retreat to my favorite chair, that I was decided. I caught sight of my paternal grand-mother, Lady Josephine, watching me. She is ageless, of course, forever capturing the bloom of our youth. As I paused and stud-ied her painting, my great-grandchildren rushed past my win-dow, tripping on their own merry shrieks. They fell in a muddle in the middle of the grounds and then, just for the glory of it, lay on their backs, spread their arms, and laughed.

I chuckled, imagining their incredulousness were they to learn my frolics were once as madcap as theirs. Lady Josephine also watched with her ever-present, coy smile. For some rea-son it brought to mind how her portrait gave me strength during those long months with my father. Something about her smile used to assure me that her antics were equally mischievous. I regret that I will never learn about them.

It is this thought that decides me.

I will for my grandchildren and great-grandchildren to know me.

Not the version they'll find archived in the newspapers. Heaven forbid they search there! I care not to contemplate the opinions they'd form. No, I will write this wrong. Let them at least judge me by truth, though who can say whether it makes me less of a culprit. Let the world think what it will. I am far too old to care, anyway. I am past the point of cowing to opinions.

It all began, of course, with my father.

Not my stepfather, William Elliston, who I believed, until that devastating night I wed Mr. Macy, had begotten me.

But Lord Pierson himself.

The second time I laid eyes on him was on my eighteenth birthday.

Mama had always made a secret celebration of that date, sneaking into my chamber before dawn. The scent of lilac clung to her rustling skirts as she'd motion me to make room for her to climb into my bed.

"You were born at this very hour." Her voice could soothe even the darkness as she settled into the down pillows.

On every birthday, even until my seventeenth, I was wont to curl against her, resting my head against her collarbone, where I listened to her heart. Rare were the moments we were granted a respite. I have little doubt we both savored those mornings.

"The sun had just peeked over the hillocks outside my window," Mama would continue, intertwining our fingers. "I was exhausted, and by the looks the midwife and Sarah exchanged, I knew they believed it was hopeless." Here, determination coated Mama's voice as if she were reliving the moment. "I fastened my gaze on that tiny flush of light and swore by the time the sun was fully risen, you'd be born. You were the only family I had left, and I wasn't about to allow either one of us to die."

I always held my breath, hoping she'd elaborate. Those birthday moments were the closest Mama ever came to speaking about her past.

"You were born just as the sun crested the horizon. Your wail was the loudest the midwife had ever heard. She nearly dropped you in surprise. Here, she thought you'd be stillborn, but you came out kicking and screaming."

Next, she'd splay her hand against mine, palm against palm, measuring my growth. It seems odd now that on my seventeenth birthday—my last birthday with Mama—our hands were exactly the same size.

"I counted your fingers and toes, over and over. You were so tiny and perfect." Even as a child I noted how her chest would rise in a silent sigh before saying, "Your father came that night. He burst through the doors and looked wildly about the room for you. He, also, marveled over you. And he, too, counted your toes and fingers over and over, as if the number would change."

Though I never had a chance to tell her, those birthday mornings were the most treasured part of my splintered childhood.

Thus for me to rise on my eighteenth birthday in order to watch the coming dawn was the most costly tribute I could pay her. It fractured me. Yet failing to honor Mama would have felt worse.

Wind shook the windowpanes as I stumbled from the bed and groped in the semidark for matches. The odor of phosphorus filled the air as I lit candles along the mantel.

During the night, the fire had burned into ashes, leaving my room so cold it hurt my throat to breathe the wintry air. I rubbed my hands over my arms as I went to my father's late wife's wardrobe and selected a thick shawl.

I glanced at the fireplace as I passed it again, wondering why the servants had not kept the fires lit. Never having lived in a great house, it was impossible to tell if the fault was the staff's or mine. It was just as likely I'd forgotten to give the necessary instruction as it was that some servant had neglected her duty.

Regardless of the reason, the timing could not have been worse. The freezing temperature served to sharpen the harrowing sensation that Mama was truly gone.

I turned my gaze toward the clock and estimated it to be about a half hour before sunrise. I knew that if I returned to the warmth of bed, I risked falling asleep and missing daybreak. Uncertain what else to do, I retreated to the window seat and brushed aside the heavy lace hanging before the window.

Though it was early morning, pewter-grey clouds layered the sky. Only traces of the previous night's snow remained on the ground, tucked amongst the roots of oak trees and glistening between the crags of rocks. A solitary snowflake floated down from the leaden sky. Like me, it didn't seem to belong anywhere but drifted from one spot to another, never quite landing. With numb fingers, I clutched my shawl closer and rested my head against the window.

"I'm here, Mama," I whispered, hoping to feel her presence.

But I felt nothing. All evidence of Mama had been successfully scrubbed from my life. Even the nightmares of her screaming warnings to me from across a chasm had stopped. My fingertips curled against the empty space near my collarbone. I hadn't even managed to keep her locket a full year. Was it only last year that she'd given me the gold necklace containing her and William's likeness? With a splurge of self-pity, I realized I still needed Mama. I wanted her to stroke and kiss my brow, telling me she hadn't been murdered, and I hadn't married her murderer. I wanted to be home, which no longer existed because Mr. Macy gave it away to prevent me from hiding from him there.

I swallowed, but it was too late. I choked out a ragged gasp before I hastily wiped my wet eyes with the hem of the shawl.

Refusing to cry further, I shifted position on the window seat and forced myself to find new occupation. Wind scattered the snow crusting the bare trees, creating a mist that waned the view where the sun worked to rise. I waited until it dissipated, then traced the grove of staggering hemlocks that filled the ravine separating my father's Maplecroft estate and the adjoining property. As if drawn against my will, I followed the course all the way to Eastbourne.

Smoke curled from the tall chimneys of Mr. Macy's vast estate, spreading ash over snow-strewn roofs, where gargoyles hunched beneath snowy capes. It appeared serene, betraying nothing of the evil that lurked there. Everything familiar to me had been stripped away within those walls, where I'd spent a week of my life . . . and betrayed Edward by trusting Mr. Macy and marrying him instead. I touched the cold pane, my stomach hollowing as I wondered if he knew yet that I was hiding from him in plain view.

As the sky grew pearlier, it became easier to see Macy's servants scurrying over the grounds, shoveling snow and attending to their duties. It was impossible to imagine that only a fortnight ago I had been amongst them, my heart soaring with the intrigue.

That period of time stood in stark contrast to the time I'd spent in my father's house.

For eight days I'd not encountered a soul, except for the timid maid who crept soundlessly into my chamber to kindle my fire and dress me. Heartsick after Edward's departure, I'd wandered aimlessly through empty rooms and echoing marble halls. My first morning alone, I'd searched the estate looking for private nooks I could duck into to read or sew if I needed solitude. I wanted time to heal and to sort through my emotions. Yet as I took each meal alone and passed hours in silence, straining to catch the sound of another's voice, I learned my search had been unwarranted. No one would disturb me. The entire estate seemed under a deep freeze, waiting for its thaw, and I'd been swallowed by its vastness.

As if to combat the thought, a warm, glowing orb of light suddenly reflected in the window. I turned in time to see Mrs. Coleman, the housekeeper of Maplecroft, entering my chamber, carrying a whale-oil lamp. The white fabric that crisscrossed her bodice showed traces of ash, revealing she'd tended duties uncommon for a housekeeper. Her eyes widened in dismay when she noted me awake. Her next thought was apparent by the despairing look she gave my empty grate.

She placed the lamp aside and straightened her shoulders. "I beg your pardon, Miss Pierson. Seven of my girls are down with a wicked chest cold. Not that it is a proper excuse, mind you."

The name Miss Pierson chafed me like carpenter's paper and made me feel as twisted as the touchwood used to light the fire. I hated allowing the staff to believe I was Lord Pierson's legitimate daughter, but until my father returned, I wasn't certain how to conduct myself.

The housekeeper cocked her eyebrows, waiting.

I frowned, feeling as though I were committing a great social blunder. Yet for the life of me, I couldn't think of how the mistress of an estate would handle such a matter. Several replies came to mind, but somehow they all felt wrong.

Apparently silence was equally appalling, for Mrs. Coleman snapped her eyes shut and gave a quick shake of her head as if to ask what they were teaching young ladies these days. When she opened her eyes again, I had little doubt as to the true mistress of Maplecroft.

"Naturally—" she stepped smartly into the chamber, the keys at her hip jangling sharply—"you wish to know whether I've summoned the apothecary and whether any of Eaton's staff is down, as well. I'm assured that at least two of the girls will be on their feet tomorrow. William, our second, has the malady, but

James is managing quite well by himself. Some of the grooms are starting to look feverish, but that shouldn't inconvenience your father when he returns home tonight."

Eaton's name I recognized as the butler's. I had only just worked out that William was a footman, because James was, when my mind seized upon Mrs. Coleman's last statement. I rose to my feet. "Did you say that my father is expected tonight?"

"That I did. 'Tis just like him too. Changing plans and returning home with a guest right in the middle of a grippe outbreak."

I gathered and pulled my hair over my shoulder as dread tingled through my body.

"You don't look well yourself." Mrs. Coleman approached and touched my forehead with the back of her fingers. "Well, at least you're cool to the touch. Nonetheless, you need to eat better. You're thinner than is healthy. You had naught yesterday except that bite of porridge and biscuit."

I gawked, envisioning members of the staff spying on me through keyholes. I had been certain I was alone when I only managed one swallow of gruel. I'd pushed the entire tray away, missing Edward too keenly to eat. Had they watched while I cried too?

"Here now, there's no need to appear shocked." Mrs. Coleman maneuvered to the hearth. "Since you arrived, the staff has been barmy with talk of you." She paused to meet my eye. "Not that I've allowed it, mind you."

Her nonchalance gave me pause. I now couldn't decide whether I had been spied upon, or if she generally meant I barely touched the tray that was delivered to my room.

"I've been waiting for you to find your way to my room," she said. "I warrant at your school they placed great emphasis on the importance of keeping a distinction between yourself and your staff. If you were to ask my opinion on it, I would tell you it was stuff and nonsense. Maplecroft, 'tis a lonely house to become acquainted with, to be sure. Your mother wasn't above coming to my rooms and visiting me, let me tell you. You would find me grateful for the occasional visit."

Her speech awoke a myriad of reactions within me, so that each word spiralled my thoughts in a different direction. It stunned me to learn that the staff had interpreted my isolation as pretentiousness. Had they expected me to seek them out, to take interest and assign them their duties? I had no right to do so, not at least until I saw my father. For I wasn't entirely certain he wouldn't ship me off somewhere. I hadn't forgotten that before the entire affair started, he'd planned to tuck me out of sight by sending me to Scotland as a servant. Lastly, the manner in which the housekeeper took it upon herself to lecture reminded me greatly of Nancy. My throat tightened, and my homesickness crested as I wondered what happened to my outspoken lady's maid.

Thankfully, Mrs. Coleman had her back to me and therefore didn't witness my struggle to hold back emotions. She knelt over the grate, raking the ashes.

"I always keep a cake in my shelf," she continued. "If you like, you are invited to join me for tea in the late afternoons. You may sit in my overstuffed chair and confide all your little secrets to me. I should rather enjoy that."

I crossed my arms, wondering what she'd do if I actually took up her offer and confided all. I allowed myself a wry smile as I imagined her too shocked to speak.

"You'll find that Master Isaac doesn't consider it below his station to come and visit me. I daresay you can trust him to determine what is right and proper, far above any nonsense your school taught you." Using tongs, she lifted the half-burnt coals from the ash and deposited them into a nearby scuttle.

I frowned, not certain who Master Isaac was, but then recalled Lord Dalry, the gentleman who'd greeted Edward and me the night we arrived.

The dull chimes of a grandfather clock sounded, filling the chamber and reminding me of my mission. I retreated back to the window. The sun had nearly risen, giving the sky a rosy tincture. With dismay, I glanced at Mrs. Coleman as she started the fire, then cast my gaze outdoors. I desired to be alone, yet there was no polite way to dismiss her midtask.

The sunrise was beautiful. Tones of gold highlighted the claret color, making the sky incarnadine. I ached, uncertain what to make of its beauty. How could the most resplendent sunrise of my life simultaneously be the most painful?

Yet as I considered the complex layers of color and light, I better understood Mama's determination that first morning. She, too, had lost her entire world. She had to fight and remain determined in order to give birth. To thrive after tragedy, one must find and draw from a pool of strength deep within oneself. Mama must have found hers that morning in me.

I gave a deep sigh, resting my head against the window frame. A newborn daughter, however, was more likely to give someone an iron will than a powerful father. Something about that thought surfaced another part of the story, which Mama had mentioned only once. I was perhaps seven or eight. After she'd described my father counting my fingers and toes, she tacked on, "I never saw a grown man weep over his child before, but your father held you against his chest and expressed such raw emotion that Sarah feared he'd drop you in his remorse."

That year, I had wrinkled my nose. If William had been weeping at the end of a long night, then he was inebriated. Even at that tender age, I could well guess he'd hidden in a pub during Mama's labor. It also stood to reason that he probably slept at the tavern, woke, and started drinking again. Knowing William's temperament, I was displeased that Mama and Sarah had allowed him to handle an infant.

But as I stood there, feeling the cold bleed through the window, I suddenly guessed the truth, and tingles spread over my body. Mama had not been speaking about William, but Lord Pierson.

I held my breath. If my father came to see me on the morning of my birth, then I mattered to him. I raised my gaze, savoring the feeling of hope that surged through me. Perhaps it didn't matter that our first meeting last month had been horrid, or why I was at Maplecroft pleading for sanctuary. All that counted was what happened next.

"'Tis a grave view, that," Mrs. Coleman said behind me, nearing me.

I had been so deep in thought, I'd nearly forgotten I wasn't alone.

She joined me at the window and frowned, glancing toward Eastbourne. "There's something evil about this, if you ask me. A bad omen, for certain."

I felt my mouth dry as I turned to look at her.

She pulled the bundle of bedclothes in her arms tighter. "Mark my words: 'twill be the coldest winter yet. Snow in October! I've been in this shire for over twenty years, with nary a snowflake before January, much less a storm."

I released a shaky breath. "You . . . you meant the snow?"

She glanced in my direction. "Whatever else could I have meant?"

Without my permission, my eyes strayed to Eastbourne.

"Humph," she said, following my gaze, then set aside her linens. With the air of a prim nanny, she surveyed Eastbourne. "Mr. Chance Reginald Macy," she finally said with distaste. "I take it you've followed his dreadful scandal in the paper, then?" She shook her head disapprovingly, the ruffles on her cap bobbing before she stalked to the wardrobe. "Best not let your father hear. He would not approve of your reading such trash. If you ask me, that girl ought to be horsewhipped within an inch of her life. Mind you, I'd like to be the first one who gives her a dressing-down. I can assure you, she'd know her duty when I finished with her."

Feeling my face grow hot, I turned my back to her. Since my arrival, I'd only glanced at the various newspapers delivered each day, never suspecting that Macy was keeping our scandal alive. I swallowed, realizing that he was still searching for me—or at least pretending to.

The heavy scent of perfume coated the room as she dug through my father's late wife's dresses. "As for him, he ought to feel the fool for allowing someone half his age to seduce him. Had he enough self-pride, he would have better sense than to keep adding to the fire, pleading for her return. He's the same age as your father, you know. Can you imagine your father making such a tomfool of himself over a girl your age? I remember a time when the two of them would ride and hunt together. The year before Mr. Macy left for Eton, he and your father were inseparable."

"They were?" Surprised by this information, I turned and studied her face. The crow's-feet that lined her eyes suggested she was only a decade older than Mrs. Windham. She'd have been too young to be a housekeeper back then, which meant she'd have been an upper maid. "What happened?"

She paused and a thoughtful expression crossed her face, as if she were reliving scenes from the past. Then all at once, she tsked. "There's no sense asking me. I was never given knowledge of the affair. Your father spent that following summer in Bath, and we scarcely saw him. Something happened there that caused the pair to fall out."

Now this bit of news interested me. Mama's past was a mysterious maze, of which I'd only learned one or two turns. One of those paths had come from Lady Foxmore. During our first tea, she stated that she'd chaperoned Mama in Bath the summer after Mama's family perished in a fire. I bit my lip as Mrs. Coleman rifled through dresses. Was it possible it was the same summer that drove a wedge between my father and Mr. Macy?

"Here. This ought to fit." Mrs. Coleman withdrew a scarlet

brocade gown. "It's none of my business, mind you, but for your mother's sake, I intend to give your father a piece of my tongue about the condition of your clothing when you arrived. I won't argue the good of teaching someone of your rank humility, but to keep her dressed in rag—" She stopped short as if recalling whom she addressed.

I pretended to view the grounds again, wanting to kick myself for showing interest in Mr. Macy. Though my common sense had been a bit woolly from the brandy, I still recalled Mr. Macy's words: *"More than one of your guardian's servants is loyal to me. I've been intercepting all correspondence involving you since your mother's death."*

I crossed my arms, willing myself not to panic, either. Thus far nothing had happened.

"What time does my father arrive?" I asked.

"Likely as not, sometime after gloaming, but with him, there's no telling," was Mrs. Coleman's stout reply as she unfolded and refolded petticoats, looking for one that would fit. "I'll have to hire girls from the village to have things readied on time. It's a blessing he didn't surprise us, considering the state of the house."

Her statement was so curious, my mouth twisted in a queer smile. I'd never seen as much as a speck of dust in the entire estate.

Aware my father could return any minute, I glanced at the clock. After Mrs. Coleman left my chambers, she wasn't likely to have the time to assist me later. If I wanted to present my best, I needed to hasten.

While Mrs. Coleman shook out the clothing she'd selected, I opened the small china boxes, looking for face powder to hide the crescents beneath my eyes. Scents of oil of tartar and almond rose from various creams, but I found no white powder. In my fumbling, one of the bottles of fragrance spilled, filling the air with rose water.

Mrs. Coleman eyed the spill as she approached, her mouth tightening. "Never mind it; I'll tend to it as you put these on."

While Mrs. Coleman pressed a linen towel against the spill, I shed the nightdress and donned petticoats too large for my frame. Shivering, I stepped into the satin gown that felt soaked in cold.

When I finished, Mrs. Coleman smoothed my hair with pomade, parted it down the middle, and completed it with a simple braid.

"With your permission, I'd like to take my leave now," she said, setting the brush down.

"Oh yes, yes," I said. "Feel free."

Her eyebrows rose as though she was surprised by my unorthodox dismissal. Nonetheless, she dipped and left with the laundry bundled against her hip.

Alone, I pulled out the pins from her hairstyle, changed my part and redistributed the pins into a more flattering style, then studied the girl in the looking glass. I heaved a sigh. I looked like a forlorn child in an oversized ruffled dress, and without Nancy, my hair lacked luster.

Even so, I was determined to be the first to greet my father.

Had I known who my father's guest was, I doubt I should have bothered.

Two

NEWS OF MY FATHER'S arrival was like a spring storm sweeping over a sere landscape, leaving verdant buds in its wake. During his absence, the brumal estate had been entombed in silence, but now it rang with life. Footsteps clattered in corridors, deliveries were made by townsmen, groundskeepers ran past windows, and smoke from the kitchen curled with greater measure into the crisp air. For the first time since Edward's departure, I finally managed glimpses of the upper maids as they bustled feverishly with pails of water, carpet beaters, and rattling coal scuttles, though they did their best to avoid me, scurrying like frightened hares down the nearest passages.

Eaton's staff likewise raced about the estate pell-mell, their eyes bright and their cheeks ruddy. Whenever they chanced upon me, instead of hiding, they bowed with such relish anyone would think they enjoyed the impossible task of burnishing an already-calendered house.

Eaton and Mrs. Coleman, too, flew about like color sergeants rallying their troops. They barked orders, inspected chambers, crawled to see beneath furniture, and measured the distances between footstools and chairs. I watched the fervor through the balustrades in the upper hall, until Mrs. Coleman upbraided a girl for missing a wilted petal in one of the flower arrangements. My stomach tightening, I quietly rose and retreated to my chamber.

There, I spent hours practicing various greetings before the ornate looking glass. I lacked the social graces my counterparts possessed, for Mama was far more concerned with deflecting William's temper than overseeing my comportment. Nevertheless, I rarely felt my deficiency. It was easy enough to compensate by imitating others.

Yet whom could I imitate?

In my village no young lady of rank graced us with her presence. My only memorable observations of a peered father-and-daughter pair had occurred in the marketplace near Am Meer during my stays with my dearest friend, Elizabeth. A carriage bearing an insignia rumbled between the buildings, causing heads to turn. When the door opened, a dainty, silken foot emerged, followed by a well-dressed young lady and her father. Elizabeth cocked an eyebrow at me, the signature mischievous look that always warned me we were about to get into trouble. Though Mrs. Windham had bid us to hasten our return, as Hannah needed the milled flour, it was a rarity to observe someone arrayed as beautifully as this girl. How could we not remain a little longer?

The pair was mesmerizing, particularly the girl. Sapphire feathers whirled about her face, accenting piles of jetty ringlets. Her dress, a brilliant bone-colored satin, fell behind her in magnificent folds, reminding me of the heavy tail of a peacock. When a group of cottage children, ten or twelve winters old, shyly offered her violets, her father beamed. Yet I noted how the girl's eyes narrowed and her smile froze with annoyance.

"Who is she?" I asked Elizabeth.

She shook her head, eyeing her in distaste. "Never seen her before. Why do you suppose she's here?"

Instead of answering, I studied the girl's miffed expression, which suddenly transformed. Clinging to her father's arm, she dimpled and tossed her curls as she bounced on her toes, pointing to Anne Goodman's stall, where a tatted lace parasol hung. "Oh, Papa, look! Can we buy it? Millicent has one similar, but that one is twice as lovely. Oh, please!"

Her father in turn preened his moustache, pretending to debate the purchase that he obviously planned to make.

"Fancy him not seeing through that act," Elizabeth murmured.

I watched the girl's rapturous face as the merchant opened the canopy and showed off her handiwork. Elizabeth frowned, and I knew it was because she'd been secretly saving for the item for months. To cheer her, I gave her a teasing jab with my elbow. "You don't suppose they're here to court Henry, do you?"

Elizabeth's mouth widened in a genuine smile as her eyes lit with pleasure. "I'd like to see her try."

I laughed, envisioning the story that Edward and Henry would carry back to us of how they handled the situation. If anything was stable in this world, it was our foursome.

Elizabeth's brow furrowed for a moment before she spoke. "Lady Foxmore is in residence this week. Do you suppose they are here for her ladyship's matchmaking services?"

I studied the girl with a newfound respect. "If so, then we might well be looking at a future duchess. It's not hard to imagine her at a court ball, is it?"

When Elizabeth made no comment, I turned and found her expression wistful. As I followed the line of her gaze, it wasn't directed at the parasol. Instead she studied the gentleman as he shook his small purse, looking for the correct coinage for the purchase. He nearly burst with pride as he pressed the coins into Anne Goodman's hungry palm.

I understood Elizabeth's sentiment better than I desired to. Neither one of us would ever know a father's approval. Trying to mask my own pain, I nudged her as the pair turned toward their carriage. "Come on, let's go see how much Anne made. Knowing her, I warrant they paid London prices."

Elizabeth shook off her trance. "'Tis a mercy, too. Just yesterday I overheard her state she wasn't sure how she was going to pay next month's bills."

As I had not yet experienced a widow's plight, her statement failed to evoke any emotion other than relief that Mama and I weren't in Anne Goodman's position. As we approached, however, hot anger sparked through me. Near Anne's stall, a gleaming snippet of purple velvet caught my eye. While Elizabeth chatted with the widow, I bent and studied the tiny bouquet of violets smashed onto the cobblestone. To my complete disbelief, the muddied footprint outlining the crushed flowers was slipper-size. It wasn't enough that the girl had to dispose of the unwelcome gift, but she'd felt the need to tread on it.

My gaze could have scorched her as her father assisted her into the carriage. My fingers curled into fists as I wondered if he had any sense of his daughter's true nature. With my foot, I nudged the violets beneath the wooden booth lest the girls learn how completely they'd been scorned.

My thoughts lingered on that incident as I waited for my father, practicing one curtsy after another. It was impossible not to feel I was somehow wronging Elizabeth. Her father died before she was born, and it wasn't likely her future father-in-law would accept her. It struck me, during that long afternoon, that as Lord Pierson's offspring, Edward's father could not easily reject me now. It hardly seemed fair to Elizabeth. I was now positioned to gain not only a father, but also the acceptance of the man we both hoped would become our father-in-law.

The longer I thought about it, the more blameworthy I felt. If anyone deserved such a twist of fate, it was Elizabeth and not

I. By late afternoon, each time I lifted my face to the mirror,
I caught glimpses of guilt.

〜〜

Well after dusk, the weary staff had trudged belowstairs, freed
from their tasks while mine lay ahead of me. I took up residence
in the front parlor, where Eaton surprised me with a tea service for one. I eyed the delicate silver teapot and extravagant
cup with appreciation. A cluster of paperwhites curled over
its pearl-handled utensils. Barley and currant scones sat on a
dainty, footed dish.

"It was Lady Pierson's favorite service," he said, setting
it down. "You scarcely touched your dinner. Mrs. Coleman
thought plainer fare might suit you."

I hid my surprise that he'd used Lady Pierson's title, rather
than calling her my mother. "It is very kind. Thank you."

Instead of leaving, Eaton pressed his lips briefly together,
then asked, "What time shall we have the maid light the fire in
your chambers?"

"The fire?" I repeated, confused.

"Yes, what time should I tell Mrs. Coleman you plan on
retiring?"

All at once I understood and envisioned the scene below me.
I pictured them around a long table, too fatigued to eat their
dinner. Doubtless they were spent, especially with so many of
the staff taken ill. It wasn't difficult to imagine Mrs. Coleman,
sitting with her aching feet propped up on a chair, her stockings
rolled just below her knees. "Use tea as an excuse," I imagined
her saying. "There's extra scones in the larder. But for heaven's
sake, find out what she intends to do."

I hated the idea of costing the staff precious hours of slumber, especially after their scramble to ready Maplecroft. Yet at
the same time, I had to hide my annoyance. Though most of
my memories of Eastbourne elicited a queer intermingling of

emotions, Reynolds had been nothing but kind; he never would have pressured me like this. In order to appear nonchalant while I thought out the problem, I leaned over the flowers and breathed their scent. I nearly coughed from their stench.

"Also Lady Pierson's favorite." Eaton bowed.

Wondering if the disliking of paperwhites was hereditary, I sat back, rubbing the tip of my nose. "Have you had any further news about my father's arrival?"

Eaton's stance relaxed, revealing that he'd hoped the conversation would take this course. "Yes. It may not be for several hours now. Likely as not, he'll expect that you've gone to bed."

I slid my hands over my skirt. Were it any other day, I'd have taken his hint and retired. But the longing to reunite with my father on my birthday proved too strong to resist.

"Thank you," I finally replied, "but I'll wait."

And wait I did.

Hour after merciless hour I sat stone still, listening to the pendulum clock beat out each passing moment. By the time the sound of silver harness bells caught my attention, my muscles ached with stiffness. Their goblin noise sent a chill down my spine and raised gooseflesh over my arms. No merry sound carried through the night, but rather a clangorous warning.

Feeling myself pale, I stood as a whip cracked, followed by a muffled "Yaw!"

The dissonance increased as horses whinnied, and the clatter of hooves trampling against stone resounded right beneath my window. I glanced at the clock. Ten minutes of my birthday were left, but suddenly I desired nothing more than to delay this meeting.

My heart beat in odd jerks as Eaton's rushing footsteps rang in the hall. I willed my body to move closer to the doors as I debated whether I should step into the hall or remain where I was. I placed my hands over my stomach, leaning forward to hear.

The front door slammed shut, and Eaton's voice carried

through the thick mahogany. My fingers felt like ice as I cracked the door open and peeked out.

Disappointment washed through me as the first person I spotted was Mr. Forrester. I nearly turned my back to the wall to remove that dreadful man from sight, but before I could, he stepped to one side, revealing my father.

I have since met many men of power and position, but none have equalled his bearing. His looks I shall describe, but they were secondary to my first impression that night. No one meeting Lord Pierson ever commented afterwards that his features were well-set. Who saw features when meeting the very definition of determination? Silver threaded the ebony hair near his temples, making him distinguished. His face was long, but with a sharp, square chin, made all the harder by the way he gritted his teeth. The bend of his brows made clear that he was not pleased. He wore a shoulder bag that looked too oiled and cared for to be a game bag. Charcoal-grey breeches were tucked into highly polished boots. His high-collared shirt, embellished by a double-knotted cravat, could be seen above his cloak. Most noticeable was the sheer energy that throbbed in the air about him. I was known for my stubbornness, but if veins of granite ran through my soul, it was only because I had been hewn from that immovable mountain.

Revulsion crawled through me as I realized he was the same age as Mr. Macy, but whether that made Mr. Macy seem older or my father seem younger, I could not decide.

My father handed Eaton his walking stick and began unfastening his cape. "How are matters here?"

"Very well, sir."

"Isaac wrote and said my daughter arrived."

"Yes, sir. Over a week ago."

"And her behavior?"

I couldn't see Eaton's face, but whatever emotion he

evinced—or perhaps the very fact he did—caused my father to look black upon him.

Mr. Forrester added his cape to my father's, tossing it on top of Eaton. "What he means is, has the girl done anything suspicious? Anything even slightly out of the ordinary?"

Eaton's shoulders stiffened. "I should think not."

"Has she entered my library?" My father peeled off chammy gloves.

"Not to my knowledge, sir."

I gasped at his bold lie, for twice Eaton had found me reading there.

"Perhaps you wish to speak to your daughter yourself, sir. She insisted on staying awake until you returned home. Shall I fetch her?"

"Oh, how fabulous!" Mr. Forrester muttered. "We're probably being spied on right now."

I grimaced, wishing some foul calamity would overtake him.

"How did she know to expect me home tonight?" My father's demand was imbued with choler. "Who told her?"

"I believe Mrs. Coleman informed her this morning, sir."

"You believe?" Mr. Forrester pulled off a red scarf, freeing his neck. "Can you be less vague? We are talking life or death here."

My father's wrath fell on Mr. Forrester as he gave him a silencing look.

"Shall I wake Mrs. Coleman, then?" was Eaton's mild reply.

"No." My father waved him to be quiet. "But before you do anything else, find my daughter; tell her I've arrived but have retired. Have hot rum brought to the library for us, and tell James to warm my robes by the fire. After that, you're dismissed."

"Very well, sir, and welcome home."

I backed from the door, praying Eaton wouldn't follow his instructions to the letter and reveal how near I was. Thankfully, his footsteps retreated down the main corridor.

As soon as the butler's footfalls dissipated, Mr. Forrester said, "I warrant the little strumpet has searched the house and combed through every one of your papers during your absence. I say we drag her in for questioning now."

"Not tonight," was my father's gruff reply.

"There's a reason he's chosen her, Roy. He's finally gained access to your life, and if you're not careful, his trollop is going to destroy everything you've spent a lifetime building."

I felt sparks of anger rush through my chest as I waited to hear my father defend me.

"Lower your tone." My father's voice was a growl.

"What? You think she's not on the other side of that door spying on us? If we whispered, she'd hear every word."

"It's my staff I'm worried about, and she's not spying on us."

Mr. Forrester chortled. "What? Shall I prove it to you, then?"

"You're being paranoid now."

"I'm not. How on earth did Macy know not to show up last night? Tell me that."

My father's snort sounded far from amused. "It wasn't her. No one here knew my whereabouts. I've had enough of this nonsense. My decision to offer her sanctuary is final, so allow the matter to rest."

"She had Edgar killed!" Mr. Forrester's voice rose a pitch. "How can you expect me to just drop that? It's nothing short of insanity that she's been allowed access to your house."

"You're allowing anger to blind you. Your groom knew the dangers of going to Eastbourne, as did you. Don't blame her."

Mr. Forrester's voice grew low, sounding as if he was moving away, and I couldn't hear his words. Whatever my father said next wasn't distinguishable either. Footsteps clumped down the hall, masking his baritone reply.

Alone, I sank against the wall, my mind racing with what I'd just learned. Surely, surely, I pleaded with the universe, Macy hadn't killed Forrester's manservant too. How could Forrester think for a moment that I would have anything to do with a matter like that? Would my father?

With a frown, I reviewed that particular night at Eastbourne, but all I remembered was how I'd sought out Mr. Macy in the middle of the night. I'd fallen asleep in his arms and woken up in my own bed. I felt my face grow hot as I realized that if I needed to defend myself, such an explanation would scarcely do.

Throughout the house the chimes of various clocks marked midnight, their sounds as dissonant as my thoughts. All at once, I felt like giving up. All that I longed for this morning now seemed laughable. How could I have been foolish enough to hope that the man who had not married Mama, who'd ignored my existence, and who then tried to send me to Scotland, would actually welcome me here?

Outside in the hall, the slight chink of glasses interrupted my thoughts. I stepped back to the crack and peered out in time to see Eaton carrying a tray of hot rum. He turned the corner and almost immediately a warm, golden light flushed the hall before vanishing when the door closed.

I frowned. If my father had lit that many lamps, it meant he planned to remain awake awhile longer.

A moment later, the same golden hue filled the hall. This time I tiptoed from the door and fled to the settee I'd occupied all evening. The only thing worse than having my father reject me was having Eaton know that I'd overheard it.

By the time Eaton rattled the doorknob, I sat slack, my head tilted back with my eyes shut. To add to my ruse, I breathed heavily and irregularly through an open mouth.

"Miss Julia." He gently tapped my arm.

I batted him away but then blinked, doing my best to look disoriented.

"I'm sorry," he said, "but I fear your father has already arrived home and retired."

I nodded, slurring nonsense words.

"I beg your pardon, miss, but I didn't catch that."

I sat up, squinting. "Home? Is he in bed?"

"He said to tell you he'd retired," Eaton replied.

I rubbed my eyes, but in truth, I felt fully awake. The precision of his wording wasn't lost on me.

"Shall I escort you to your chamber?" he asked as I studied him anew.

I shook my head. "No, but will you see to that tray? I don't want my father to find it."

He glanced at the untouched tea before his white gloves flashed in the semidarkness. "With pleasure. Sleep well, Miss Julia."

I stood, pretending to find my balance. I waited until I was certain of his departure, then fell back into the chair and hugged myself.

Why should it matter, I thought, what opinion my father and Mr. Forrester had of me? Hadn't my father said he was offering me sanctuary? Wasn't that all I wanted? Hurt turned inward to bitterness. Had I so soon unlearned the lessons I'd picked up from William—not to expect acceptance or love? Perhaps it was better not to form any attachments while here. It would only complicate matters later. And why should I feel hurt that he'd not bothered to defend me against Mr. Forrester's disparaging remarks?

"Let people reveal themselves first," Sarah, my nursemaid, used to intone.

Well, my father most certainly had. I now saw he was a cur of the worst sort. And I despised him. Tears clotted my throat, but I refused them. If I detested my father on the night I married Mr. Macy, that emotion was impotent compared to this.

I had no need of family. None.

I crossed my arms, imagining how good it would feel to march down the hall and tell them both exactly what I thought. Only I had nowhere else to go, and I knew it.

"You did what?" Forrester's scream tore through the night and echoed down the hall, followed by, "How could you!"

The chair creaked as I stood. Though I wasn't certain, I thought I still heard his voice. Knowing their argument was probably about me was maddening.

A few more steps found me at the door, which I eased open.

For a moment, all was silent. Moonlight streamed through the hall, washing a ghostly light over the ancestral portraits lining the stairs. Earlier that week, I had carefully looked for any trace of myself but hadn't found any except for the young girl at the bottom of the stairs—my look-alike.

Hoping to hear more, I tiptoed into the hall and shut the door behind me. At best I picked up the occasional lilt of a male voice, but it was impossible to distinguish words.

As I continued to creep toward the library, my look-alike watched from her elaborate frame. Something about the utter boldness in her eyes made it clear that she wouldn't hesitate to go and eavesdrop.

I bit my lip. Edward would never condone spying on my father, especially with Forrester here, accusing me of it. Besides, it was too risky. If I were caught, I had nowhere to go except back to Mr. Macy.

Nevertheless, I also knew that Henry and Elizabeth would fully approve of my spying. That thought made me ache for our foursome. I could almost envision the fight we'd have over this. Henry would grow impassioned, telling Edward he was an absolute ninny not to advise me to go and learn as much as I could, considering. Elizabeth would only frown and keep her opinion to herself as long as possible. Edward would demand to put it to a vote, which Henry would adamantly refuse. As a rule, no matter what, Edward and I solidly took each other's side—thus Henry and Elizabeth never agreed to a vote.

Once more Mr. Forrester's voice escalated as he argued some point.

I wiped my palms along the sides of my dress, considering the arched corridor I wanted to take. Even in the dark, the black-and-white tiles stretched so far back they looked distorted and staggered. There wasn't even a plant or statue I could duck behind, though it was possible to flatten myself in the molding of one of the arch windows, provided no one passed by the opposite side. I pressed my lips together. I'd never done anything this daring alone, and I wasn't sure I wanted to.

Especially when it would have had the four of us heatedly divided.

I lifted my gaze, as if I would find an answer inscribed on the painting, and was struck by the idea that if she could vote, she'd take Henry and Elizabeth's side. My mouth twisted as I pictured a future date when I'd have to tell Edward that we'd been outvoted, and what did he expect me to do?

Certain that I would regret taking imaginary advice from a dead woman, I picked up my dress and tiptoed to the library door.

Three

A NARROW SLIVER of light streamed through the dark hall as I pushed the library door open ever so slightly, thankful to find that Eaton hadn't fully latched it.

"What did you expect I'd do?" My father's was the first voice I heard.

"Macy couldn't have planned your downfall better! They may forgive you for having an ill-begotten child, but to lie about it is committing political suicide. You can't honestly think you can hide her identity from that lot!"

I took measured, tiny steps forward, fearing the door might creak and give me away, before finally taking my first glimpse. Inside, a roaring fire cracked and hissed, casting a glow on the heavily polished wood. At the hearth, Mr. Forrester spread the tails of his frock coat apart as he warmed his backside.

My father sat, bent over his desk, carefully writing out a document before him.

"She doesn't even resemble your wife." Mr. Forrester dropped his tails. "Nor does she possess grace or manners. How are you going to convince anyone she's lived her life in a finishing school? What school produces something like her?"

The uncomfortable look that passed over my father's face as he dipped his pen told me he secretly agreed with the assessment. "You can keep wasting your breath," my father said, "but I'm going forward with this. Either help me or leave."

"Of all the stupidity, Roy. Tell them it was a misprint. Or send her to a real finishing school."

My father picked up the page and perused it. "No."

Mr. Forrester hit the oak mantel with his fist. "What about marrying her off?"

To my dismay, my father chuckled. "Is that an offer, Robert?"

Forrester sneered before slumping into a nearby chair. "No, absolutely not." He paused a moment as if winding up again. "And what are you planning to do when it's time to present her at court?"

My father dipped the pen, ignoring him.

"Who do you think is going to sponsor her? Have you even thought of that?"

Still my father didn't answer.

"What? Are you just going to sit there and ignore me now?" Mr. Forrester asked. "You haven't a clue, have you?"

"If necessary, she'll come out this season and take her place."

There was a derisive huff. "As what? Mrs. Macy?"

"She's no more his wife than I am," was my father's response. "And you know it."

"I know nothing of the sort." As if at wits' end, Mr. Forrester grabbed his hair and held it in his fist for a second. "Even if she's not placed here by Macy, she'll ruin you. She's mannerless, rude, short-tempered. One morning I found her whiskey-slinging before breakfast! No one is going to believe the story you've concocted."

"Isaac met with her before determining how to handle this. He thought her capable."

Mr. Forrester scrambled to his feet, knocking over a nearby glass. "After all he's sacrificed for you, you're destroying his career along with yours. Have you even considered how selfish you're being?"

My father's features hardened before he retrieved his pen, dipped it in ink, and started to write again. "I'm not doing anything to anyone. He and I discussed this possibility before I left, and he chose to take it."

Mr. Forrester's mouth pulled downward as his jaw jutted. "I wish I'd never laid eyes on your daughter. Had I known any of this would happen, I never would have fetched you that night."

Instead of a reply, my father considered Mr. Forrester. "Would I better gain your support, Robert, if you knew that this measure thwarted Macy?"

Mr. Forrester hesitated. "How do you mean?"

Sighing, my father leaned back and opened a bottom drawer of his desk. "Look over some correspondences between her mother and myself. Simmons collected all documentation after her death, so you'll find my letters in there as well. You'll see that Macy has been planning to collect Julia for some time now." He slid a black portfolio across the desk.

I gasped, but thankfully it went unheard.

Mr. Forrester gave an exasperated breath and sprawled himself into one of the teak chairs planted before the desk, leaving his arms and legs dangling. "It makes no difference. Even if Macy planned this years ago, your daughter is his strumpet now. Her loyalty sleeps with him."

Nevertheless, he opened the portfolio with a flip of his hand and withdrew a sheet.

Sight of that first letter tortured me. After Mama's death, I'd spent months searching for the mysterious missives that frightened her. I'd emptied her desk, torn apart her wardrobe, dumped out every drawer, and overturned her mattress. The passion seized me one afternoon after staring at the endless rippling circles the rain had formed in puddles. Like a feeble-minded woman, I went from despondent to frantic. Believing Mama had taken her own life because of a series of correspondences, I wanted answers. And I would not be put off. I had searched and searched until Sarah finally found me sitting in the middle of a wrecked room and begged me to cease.

Even from my distance, I recognized Mama's stationery and had to resist the urge to rush into the library to snatch up the file.

I couldn't see Mr. Forrester's face, for he turned, but he made quick work of the first letter, then picked up the next. Again, I felt desperate. I recognized that letter too. It bore a tea stain from the time Mama's hand shook so much, she overturned her cup while reading it. I wanted to scream. It was maddening that for once in his life, Mr. Forrester wasn't giving commentary.

My father waited in silence, using his thumb to twist a ring on his fourth finger.

Mr. Forrester turned over the last page in the file, then hooked his elbows behind his chair. "I don't understand."

"Neither do I, but I do know that we're disrupting something he's been scheming for some time now. It's why I'm keeping her here." My father sanded the document he'd been working on, folded it, and slid it into the shoulder bag he'd worn home that evening.

Mr. Forrester shifted in his chair, allowing me to see his face. "This is Macy we're talking about here. How do you know he didn't plan this too?"

My father withdrew a new sheet of paper. "Because no one would expect this bold of a move. Consider it from my point of view, Robert. I never wanted her here either. But now that Macy's forced my hand, I'm calling his bluff and raising the stakes."

Forrester snorted with derision. "And what if he's not bluffing?"

"He's stalemated, and he knows it." My father's voice softened as he picked up his rum. "Think on it. The legality of the union is debatable at best, and even if he could prove it, he lacks proof that she's the girl."

Mr. Forrester lifted the portfolio and waved it in the air. "No proof?"

My father glowered. He looked askance, taking a swallow of the rum. A look of sadness crossed his face before he stood and held out his hand. When Forrester handed him the portfolio, he hesitated for a second as if regretting the action, but then, seemingly devoid of emotion, he tossed the entire sheaf into the flames.

Part of me felt tossed into that inferno too. I rested my cheek against the doorframe and watched helplessly as the fire devoured the documentation that held the answers to my questions. Now I would never fully know what Mama's last thoughts and days were like.

Mr. Forrester looked as though he'd smelled something offensive. "I still say this is a trap and you're walking right into it. How do you know that Macy hasn't managed to create copies?"

It was clear my father hadn't considered that. His gaze was trenchant as he studied Mr. Forrester. "I trust my staff implicitly."

I held in my groan, knowing any one of my father's servants could be a traitor. And if my father was unaware, then of what else was he ignorant? I crept away from the library, feeling I'd consumed as much news as I could handle in one night. I wanted time alone to ponder it.

～⌒～

The following morning, I sat fragmented as hot water was poured from a copper pitcher into the hip bath. The hurt that had blustered into anger and roared the previous evening had expended itself, leaving behind vast emptiness. I could stir no emotion as clouds of steam rose and mingled with my breath. Despite the fact that I was unaccustomed to bathing in front of more than one servant, I couldn't even arouse a sense of modesty. Nothing mattered.

"She's expected downstairs in the library in less than ten minutes," Mrs. Coleman shouted into the next room. "Where's Mary with the rinse water?"

"Shall I go look for her?"

"No. Stay put. I'll need your help dressing Miss Pierson."

I draped my arms over my knees, ignoring the chill that developed as rivulets of water ran down my back from my wet hair. I stared unseeing at the far wall, not wanting to meet my father. Having observed him last night, I could foresee no possible relationship between us now.

With a soap-covered hand, Mrs. Coleman pushed back a wisp of hair that had fallen over her eyes and studied me with a mild panic before glancing at the shelf clock. A girl raced into the room carrying a steaming pitcher, which Mrs. Coleman took with brows knit together.

The next batch of water nearly scalded me. Mrs. Coleman frowned as I winced, then set the pitcher down with a clang. "'Twill be a mercy when Miss Moray arrives to serve as your lady's maid."

The mention of a lady's maid brought to mind Nancy, the brash girl who served me at Am Meer. Memory of her bossy manner finally stirred emotion—one of the worst in my collection, a deep, aching loneliness. I felt it as keenly as I had the week Mama died. Despite my efforts, tears welled. I stood to leave the tub. If I remained here one more moment, I'd be crying. Water trickled down my body, raising gooseflesh.

"Mary!" The floorboard creaked as Mrs. Coleman struggled to stand. "Fetch Miss Pierson's dressing robe. Ann, run and fetch the dress being altered. Step lively."

"Yes, ma'am!"

While she waited, Mrs. Coleman rubbed a linen towel through my hair with a vigor that made me see lights.

The girl raced toward me again, carrying a fluttering robe of silk and lace. As she approached, she held out the garment, dragging its hem through the puddles surrounding the tub.

I accepted the useless robe without comment. What did I care that she should have selected a thick woollen one or should have warmed it by the fire?

"Best make haste." Mrs. Coleman ushered me toward the main chamber. "Your father is in one of his moods. If you're late, there's no telling what he'll do next."

Tying a knot in the robe, I left the dressing room and retreated to the blaze in the main compartment of the bed-chamber. Here, shadows competed with the lambent firelight shimmering over the walls. I eyed the movement, wondering what would happen if I refused to present myself to my father.

Tucking a wet clump of hair behind my ear, I leaned against the hearth. What was the worst he could do? Send Mr. Forrester in after me?

Mrs. Coleman entered the chamber, her arms full of wet linens, commanding the unfortunate Mary, "Don't just stand there. Fetch the good lace petticoats!" She went straight to one of the wardrobes and reached for wooden boxes stacked inside. "Remind Eaton to iron Lord Pierson's newspaper. If he acts sour about it, remind him that *his* footman neglected to iron the papers a fortnight ago. Grippe is no excuse. Tell James, too, that I'll be inspecting the crystal goblets for fingerprints."

I shivered and pulled the flimsy robe tighter. Mrs. Coleman glanced at the mantel clock as the maid raced through the room. "Five minutes!"

The door swung open and a chambermaid entered, lugging a massive gown. She breathlessly bobbed to me before turning to Mrs. Coleman. Straggles of loose hair hung from beneath her cap. "Lord Pierson's going to be furious."

"You've got cheek standing there, speaking of him thus. Talk like that again, and I'll give you a temper more terrible than any of Lord Pierson's." Mrs. Coleman blotted her brow with her apron. "Has he entered the library yet?"

The girl shrugged.

"Hurry. If he hasn't, see if you can get James to stall him."

The girl dipped before I caught sight of her thin legs amidst the swirl of petticoats.

"There's trouble a-brewing," Mrs. Coleman said to me with a shake of her head. "Your father's not been this surly since the Reform riots. If you ask me, it's that guest of his feeding his ill temper. I wager a month's pay that Mr. Forrester is the one who clumped mud over my floors, not that it's any of my business."

Mrs. Coleman made quick work of helping me from my robe and into undergarments too large for my frame. Silently, I submitted to the flurry of being dressed. Pantaloons, layers of petticoats, and an ivory satin gown all flew at me in various shades of white.

Eyeing the hands of the clock, Mrs. Coleman smoothed my wet hair with pomade and tucked it under in a simple chignon. "Make haste!" she urged when I made no movement to stand. "There's not time for more!"

Feeling out of sorts, I grabbed a grey shawl that lay over the back of a chair. Knowing Mr. Forrester was already awake and about certainly didn't put wings on my feet.

At the top of the stairs I paused to view the entrance hall of Maplecroft. Frost clung to the windows, blocking all views, enclosing the house. Light radiated behind the large oval dome above the ancestral portraits. I descended, keeping my eyes upon my look-alike.

At the bottom step, I stopped to read the engraved brass plaque screwed into the bottom of the frame. *Lady Josephine Anna Pierson.* I touched her name, trying to draw strength. Now that Mama's locket was no longer my talisman, perhaps here was my replacement.

I turned from her and studied the hall. In the weak daylight, the plaster rosettes and ornate moldings contrasted against the Wedgwood blue, making it seem like an ice palace. The mawkish gown I wore had the weight of three dresses and completely swallowed me. But I no longer cared about my appearance.

The clack of footsteps announced that someone else had entered the hall. I turned to find James carrying a tray of piping-hot coffee and tea. He was wigged and dressed in heavy velvet. His expression was one of annoyance, and he held his arms at an odd angle, as if the thick suit of clothing chafed him. His eyes widened as he spotted me, but without so much as rattling a teacup, he assumed a formal stance. "Good morning, Miss Pierson. I am also en route to the library. Shall I escort you?"

Two emotions finally stirred. Until that second, I hadn't realized how badly I needed even a small gesture of acceptance; thus it warmed me. Yet panic also lit through me. My ability to survive depended upon being able to shut off feeling. I had always survived that way.

"Yes, please," was all I managed.

"The library is just ahead." James inclined his head toward the correct door as we approached.

I nodded, nervously running my fingers over my throat as guilt washed through me at the memory of last night.

Balancing the tray on one hand, James managed to give the door a solid rap, despite his gloves.

"You may enter." My father's voice resonated from deep within the chamber.

I hesitated, allowing James to go first. Keeping out of sight, I heard my father's greeting. "Yes, thank you, James. Set the tray there. Is William feeling better?"

"Yes, sir. He hopes to be back at duty tonight."

"Good, good."

Hoping to arrive unnoticed, I stepped up to the threshold. My father still sat behind his desk, this time clutching an old-fashioned quill pen so tightly between his fingers that it was a marvel the shaft didn't snap. He must have seen me from the corner of his eye, for he lifted his head. He frowned, deepening the jowls about his mouth. "James, you're dismissed."

While James took his exit, I curtsied, feeling clumsy.

"What time did I ask you to meet me here?" my father asked.

I placed my hands on my bodice. "Seven . . . sir."

"What time is it now?"

My gaze flitted about the room and found yet another ornate Maplecroft clock. "Ten after."

Mr. Forrester gave a disapproving shake of his head as he added cream to his brew. "Maybe you can tell everyone her finishing school forgot to stress the importance of timeliness."

My father shot him a warning look but returned his attention to me. "When I summon you, I expect you to be punctual. Not one minute early, not one minute late. Is that clear?"

I barely managed a nod.

My father jotted a few more lines and then, without looking up, pointed to the door behind me with his pen. "Shut the door, Daughter."

When I'd done so, I approached his desk, keeping my feet turned outward and my steps refined as I had practiced with Mama long ago. Refusing to so much as glance at Mr. Forrester, I dropped into a chair.

"I did not grant you permission to sit." My father dipped his pen twice in the inkwell, still not regarding me. "You will go outside, knock, and enter the room again. This time as a young lady."

I shifted my gaze to Mr. Forrester, who smirked and swirled the coffee in his mug.

Mortified, I stood and retreated from the room as quickly as possible, then leaned against the plaster wall. Humiliation burned in my chest. It took a full minute for me to be willing to demean myself, but I knocked.

"Enter."

The tightness in my throat made it ache, but this time I

remained at the threshold, pulling my shawl tighter. My father scratched out a few more lines. "You may be seated if you desire."

Taking care to walk in the manner taught me so long ago, I crossed the room. When I sat, I clasped my hands in my lap and kept my head poised. It had been years since I'd been forced to remember the rules of etiquette.

My father finished his letter. In no apparent rush, he blotted it, then laid a large book on top, covering the text. Mr. Forrester took to his feet, setting his coffee down. He opened his mouth, but my father held up a hand for silence. For a moment, I suspect he saw how vulnerable I felt, for he shifted uncomfortably in his seat and his face softened. "Have you been well cared for in my absence?"

I clenched my hands and drew them toward my stomach. "Yes, I've been very comfortable; thank you."

Mr. Forrester made a huffing noise, as if frustrated at the waste of time, before throwing himself back into his seat.

My father's jaw tightened as he ignored him. "Tell me how you made use of your time."

"I . . . I explored your house."

"My house?" He sat back in his chair and poured himself coffee. "Maplecroft is now your house too. What else?"

My mouth felt dry as I tried to think of something useful I'd done. "Th-there is nothing else."

He angled his head, displeasure bristling his features. "Do you mean to sit there and tell me you spent nine days doing *nothing*?"

When I glanced at Mr. Forrester, he smirked again and further swirled his coffee. I struggled to compress my rising anger toward my father for lecturing me before that man. Gritting my teeth, I answered his question. "Forgive me, *sir*, but what else was there to do?"

"Oh, I don't know." Mr. Forrester leaned back and crossed his legs. "What about leafing through your father's documents and smuggling them to Eastbourne?"

JESSICA DOTTA ❧ 39

"Robert," my father warned him.

"We agreed this was necessary," Mr. Forrester spat back. "You know as well as I do, this won't work if you interfere or try to turn this into tea. Let me question the girl already."

My father studied me a long moment, the burden of his thoughts causing his shoulders to sag. With a stricken expression, he stood and waved permission to Mr. Forrester. "All right. Go ahead."

The chair creaked as Mr. Forrester put his cup aside, then leaned forward and scrutinized me. "Look at that," he said, his eyes narrowing. "You didn't sleep last night, did you?" His gaze darted to the library door before returning to me. "What were you up to?"

I fisted my skirt and pulled a layer of it toward me as fear webbed through me. "I'll thank you not to make assumptions. How would you know whether I slept or not?"

Mr. Forrester's grin would have done a cat justice. "You forget, luv, I know what you look like the morning after you've spent your night unsupervised with Macy."

My breath felt stolen from me as I stared back at him. Perspiration soaked my chemise. With a pleading expression, I begged Mr. Forrester to stop. I could bear the stigma of my scandal, but not with my father present.

"So where were you?"

It felt like fleece lined my throat, but I finally managed, "Bed."

Beside me, I heard my father stand, uncork a bottle, and pour a drink. Mr. Forrester frowned in his direction as if disliking the interruption, but he rubbed his palm over the top of his trousers and, after clearing his throat, started anew.

"Tell me about Dillyworth."

I gave him a confused look.

"Leatherbarrow?"

Pulling my shawl tighter, I shook my head.

"Colburn? Ripley?" Mr. Forrester's voice grew in intensity.

My fingers felt hollow as I pieced together that these names must belong to men who'd had dealings of some sort with Mr. Macy. I shook my head, denying any knowledge.

"Oh, come now!" Mr. Forrester screamed, jumping from his seat. I cringed as he stomped toward me. "Do we look that stupid? Do you really think we'll be fooled into thinking you have *no* knowledge of these men?"

Terrified, I looked to my father for help. He stood angled away from the scene, his entire body stiff as he heaved gulps of air through his nose.

At that juncture in my life, I did not understand that this was no less of a trial for him. All I saw was a man who stood idly by as his daughter was bullied. Any trust I might have placed in him vanished; thus we began our relationship like two dance partners out of step.

I would like to write that when I returned my attention to Forrester, I let him know in no uncertain terms that I was innocent and would not be spoken to that way. It is tempting to gloss over my faults, especially as my age now makes me the sole survivor. Who is left to contradict?

But here is the truth. My response was as cowardly as my father's. Like him, I throbbed with anger, but something far more sinister stirred. I felt my lip curl, wondering what Mr. Macy would do if he knew I was being treated in such a manner. I grabbed the only source of power I could find, and that was the satisfying thought that I could probably have Mr. Forrester killed, and *I* wasn't at his mercy, but rather *he* was at mine.

Such are the lies we tell ourselves.

"Tell me," Mr. Forrester shouted, "about Marwick and Whiteclay!"

"Enough." My father slammed his glass to the desk. "She doesn't know. Julia, you may leave."

Mr. Forrester positioned himself in front of my chair before

I even realized I'd been dismissed. "You swore to me I could question her."

"Look at her face. She has no knowledge."

"What do you think you're protecting her from?" Annoyance threaded Mr. Forrester's tone. "She spent her nights alone with Macy. She has no innocence."

Instead of answering, my father stormed to the hearth. Red splotched the back of his neck as he gave the flames a brusque nod, allowing Mr. Forrester to continue.

"How many men does Macy have?" Mr. Forrester asked.

Slowly, I turned my gaze to Mr. Forrester's jeering face. "You were there. You saw his servants."

"Answer the question."

"I-I met Mr. Greenham and Mr. Rooke."

My father stiffened as though the mere mention of these names upset him. Mr. Forrester leaned on the edge of my father's desk, his arms crossed. "So let me make sure I understand this. You married Macy, and the *only* two gentlemen you have knowledge of, out of his *entire* organization, are the two men that I'm already aware you're acquainted with."

"She has no acquaintance with them." My father's tone became feral as he faced us. "You've questioned her long enough."

Mr. Forrester flung out his arms. "This is ridiculous. He's planted her here, and because you're afraid to allow his trollop to hear a few unsavory names—"

"That's it!" My father's shout seared the room to silence. His face had turned bright red, almost purple, as he dashed his tumbler to the floor.

To my dismay, he made straight toward me, wearing the expression he'd worn the night I married Mr. Macy. Before he could grasp my arm, I flung myself from my chair and stumbled into a table stacked with books.

"Now look what you've done." My father turned his full tempest on Mr. Forrester.

"Me!" Mr. Forrester thumped his chest. "You're the one bellowing like a bull. All I'm trying to do is ask a few simple questions about her husband."

"For the last time, he's not her husband!"

Mr. Forrester opened his mouth to argue, but thankfully before he could speak, a loud clamor filled the front hall.

"Are you expecting someone?" Mr. Forrester asked.

My father stilled with a stricken look. "No. You don't think . . ."

Mr. Forrester slid a hand into the opposite side of his frock coat as if ready to draw out a firearm. He backed away to take a position near the door.

My father's face became drawn and grey. The lines about his eyes deepened before his uneasy gaze fell on me. I stared back, breathless, wondering if this was the last interaction I'd ever have with my father.

Male voices boomed in the hall, approaching.

It was impossible to imagine Edward looking so resigned to fate if he were in the place of my father. Edward would have grabbed my hand and already have been testing the windows. Fear roiled in my stomach as I wished I'd never come. Then, resolved to at least show courage, I lifted my chin and shoulders, prepared to face my husband.

The door burst open. But instead of Mr. Macy, two smiling gentlemen entered, holding brown-checked hats as if they'd doffed them in a hurry. One sported a rifle, cocked open for safety. Five spaniels with silken ears and docked tails followed them and pranced in and out of the doorway, spreading muddy prints everywhere.

The shorter man I recognized. He had been amongst the party that crashed Eastbourne the night I married Mr. Macy. At that point I didn't feel warmth toward anyone who had witnessed that night of my life. Yet I can now attest that Colonel Greenley is one of the most warmhearted men I've known.

"Did you see their bleeding faces, Greenley?" the taller man declared with a laugh. "Thought we were Macy, did you? I suppose I'd look like a seasick sailor too!"

A vein throbbed in my father's forehead. "You dare to speak that name openly in my house—"

"Oh, come now!" the shorter man, Colonel Greenley, soothed. "Surely amongst ourselves—"

"Never mind me," the tall man interrupted. "I hadn't meant to stir up trouble. We came to find out if the plan worked. But from your reactions, I take it you have not apprehended Macy."

My father and Mr. Forrester only glanced at each other.

"But you jolly well got the girl!" Greenley noted, rubbing the ears of one of the hounds. "So you must have had some measure of success."

"It means nothing. She arrived during our absence," Mr. Forrester said.

"Well, what happened? I thought you had him for certain this time."

Mr. Forrester picked up his coffee cup and jabbed it toward me. "I'd rather not say with her present."

"Dash it all, then." Greenley rocked on his feet. "We came figuring you needed a distraction from this messy business. It's a brisk morning, but there's game to bag. What do you say, Pierson? You can tell us the whole affair."

"A bit of fresh air will clear the lungs and clear your head," the tall one said, "as your father used to say."

My father's eyes panned the soiled floor, slowly taking in the paw prints, which had spread over the floor and carpet. Two of the squirmy dogs had wiggled their liver-colored heads against my leg, making a plea for affection. I rubbed their velvety ears between my fingers as their feet dirtied the bottom of my dress. I braced myself not to care if my father abandoned me our first morning together.

"Oh, leave off," Mr. Forrester said, setting down his drink.

"It's not as though you can't afford a new rug." He faced the men. "Yes, we *will* join you. Roy, you need this more than anyone. They're right."

For a fraction of a second, my father glanced at me. His mouth pursed in unease.

"You're acting worse than Tinsworth, now," Greenley said, slapping gloves against his arm before squeezing his hands into them. "The girl will be fine. We shan't even leave your property. Come on, man!"

My father gave a reluctant nod, then frowned.

The tall man thumped my father's back and smiled at him. "We'll await you in the stables. Forrester, a word with you." He gave a whistle, and all five dogs' heads perked at the sound. They wasted no time bounding after Mr. Forrester and the other man as they trundled down the hall.

At the threshold, my father paused and faced me. Twice he looked ready to speak but seemed to change his mind. All at once his face hardened, and he gestured to the dirtied chamber. "Have Mrs. Coleman tend to this at once!"

I dropped my gaze, refusing to meet his eyes.

"I say." Colonel Greenley eased the door closed. "You're going about it all wrong. You won't get anywhere with the girl, barking orders at her like that."

The door shut, leaving me alone. Smears of mud covered the bottom of my dress, and an ivory chair sported paw prints, as if one of the canines had leaped over the arm and sprung off the seat before it left. Recalling that the staff was already short-handed, I felt a wave of pity for Mrs. Coleman as I found the bellpull, gave it a yank, and then turned to leave.

As is often the case in life, the truest damage from that morning was invisible, exacting a toll that would prove to be far more costly than we were prepared to pay.

Four

I WOULD LIKEN the next four days to being adrift in a rowboat, without oars, borne amidst a thick gloom, on an ever-moving current. I found myself sitting in window seats, passing hours, subsisting on little more than an inner reality.

When Edward left, he'd carried a letter to Elizabeth from me, so I had held off writing Am Meer until I'd met with my father and had news. I now wished to write and communicate what had befallen me—especially Mr. Forrester's interrogation and how my father hibernated from sight afterwards.

I made no attempt to write, though, for I realized my father would never allow evidence of my true identity to leave Maplecroft. Nor did I desire to risk placing my post through one of the servants, lest I choose the wrong one and it fall into the hands of Mr. Macy. For there was little doubt by then that Mr. Macy knew my whereabouts. From snatches of conversation, I pieced together that a notice had been placed in Forrester's newspaper saying that Lord Pierson's daughter had returned home from school. Late in my life, I saw a brittle yellow copy. It was one of those mindless snippets that typically filled the society page.

A rather bold move on my father's part. He must have known his announcement would ripple shock to the highest rank of government. I have since been told the young queen herself sent for Lord Melbourne that very day and demanded explanation. Who would have guessed that during the season I felt most unseen, my existence was being discussed and questioned all over London. At that time, I would have compared myself to one of those foreign women I'd seen in engravings. The ones covered in veils from head to foot, standing in the background while the men talked, seeming to have no mouth, just eyes that observed.

After being accused of doing nothing, I made it my habit to occupy myself with knitting and monitoring the household. But as often as opportunity afforded, I'd drop my work, shut my eyes, and conjure up images of the past.

I recalled summer days of our foursome standing atop grassy knolls during windstorms, our arms spread wide, scarcely able to breathe as gale-force winds struck us. Elizabeth and I would stretch out our shawls behind us, allowing them to fill like sails before we'd race to the bottom of the hill.

Many times during these reveries, I'd rest my head on the side of an armchair, looking at the straggling hemlocks outside of Maplecroft, particularly recalling the hidden grove of pine trees we'd discovered in Farmer Baker's field. That summer we'd held countless picnics beneath its feathery branches, spreading our blankets atop the thick carpet of fragrant needles. How good they smelled when warmed by the honeyed noontide light. That bower of trees became our faerie hall, though Mama and Mrs. Windham constantly bemoaned the sap and pine needles they found worked into Elizabeth's and my best clothing.

"It's growing dark," Mrs. Coleman said from where she was seated at the chimney nook, breaking one such succession of thought.

My concentration broken, I looked up from the papers I'd elected to work on in her chamber. I rubbed my eyes and glanced at the clock. To my astonishment, I'd been in her cramped sitting room, looking at five handwritten requests, for the past two hours.

Mrs. Coleman rose and set her knitting aside. "Perhaps you'd like to consider them in the morning."

"No," I said, trying to sound forceful like my father, whom no one questioned. I moved a new paper to the top of the stack. It should have taken me less than a quarter hour to finish these, but I'd purposely dallied as to attain some measure of company.

Mrs. Coleman's voice turned less patient. "Perhaps you'll want the time to dress for dinner."

Not having been invited to dinner, I gritted my teeth. I'd not seen my father once, despite two attempts. For the last four days I'd selected his menus and approved which sheets he slept upon but somehow couldn't gain an audience. I shook my head. "I'll have a tray brought to my bedchamber as usual."

Mrs. Coleman's lips turned white as she pressed them, but she repositioned herself in her rocking chair and lifted her yarn and needles. Every few seconds, she peered over her spectacles.

I shifted under her gaze, feeling a headache lurking. Perhaps it was cruel to keep the housekeeper from her duties, but I needed company whether she wished to be here or not. I was sick with wandering about lifeless rooms under the dreary gaze of my ancestors. Thank goodness Mrs. Coleman only had amateur watercolors of irises. It was a refreshing change.

"Which request is that one?" Mrs. Coleman asked, her voice as tight as her smile.

"Eaton's."

The cadence of her needles increased. "Ah, and will you be approving it?"

I folded down the corner of the paper in my hands. The butler requested approval for a new set of china and serving dishes. It had been nearly two years since new sets had been ordered. Ours were feared to be gaudy now that fashion had changed.

I pressed my lips, wondering how I was supposed to know the correct answer. I hadn't been raised to this.

"I wouldn't fret so much over the decisions." Mrs. Coleman jabbed the coals with her poker. "Your father will neither care nor notice whether you order new dishes. You may trust my advice, I assure you."

I lifted the bottom corner of the paper in order to see Eaton's suggested budget. The sum was outrageous, spreading quick fire through my limbs. Here I had lived in near poverty, and my own father had apparently thrown money everywhere except to Mama and me.

"There, there," Mrs. Coleman said, misunderstanding the sudden hurt that must have evidenced itself on my face. "Is that the cause of all this shilly-shallying? Do as you wish; your father is more than generous with his money. There, at least, you'll find no fault."

I stared at her, too horrified for words. My prior circumstances had been so mean that at times I had been ridiculed for my lack of funds. My mourning dresses had been rags, the sleeves so short they exposed my wrists. After William's death, Mama and I had given up our horse and carriage, let go of all servants except Sarah.

Firm footsteps rounded the hall, doubtless a footman. Mrs. Coleman looked up expectantly, and I took the opportunity to rise and retreat to the window to hide my pain. A miserly rain hung on the panes like beads, as impenetrable as a thick fog.

"Good evening, Mrs. Coleman," said a male voice behind me. "I came here with the hopes you could tell me where Miss Pierson was, but I see I've found her."

The confident tone was not that of a servant. Startled, I turned.

In the doorway stood the gentleman I'd not seen since he departed with Edward.

Imagine how differently we'd treat people if at the beginning of an acquaintance we were given opportunity to know how that person would affect our life. How joyously we would greet some we might otherwise act cool toward, or how deep our antipathy would run toward others we might initially feel attracted to. Naturally, I had no knowledge of the sort of soul Lord Dalry possessed. Thus I turned and greeted him with a wary eye.

"Good merciful heavens!" Mrs. Coleman stared at his clay-caked boots. "Isaac, you didn't walk through the house like that? When did you arrive? Does Lord Pierson know you've returned home?"

He tore his gaze from me as if unwilling. "Not yet, and you're not to inform him. I need a few minutes in private with Miss Pierson before my arrival is generally known. Will you help us?"

The papers slipped from my fingers as I envisioned Edward. "Why? What's wrong?"

"Alone! And me knowing?" Mrs. Coleman's scandalized voice drowned out my frantic whisper. "No. Absolutely not. Can you imagine Lord Pierson's temper if he discovered—?"

"I'll manage him," Lord Dalry said. "I wouldn't ask if it wasn't of the utmost importance."

"Isaac." Mrs. Coleman planted a hand on her hip, then slowly looked my way. Her gaze lingered over the papers that had dropped from my hands to the floor. Relief flooded her countenance. "Yes, yes, do take her." She bent and scooped up the pages. "Only give me your promise to help her decide on these household matters." She thrust the pages into Lord Dalry's hand.

"Have James bring us tea in the back parlor." Lord Dalry slipped the loose pages under his arm. "James, mind you; not William or Eaton. Understand?"

Her mouth pursed, and for half a second she looked as though she doubted her decision. "No shenanigans. I want your sworn word."

His reply was a direct stare, which brought color to her cheeks. Even I shifted, uncomfortable with his evident displeasure. "Have I ever acted unseemly? Even once in memory?"

Her color deepened and she mumbled something inaudible.

"Move along with you, then." Lord Dalry stepped from the doorway, allowing her to pass. "Be quick about it. Simmons is also on the prowl. Be forewarned; there's bound to be another quarrel between us tonight."

I frowned at the mention of my father's steward.

"Good gracious," she said, entering the dark hall. "Here I've been waiting for you to come and settle things, not stir them up worse."

His eyebrows elevated before he turned and favored me with a bow as Mrs. Coleman pattered away. "Forgive me this unorthodox greeting, but if you wish to hear the particulars of my journey, we must act now."

"Please." I advanced toward him, scarcely able to level the panic in my voice. "Is he all right?"

Lord Dalry extended his arm, and as he did so, homesickness nearly buckled my knees. Traces of Am Meer's scent clung to his clothing. "I assure you, I left Reverend Auburn in excellent health." Even then, I noted how he made sure our eyes met when he said Edward's name, only I couldn't guess the reason. "Please, the moment your father learns I'm home, he'll summon me. Once he learns what has passed, I'll have no opportunity to furnish you with the particulars. I promised Miss Windham I would do my best to deliver her message to you."

"Elizabeth?" Her name alone threatened to dissolve me.

Lord Dalry placed the tips of his fingers beneath my elbow in the lightest of touches. "This way."

For several minutes nothing was spoken as he guided me through passages of Maplecroft I'd not yet explored. My slippered feet made no noise while his boots echoed over the vast marble halls. His conversation with the housekeeper and his working knowledge of the passageways made me feel more alien in Maplecroft than ever.

"Turn in here." Lord Dalry opened the door to a white-pillared room whose walls were glazed the color of weak tea. Gold glinted off various mirrors, and gilt-edged wreaths embossed the sides of tables. Opposite us hung a carriage-size painting of my ancestral look-alike. From high in her massive frame, she watched as I pulled my shawl tight. A smile curved her lips and welcome filled her eyes.

"Lady Josephine," Lord Dalry said, slipping past me and into the chamber. "Your father's mother. This was her private parlor."

My gaze settled on the large center table, where speckled green and brownish-red pears sat in a porcelain bowl next to dainty white flowers. Near them, a bronze sculpture of cherubic children played with boughs of flowers. An awkwardly decoupaged box sat beneath an intricate jewelry box. Plain next to fancy. Earth next to art.

"My grandmother," I whispered, returning my gaze to the smiling portrait. My father's harsh words, spoken the night I married Mr. Macy, cycled back.

"There's also a handsome living left to you from my mother. . . . She learned of your existence and took pity. I'm glad she died, sparing herself the knowledge of how shameless you are."

"So it was her," I whispered, studying her portrait.

I crossed the room and touched the crackled paint. Had she wondered about me, perhaps yearned for her granddaughter? The thought contrasted so greatly with my father's treatment that my nose tickled as I held in tears.

"At least the fire is lit," Lord Dalry said behind me, unaware of the transformation taking place within me. "It wasted precious time, but it would look odd if your father found us sitting in a cold, unused portion of Maplecroft."

"There you're mistaken." I reluctantly turned from Lady Josephine and found Lord Dalry crouched before the kindling he'd lit. "It makes no difference to my father what I do."

Furrows lined his brow as he rose and dusted his knees.

"That, I can assure you, is far from the truth. Whatever led you to believe that?"

Here was a dispute I had no desire to enter. I sank into a chair, realizing I'd said too much. "Please, just tell me about Edward."

Lord Dalry took a seat opposite me. His eyes stayed trained upon me, observing me as keenly as Mr. Macy used to, but without his mocking humor. "Here." He extracted two letters from his waistcoat and held them out as though he regretted their contents. "I promised Miss Windham I'd say nothing until you'd read her letter first. She felt it would be better if she were the one to communicate what transpired."

Had I been shoved off a cliff, I could not have felt more panicked. My fingers trembled so much that after I took the letters, I couldn't loosen the wax. The pitying manner in which Lord Dalry watched me made it all the more chilling.

The distinct clack of china broke the silence, and I turned to the sight of James rolling a tea cart. Though he looked void of expression as he stepped through the threshold, he gave Lord Dalry an exaggerated shake of his head and mouthed, *He's coming.*

Behind him, more footsteps pounded.

Without pause, James pulled a folded table from the wall and raised its leaves while Lord Dalry stood, placing his hand beneath my elbow, encouraging me to rise as well. Certain it was my father, I tottered to my feet, not ready for another encounter.

Within seconds my father entered, accompanied by Mr. Forrester. My father's sharp gaze went to James and then to the empty chairs. His face mottled red. "Isaac, what the devil is going on here?"

To my amazement, Lord Dalry looked perfectly calm. "I beg pardon, sir?"

"Don't give me that. How long have you been home? Why is she with you?" He spun around, passing over me with his probing gaze. "And where is Simmons?"

"Here I am," came the sour answer from the hall, "though Master Isaac did his best to slip past me."

My father's steward entered. His wet hair lay in rows where he'd hastily combed it. Oppression fell over the space, as though unheard music suddenly struck the wrong notes. As if magnetized, the steward's gaze flew to the letters still in my grasp. He made a noise like a choke and a snarl rolled into one. "I forbade you to give those to her without Lord Pierson's approval."

My father finally acknowledged me with a glance. "Give her what?"

I resisted the urge to stash the letters down the front of my dress, where no man could be permitted to retrieve them. My father's temperament was unpredictable. Having already been raised in such a household, I knew better than to escalate matters during a tense situation.

"Master Isaac brought back letters for your daughter." Simmons hefted a leather satchel onto the empty desk and opened it. "I explicitly forbade him to pass them on to her."

"Pray, you'll have to forgive me then." Lord Dalry returned to his seat and motioned for me to do likewise. "But I'm not in the habit of obeying your orders. The last time I checked, I live here of my own volition."

"She's my master's daughter." Simmons withdrew a leather book and clomped it open on the desk. "And as such, she falls under my jurisdiction."

"There you are mistaken." Lord Dalry removed a ring from his hand and turned it about in his fingers. "It is my understanding that Miss Pierson has taken up the duty of directing the staff, which means you now fall under her authority."

"Impossible!" Simmons shifted his nasty gaze to me.

I looked at Lord Dalry, wondering how on earth he'd obtained that bit of information already. The room felt suddenly deprived of air, and I sensed I'd been thrown into a clash that had been ongoing for years. At stake were my letters, which I desperately needed to read.

The repose with which James unfurled the milk-white table-cloth amazed me. If it were possible for someone to be unaware of the tension, he would have looked exactly as James did—half-bored, as if his mind were too replete to be bothered by our buzzing conversation.

"It matters little who's in charge of whom," Mr. Forrester said behind me. During the drama, I'd lost track of him but now found him behind my chair. He plucked the letters from my grasp. "The fact is, Miss Pierson is not allowed to receive any outside correspondence. No matter who wrote it. No matter who's delivering it. It's too dangerous, and we all know that."

"Of all the nonsense." Lord Dalry faced my father. "Honestly, sir, what harm can there be in reading a letter from her former home?"

With a frown, my father stepped toward me and stretched out his hand. "Robert, I'll take those. He's right, Isaac. She's not permitted contact."

Helplessly, I watched as my father opened the first of the two missives. James used this opportunity to escape, shutting the door gently.

"Personally, knowing the source, I'd burn them." Simmons perched on a chair and pulled an inkwell toward him, no longer watching us. "There can hardly be anything sensible therein."

My father made no reply as his eyes raked over the unfolded letter. His gaze tarried on certain parts, the jowls of his cheeks deepening. When he finished, he lowered the page and glared at me.

I folded my hands over my stomach, my sense of shame growing warmer by degrees. What could Elizabeth have written to merit such a response? My heart wrung. What had happened to Edward? Our scandal?

When I said nothing, my father tore open the second letter. He winced, then held it at arm's length. Heavy perfume clouded the room as he turned his head to escape the overpowering scent. Light passed through the thin paper, revealing large tearstains and inkblots.

"Who on earth is Mrs. Windham?" My father squinted at the scrawled signature.

Simmons didn't even glance up as he wrote. "The widow your daughter formerly stayed with."

My father cocked an eyebrow, then started reading. The more he read, the more his disgust deepened the creases on his face. "This is the woman you chose?" Anger seeped into his tone as he flapped the missive. "Is this how you handle all the tasks I give you?"

Simmons looked up, seemingly as irritated as my father. "Under the circumstances, I thought I did rather well by allowing the visit." He began counting off fingers. "She lived far removed from society. Had no friends of consequence. Occupied a neighborhood where your daughter hadn't half a chance of finding a husband without a dowry."

My mouth fell open as I learned why I'd been granted permission to visit Am Meer before being sent to Scotland. My father shot Simmons a silencing look, then jerked his face from sight.

"Ah yes," Mr. Forrester gibed, surveying the platter of pastries James had set out. "Someone who took her to Eastbourne to look for a husband. Good show, Simmons."

"I hardly require your approval." Simmons threw his black pen down. "Lady Foxmore was not listed amongst those she was acquainted with. And heaven knows, I never suspected Lord Auburn would actually permit that Windham woman into his house."

"How unlucky your lack of foresight proved to be for his youngest son." Mr. Forrester bit into a raspberry Danish, holding one hand beneath his mouth to catch crumbs. "His good name lost over that tart sitting there."

My father grimaced. "And the meeting with his father?"

"Lord Auburn plans to remain ignorant, but at cost. You may want to sell a mine when you learn how much." Simmons frowned, nudging his head toward me. "He also requires you prevent chance encounters since he's met her before. If they cross paths, he'll be forced to go to the authorities to keep from being an accomplice."

My father kept his face turned from me but pushed back the tails of his frock coat. "Isaac, remove Julia. She needn't be privy to this."

Lord Dalry found his feet and gave a graceful wave of his hand. "Normally I would be glad to, sir. But if you recall, it was your party who disturbed our tea. It would be far more seemly if you left and took the conversation with you."

"Isaac!"

"I'm perfectly serious, sir." He turned and gave Mr. Forrester a curt nod. "No matter what their opinion of her is, it doesn't change the fact that she's Lord Pierson's daughter, and, as such, she'll be treated graciously and not insulted."

"No one insulted that piece of work," Mr. Forrester said between mouthfuls, setting his Danish into an empty cup to comb over the other selections. "We were discussing Simmons's faults. Not hers."

"This conversation is finished. Isaac, I know what you were attempting, and it was ill done. What happened to Reverend Auburn is of no concern to her. Or us, for that matter." My father tossed the two letters into the fire, now crackling merrily. Mrs. Windham's missive, unfolded, fluttered and made an open show of going to its death.

"Isaac, finish here," my father commanded, "then join me in the library. You should know now, we leave for London in the morning."

"London!" Lord Dalry bent his head, making a petition. "But it's not even the season yet! I hoped at the very least to spend a day or two with Kate and Mother."

"There isn't time. I've been waiting for your return. It'll take both of us controlling the damage if we're going to pull this off. Tell Eaton to send them word that we're leaving."

"With all due respect, sir, I'll ride over and tell them myself."

My father looked about to deny the request. "Honestly, Isaac! Fine. Only I expect you to dine here."

Lord Dalry seemed surprised, even annoyed, at the command but acquiesced with a nod.

"Robert." My father turned and, without waiting to see whether Mr. Forrester followed him, left. His voice rang from the hall. "Simmons, stay and chaperone."

With a shrug, Mr. Forrester abandoned the tea tray and wiped his hands over the front of his frock coat as he left the chamber.

There was no recovery from such an action—from this conversation. I pressed my fingertips against my forehead and my cheeks as if to ascertain this wasn't a horrible nightmare.

"I am truly sorry, Miss Pierson," Lord Dalry said in a low voice. "I had hoped we'd have a few more minutes in private."

I stared at the fireplace, where my former life turned to ashes. If I could have trusted my feet to carry me, I would have fled the scene. What tidings had Elizabeth thought would be best coming from her? Had the bishop come? Had Edward been tried as an adulterer? Was Nancy hurt?

"Tea, Miss Pierson?"

Rendered speechless, I turned to view Lord Dalry, my restless fingers now tangled in the hair at the nape of my neck. Could he not see I barely clung to sanity? But he did see. Compassion punctuated his every feature.

"I assure you, matters could have been much worse, and Reverend Auburn fared rather well through the entire ordeal."

"Isaac," Simmons warned from the desk in the corner.

"Surely even you cannot object to me offering that morsel of comfort."

"You'd be surprised at what I could object to," was Simmons's response.

"This may sound odd, but I cannot tell you how much I enjoyed my time with the Windhams," Lord Dalry continued as if not hearing him. "The glimpse at your former life was most profitable; indeed, I almost envy you the freedoms you enjoyed there."

I stared at him as though he were addled before the idea seized me that he was trying to lay the path back to normalcy, step-by-step help me adapt from the scene that had just unfolded.

The nonchalant way he waited for me to meet his gaze bespoke a silent command that the elite never permitted themselves to act emotional, to show weakness, to betray a thought.

At the desk, Simmons stopped tallying his books and observed us.

I looked between them, wondering if they truly expected me to continue on as if I'd not heard how my father tried to tuck me out of existence, as if my feelings were of no consequence.

"Tea, Miss Pierson?" Lord Dalry pressed again in his emotionless voice. Again, he watched me, waiting.

I drew a shaky breath and allowed my hands to drop to my lap, stunned that he was expecting it. "Tea!"

"Mrs. Windham had a charming blend, though I can't say that I'll continue her practice of adding rose petals." He picked up the silver pot. "May I?"

I stared, shocked that he'd just continued on, but then, wondering if he was attempting to find a way to talk about Am Meer, I nodded agreement.

Lord Dalry's smile was approving before he selected an extravagant black and gold-gilt teacup, which he arranged over a saucer. The delicate china never slipped or rattled under his care. "I am sorry that Miss Windham's letter was burned." He set the hot cup in my hands. "I know she felt the loss of your companionship most keenly. One day I hope to have the pleasure of seeing your friendship with her restored. I found her to be the perfect model of discretion."

Simmons harrumphed, flipping over a page. "Yes, and her

mother the perfect lack thereof. If you ask me, Miss Pierson would be wise to forget she ever knew such rabble."

Lord Dalry did not glance at him but concentrated his gaze on me as if willing me not to respond in any manner. This situation scarcely felt real. The desire to scream and smash everything in the room came over me, yet as long as Lord Dalry kept his focus on me, I felt unable to do anything except sit. Behind him, Lady Josephine gleamed from her portrait with approval.

"We stayed at Am Meer for nearly a fortnight," Lord Dalry eventually said. "The cottage is decorated rather charmingly. Have they lived there long?"

I gave him a strained look as questions screamed at me: Why did they stay at Am Meer? Why a fortnight? Had Edward been on trial? Impatient to hear the real news, I gave a curt nod. "Yes, yes . . . I believe many years now."

"Ah, that would explain the grounds. Mrs. Windham spent half her time planting bulbs. Even this time of year I could see how magnificent her garden must be."

All at once I realized this wasn't his way of giving me tidings, but his way of training me. Like one waking from a trance, I dumped my teacup on the nearby saucer. Lord Dalry could hope all he wanted that I'd just sit there having tea while my life was being destroyed, but I wouldn't. Never!

My breath came in hard pants as I resisted looking in Lord Dalry's direction again.

"I have nothing more to say to you." Unwilling to subject myself to his influence, I found my feet. Yet even as I did so, the urge to curtsy and formally take my leave proved stronger than my resistance. I dipped. "If you'll please excuse me, Lord Dalry."

He likewise rose and bowed.

Cold air enveloped me as I rushed into the hall and escaped the bizarre encounter. I braced myself against the wall, fighting tears. I pressed my fingers to my temples, knowing I needed to find a way to contact Edward and have him come and get me. But how?

"Pity," I heard Simmons say after a few seconds. "You nearly had her acting ladylike."

"Quiet." Lord Dalry's command was soft, yet unbending. "She doesn't need criticism, but our aid."

I heard a book slam shut. "I'll not welcome one of Macy's girls, even at your command. It was folly to risk everything on her."

"Well, there's no helping it now. The plan is already in motion." This time Lord Dalry's tone contained irritation. "There's little we can do now but hope for the best."

Simmons let out a huff. "Were I you, I'd be clambering to find an escape from your part of this scheme."

"Keep your concern. I don't need it."

Simmons snorted and papers rustled. "Only a fool steps so directly in that man's path. Don't expect me to weep when you're killed. You do realize you are the only one whose life is primarily in danger."

I held my breath to ensure I heard the reply, but it was unnecessary, for a jovial laugh followed the remark. "I never presumed you to feel one of the worthier emotions. Besides, Forrester is the one I wouldn't trade places with. My danger is nothing compared to his."

"Don't count upon it," Simmons said. "Stealing a man's wife right out from underneath his nose! This is the most reckless scheme I've ever been forced to embark on. For my own part, I wish myself far from here."

"Well, no one's asking you to do anything except manage Lord Pierson's properties and keep quiet." China clattered as Lord Dalry presumably dumped his cup and saucer onto the tray. "I'd best move on to the library now."

Having no time to flee, I stepped into an empty room and pressed my ear against the door. Lord Dalry exited and made his way down the passage.

Five

I DID NOT FIND the solace I sought in my bedchamber that afternoon. After locking myself inside, I spent all emotion and fell into a shallow slumber.

There, I dreamed of Mr. Macy.

In my sleep, I thrashed against the sheets that weighted my legs, making it impossible to run. I sobbed and fell to the marshy ground, knowing I was in a dream but unable to wake.

Wind pierced the wintry brume, raising the stench of rotting leaves and stirring the ground fog. In the haze, the urns and half-toppled columns jutting from the sloping ground resembled broken teeth.

Julia . . .

Mr. Macy's voice, soft as a whisper, demanding as a general's, took on an ethereal quality; just as in real life, there was no pinpointing which direction he would next come from. At times his voice arose from crumbling gravestones, and at others I caught sight of a shadow in the spinney of ghostly birches. My heart pounded as I waited for his approach, waited to awaken. Though my throat burned, I sobbed. From the distance, the sound of nails being hammered into coffins filled my ears.

"Miss Pierson!"

Gasping for air, I lurched up in my bed, clutching my covers to my chest. The hammer's ring weakened into someone knocking on my chamber door. Slowly the fabric of my dream receded under the icy slap of sleet beating against the glass. I drew my knees to my chest and hugged them against me.

Keys rattled and my lock groaned before Mrs. Coleman cracked open the door, her round eyes illuminated in the orb of light from her single candle. "Are you all right?"

I shook my head. I would never be all right. My life had gone irrevocably off course, and I would never be able to set it right.

Mrs. Coleman placed her tiny flame on my nightstand. Tenderness filled her face for a second, but instead of comforting me, she took a deep breath and gave me the same look I'd seen her give an undermaid. "Well, chin up and dry those tears. I'm to fetch you for dinner. Your father is not one to tolerate a young lady weeping at his table, to be sure."

I wiped away the wisps of hair plastered to my face, scarcely able to contain the sudden rush of belonging. "My father ordered me to dinner?"

Regret flickered through Mrs. Coleman's features. "Master Isaac sent me."

I started to pull the counterpane back over my head.

Her chest puffed as she stopped the motion. "What difference does it make who insisted you join? If you want your father's approval, now is the time to go claim it. Be glad for the opportunity to prove yourself."

My eyes burned from my earlier weeping. "Is Forrester attending?"

"Are you going to let a man like that stand in your way?" Without waiting for my response, she pulled back the heavy counterpane. Her eyes locked on me. "Mercy, child, did you have to sleep in your dress! Well, never mind it. Master Isaac stressed timeliness. I'll comb and pin your hair. It's the best we can do. James is waiting at the foot of the stairs. We need to get you to him before Eaton sees him."

"You're wrong, you know," I said, sliding from the bed.

"How so?" She hastened me to the vanity.

I fell to the vanity bench and frowned at my image, trying to overrule my own feelings. "I could hardly care less what my father thinks."

The good woman laughed outright. "I'm a mite wiser than you think. Lucky for you, I've handled the Pierson temperament longer than you've been alive. I warrant I know the two of you better than you know yourselves."

Ten minutes sufficed to find me in the hall, wearing a deeply creased dress, with my hair pulled tightly into a bun. I clomped down the stairs, listening to the rain that pelted every window, amplifying the dreariness of Maplecroft.

James's eyes sparkled as he stepped forward, which warped my emotions. I disliked Lord Dalry with each downward step I took, for I predicted the dinner would be a dismal failure—and because of his interference, key staff members were now hoping for a happy ending, increasing my embarrassment at being continually rejected by my father.

The closer I moved toward James, the more his smile died. He took in my dress with consternation. I nearly laughed, picturing how amused Edward would be by his reaction. James bowed, unable to take his eyes off the mass of wrinkles covering my dress. I gave him what I hoped was a distinguished nod; then, feeling like Anne Boleyn going to the execution block, I picked up my billowing skirts and followed him.

～～

"No, we'll let Isaac be the one to persuade him." My father's voice resonated with authority as we approached the threshold.

"The first evening we're back in London, go to our club and straighten out Lord Alexander."

"I highly doubt he'll listen to me," came Lord Dalry's vexed-sounding answer. "He never even hears a word I say, but sits blowing smoke rings. You should be the one to refuse him."

"Nonsense." My father's tone stopped me cold. "I know you don't care for his character, but it's time you overlooked it. We need his continued support."

Mr. Forrester's obnoxious laugh followed the clinking of a glass. "Isaac's right, Roy. If he's the one to inform Lord Alexander, he'll only see it as a challenge. It might aggravate the situation. You shouldn't have advertised her. Had you listened to my counsel, we wouldn't even be in this position."

"Your counsel? Since when have I ever required counsel from you?"

"I'm reminded," Lord Dalry said. "During my absence, was there a correspondence from Burns?"

"No," my father replied, "but Palmer received quite an earful from Lord Auckland." I stepped up to the threshold just as my father reached for his wineglass. A full course was already set and on the table. "I'm anxious to glean his thoughts about Dost Mohammed; the last I heard—"

"Ah, Miss Pierson!" Lord Dalry rose with a smile.

My father visibly started to see me before he muttered a low oath. He removed the napkin from his lap and stood. "Daughter?" His tone was stern as he avoided eye contact. "Is there something you require?"

I lost mastery over my feet and paused in the doorway. Opposite me, on the wall, a snowy-haired version of Lady Josephine watched me with an arch smile. I fastened my eyes on her portrait, envisioning that if she were alive, she would rise to greet me, holding out her arms in welcome, the emeralds glinting in her cottony hair.

Lord Dalry was at my side before I regained enough sense to

retreat. "I'm delighted you decided to join me. Come, sit with me. We'll leave politics to your father and Forrester."

My father's mouth twitched with anger as he retook his seat. "Isaac, you know I do not tolerate tardiness in my house."

"Well, sir, it is rather hard to make a timely entrance when you're uncertain you're invited to the event." In a fluid movement, Lord Dalry gathered me with one arm and moved me to the table. With his eyes, he indicated that I should follow his lead.

I couldn't help but glance nervously at my father.

One finger pressed deep into his cheek as he frowned. "The next meal, you will be on time or you will not join us. Is that understood?"

Whereas other people might have felt resentment, I only felt hurt. My face burned with humiliation as I took a seat.

"Young ladies do not turn scarlet at the table, either." My father waved for more wine.

"Ah, then someone should tell Miss Anna Knight," Lord Dalry said with a soft laugh, lowering himself into the seat next to me. "She has a dreadful habit of becoming tongue-tied and flustered during every dinner we've attended. Have you not noticed it?"

My father's bottom lip curled out. "With an aunt as prestigious as hers, she can better afford nervous fits."

Lord Dalry's eyebrows rose. "I assure you, your own prestige quite matches Miss Knight's aunt's. Therefore, we can conclude that if your daughter blushes, it will be overlooked."

"I highly doubt your daughter has control over her color," Mr. Forrester said with a sneer. "All it takes is a certain *unnamed* gentleman whispering in her ear, and within a blink, she's red all over."

My stomach tightened with panic. I started to push away from the table but Lord Dalry touched my forearm, stopping me.

"I'll ask you not to spy on Miss Pierson and me." His voice contained a note I'd not heard before. It was inflexible, worse than my father's temper, and yet somehow calm. He shifted in his seat to view my father. "Sir, please accept my deepest apology. While I might have stolen a moment in private with your daughter earlier, I can assure you, I said nothing unseemly."

It took a moment for me to realize that Lord Dalry had spoken thus for the sake of the butler and footmen watching from the sideboard. My father, however, seemed unable to recover from the allusion to Mr. Macy. His face flushed as if he had suffered an apoplexy.

"The next course, if you please." Lord Dalry addressed Eaton, making a motion to clear away the untouched plates. "Send Pierrick our assurances it was not the hare. Tell him the start of our dinner was delayed, nothing more."

"Yes, sir." Eaton bowed and nodded for James and William to step forward and clear the fricasseed rabbit.

Mr. Forrester garnered a few shelled walnuts from the bowl, meeting me with his challenging gaze. "It's interesting how our Miss Pierson always shows up late for dinner. I seem to have memory of her arriving shamelessly late to another dinner, scarlet from head to toe. But of course, as our acquaintance has been short, I must be recalling nothing more than a dream."

A vein rose across my father's brow.

Tingles of heat ran up and down my neck and face as I glanced at the expressionless footmen.

"Odd that you're dreaming about Miss Pierson." Lord Dalry's voice held disgust. "I'll have to ask you to refrain from mentioning them as well."

The twitching of Mr. Forrester's mouth was the only indicator he'd been offended.

"Sir." Lord Dalry faced my father. "I wasn't going to bring this up during dinner, but I feel compelled to now. The staff is rather disturbed by Mr. Forrester's alarming fascination with your daughter. They do not like his method of courting, nor do I."

Mr. Forrester nearly choked before he spewed a piece of walnut onto the table. Wiping his mouth, he glared at Lord Dalry.

"Naturally, at first I dismissed it as nothing more than a rumor." Lord Dalry strummed his fingers on the arm of his chair. "But then I learned he's been spotted rifling through her bedchamber. Mrs. Coleman informed me that he comes to her nightly and demands to know what your daughter did that day. Another servant informed me Mr. Forrester is up all hours of the night pressing his ear against her chamber door."

My father pinched the bridge of his nose, lowering his chin.

"Most disturbing, however," Lord Dalry continued, "is the report that he's peeped through her keyhole." Lord Dalry held up one finger, telling Mr. Forrester to wait, when the man gave a threatening glare. "Upon further investigation, two of the maids confessed that he's paid them to enter her bedchamber and check on her while she slept. Is that not so, James?"

The footman kept his eyes on the dishes as he cleared them. "Yes, sir." Then he quickly added, "'Tis hardly the half of it."

"To be frank." Lord Dalry still addressed my father but shifted his gaze to Mr. Forrester. "I find your guest's preoccupation with her repulsive."

"Ha-ha, Isaac." Mr. Forrester thumped the table, his face flushed with anger. "Very humorous."

"I'm not laughing."

"Well, you ought to be. You're playing the role of the fool. Can't you see what she's doing? Dividing us?"

"Eaton." The heavy voice of my father fell upon us with authority. "You're dismissed. Take James and William with you. We'll ring when ready for the next course."

"Yes, sir." Eaton's expression remained dry as he did an about-face.

Not a fork slid nor a glass clinked as they crossed the chamber and left, shutting the door behind them. With the staff gone, my father leaned back in his chair and lapsed into a silence that we dared not break. Little by little, his face returned to a normal color.

"Isaac," he said first, lowering his hand.

"Sir, he's forcing my hand."

"You have no idea the fire you're playing with, Isaac." Mr. Forrester yanked his napkin from his lap and rose. "You've just destroyed my ability to keep her in check, destroyed my credibility with the staff here—"

"What do you think you've done to hers?" Lord Dalry also rose, but he appeared calm and his voice stayed level. "Did you think I would sit by quietly while you openly attacked her?"

"Enough!" My father's bellow roared through the room, causing me to cover my ears. "Not one more word from either of you!"

"Oh no!" Mr. Forrester shook his head, jabbing his finger into the table. "Oh no, oh no! We've not even begun this discussion. If I don't disillusion Isaac right now as to what she is, what she's capable of, he'll be her next victim. I'm nowhere near finished speaking."

"Oh yes, you are." My father's voice rumbled like thunder in the distance, promising a great and terrible storm. "You're both going to cease this minute and sit down and eat dinner like civilized people. Robert, if ever I catch you at her bedchamber door, I'll personally drive you with a whip from my house. And, Isaac." My father allowed the full wrath of his glare to fall on Lord Dalry. "This is not how I raised you. This is not acceptable behavior. Robert is a guest at my table, whether you approve or not." He braced his hands on the table and leaned forward. His voice came out in a growl. "Need I remind the two of you how important this alliance is?"

Lord Dalry's eyes communicated his ire at Mr. Forrester before he directed his gaze toward me as if to see how I fared.

I had grown up in a house of conflict, one where insults and harsh words were flung like cabers in Highland games. Reacting only exacerbated the conflict; waiting was always the wisest choice. Besides, I knew their emotions were so heated that nothing I said would be heard regardless. When tempers flare, people are always far more interested in expressing their hurt than in seeking solutions. It was far better to stay out of the fray and listen. I planned to sift through the accusations later and weigh them, one by one, to determine whether they were statements made in anger or something I needed to beware of. Thus, for most of the argument, I simply folded my arms over my stomach and averted my gaze.

When Lord Dalry questioned me with his look, however, his brow furrowed as if he couldn't make sense of my response.

"Isaac, Robert." My father's voice was nearer to my seat, and I realized he'd risen. "Both of you to the library. Julia, have a tray sent to your bedchamber if you're still hungry."

I jumped in my seat as my father placed his hand on my shoulder and gave it a slight squeeze. Lord Dalry crossed his arms, studying me as if taking note that I startled when touched. Between his evaluation and my father's unexpected gesture, I felt unable to collect myself.

"Sir, may I have a private word with your daughter first?"

"Isaac!"

"One moment. Please."

My father must have answered with a nod and then motioned to Mr. Forrester, for they marched from the chamber. Not certain what Lord Dalry wanted, I fastened my gaze on the heavy wine goblet before me, refusing to look at him. He, however, laid his forearm over the table and leaned into my view.

"Listen," he said, his tone soft. "Mr. Forrester will likely leave for London tonight, as your father now sees benefit in having him gone. I'm not certain I shall be back in time for breakfast, but I'll try. I promised my mother and sister they'd have time with me during the off-season. I gave my word months ago, and I've been remiss in that promise twice. This time of year, your father takes his breakfast at eight. Be certain you are timely."

I cocked my head. "Why are you telling me this?"

He gave a sad smile, then leaned back in his chair and viewed the dining chamber with different eyes. His mouth pursed as if he'd tasted a sour wine. When he spoke, I barely caught his next words. "Trust me, I know better than you realize what you're undergoing. It becomes easier from here."

Then, like a true member of the gentry, unaffected by the ripples of change, he rose, bowed, and left.

~~~

Sometime after midnight, the sound of a horse's whinny woke me. I opened my eyes to a dimly lit room. A feeling of calm had replaced the heaviness I'd taken to bed. I rubbed my eyes, trying to account for the change. Gradually I became aware that firelight burnished the walls, warming the chamber. I sank back into the pillow, noting that Mrs. Coleman must be happy for the recovery of her staff.

Once more a horse nickered, only this time it sounded closer. Curious, I slid from bed, lit a candle, and retreated to the window. In the ravine, the outline of Eastbourne could barely be seen as it was barraged by precipitation.

A wide circle of lantern light turned the corner of Maplecroft, followed by a groom holding the light aloft. Behind him, a man sat upon a steed. I leaned forward, squinting. It wasn't difficult to recognize Mr. Forrester's rumpled silhouette. Thankfully, darkness hid his expression, though I could well imagine it as he caught sight of me, then turned toward Eastbourne as if to ascertain what I'd been looking at. I frowned, considering what he'd tell my father.

Looking over his shoulder, he studied me for a moment as if wanting me to feel the weight of his accusation, before his shoulders squared and he lifted his reins. Despite the mud, his horse picked its way down the road that led from Maplecroft and past Eastbourne.

I sighed with relief, glad I needn't be worried about his loathsome presence in the morning. Though I didn't want to care, a small part of me hoped that with Forrester gone, there might now be a chance of winning my father's approval.

Six

ICY SHARDS of rain slanted inward and blended with the muddy footprints that had been trampled indoors by the servants. I paused midway down the stairs to watch. Pallid faces huffed with exertion as they hefted trunks and carried them outdoors, where the remnants of night waned. Beyond my view, the crunch of carriage wheels on cobblestone combined with the slap of leather against horseflesh.

Simmons looked over from where he supervised. With a frown that made his bushy eyebrows extend over his spectacles, he jabbed the air in the direction of the breakfast chamber, an indication of where I was expected to go. "No slacking," he barked at a stable hand who stopped to tip his hat. "Back to work. Now!"

I folded my arms against the cold that streamed through the open door, then hurried down the last few stairs and hastened to the breakfast chamber. As I reached the threshold, however, a burst of girlish laughter sounded from within. Stunned, I paused and peeked inside.

To my astonishment, Lord Dalry had returned. He sat at the

far end of the table, concentrating hard on a small leather volume. A girl dressed in pale-yellow travel attire sat next to him, waving her spoon within his line of vision as if trying to break his attention. Glossy amber-colored hair was piled high atop her head, but it was so curly that natural ringlets had escaped, framing her face and gracing her neck.

"You can ignore me." Her voice was singsong. "But I know you can see me."

Lord Dalry did not so much as blink, though he gave a slight sigh, bringing about another round of girlish laughter.

She turned in my direction and gasped, grasping his arm. "Oh, Isaac! She's here! She's finally here!"

Lord Dalry lowered his book and regarded me. He kept his debonair expression as he stood. "Miss Pierson, may I have the pleasure of introducing you to—"

With a toss of curls, the girl rushed to me and grabbed my hand. "Oh, we are to be the very dearest of friends! I just know it. Oh, how I know it. Just you wait! You'll see I'm right. I'm always right about these sort of things."

Uncertain what to make of her sudden rush to offer me friendship, I took a step backwards.

She leaned closer. "Doesn't it feel like we're already sisters! I nearly spent the last fortnight weeping in anguish for you. Every time I thought about—"

"Kate!" Lord Dalry's tone brooked no argument. "Miss Pierson is a young lady of good breeding. Do not display your lack of refinement. You are not to speak unless she asks you questions. Take your seat this instant."

Kate dipped her head as though humbled by his rebuke, but carefully keeping her face shielded from his view, she smirked at me, rolling her eyes.

"Your father has invited my younger sister to join us," Lord Dalry explained as he held out a chair for me. "He thought you would enjoy a travelling companion."

Kate stifled a laugh. "And he woke us up at three in the morning too! Mama was beside herself to ready me in time."

The rate at which this girl poured out her thoughts and feelings to others was overwhelming.

I took my seat, wary of the both of them as I made them my study. Their ease struck me first. They sat with the carefree manner of those who know they belong in their surroundings. I scanned the table next, surprised to discover their plates were full.

Lord Dalry took his seat, his blue eyes trained on me. I refused to meet his gaze.

When Eaton announced my father a moment later, Lord Dalry smiled with affection and stood. I bunched a fistful of my skirt, uncertain whether to rise. I took my cue from Kate, who remained in her seat, staring wide-eyed.

My father's eyes crinkled as he went straight to Lord Dalry and patted his arm. "Son, thank you for joining us on such short notice."

Jealousy and wistfulness stabbed my heart at the realization that my father called Lord Dalry son. I straightened, awaiting my greeting.

Instead, he turned toward the girl. "Ah, Katherine, so you decided to accept my invitation? I am certain my daughter will greatly benefit from your example and companionship."

Miss Dalry covered her mouth, giggling. Beneath the table, something bumped the table leg, so I assumed she'd swung her legs too. My father gave her an indulgent smile; then either not seeing or ignoring the fact that I awaited his acknowledgment, he sat and took an orange from a silver bowl and began peeling it with a knife.

Lord Dalry, however, carefully measured my reactions. I tried to pretend I cared not and fumbled with my napkin.

A moment later, Eaton delivered a stack of newspapers, all cut and ironed. The interested expression my father gave them ended any hope that he'd speak to me next.

Lord Dalry set aside his book. "May I see the *Morning Gazette*? I wish to read the article Forrester told us to expect today."

My father nodded permission and unfurled the *Times* for himself. I stared at the paper barrier between us, unable to believe he'd not even wished me a good morning.

Kate leaned over her plate. "Excuse me, sir, but have you learned whether the Prescots will host their annual ball this year?"

I cringed, waiting for his rebuke. Lord Dalry stopped reading, but it was me he studied.

My father dipped his paper, making a crinkling sound. Teasing filled his voice. "I might have overheard some nonsense about a dance."

Kate squealed, clapping her hands, and turned toward me. "I can't wait for you to see their ball. They empty the entire downstairs to—"

"Kate," Lord Dalry said after glancing in my direction, "do not speak at the table unless you are spoken to."

"No, no." My father leaned back with a smile. "Allow the girls to prattle."

I felt my eyes widen with indignation as I signalled James for tea. *Prattle,* I thought, clenching my spoon. Had I prattled? Had I even spoken one word?

Across the table, Lord Dalry continued to observe me with a look of concern.

Kate propped her elbows on the table and faced my father with shining eyes. "I already know what I'll wear! Remember that darling velvet gown you sent for Christmas?"

My spoon clattered to my saucer, drawing Lord Dalry's full attention, for he folded the paper and set it aside, keeping his eyes trained on me.

But I didn't care. A chasm of hurt opened in my soul. There hadn't been meat or coal at my house last Christmas. My dress had been in tatters, literally threadbare at the elbows. Yet my father had sent this giggling girl a Christmas present?

I viewed the table laden with food before me, realizing more was wasted at breakfast here than Mama and I had eaten in a week.

Once again, as if able to read my thoughts, Lord Dalry looked pained for me as I tried to adjust my emotions.

"Julia, answer her question!" my father ordered.

Pulled from my thoughts, I realized Kate had spouted some nonsense in my direction. "What question?"

"About dances! Did you dance at your school?" Kate leaned forward with excitement.

"No," I responded. "We were far too hungry and too poor to think of such nonsense!" Then with a sudden rush of anger, "One time we spent an entire afternoon picking mealworms out of the flour, just so we could have something for dinner."

Kate gaped, stunned to silence.

"Of all the lies—" My father fisted his napkin, red creeping up his neck.

"Sir," Lord Dalry said quietly, "my sister's place is below that of your daughter. As hostess, if your daughter wishes conversation, allow her to lead it. Kate, no more talk. Be quiet."

My father grew remarkably red in less than a second as he continued to glare at me. "How dare you act so—"

Lord Dalry placed both hands on the table as if ready to rise. "You'll have to forgive me, sir. But the offense is Kate's. It wasn't her place to push Miss Pierson when it's clear she desires peace. This is her house. This is her table. She should not be forced to accommodate my sister."

"Her house? Her table? Isaac, even you forget your place. My daughter's duty is to grace the table, not sit there and spin tales of woe. And if you think I'm going to tolerate her fibs—"

"I detected no deception, sir."

"Are you suggesting that I allowed my daughter to live in unfit circumst—?"

"I'm suggesting that you were unaware, sir. Please, do not add to her burden by punishing her for speaking truth."

My father set down his newspaper, choking on his anger. "Eaton, tell Simmons to prepare a separate carriage for my daughter and Miss Dalry. Isaac and I will ride alone." My father clenched his fists. "Apparently there are matters we still need to discuss."

Lord Dalry gave a sigh as he set down his cup and looked in my direction with a hopeful expression, but I would not acknowledge him.

His ability to sense my thoughts was too unsettling, for I could not yet read him.

～

"Be sure to keep your feet dry." Mrs. Coleman tugged at the top button of my mantelet.

I nodded and adjusted the cuffs of my sleeves, surprised by my desire for tears.

"I daresay you'll find the London House staff as efficient as ours." She gave a sly smile. "You may coop up Mrs. King all hours of the day now if you like, though I warrant you'll be far too busy for that."

I tugged on my gloves, then clasped one of her hands between mine, realizing that she'd become my refuge at Maplecroft. Tears lodged in my throat as I wondered if I could convince my father to allow me to stay at Maplecroft with his elderly housekeeper. He stood a short distance away, speaking in terse whispers to Simmons, who held open a large leather ledger and trailed down one column with a gnarled finger. Their expressions alone killed any hope of approaching them.

I gave Mrs. Coleman a teary smile. "I don't know how I shall ever manage without you."

Her mouth pursed as she stepped back, though her eyes glistened. "Nonsense! You'll be perfectly fine. Master Isaac will see to that." She glanced over my shoulder. "Never thought the lad would come to mean so much to the house." She shook her head.

"I still remember the day Lord Pierson set the boy down in the foyer and announced his intentions to raise him. Such a sight, Master Isaac fresh from his father's grave, too old to be sucking his thumb.

"Sad days those were. I could tell you stories that would make you thankful your homecoming wasn't Master Isaac's." All at once, she straightened, dusted off her hands, then addressed me in a no-argument tone. "If you'll take my advice, you'll let go of your prissy ways and accept all the help that lad gives you. You'll never find a truer soul on God's green earth, and that's a fact."

Winding a muffler about my neck, I looked farther down the hall, where Lady Dalry had come to bid her children farewell. Her picture was the opposite of my father. The kindness in her smile and eyes quelled fear. She stood with one hand on Lord Dalry's cheek, gazing up at him. They spoke their own silent language, one that gave utterance to something full of tender mercy and yet unyielding strength.

I stood transfixed as volumes of instructions and information passed between them, none of which I could translate. Their look made me think that if I could understand, I'd find something wonderful and transforming. Lady Dalry's other arm was draped over Kate, who had no clue as to what transpired above her. With both arms wrapped about her mother's waist, she sobbed bitterly.

I can still see the picture Lady Dalry made that day.

Tawny hair pulled into a loose braid that wound about her head complemented the crocheted, homemade-looking shawl pinned about her shoulders. Her dress was nothing more fancy than serviceable muslin. Her red jacket was faded. She was the first lady I'd ever encountered in homemade attire, making her a novelty.

As I studied her, she suddenly turned toward me. Whatever expression she saw on my face instantly warmed hers. As easily as someone pulling out miscounted rows of knitting, she disentangled herself from Kate and floated in my direction.

"Miss Pierson," she said, her voice as amber as honey. With the gentlest of touches, she cupped my cheek. Then staring at me with glistening eyes, she stated, "Oh, Roy, she's truly lovely. Lovely."

At that moment, my soul was laid before her, and as I'd experienced with her son, I had no ability to hide it. My bottom lip trembled as I tried to wall her out. I doubted not she saw everything: my grief over Mama, my fear of Mr. Macy, my longing for Edward, my resistance toward the friendship her children offered me, and the burning anger I felt toward my father. Compassion softened her features as I tried to deflect her direct stare by dropping my eyes.

My father glanced at us, looking choked before he fisted his hands. Instead of answering her, he pulled out his pocket watch and peered at it. "It's time to leave," he called out. "Isaac, see the girls to their carriage." He turned back to his conversation with Simmons before the two of them stormed outside, leaving the front door open in their wake.

Lord Dalry approached, studying me as keenly as his mother had, his expression giving away only what he chose, which was nothing.

"Take care of her, Son." Lady Dalry gave him a worried look, stepping back. "The situation is more fragile than I realized."

"I agree." He kissed her cheek. "I'll proceed with utmost care. Are you ready, Miss Pierson?"

My throat clogged with tears as I uncharacteristically grabbed Lady Dalry's hand, then leaned over and whispered, "Do you . . . do you ever come to London?"

The tenderness in her expression pierced my heart as she tipped forward and kissed my cheek. "No, child, but when sessions are over, you must come and spend hours and hours with me."

I nodded, disliking that I was now acting as forward as Kate.

Yet Lord Dalry beamed with approval as he offered his arm. Though I had extended my friendship to Lady Dalry, I still hadn't accepted her children's. I have no doubt my face became petulant, for Mrs. Coleman huffed with disapproval as I unwillingly took his arm.

Wind-driven rain stabbed my cheeks as we hurried to the carriage. James opened the door, looking strange without his powdered wig. Brown hair caked his forehead. To my relief, his thick greatcoat and hat heralded that he would accompany us.

I glanced over my shoulder at Eaton to determine whether he would attend as well. His pale fingers, however, gripped nothing more than a lightweight cape thrown over his shoulders as he listened to Simmons's instructions. I felt overwhelmed at the thought that I would have a new butler and housekeeper.

"Who's the footman for this carriage?" Lord Dalry raised his voice to be heard over the hard slap of rain.

James grinned and drew the collar of his cloak about his face. "I am, sir."

"Good." Lord Dalry offered his hand so I could climb up to the open barouche door. "It will be dark by the time we reach London. Keep your wits about you. No one approaches this carriage. Is that understood?"

James gave a sharp nod. "Aye, sir. You can depend on me."

I entered the barouche, losing their conversation to the drumming on the roof. Moist air penetrated the carriage, deepening the scents of oiled leather and axle grease. After a few minutes, Kate dipped her head and entered. Her eyes were exceedingly bright for someone who'd just been crying. She brushed rain from her coat sleeves.

"You are not to disturb Miss Pierson's peace during the journey." Water dripped from the brim of Lord Dalry's hat as he wedged his head in the door before closing it.

Kate turned toward me, dimples denting both of her ivory cheeks. Her eyes sparkled, informing me she had no intention of remaining silent. When Lord Dalry latched the door, she smeared the window with her gloved hand. "Isn't Mama wonderful? You should have seen your face as you spoke to her."

Sinking against my seat, I stared at the hazed-over window, embarrassed that there were witnesses to that moment of weakness. With luck, she'd take the hint that I had no desire to talk. I removed my damp gloves, then started on my bonnet. Already the pheasant feathers Mrs. Coleman had faithfully groomed drooped over the brim.

"Here, allow me." Kate bounced on the edge of her seat as she reached under my chin. "You mustn't feel uncomfortable, now." She giggled and grasped my arm. "Not when you consider our future." Her smile revealed dainty teeth as I questioned her with a look. "We are to be the best of friends. I just know it! We shall be better than sisters! Shall I sit with you?"

She started to remove her handbag and gloves as she stooped.

"No, please remain in your seat."

Kate obeyed by falling back to her seat and pressing her forehead against the glass, eagerly drinking in the bevy of servants scurrying about. "I wish I could have been here the night you arrived! It must have been so romantic! I feared you would die of a broken heart from missing your school chums before we could meet. Wouldn't it be wonderful to die of a broken heart?"

The carriages lurched into motion, and she had to clutch the seat. Weariness took over, and all at once I felt the effects of waking so early to be hustled out the door. I shut my eyes and leaned back in my seat. Though I doubted I could sleep, I hoped it would encourage silence.

"You mustn't sleep yet." Kate laid a hand on my forearm. "We're to drive past Eastbourne. You must see it for yourself. Oh, you must!"

"Eastbourne?" I straightened, alarmed. "You've been there?"

"No, of course not. No one is allowed inside." She grabbed

my hands. "But Mr. Macy is another romantic soul! He's spent years locked away, refusing to admit anyone into his estate. A lost love kept him there, I just know it. Then after all this time, he married someone our age, only she was unfaithful and ran away with a clergyman."

I felt paralyzed as our carriages did indeed come alongside the ancient section of the estate. Coldness enveloped me as I viewed the path near the stable where Mr. Greenham had declared he was Mama's murderer, then the bench where I had tried to tell Edward of my engagement, and the greenhouse where I pledged my troth to Mr. Macy.

Kate leaned forward. "He was so devoted to her, too. For weeks he pleaded in the papers for her return. She must be very ungrateful, for she wasn't even a peer—"

"Hush." I frowned, feeling out of sorts. "The story probably isn't even true."

"Oh, but it is! It really is." Kate nodded so furiously that one more curl came loose from her style. "All the newspapers carried it, and everyone whispers about it when they think I'm not listening."

We passed from view of Eastbourne, and I sank against the back of my seat, contemplating how one week of life had changed everything. The weight of my blame settled into the hollow of my chest.

I closed my eyes, wishing myself home. To combat the ache, I opened the cache of memories comprised of my summers with Edward. Each memory was a paragon, transcendent. The one that kept surfacing was of a rare, jewel-like day in June, when the azure sky was filled with masses of clouds that look like beds of down.

Elizabeth and I had dressed in white lawn dresses and tied pink ribbon sashes about our waists, then hastened away from Am Meer before our mothers could question us. Even though I was a child, as we approached the ancient oak where the boys waited, the pride on Edward's face was unmistakable and I felt right again.

Silence was our bond while laughter was Henry and Elizabeth's; thus we ambled at our own pace. We passed through fields and pastures bathed in sunlight, over mossy stones embedded in trickling brooks.

When we arrived at Henry's planned destination, Elizabeth gasped in amazement at the large, early field of sunflowers. Rays of sun touched down upon the golden heads, which nodded in the breeze. They had always been her favorite.

"We'll have to make certain we don't break any," Henry said, "but I explored it earlier and found a gap where they planted around a stone. We can eat there." He faced Elizabeth, grinning. "Ready?"

An adventurer about to embark, she gave a gay laugh, and despite Henry's admonition, they left a path of bent stalks, strewn leaves, and yellow petals in their wake.

I stared at the oversized flowers, wishing we hadn't come. Though I didn't fully understand, this particular flower was a source of tension between William and Mama. They were banned from our house, though she longingly touched the ones that found their way into market stalls. Thus, I associated sunflowers with wrongness. To walk beneath those heavy-headed disks felt unchaste.

When encountering a disjointed part of my soul, Edward knew better than to speak. Words cause so much damage, and even at that tender age, he had the uncanny wisdom to use them sparingly. And though it was irrational to fear walking beneath sunflowers, he simply offered his hand, then his gentlest smile. Not a smile laced with pity, for that would have communicated only how different I was, but a smile of acceptance.

Nothing more was needed to untwist that part of my soul. I took his hand, willing to trust, and plunged into the leafy copse, where I found nothing bad happened. We ate a horror of confections that only children would pack: chocolates, toffee, and sweet biscuits, all guzzled down with lukewarm water from a flask. Yet it was a golden feast, as epic as any king's.

Thereafter, when Mama would grow sad and touch the sunflowers in the marketplace, I'd lean against her and join her lament, though I did not know what we cried for.

Seven

AT SUNSET, Kate and I had our first view of London. Buildings crowded each other, silhouetted under a bleak sky filled with soot and smoke. The rain had receded hours after we left Maplecroft, but the aftermath wrapped the city in a heavy blanket of fog, so that as we entered the city, it became impossible to see farther than a few feet out the window.

London is not the same city today that it was then. The farther we progressed, the stronger the reek of manure and sewage. In the hazy glow of lampposts, ragged children ran past our carriage with brooms, cleaning the muck of horse droppings off the cobblestones. Once a beggar approached the carriage and clung to the side, babbling at us. From his perch atop our barouche, James beat him off with his crop.

Coaches, omnibuses, and wagons came from every corner. More than once we were forced to a standstill while an entangled mess cleared. My father's wealth became evident, for police always carved a path for my father first, tipping their hats, wonderment on their faces.

"What if we become separated?" Kate whispered as my father's carriage crossed a street, leaving us to wait in the murk for another clearing.

"Hush." I waved for silence, disliking the tingling fear that washed over me. "Even if we did, the coachman knows where he's going, and James is with us."

Kate shifted to my seat as she stared after my father's disappearing carriage. Realizing she needed comfort, I allowed her to sit next to me and take my hand as I observed the streets. If you were to count the number of people I'd met in my entire life, they would have easily been outnumbered by the people we'd just passed in one evening. I eyed beggars sitting in doorways, gaunt with vacant stares, realizing how minuscule my woes would seem compared to theirs. Children in rags that displayed thin legs, digging through rubbish piles, presumably searching for food.

I studied their piteous condition, stunned. If these were some of the realities that Edward faced as a clergyman, no wonder he'd become fanatical during my absence.

My heart burned with compassion everywhere I looked. Under the feeble gaslight, hard-faced women sold oranges and flowers out of boxes that hung from straps around their necks. Even though it was dark, peddlers still called their wares while others packed, presumably to go home for the night. In one building, women leaned out of windows, their arms folded beneath their bosoms. They wore nothing but low-cut chemises and hopeless expressions.

As the streets darkened into night, a herd of cows hemmed us in, delaying us further. Kate whimpered when my father's carriage turned completely from sight. Sounds of the coachman's and James's voices could be heard yelling at the herdsman. With his crop, James began to beat the cattle away.

Without warning, the hefty man reached up and pulled James from the carriage.

"Get off him," our coachman yelled, and the carriage shifted as though he stood. Using the horsewhip, he lashed at the rogue. Cattle reared their heads, lowing. From the sidewalks, people began to shout, laugh, and throw garbage as James broke free and also beat the vagrant. A cow crushed against the side of the carriage, rocking it, making Kate scream. Then as suddenly as it had started, it ended. The herd made their crossing and their caretaker ran after them.

His lip swollen, James pulled at his ripped velvet greatcoat, then climbed aboard the carriage. Neither Kate nor I spoke but sat clutching each other's hands. I ceased to watch the activity until we reached the richer section. Here the air felt less oppressive. Instead of shops, clusters of houses were lit. Bobbies walked the streets in lesser numbers. When the carriage halted, I breathed relief that we'd safely made it.

The door jerked open. To my surprise, my father stood outside. With an ungloved hand, he reached in and touched my cheek. Even in the dark, I could see relief replacing the fear in his eyes. He looked me over from head to toe before reaching out both hands to aid my descent. Fury filled his features as he faced the box seat. "What street did you take?"

"The same as you, sir." The coachman alighted, rocking the carriage. "Only we were stuck at a crossing with cattle between us."

"Could you not have gone around them?"

"Not if I was to take the exact streets as you ordered, sir."

My father's fierce look stole my breath. "When I entrust my sole child to your care, I expect better than that performance!"

The coachman turned his hat in his hands, not daring to look up. "Next time, sir, should I disobey your orders, then?"

"Are you questioning me?"

The poor man rubbed his balding spot, opening and closing his mouth.

I flinched at my father's outrage, even while another part

of me thrilled that he'd been worried. I tapped his arm. "He couldn't help it. There were cattle—"

My father's ire turned on me. "Did I give you permission to speak?"

"If I may interject?" Lord Dalry stepped toward us, his voice serenity itself. "All's well that ends well, sir. Your daughter is here, safe and sound. Hudson, thank you for your service. You did well to heed Lord Pierson's exact instructions."

My father glared a second longer at the coachman, then forcibly moved me toward Lord Dalry. "Take her indoors. Do not leave her side until all the baggage has been unloaded, the servants counted, and the doors locked."

"Sir, I hardly think the precaution—"

"Isaac, now!"

Lord Dalry caught my father's attention and nodded in my direction. "You asked me to remind you."

My father's brows knit, and he looked as though his temper was near giving way, but then he ran his fingers through his hair, looking awkward. "Julia, in London I'm a busy man; nonetheless, we should become acquainted. Would a nightly meeting work with your schedule?"

I still hadn't recovered from the sting of having been yelled at; therefore I didn't trust the sudden change. I felt my brow wrinkle as I tried to work out whether I wanted to agree to his plan or not.

My father frowned, deepening his jowl lines, as he shot Lord Dalry a look that asked what he was doing wrong.

Lord Dalry stepped forward. "What do you say to designating a time, sir?"

My father eyed him as if not trusting his take on the situation. "Fine. Ten. Now take her inside, Isaac." Lord Dalry looked about to speak, but my father leaned in our direction, his voice a low growl. "Now, Isaac, now! I want her out of sight immediately!"

Lord Dalry placed his hand beneath my elbow but turned to

the carriage. "James, escort Kate and find the housekeeper. Ask her to allow my sister to wait in her chambers until I'm finished."

Lord Dalry ushered me toward the house, and I drew in a stunned breath as I viewed my father's London residence. The immense structure stood at least three stories high. Its breadth matched its height. Gabled roofs angled over every corner and stuck out past tall brick chimneys. My father apparently wasn't afraid of the window tax, for his house boasted casements even below street level. My breath caught as I wondered exactly how rich my father was to be able to afford an estate as expansive as Maplecroft in the country and a house this size in the city. I clutched my skirt and turned in time to see an open carriage draw to the curb and stop.

Three men rose and tipped their hats at my father with solemn expressions.

"Who are they?" I asked, feeling mild panic. "What do they want?"

Lord Dalry glanced over his shoulder and laughed a wondrous, clear laugh. "Oh no! And your father wanted to keep our being in London a secret. Those men are our staunchest supporters. Each one hopes to be on my cabinet if I become prime minister." His voice lowered. "They actually believe I'll allow your father to choose my cabinet. Their obeisance is vain; nevertheless, commit their faces to memory, for you'll see them often and need to recognize them."

I dropped my skirt, too stunned to speak. "Prime minister?"

Lord Dalry looked all astonishment and halted. "Did you not know our aim?"

I felt my nose wrinkle. "But . . . you're not old enough!"

His laugh was genuine. "Well, I was rather hoping time would amend that problem."

Confused, I glanced back at my father. "I don't understand. Why would you do this, then? Why would either of you risk such consequences by pretending I'm his daughter?"

"Because you are. Now if you'll please follow me. He'll have my head if we remain on this stoop one more minute." Lord Dalry urged me up the stairs.

The moment we stepped inside, I felt my fate change.

Some sort of hidden magic seemed to rise from the streets of London, through the brick and cobblestone, and into this mansion. Entranced, I took a few steps forward. A fireplace of hewn stone—fashioned to look like a castle, complete with turrets—warmed the entrance hall. Dark polished staircases ascended on both my right and my left. The vestibules of the second and third stories could be viewed behind ornate spindles, so that a person could stand on the third floor and look down on the second and entrance hall. From our vantage point, I saw room after room spilling from behind arched doorways. The walls were a mixture of bold colors and Gothic stone.

"I knew you would feel it too," Lord Dalry said. "I knew it."

I felt too amazed to speak.

"Your father could have afforded a house on Park Lane, but he chose Audley because of this house. The housekeeper didn't get notice of our arrival, so your bedchamber is being readied even now. While we wait, I'll show you the library, where you'll meet nightly with your father."

"Why didn't the notice arrive? What could have waylaid it?"

Lord Dalry shrugged. "It happens occasionally."

"It shouldn't," I pressed, wondering if Macy could have intercepted it. "Who was responsible for overseeing it?"

His shoulders lifted, as if such a detail were of little concern, before I was distracted from the thought by an agitated voice crying behind me. "Josephine!"

I spun and beheld an ancient man, who, with shaking hands and feeble steps, reached out for me. Cold hands clutched mine. Tears streamed from his cataract-clouded eyes. "You've finally returned."

"This is not Lady Josephine, Kinsley." Lord Dalry placed a

steadying hand on my shoulder. "This is her granddaughter, Julia."

"No." The man tightened his grip, looking angry. "'Tis Josephine. I would know her anywhere."

Lord Dalry didn't argue. "She's had a long journey and needs time to recuperate."

"Shall I have your special tea made?" Kinsley asked me.

I nodded and smiled, sensing he needed some reassurance from me. "Yes, please. That would be lovely."

Chuckling to himself, the man pattered away. Lord Dalry went as far as the end of the hall, watching the old man's progress for a full minute. When he turned, his brow was creased with grief.

"Wh-who is that?" I asked.

"Kinsley, the London butler."

"He manages to run a household?"

Lord Dalry swallowed as though burying sorrow. "No. Yes." Sadness tinged his voice. "Your father is going to take this news hard. Will you please allow me to inform him of what just transpired? It would be better coming from me in private."

I agreed, glad not to have the duty, as Lord Dalry directed me toward a stairwell on the right. Beneath the stairway, there was a small door, just large enough to enter, but once past the alcove, it opened to a vast room.

Glowing lamps welcomed us, their light reflecting off the wood. Massive mahogany shelves, protruding in rows, held volumes of calfskin books with gilded words. Buttoned sofas with fringed pillows filled the sitting area. Warm light brightened the space, making it as lovely as anything I'd encountered before. I stepped to a large desk situated near the fire and ran my hand over its smooth surface. The clean scent of linseed oil greeted me. This house had a more magical effect than Eastbourne. For some reason, I felt free, almost on the verge of a faerie tale.

It was then that I first noticed the glint of quince yellow, bright blues, and aqua greens in a small painting. The bright colors so greatly contrasted with the sober hues in the other artwork that I felt compelled to cross the chamber in order to study it.

Further inspection heightened the art's impertinence. Clearly this artist's work was nothing like the other prodigies that hung in their grandiose frames.

But it was the subject matter that held me mesmerized. It contained a single sunflower, off center, showing a blue-green center. The petals blazed like the sun, uncontainable and free. I stood riveted, sensing the wild soul of the artist. I was so captivated, I touched one of the fiery petals before noticing the initials at the bottom: *LC*.

A chill tingled through my arms as I stared at the first letter and realized the painting was Mama's. I knew the distinctive way she looped her *L*s. And her maiden name was Cames. I had once seen it scrawled in a book.

I stared, frozen. How was it possible that Mama had once been a painter? The idea was so ludicrous. I wanted Elizabeth or Edward there so I could show them this impossibility.

Then sadness engulfed me as I lifted my gaze to the blazing petals. There had been so much passion, so much life. What could have quenched her soul?

"Your father," Lord Dalry said, approaching, "can stare at that painting for hours."

"Where did he get it?"

He shrugged, giving Mama's nonesuch only a casual glance. "Bath, I believe?"

I considered telling him it was my mother's work, but then decided against it. I liked having knowledge about my father that he did not.

"Here, may we sit and talk?" Lord Dalry asked when I'd been silent a minute. "I'm anxious to open a certain subject that I wish to be frank with you about. Please, be seated."

Reluctantly, I tore my eyes from the work. I glanced at the couches, having no desire to talk. A day in the carriage with Kate was nearly as trying as one with Mrs. Windham.

I glanced at the door but decided it was better to have whatever he wanted to discuss over all at once, like swallowing a spoonful of castor oil. I dropped to one of the couches.

His eyes widened, giving me a dart of satisfaction. Likely, Henry would have snickered too, that my plopping onto a couch had tongue-tied this proper gentleman.

Giving his trousers a slight tug, Lord Dalry took the seat, but for a minute he did nothing other than look thoughtful. "Your father asked me to discuss with you the terms of this . . ." His mouth moved as if he were tasting the word before releasing it. "This . . . arrangement."

I narrowed my eyes, not following him.

He spread his hands. "On the night you arrived, I fear I may not have fully appreciated how matters would turn out. I assumed, of course, that by the week's end, Mr. Macy would be exposed and an investigation launched. But as it turns out, the evidence was stolen and your father had to make some hard decisions."

I waited, knowing he'd expound.

"Had your father managed to expose Mr. Macy, we could have easily handled the few people who learned about you and, with some slight embarrassment, swept this entire affair beneath the carpet, allowing you to return to your prior life."

My mouth dried. "And now?"

He paused, reminding me of the way the apothecary hesitated before revealing his opinion that Mama had committed suicide. "Our efforts to expose Mr. Macy were vain, leaving your father in a rather difficult position to know how to protect you. He decided upon a rather bold campaign, and, as such, he has declared to the newspapers that his legitimate daughter has recently returned home from finishing school."

I nodded, as this was not a surprise to me.

"I don't think you fully grasp what I'm saying." He leaned forward. "Consider the implication of what it means to be Lord Pierson's daughter. In order to keep you from Macy, this is no halfhearted effort. This alters everything."

I kept my gaze fastened on him, not certain what gravity he waited for me to discover.

"Think upon what it means to be the sole child of Lord Pierson and what the next step would be," he prompted. "You're an heiress, just returned home from school. Everything you do is now a matter of politics with a vast fortune connected to it."

I placed my hand over my bodice, unwilling to even allow my mind to go there. I shook my head. "No. This is a temporary arrangement only!"

"Yes, well, that brings us to my point. There's no undoing a measure like this. Before your father took this step, he wrote to ensure he had my full support."

I opened my mouth to demand that he take his words back, but instead kept shaking my head. If I was truly the daughter of a peer, debuting and finding a husband was the expected next step. Which meant that my father had written Lord Dalry beforehand to ensure that the gentleman in question would marry me.

The concept was so jarring that angry tears rose in my eyes. Lord Dalry was saying something, but the words dissipated around me in a murmur. I held out my hand for quiet, wishing he would disappear too, so that I could think.

I tried to recall exactly what I'd overheard my father and Mr. Forrester discussing that first night. Yes, I had gathered that they'd failed to entrap Macy, but what on earth made my father assume I'd be his pawn? It was one thing to act as though I were legitimate within his own household, but quite another to carry it through among the elite and powerful.

And Lord Dalry? I paused to stare at him in disbelief. His

presumption was unparalleled. He'd seen Edward and me together. He knew of our troth. He'd been to Am Meer—and probably slept in my bed there, for heaven's sake. He must have met Henry and Elizabeth and realized the depth of our bond. I challenged Lord Dalry with my eyes. "How dare you!"

The door swung open.

"Isaac, what the deuce are you doing?" My father's booming voice added to the already-present tension in the room. "You can't be alone with her. We're fighting an uphill battle as it is. Leave no room for servants' gossip."

"Sir, forgive me; I—"

"Don't!" My father's left hand shot up, silencing Lord Dalry, while he rummaged through a desk drawer with his right. "It's not an issue of trust. Just call Kinsley in the future." He grabbed a stash of papers. "Your duty is finished here anyway. The house is locked. I want you in the smoking room. We have a problem."

"Now, sir?" Lord Dalry asked, rising. "I would much rather not leave our conversation off where we did. May I not at least finish it?"

"There's not time for it. Within the hour, all of London will know we're back." My father strode away, one of his papers falling to the floor. "Say good night. No delays."

"Yes, sir."

The door banged shut.

Lord Dalry sighed but kept a refined expression as he bowed. "Forgive me, but I must leave. I did not wish to add to your distress. Perhaps tomorrow we can finish our conversation in private." Anger rippled through me, but before I could assure him we'd *never* finish this conversation, he continued. "In the meantime, wait here. I'll have a servant fetch you when your chamber is ready. Don't forget your meeting with your father at ten. He doesn't tolerate tardiness."

I glared as he withdrew and shut the door. Alone, I sank beside the fire, my dress ballooning about me. The entire situation felt insane. Shutting my eyes, I rested my forehead against one of the marble columns that flanked the fireplace, wondering if I had correctly interpreted where Lord Dalry was leading me.

Part of me couldn't put stock in my understanding. Surely, Lord Dalry hadn't been hinting for me to expect a marriage between us. Considering that I was already married to one man and engaged to another, he'd have to be mad to believe such a possibility existed. As would my father.

I glanced at the clock, increasingly anxious for an audience with him. There were at least two hours to wait. I folded my arms over my churning stomach, not certain I could last that stretch of time with this desire to vehemently argue with him.

❦

Fingers tucked a stray curl behind my ear. Memory of Mr. Macy's arousing touch woke me. I opened my eyes and pushed against the velvet upholstery. At first, I only saw flickering shadows dancing in slow adagio over the books. Then my gaze fell on Lord Dalry, kneeling at the curved arm of the settee.

"Why are you not in bed?" he asked.

I felt too confused to answer. Just a moment ago, I'd been sitting with Edward atop a hill, overlooking his parish. I shut my eyes, wanting to go back.

"Why is she here? Did you not give her my message?"

"I passed the message to Kinsley," James said behind me.

I reopened my eyes to find Lord Dalry's squeezed shut. He pinched the bridge of his nose, making me wonder if his head throbbed.

"Well, sir?" James asked.

"I don't know. I'm thinking," Lord Dalry said. "There's a good chance they are coming here next. Imagine if Lord Melbourne were to stumble over her now. But I can't sneak her upstairs without them noticing."

"No one would be to fault, sir."

"No." Lord Dalry sounded annoyed. "It would be mine. I told Lord Pierson she'd gone to bed."

"On my honor, sir, Kinsley swore he'd tend to it."

Lord Dalry waved for James to hush and looked toward me. He seemed relieved to find me alert, but before he could speak, the library door creaked and a ribbon of light striped his face.

It was nearly imperceptible, but Lord Dalry winced.

"Isaac?" My father's voice carried from the door. The room flushed with light as the door opened farther. "What is this?"

"Sir." Lord Dalry stood. "It's my fault. I failed to deliver the message that you wouldn't be joining her this evening. She must have fallen asleep while waiting."

"Is that so?" The displeasure in my father's voice settled upon the room with a chill.

"It's just as well, Pierson," came a voice behind my father. "No more excuses why we can't see the girl tonight. Let us settle this matter once and for all."

"Lord Ramsden." Lord Dalry gave a nod and rose.

A walking stick rapped the floor as two men entered.

"Lights. Bring in lights. I wish to view her face."

Like chess pieces returning to their rightful places after a game, everyone moved at once. James ran about the room, touching his candle to the lamp wicks. My father went straight to his desk, uncorked a decanter, and poured whiskey. He shot Lord Dalry a glowering look.

Having already sensed that Lord Dalry was my best resource, I looked to him for help. His expression was serious.

Two gentlemen entered and stopped before me. They were well dressed, their clothing tailored to fit, the material costly.

Lord Dalry placed a firm hand under my elbow and impelled me to rise. "Lord Melbourne, may I be the first to have the honor of presenting Miss Pierson?"

The gentleman bowed his head and waited. Etiquette

demanded I give him some token greeting. "Sir . . ." My legs went trembly. The name Lord Melbourne pounded against my memory as someone terribly important, only I could not place him.

Finally, Lord Melbourne's companion grunted with impatience.

"So this girl is your daughter, Roy?" Lord Melbourne asked at last, turning to my father.

"She is."

Lord Melbourne frowned, clasping his hands behind his back. For a length of time he studied me, then shook his head. "Why did you not consult me? We could have found some way around this."

"Consult you? About what?" My father shrugged before taking another sip of his drink.

Lord Melbourne's mouth slanted downward before he stepped toward me. His voice grew gruff. "Are you, or are you not, the daughter of Lady Pierson?"

Caught off guard, I glanced at Lord Dalry for my answer, but when my father set his drink on the desk with a plunk, my gaze went to him. Grey tinged his face, making him look stricken.

It wasn't possible to destroy him in that moment. Regardless of the fact he'd virtually ignored me since birth, something inside me stirred with compassion. Henry always claimed there were more solutions than problems if you were willing to take paths no one else would. Whatever lunacy Lord Dalry and my father planned, I could handle later.

"Well, girl, have you no voice?"

"I—I—have no memory of my birth. Like everyone, I rely on others to tell me who my parents are." I swallowed. "I've never known my father to lie."

Splotches crept up Lord Melbourne's neck. "Pierson, if you're expecting to present an illegitimate child to the queen, you know I can't allow it."

"Forgive her hesitation." My father stopped leaning against

his desk and straightened. "This is all new to her. Until recently, to keep her from fortune seekers, she thought herself orphaned and living on the charity of her boarding school. I can furnish records of her birth and witnesses to this peculiar arrangement. But imagine being wakened in the dead of night, by a person of your status. Who wouldn't be flustered?"

Lord Dalry's hand perspired where he supported my elbow, but he kept a refined, bored expression.

Lord Melbourne ran his gaze over me again, as though trying to find any semblance at all to my father's wife. "Take no offense at this, but if you're lying, confess it now."

My heart pounded in my chest, uncertain as I was whether I wanted my father to confess or not.

"There's no deception here." My father jammed the glass stopper into the decanter. "And I do take offense—great offense—that you suggest such unsuitable things within the hearing of my daughter."

Lord Melbourne tapped his walking stick, in turn looking uncomfortable. "What else is a body to think? Why in mercy's name would you hide a daughter at a finishing school and then shock the whole of London by bringing her home unannounced and unexpectedly? Explain yourself."

"She attempted to marry a rogue without my permission." My father crossed his arms. "The elopement was scarcely prevented, and I was forced to remove her immediately."

Heat seared my cheeks and ears. This was humiliating—and too close to the truth.

Lord Melbourne stroked his chin, studying me before slowly nodding. "Then she'll keep up with the blue bloods?"

"Her manners are faultless," my father said.

"Yes, as I saw by our introduction." Sarcasm coated Lord Melbourne's companion's voice.

"She's travelled all day and woke in a new place," Lord Dalry said. "You can scarcely expect Miss Pierson to perform."

A ghost of a smile played on Lord Melbourne's lips as his gaze moved to Lord Dalry. Respect shone in his eyes. "So you bolster her claim as well?" He gave a huff, lifting his shoulders as he considered Lord Dalry intently. "All right, if Dalry supports this, so will I." He turned to my father. "Send me the paperwork. Have Lady Beatrice write and request a private court presentation. As long as she confirms your story by sponsoring her, I'll allow it." Lord Melbourne moved his gaze to Lord Dalry. "It would be wise to settle the issue of her marriage sooner rather than later. I've already been approached by three members of the gentry, hoping I'll persuade you in their favor."

"She'll be wed before the finish of the season."

Chilled by my father's words, I lifted my eyes and met his with a defiant stare. If he understood me, he gave no acknowledgment. He knew as well as I did there was still Macy to contend with. I had no choice but to aid the ruse. Nevertheless, I felt like a bird that had been lured into a cage with an offer of rest, only to have the door lock shut behind it.

"Allow us to leave you gentlemen in peace." Lord Dalry escorted me toward the hall.

To my surprise, my father advanced, laid a heavy hand on my shoulder, and gave it a squeeze as he opened the door.

Eight

THAT NIGHT I tossed relentlessly between my sheets as the clop of hooves and jingle of harnesses carried from the cobblestone below. The few times I managed to slumber, my dreams were a tumult of images, primarily Edward and me trying to hide from an angry sunflower sun.

Each time I awoke, my conversation with Lord Dalry in the library came to mind. That I had unwittingly been forced into such a position vexed me to no end. I desired to be angry. Then I could at least vent. Yet I felt too rational to blame my father. He obviously hadn't planned on this either. And anger toward Lord Dalry went nowhere. There was little point in disliking a gentleman who politely warned people to be on their guard against him.

Sometime after dawn, when the last of the raucous laughter and wine-slurred songs died on the streets below, a tangled-haired Kate creaked open my chamber door. Puffy eyes evidenced that she, too, had wept.

She sniffled, wiping her nose. "May I sleep with you?"

I sighed, debating. I hadn't invited her into my world; she'd just barged in. Furthermore, I knew my desire to befriend her stemmed only from my own misery. It wasn't fair to her. Who wished to be befriended only because there was no alternative? It went against every principle I had always stood for.

Kate's lower lip protruded when I made no response.

"Oh, dash it all!" I lifted the counterpane and waved her to me. Henry and Elizabeth were always this reckless in their treatment of others. Maybe just once I could bend my own rule.

I laugh now at the measures I took to shield myself from the knowledge that I, too, was vulnerable and needed love and friendship.

Kate bounded toward my bed and clambered over the side. She rested her head against my shoulder and closed her eyes. "I dreamed Ben kept screaming in pain, and I couldn't find him."

I tucked the covers about her, warmed more than I liked to admit. "'Twas but a dream. Sleep."

Sniffling, she settled down and closed her eyes. I sighed and listened to her heavy breathing, wishing slumber were that simple for me. Yet it must have been, for when I next opened my eyes, it was no longer grey but bright with streams of sunshine.

A soft knock sounded again on the chamber door.

"Miss Pierson?" Lord Dalry called from the other side.

I glanced at Kate. She slept amidst a gnarled mass of cinnamon-colored hair. With a sigh, I sat straight and waited for my head to catch up to the motion.

Lord Dalry knocked again. "Miss Pierson, it's rather urgent."

I eyed the door. He was the last person I wished to see or speak to. I shut my eyes, hoping that I could convince at least one member of the Dalry family to just go away.

"Please," he said again from the other side. "Lady Beatrice is demanding an audience with you. If you don't open the door . . . well, forgive me, but I'll have no choice but to open it myself."

Rolling my eyes, I slid from the bed, imagining how Henry would have roared with laughter at such a mollycoddle threat. "Spare yourself from such *drastic* action," I called. "I'm coming."

I caught sight of myself in the looking glass as I passed. Wisps of hair had escaped my Quaker bun, reminding me of the plume on a young robin's breast. Last night, I'd not bothered to change; thus once again my dress was creased.

When I opened the door, more light streamed from the hall, filling in the gaps, softening the angles. Lord Dalry waited, dressed in a charcoal frock coat with a puffed black silk tie and gold waistcoat. My nose tingled with the scent of cedar blended with fuller's earth. If I was stunned at how richly attired he looked, he was equally stunned at my mussy appearance.

Concern etched his brow. "Do you always sleep in your dresses?"

I cast him a resentful look. "No."

"This cannot be happening," he murmured to himself as his panicked gaze swept over my form. "Remind me to check on your lady's maid. But in the meantime, we cannot present you to Lady Beatrice like this. Have you a large shawl? Can you at least comb your hair?" Before I answered, he spotted his sister. "Kate! What on earth? Stop bothering Miss Pierson!"

"It's not her bothering me," I muttered.

Kate scrunched her mouth in a pout before pulling the covers over her head and turning away.

Lord Dalry glared at her caterpillared form. "I am so sorry, Miss Pierson. I promise you, I shall speak to her."

"She's fine. She had nightmares about someone named Ben." I opened my trunk and selected the first shawl I found. A flush of pleasure rose through me that it utterly clashed with my dress. "Whatever she dreamed, it sounded awful. Do you know—?"

I turned and found the blood drained from his stricken face. But whatever thought arrested him proved less urgent than his current mission. "We must hurry. Your father and Lady Beatrice should not be left together for any length of time."

Not certain how this gentleman had managed to step into my life and take charge, I donned the silk shawl, then released and recombed my hair into a loose bun.

Lord Dalry scrutinized my appearance and, with reluctance, nodded. "We can't afford to leave them alone longer. Do you understand the importance of this visit?"

"I recall Lord Melbourne mentioned the name." I desperately tried to coax the wrinkles from my gown by smoothing it. "But who is she?"

"Your father's mother-in-law. If she claims you are her granddaughter, then not a soul in London will dare question your heredity. Only there's a catch." Lord Dalry took my arm and started us down the stairs. "She has a particular aversion for your father, which is why Lord Melbourne required her sponsorship. We must not fail."

⌇

Warmth bled from the air as Lord Dalry slid open the pocket doors to the drawing room. My father sat sideways behind a writing desk. The nearby blaze cast an orange glow over his morning attire. He stopped midsentence and jerked his head in my direction. He glared at Lord Dalry a full second before saying, "Julia." His abrasive tone cut the room. "Come in and shut the door."

Self-conscious about my creased gown, I drew myself to full height. My courage dissolved as I surveyed my surroundings. Mr. Forrester stood tapping his riding whip against his polished boots with a disdainful expression. The last occupant of the room, however, made me forget all else.

A matriarch, dressed in second mourning, sat upon the settee with two pugs snuffling around her feet. Tight ringlets frizzled in a pile over her forehead. Her bonnet remained tied tightly beneath her sharp chin. Judging from her carriage, the arch of her brow, and the refined way she turned to view me, she held the firm opinion that she was a great lady.

Two fingers dented her craggy cheek as she tilted her head, observing me. Under her captious stare, my mouth grew parched. Her gaze travelled over my appearance, and I knew that she saw every flaw because one by one I became aware of them myself.

Finally, my father stood, tugging his frock coat and clearing his throat. He frowned once more at my general appearance but gestured to the woman. "Julia, may I present you to Lady Beatrice, your maternal grandmother."

I scarcely managed to dip.

"Have you any idea, Roy," she said with a needled tongue, "how mortifying it is to have a granddaughter announced in the papers?" She rose and twisted to view him. "Did you actually think I'd play along? Do you even feed the sickly thing?"

My father took his chair and folded his arms over his chest. "Am I to understand you intend to deny your only grandchild?"

The woman snorted. "Oh, come now! Do not disgrace yourself further. There's not even a shred of resemblance. Whose whelp is this?" She circled me, her skirts crackling with each step. "Where have you housed your mistress all these years?" With her closed ebony fan, she lifted my chin. "Hmm, I take it your kept woman wasn't very pretty."

Heat rose through my neck and cheeks.

Lord Dalry stepped forward and removed her fan from beneath my chin. "If you don't mind, Grandmamma."

When she met his gaze, she shrank to nothing more than an old, bitter woman, but she swept her skirts and faced my father. "Well, Roy? I think I deserve answers."

"Robert." My father gestured to a glass-shaded lamp. "Will you be so kind as to light that? This room is rather gloomy."

Mr. Forrester made a point to stomp as he complied.

"I believe your nephew is still interested in Northfield, is he not?" My father leaned forward and opened a leather portfolio, scarcely glancing at its contents. "Simmons tells me the rent this year should yield a healthy capital, but I regret purchasing the estate. Now that there's better light in the room, look upon your grandchild again. I'm certain somewhere in the Kelsey or Browning line there's a raven-headed ancestor."

Lady Beatrice pressed her lips shut and curled her clawlike fingers. "You wheedled that property for Isaac."

"I relinquish all claim." Lord Dalry dipped beside me.

I stood, scarcely able to draw breath. I had no desire to be placed under obligation to him.

Lady Beatrice's gaze shifted to the portfolio. With mincing steps she approached the desk, then spread the papers in a trail over the surface. "Now that you mention it—" her voice soured as she tugged off her gloves and started to untie her bonnet—"I might recall that Great-Aunt Sarah had darkish hair."

"And isn't it a comfort to finally see someone who resembles Great-Aunt Sarah?" My father rested his chin in his hand, but his body remained taut.

"I said she *might* bear a slight resemblance. Since you've already had the audacity to announce her in the papers, quite a bit rests upon my memory, does it not?"

"I hoped it wouldn't come to this." My father's chair creaked, and I turned to see him place a stack of opened letters upon the desk. "Eramus is over seven thousand pounds in debt, and that's only what I've been made aware of. Every week a new creditor writes me."

"Am I expected to believe you'll allow him to go to debtors' prison?" Lady Beatrice stooped and snapped her fingers. The pugs came bounding toward her, and she scooped up the larger one. "You're grasping at threads, Roy. I cannot begin to tell you how much I'm going to enjoy seeing you squirm for once. By announcing your bastard child, you've finally made a mistake you can't cover. If you expect me to keep the truth from the papers, it's going to cost far more than a meager estate."

My father chuckled and gestured to Mr. Forrester. "Have I neglected to mention that Forrester is co-owner of the *Morning Gazette*?"

Mr. Forrester curled his lip in distaste and turned from the conversation.

"Depending on what happens during this meeting," my father said, "tomorrow's paper will carry either an announcement that you're overseeing your granddaughter's introduction into society or a detailed account of Eramus's debts and the houses in which he amassed them."

"You wouldn't have the audacity." Each word came out distinct and gnarled.

"Shall we test that theory?"

"I'll expose you, and you know it."

"How? She is your blood granddaughter, whether you acknowledge it or not. Society will find it rather curious that you only denied her after I refused to pay your nephew's debts. You didn't deny she was your granddaughter when the story first ran."

Lady Beatrice's chin quivered in anger, and her nostrils flared with every breath.

I tried to wet my lips, but my mouth was too dry.

"If I parade her as my own, I'll tolerate no interference from you." Lady Beatrice spoke through clenched teeth.

"Fair enough. All I require is that she comes out, and then you'll be free from our agreement."

"She'll need better clothing."

"Done."

An unkind smile spread over her lips. "I *alone* will oversee that part."

"Agreed."

She circled me again, bringing to mind a carrion bird

looming over its prey. She clutched my chin, pressing her nails into my skin. "What foreign languages can you speak?"

I swept my lashes down, fighting panic. "None."

Mr. Forrester looked over his shoulder, returning to the conversation, wrinkling his nose in aversion.

"What instruments do you play?"

It felt like Lady Foxmore's interview all over again, although my ill opinion of her lifted under Lady Beatrice's predatory gaze. "None."

The brown of her eyes slithered in my father's direction. "What did you do, Roy? Raise her in a dungeon?" To me, nearly inaudible, she added, "He's never cared for anyone but himself, has he, child?"

Her statement sliced as intended, and an odd anguish fell over me.

"I take over her education." Lady Beatrice released me and gathered her gloves and bonnet.

"I'll not question it."

"I choose her husband."

My father's deep chuckle resonated. "I think not. You know full well I've already selected her husband."

I tried to swallow as I shot Lord Dalry an accusing look. His jaw tightened.

Lady Beatrice gave us both a withering glance, then slid her fan over her wrist. "She's to live with me until her introduction. It's the only way I can have her ready on time."

"Ready on time?" My father frowned and pushed back his frock coat, exposing his tailored vest. "She spent her life at the best finishing school money can buy."

Lady Beatrice swished her skirts to the side. "Yes, that much is evident, Roy. We can only hope it's not too late. My carriage is outside. I'm taking her home with me tonight."

"No. She does not leave the protection of my household."

"Protection? From what?" Lady Beatrice laughed as she

tied her bonnet. "She's lowborn, positively vulgar. Look at her posture, her movements, her expression. What do you expect me to do with her except hide her from view and pray I have no callers?"

I turned my head to keep from seeing my father's embarrassed response.

"You may work with her *here*," my father said.

Lady Beatrice shook her head and cackled. "I think not, Roy. You'll interfere too much. No. You're not invited to our little tête-à-tête." Lady Beatrice walked over to the desk and picked up the portfolio. "I shall educate your daughter at my house or not at all."

"I'll allow it only if Simmons accompanies her."

"No," Lady Beatrice said. "That killjoy never sets foot under my roof again. Never. Send your footman, since your butler is decrepit."

"I'll allow you the hours between breakfast and tea. No more."

Lady Beatrice smirked and paused on the threshold. "I fail to see how you are in a position to make demands. I'll fetch the girl tomorrow and decide for myself the hours I keep her."

When the hem of her skirt disappeared from sight, the pugs lifted their flat, wrinkled faces from the carpet and scampered after her, their curly tails upright.

Nine

"WELL, SHE'S KEPT her end of the bargain and then some." The following morning, my father threw the *Times* of London on the table, placed his elbows over the front page, and rubbed his eyes. Dust filled the morning slants of sun that fell over his back. He turned toward Lord Dalry, exposing the silver threading the hair near his temples. "She knows we're not prepared to handle this."

Lord Dalry set his fork down, clinking the crystal saltcellar, something akin to a frown marring his normally placid features. "Handle what, sir?"

Ignoring him, my father seized the paper, scowled, then tossed it in my direction. Kate's eyes widened with curiosity as I leaned forward to retrieve it and flattened it over my lap. The front page read:

EMERALD HEIRESS TO BE INTRODUCED

London is most pleased to welcome the return of her beloved son Lord Pierson and anxiously awaits the forthcoming of his daughter, Miss Julia Pierson. We are pleased to report that last night, after a lengthy and heartfelt isolation, Lady Beatrice Kelsey and Miss Pierson were reunited with much mutual affection and pleasure. The shadow of Lady Pierson's death marred their otherwise-joyous reunion, and many tears were shed as grandmother and granddaughter sought solace together. This matriarch and gentle lamb have endured a grievous and long separation, and while it remained necessary to sequester the girl, who is perhaps England's richest heiress, from fortune seekers, Lord Pierson finally yielded to the relentless pleas of Lady Beatrice Kelsey and brought his most guarded treasure back to her native soil.

With no direct male heir left in the Pierson line, Miss Pierson stands to inherit a vast birthright, consisting of four estates; a London home; African emerald mines; holdings in India, which include three tea plantations; and numerous other profitable ventures. Lady Beatrice Kelsey hints at a possible attachment between her nephew Mr. Eramus Calvin and her granddaughter; however, equally trusted sources inform us to keep a close watch on Lord Dalry. We find it noteworthy that Lord Dalry's sister has been chosen as Miss Pierson's sole travelling companion. Thankfully, we shall not wait long to resolve for ourselves which young gentleman, if either, is favored by Miss Pierson. Lady Beatrice has set her presentation at court to be in three weeks. She has informed us that her granddaughter will likewise make her first public appearance that night, during Lady Northrum's ball scheduled for the 30th of November, which Lord Pierson has generously offered to now host. London, we are pleased to predict that we have found the toast of the Season.

Three weeks! The season wouldn't even start for another two months. I folded the dreadful words, wishing I could so easily rid myself of this state of affairs. Not only had London learned that my father intended for me to wed, but so would Edward. I lowered the paper with disgust.

"What is it?" Lord Dalry asked, sounding alarmed.

"Such a long face for someone who just discovered her worth." My father glowered at me, then yanked the paper from my fingers. He handed it to Lord Dalry, then tapped his broad fingers against the table, waiting for his protégé to finish.

Lord Dalry wore his urbane expression as he read the article. The slow ticking of the mantel clock carefully measured the passing seconds of silence, each one lasting longer than the previous.

This situation had turned into nothing short of disaster. Surely, I reasoned, somewhere Mr. Macy leisured over breakfast, reading this very article. I eyed the stack of papers placed at my father's side, wondering which one Mr. Macy had used to plead for information for my whereabouts. I knew better than to ask.

Across the table, Lord Dalry lifted a brow, making me wonder if he'd reached the part with his name.

"Well?" My father cut the silence.

Lord Dalry lowered the newspaper and slowly folded it. "This is quite a bit sooner than expected. I daresay her ladyship is punishing us."

Kate stretched out her hand. "May I see too?"

Lord Dalry studied me as he passed the paper to his sister.

"Can you have my daughter ready on time?"

"It's not an issue of her performance." The tightening of the muscles around Lord Dalry's mouth was the only visible sign of his stress. "But rather whether she'll be sufficiently recovered from prior events."

Beneath the table, I bunched my scarlet skirt into my clammy fists, recalling the words my father had spoken our first night here: *"She'll be wed before the finish of the season."*

"Time heals all wounds, Isaac," was my father's dry reply.

My chest heaved in silent protest.

"It's scarcely been a month—"

"I'm not discussing this." My father's voice rose, as did

his color. "The sooner her engagement is settled, the better. Besides, this isn't your decision; it's mine."

Lord Dalry's eyes narrowed. "I beg to differ—"

"Isaac?" Kate's horrified whisper interrupted their conversation.

Lord Dalry shot his sister a warning glance. "Not now, Kate."

Paling, she set down the paper. "But did you read it all?" She met her brother's eye with a look of horror, making me wonder what she'd seen that I hadn't. "It mentions—"

"Kate!" Lord Dalry's voice rang sharp. "We'll discuss this later."

A cool anger glinted in my father's eyes. "Am I to expect interruption at my own table every morning?"

"She'll not interrupt again, sir," Lord Dalry stated.

"See that she doesn't."

I gripped the edge of the table as I considered just how precarious my situation was. The fact that my father could act indulgent with Kate one moment and be impatient the next didn't speak well.

Before I could sort out how this would affect me, the door opened and James poked his head inside. "Excuse me, sir, but a carriage has arrived from Lady Beatrice. Her driver says she expects your daughter within the next quarter hour."

My father's face grew dusky. "Take that silver platter, James; go to the stable yard and collect the freshest pile of—"

"Sir!" Lord Dalry winced as if picturing it. "Be reasonable. We still need her sponsorship."

My father gestured to the morning paper. "If that woman wants to play games, we'll play games. She can't very well back out now. After that jugglery, let's allow her time to stew on whether or not she'll be humiliated alongside us."

"Honestly, sir."

My father sat ensconced in his chair like a fabled god. Tall, strong, immovable. But I saw through the illusion and despaired.

Ten

ONE OF THE MOST jagged paths I know is that of rebuilding a life that has been completely riven. Few understand the difficulty of such a task. Not everyone will understand my actions on paper, even though it is the human experience.

That first morning, after gaining a clearer view of my father, I quietly withdrew and sought a private space for myself. I had long been in the habit of seeking solitude in which to work out solutions. It has ever been my personality not to speak, or act, before I have devised a plan. In addition, my soul required release after tragedy—and tragedy I'd already had in full measure.

As I left the breakfast chamber, heaviness gathered in my chest, denser and weightier than stone. I needed to vent the ferment. I needed to cry as desperately as I needed air. And for that I wanted privacy.

Generally a person can collect himself without such extreme measures, especially the elite. Though I'd not been raised in that sphere, had I been given enough time between catastrophes to adjust and heal, I believe I might have carried myself more nobly.

The past eight months of my life, however, had contained one blow after another. The fact that Mama had been murdered was enough to make any person reel emotionally; never mind that I'd married the man responsible. Add to the equation the heartbreak of being separated from Edward, the longing for Elizabeth and Henry, and the fact that I'd just lost my identity by telling Her Majesty's government a falsehood.

It was none of these concerns, however, that drove me to seek time alone. I'd seen enough to make me believe my father would trample me underfoot, and much as I loathed agreeing with Lady Beatrice, it seemed she was right that no one's welfare mattered to my father except his own.

That was what I wished to mentally address, but each time I tried to logically map out how to contend with it, my desire to cry became so sharp that I couldn't focus. To be able to think again, I needed to purge some of the pain.

I checked the nearest room, fearing Kate would follow me if I didn't disappear quickly enough. Near the entrance, I found a chamber that looked unused. A table with ornate legs sat in the middle of the space, with an upholstered green velvet chair behind it and two others on its flanks.

Hearing Kate's voice emerge from the breakfast chamber, I slipped inside.

I waited near the door until all voices and footsteps receded. Then, convinced I was alone, I sank into a chair, covered my mouth, and silently keened.

To my dismay, within three minutes, footsteps sounded outside the door. It was too late to do more than swipe my cheeks. The door opened to reveal Lord Dalry and Kate, who both gaped to find me crying.

"Must I trip over a Dalry everywhere I go?" I shouted, dabbing my eyes with my shawl. "Are the pair of you incapable of leaving a body alone for ten minutes!"

Kate's face went from sunshine to storm before it crumpled

and she, too, burst into tears. She turned and fled down the hall, her hard-soled shoes clattering toward the back of the house.

Lord Dalry hesitated, seemingly torn as to which one of us to pursue; then with a slight sigh, he slipped into the chamber and shut the door. He divested his waistcoat of a silken handkerchief, which he extended toward me.

All at once, I felt contrary. No, more than contrary. I felt positively obstinate. I'd had enough of him and my father. I made movement to rise, but before I found my feet, he spoke.

"I know this may be difficult to accept, Miss Pierson, but I truly am your friend. When you've been hurt enough, it's not always easy to tell the difference between those who wish you harm and those who intend you good. But I am on your side. So is your father."

I scoffed before I could help it. "There you are wrong. I mean nothing to my father!"

His astonishment could not have been more complete. "I grant you," Lord Dalry said slowly, tugging on his trouser legs as he took a seat, "your father is acting a bit surly, but certainly you can make allowances, considering the direness of the situation we're currently—"

"A bit surly?" My voice closed in on itself. "That man cares for no one except himself! He is selfish, mean, and a bully."

Lord Dalry angled his head, assessing me. "I fear you do not yet understand your father, Miss Pierson."

"Oh, I understand him! I can see him exactly as he is."

"Can you?" His voice held a mild rebuke. "Because I am looking at a very different portrait. When I look at your father, I see someone who risked his life and reputation to shelter his daughter, which I find courageous. I see a man who stepped into the path of one of London's most notorious criminals, despite the high risk. I see a man willing to accept the anger and wrath of Lady Beatrice to gain sanctuary for you."

His views were so disjointed from my own, my tears dried as I stared at him.

"I also see a scarred and broken man, one who needs healing as desperately as his daughter obviously does. Lastly, I see a man who fears to love his daughter, who fears facing his past failures."

His speech was jarring. It reawakened desire and unleashed hope that I feared to accept. "He told you that?"

Lord Dalry frowned slightly, then rubbed behind his ear. "Not directly. Call it an innate ability, if you will. I've always been able to see people as they were intended to be—not merely who they are now, but what their full potential is. Your father has the capacity to be one of the greatest men in my acquaintance." Lord Dalry leaned forward, making certain our gazes met. "If I may remind you, you did seek his protection, did you not? Was it truly your life that was disrupted or his?"

I stared at the fire, wrestling with this new concept. Some of what he said made sense, but I needed time to examine it for the flaws.

"Imagine the insult it would be to your father to learn that his daughter left the breakfast table in order to sit alone in a parlor to cry, when he's offering you all that he has to give."

I viewed my hands, badly wanting to believe him.

"You are the one choosing your own unhappiness just now," Lord Dalry said. "If you wish, I will leave you here to your melancholy, but you are the *daughter* of Lord Pierson. It is not fitting for you to weep here. I hope that instead you will put aside tears and allow me to see you to the library, where your father has tasks he wishes to assign to you."

He rose, expressionless, and studied me as if waiting to see if I would willingly join him.

My nose tingled and felt runny as I stared. To be frank, I wasn't certain what to think. But before I could fashion a sensible thought, the doorknob rattled, followed by a pounding fist.

Simmons's voice carried from outside the door. "Master Isaac? Are you in there?"

"Yes," Lord Dalry replied in an irritated voice.

"Is Miss Pierson with you?" Simmons demanded.

Lord Dalry crossed his arms with a sigh, clearly frustrated that we'd been interrupted at such a crossroad. "Yes."

"And your chaperone?"

"Honestly. Have you any idea how ridiculous this is!" Lord Dalry turned and argued with the door. "Do you truly think you have to monitor us?"

"You can shut all the doors you want after you're married," Simmons replied. "But for now you will open this door!"

Lord Dalry pinched his nose in a rare gesture of exasperation but then wordlessly crossed the room and opened the door.

With an armload of books, Simmons cast his hooded gaze at the two of us, then sniffed. "The next time I catch the two of you alone—"

"Spare us," Lord Dalry said, returning to me. "I'm in no mood for a lecture. Have you work to do here?"

Simmons deposited his books on the desk and began to lay them out. "Yes. If I were you, I'd hurry along. Lord Pierson was quite impatient when I left, and that was ten minutes ago."

"Yes, yes, thank you." Lord Dalry returned to me and offered his arm. "Miss Pierson, if I may see you to your father."

Though I took his offered arm, I did not look directly at him. For I still had not made out whether or not his logic was faulty or whether his speech angered me.

"I wouldn't let her show up looking like that." Simmons opened a desk drawer and thumbed through files. "Her eyes are positively red, and if there's anything his lordship hates, it's weepy eyes."

Lord Dalry flashed him a warning look.

"That reminds me." Simmons patted his pockets, looking for something. "Lady Beatrice sent a note, demanding explanation as to why Miss Pierson's neglected her duty. I thought I placed it . . ." He frowned. "Well, never mind. Her ladyship will only accept explanation from you. Best pencil her into your day, as well."

At the threshold, Lord Dalry gave him a slight bow. "Fine."

Shafts of sunlight filled the front of the house as Lord Dalry shut the door and frowned at it.

His behavior was so curious, I hugged myself and inquired, "Why don't you care for Simmons? Does he not have great potential too?"

"Hmm," was Lord Dalry's disinterested reply.

"What about Kate?" I ventured, testing this new theory. Part of me longed to believe what he'd said about my father, but so far, my stepfather's teachings seemed more sensible—believe only what you see. "What are her prospects?"

Lord Dalry's expression was poised as he turned his full attention on me, making it impossible to tell his thoughts. "She's a generous, funny little soul, isn't she?"

I said nothing. His answer was of no help.

"When we reach the library," Lord Dalry instructed en route, "I recommend you call your father Papa."

"Papa?" I felt so stunned I stopped walking.

"Yes. Besides the fact that all the fashionable young ladies call their father that, it will go a long way toward winning his heart."

"You mistake me. I have no desire to win him."

Lord Dalry's gaze gave the impression that he saw through my dissembling. "I'm only trying to be of assistance. If you wish to break through this wall separating you, start by calling him Papa."

I frowned, pulling my shawl tight, deciding that Lord Dalry might choose to walk in the realm of possibilities, but I would keep my feet on the solid ground of reality.

Nonetheless, upon reaching the library, I carefully studied

my father's features as he gave me instructions on how to answer his social correspondences. In vain I searched for a hint that he, too, desired relationship.

His jaw tense, he jabbed his finger toward a basket of posts. "Any invitations from a marquis or higher rank, set aside. I may need to attend those events. Decline all others. Listen carefully, for this will be your duty for some time. Members of the royal household receive embossed stationery with our emblem." He splayed his fingers over a stack of papers. "Tell Simmons when we are low. It takes a month to order new." He turned toward me suddenly, his face distrustful. "Don't waste it. It costs over a pound a sheet!"

Seeing that he expected some sort of reply, I managed, "Y-yes, sir."

"For those of our rank, use the vellum with my monogram. Those below our rank, use plain paper and make certain to affix it with this seal." He set forth a brass. "Otherwise, use the gold seal, the larger one for royalty." He paused, looking over the table. "Unless it's Baron Van Tross. Set any of his aside. Do not read them. Oh yes, and for the speaker of the House of Commons, use the monogrammed vellum. I don't need to cause problems between him and Isaac."

He dumped his instructions upon me too quickly to grasp them fully, then gruffly demanded, "Am I clear?"

While his instructions weren't, his nonverbal cues were— I was expected to agree. Across the chamber, Lord Dalry also gave me a quick nod, as if to say that now was the hour to call him Papa.

I tightened hands into fists, refusing to reward my father by calling him Papa while he was in that temper. "Yes, *sir*."

"See to it, then." My father placed his hand on my back and steered me toward the hall, past where Lord Dalry stood at the threshold. He thrust the basket of correspondence into my hands and the door closed behind me, but I heard my father say,

"Russell is intending to ask for an increase in the Navy. I want you to have an argument prepared, ready to send to Palmerton by tomorrow, as to why we should approach Russia with negotiations about manning the Baltic first . . ."

I listened until his voice drifted to the other end of the library, then hugged the basket against my stomach.

Knowing Simmons occupied my former chamber, I tested the room where I'd met Lady Beatrice and found it open. With a sigh, I dumped half the basket's contents onto the small desk. The sheer number of invitations amazed me. It would take me hours to finish the task.

The first post I opened was from someone titled Master of the Horse. I frowned, not knowing the rank. It sounded as if it had something to do with the queen, which would have meant the expensive stationery. Yet that felt wrong.

Someone sniffled loudly from the direction of the settee. Frowning, I turned and found Kate sullenly watching me, her lower lip trembling and her downcast eyes glistening.

All at once, I wondered if that was how I must have appeared to Lord Dalry—childish and full of self-pity. Despite myself, I smiled, then chuckled at the image.

She stood, lifting a haughty chin.

"I'm sorry, Kate," I said, trying to hold in my smile, determined not to allow myself to act in such a manner again. "I'm so sorry. That was awful of me."

She blinked as if considering, then raced to me and flung her arms about my waist. "It's not all your fault," she cried, her tone plaintive. "I heard Isaac tell Mama we'd have to take care, as you had your father's temperament, and Mama told me I would need to be extra patient with you."

I stiffened, not certain what to make of that statement. Rather than tackle it, I redirected her. "Any chance you can help me sort through the ranks?"

Kate peered over her shoulder before releasing me to skip

over to the basket. Drawing out a large handful of posts, she said, "Don't let your father find out you've not properly memorized precedence. Isaac also told Mama that Lord Pierson is angry at how poorly you were educated."

I did my best to look aloof, though each word stung. Starting a pile of letters, I shrugged. "Well, he has no one to blame but himself."

Kate's amused eyes met mine. "That's what Mama said too!"

～

Gold wax oozed from beneath the signet, and the smell of burnt paper filled the air. The last *We regretfully must decline* had been penned. I set the seal aside and massaged my cramped hands.

I reached my arms over the desk to loosen my shoulders, then sank against the back of my chair. I'd sent Kate to bed hours ago when her yawns became contagious, but now I was the one hardly able to keep my eyes open. Sun stretched across the room, warming my dress, tempting me to nap. I shut my eyes, but to stay awake, I favored a mental picture I kept of Edward. Once again, I recalled how pale he looked that morning in the front parlor of Maplecroft, knowing he would soon leave. How well I recalled his silent anguish and how tightly he held my hands in his.

"It's just for a little while," he had whispered between kisses near my ear. *"This too shall pass, and nothing will ever separate us again."*

I'd clung to his neck, sobbing.

"We've always done this," he'd assured me. *"Just one more separation. That's all this is. Just one more."*

A bell clanged in the front hall, breaking my train of thought. All morning men had come in and out, most of them seemingly important.

Careful to keep the floorboards from creaking, I crept to the door and peeked out. Kinsley plodded past, keys jangling at his hip. The brass ring looked all the heavier against his frailness.

When the door swung open, a middle-aged gentlewoman entered and dropped a travelling bag. She looked around her as she tugged off gloves, then unwrapped a veil from around her hat and face. She viewed the towering balconies of London House with an air of disgusted familiarity.

Kinsley shut the door and took up the silver tray next to it. "Your card, please, miss."

The woman turned and faced him, her movements as elegant as her dress. "Kinsley?" She placed a hand on his shoulder. "Do you not recognize me?"

"Miss Josephine never sees visitors without a card. Your card, please."

"Miss Josephine?" She stooped into his view. Tears coated her voice. "Kinsley, look at me. Who am I?"

The butler raised a trembling hand as clarity filled his eyes, and he clutched her fingers. "Why, Miss Moray! How delightful."

Her eyes crinkled with emotion, exposing crow's-feet.

I slid from behind the door and entered the hall, trying to look as dignified as I could. Holding my head high, I approached her. "May I help you?"

She scarcely gave me a glance before waving her gloves toward her satchel. "Yes, take my bag to my room. Ask the housekeeper if you aren't sure which one it is. Then run and inform Miss Pierson that Miss Moray, her lady's maid, has arrived. Do not dawdle in your task or I shall inform your mistress of your slovenly habits."

Cool anger filled me. "I am Miss Pierson."

Steel-blue eyes bored into me as Miss Moray surveyed me from head to toe. Strands of iron grey intermingled in her dark hair, tightly pulled into a bun. She blinked, alternating her stare between the grandfather clock and me, as though timing her silence. When she had redeemed enough seconds to satisfy her, she folded her arms. "Yes, I see traces of Lord Pierson, but I only served Lady Pierson while she lived. Go fetch your father. I highly doubt I am the lady's maid he wishes to employ."

Memory of Nancy's freckled face clashed with the dreadful woman before me. I highly doubted she was the right person for the job either. Attempting to regain control, I gave her a cold look. "You will remain here. Touch nothing."

Miss Moray lifted a proud eyebrow.

My steps felt stiff as I turned and opened the library door. The chamber was empty. I glanced over my shoulder and saw her tapping her foot with contempt. Rather than allow her to see my vain search, I set out to find James, in hopes he'd know my father's whereabouts.

Near the back of the house I caught a strong whiff of cigars, followed by the sound of my father's voice. Knowing I was supposed to have spent my life in a finishing school, I resisted the urge to fly into the chamber. Instead, I inspected my dress, smoothed my hair, then rapped on the door.

After some shuffling, my father opened the door, holding a cigar. His face flushed red and his eyes narrowed. "Gentlemen," he managed in a calm voice, "my daughter."

Behind him, two men rose and hastily hid their cigars behind their backs. They both bowed. The younger one's eyes beamed mischief beneath his dark brows.

My father set his cigar on a nearby table and urged me into the hall. "If you'll please excuse us." The moment the door shut, my father grabbed my arm. I winced in pain, which only infuriated him further. "Do you have any idea how important those men are? What on earth merits disturbing me in the middle of a meeting?" He stalked down the hall, maintaining a firm grip.

"Miss Moray is here. She . . . she accused me of not being Lady Pierson's daughter."

My father's eyes bulged. "Where?"

I pointed before I remembered to answer verbally, but he'd already dropped me and stormed toward the main hall.

My arm throbbed. I despised him, and I wanted to knock down every painting in the hallway. Yet, determined not to show emotion before Miss Moray, I composed my features, then hurried down the corridor after him.

In the front hall, Miss Moray clutched her bonnet by the ribbons, with a demure, empty expression, as she listened to my father. She lifted her gaze to me and curtsied as I entered.

My father waved impatiently. "Kinsley, see that her baggage is brought to her chambers." He turned toward me with a scowl. "Do not ever disturb me during a meeting again." With heavy steps, he returned along the passage by which he'd arrived.

Miss Moray's demure expression dropped once my father disappeared. Her lip curled in scorn as she swept by me and marched up each step.

Eleven

❧

HOW LORD DALRY spent that day, I cannot say. But he returned
to London House well past dinner with an exhausted Kate. She
went straight to bed, but though his eyes evidenced exhaustion,
Lord Dalry ordered James to light Lady Pierson's office.

To my surprise, he summoned me and sorted through the
various posts I'd worked on earlier. Cupping the side of his face
and keeping his eyes closed as if too worn to sit straight, he verbally discussed with me each invitation. Thereafter, we worked
out the proper way to address every person: his rank, his political
leaning, and my father's view of him.

After an hour, he grew so still that I paused in my recitation
to study this strange gentleman. Every inch of him was courtly
and polished, though to memory, I hadn't yet caught him preen-
ing before a mirror. His handsomeness was overall, in a sort of
scholarly way. His clipped brown hair was meticulously waxed
into place, accenting the angular lines of his jaw. His chin had a
unique round ending, one which added to, rather than detracted
from, his looks.

"Did you forget?" Lord Dalry's words slurred as he opened his eyes. "You drop the *of* and address an earl with the title Lord and the name of his locale. So instead of the Earl of Danbury, you'd call him Lord Danbury."

I swept down my lashes, embarrassed to have been caught openly studying him. "I thought you were asleep."

He straightened and rubbed his eyes. "Forgive me. I confess I am weary, but it was remiss to show it. What do you say we leave off studying the peers until tomorrow night? I see little need to quiz you on current affairs yet. Your father will prefer you to keep those opinions to yourself. Tell me instead about your studies in Scripture today."

For a second, I was too stunned to speak. "My what?"

He sat straighter, seemingly puzzled by my expression. "You're not the first to neglect your studies once in London, but trust me, Miss Pierson, it only grows more difficult from here. Tell me where you last studied, form a theory on it about a spiritual principle, and we'll take opposing views and practice our logic."

I didn't know whether to envy him his education or despise him for his utter foolishness. "Have you no clue who I am?" I finally managed.

He waited.

"My name is Julia Elliston, and I am—" I felt heat rise. "Well, I *was* the daughter of the famed atheist William Elliston."

He met my protest with no expression but maintained the expectation for me to complete his assignment.

I spread my hands, showing my offense. "Do you really desire to pick up where I left off? Well, I believe it was a triple-chinned vicar's assessment that I was bound for eternal torment unless I repented of my father's blasphemy. Never mind his own gluttony."

His brows knit slightly. "I observed no such tendencies in Edward."

"Don't you dare," I warned. "Don't you dare speak lightly of him to me."

"Forgive me. I meant no offense. But I had assumed that spiritually speaking, you were under Edward's care."

I longed to escape the interview. My discussions with Edward in regards to spiritual matters were far too intimate to share with another soul. My burgeoning steps toward belief were at great cost, for they required that I accept the beliefs of the very people who had wrought the most damage to me. To state that I had no faith wouldn't be fully true; I was reconsidering. So I simply said, "I have not enough knowledge of Scripture to debate you."

"But you have some knowledge?"

"None."

Had a brick of weight been added to Lord Dalry's load, this additional burden could not have been more evident. He sagged against the back of his chair but said nothing while he mentally adjusted. "I'm at a loss as to how to proceed." He set his pen on the desk, then sat back and looked at it, gripping the arms of his chair. "We've only three weeks, and now we have this to tackle as well."

"I fail to see how my viewpoint has bearing on anything."

He leaned forward. "Because you arrived with Edward. No, you don't see. We've already been telling everyone—your father and I, that is—that you've been at a religious institution. They're all curious about you, and you're shy, which means out of politeness they're going to look for subjects you'll excel in."

"Why did you tell them that?"

"Well, we needed something to explain you." Though his expression did not change, his voice indicated mild shock. "How can you be completely unversed in Scripture if you've been planning to marry a vicar?"

"I wasn't planning on marrying a vicar. A vicar! William Elliston's daughter? Why do you think I was tempted to marry Macy in the first place? It was because Edward took ord—"

Before more could be said, the door flung open. The candles

flickered in the swirl of air. Half died, plunging the room into gloom, piping smoke into the air.

Miss Moray stood in the doorway, appearing as sour as rancid milk. She started to speak but saw Lord Dalry as he rose. "Master Isaac!"

Lord Dalry looked over his shoulder before joy lit his face. "Miss Moray! When did you arrive?"

"This afternoon."

He crossed the room and kissed each of her cheeks as she clutched his sleeves. "No one told me or I would have greeted you. How wonderful to see you again!"

Stunned by the joy of their reunion, I pinched my mouth tight.

"Look at you!" She stepped away. "This can't be the lad who used to steal extra tarts from the tea tray."

Lord Dalry laughed. "No need to tell Miss Pierson my past faults, if you don't mind."

Miss Moray's smile vanished at the mention of my name. She released him and brushed off her skirt. "Yes, which reminds me, I've come to collect the girl for her evening facial."

Lord Dalry's smile likewise ceased. "She meets nightly with her father in the library and is due there any moment. I suggest in the future you check her schedule before arranging it."

Miss Moray's mouth curdled as she dipped.

Lord Dalry nodded toward the door. "You're dismissed."

With a face of stone, she left. Lord Dalry stood by the threshold, his head bent in thought. He must have disliked the conclusion he reached, for he shook his head as he turned toward Kinsley, who slept in a nearby chair. He squatted before the elderly man and touched his shoulder. "Wake, Kinsley. Miss Pierson and I are finished."

With a snort, Kinsley awoke. "Eh? Don't forget to set out Master Pierson's slippers."

Tenderness filled Lord Dalry's face as he offered the aged

butler his arm. "I'll make certain it's done. Come with me. I'll escort you to your chamber."

Firelight shone through Kinsley's thinning hair as he tottered to his feet, supported by Lord Dalry's steady arm. As they passed me, Kinsley reached out and grabbed my arm. "Be careful, Miss Josephine. It might rain."

"Wait here," Lord Dalry advised me. "I'll return and escort you to your father. I wish to have a brief word with him."

"Will I be late?" I asked. I'd been staring at the shadows in the hall Miss Moray had disappeared into. My fear of keeping his schedule had begun to infect me as it did every other member of this household.

"Yes, but so long as you arrive with me, it won't matter."

⌇

In the library, my father stood before the blaze and shuffled through papers. Miss Moray waited in an armchair, watching him so intently she didn't notice our arrival at first. When she did, she rose and curtsied. "I'll go wait in Miss Pierson's chambers, sir."

"Thank you." My father scarcely glanced up from his work as she departed. "Close the door, Isaac, and come here." He placed the parchments on a reading table and glowered as Lord Dalry approached. "Have I or have I not asked you to keep a chaperone on hand when you are with my daughter?"

"You have, sir."

"Then why are you disregarding my orders?"

Lord Dalry took a seat and crossed his legs, then leaned back, lacing his fingers over his knee. "Is this because I was speaking briefly to your daughter when Simmons found us?"

My father raised an eyebrow. "No. This is because Miss Moray found the two of you in a dark room alone."

I almost choked on my readiness to defend us, but Lord Dalry held up a finger to me when my father focused in my direction, forestalling the thunderclap that would have followed my interruption.

"We weren't, sir. She opened the door suddenly and some candles blew out. Besides, Kinsley was with us."

My father strummed his fingers over the table. "I questioned her quite thoroughly on this. Are you suggesting that she lied?"

I clenched my fist, wanting to demand that she be called back into the room and accuse us to our faces. Lord Dalry, however, only looked at his fingernails. "He was asleep in a chair that faced the fire. I suspect she failed to see him."

"She asked to become your chaperone, and I'm half considering it."

Lord Dalry almost looked bored as he met my father's eyes, then gave him a lazy smile. "Well, sir, for obvious reasons we prefer Kinsley."

My father darkened as he planted his hands on the table and leaned over it. "What exactly were you two doing?"

Lord Dalry looked mildly surprised. "I'd much rather not say, sir. It would only start a bad precedent, for I have no intention of disclosing all our doings."

My father glared but then shook his head with a chuckle. "If it were anyone except you, Isaac, I'd have him thrashed and thrown out on the street for such answers. Very well; keep your secrets if you must have them."

"And may we keep Kinsley too?"

"Yes, yes, keep Kinsley. You know I trust you." My father waved for me to leave. "In another vein, I want you to take my place and join Crawlsley's hunting party. He's gotten hold of Thomas Carlyle's pamphlet and has been making arguments for the movement. I need someone who can argue sensibly with them. Would you like a brandy?"

Lord Dalry uncrossed his legs. "No, sir. I'm intruding upon your time with your daughter. Allow me to leave."

My father looked up and saw me. "You're still here? I thought I'd dismissed you. Miss Moray informs me that she requires you for beauty treatments in the evenings. I'm sorry. We'll be unable to meet."

Lord Dalry leaped to his feet. "Sir, that's the only time available for you to spend with your daughter. Make Miss Moray wait."

"She'll clamor to Lady Beatrice then. You remember how they were." My father poured himself a tumblerful of brandy. "Besides, the Lords Hardwicke and Alexander were here today. You wouldn't believe the politics that are happening at the clubs. We have work to do, and there's no time to spare. I've arranged our key points, and we need to revisit them."

"I wouldn't trust a word Lord Alexander says," Lord Dalry said. "And no matter what is happening politically, can you not spare one hour for your daughter's sake?"

My father ignored the hurt that I could feel fashioning my face and turned toward Lord Dalry. His chunky gold ring clinked against the side of the glass. "Do not question me, Isaac. You know as well as I do the problems that will crop up between Lady Beatrice and Julia. Let her have her cursed beauty treatments."

Lord Dalry met my father's intense gaze with one of his own. "If you'll excuse me, then, I'd like to walk your daughter to the stairs."

My father sipped his drink, waving his fingers for Lord Dalry to do so. That my father would so easily dismiss our evenings brought me closer to tears than I liked. I turned and fled, not waiting for Lord Dalry.

He caught up to me in the hall. "I'm sorry, Miss Pierson," he said, and he sounded it. "I know what this time with your father meant to you. It's only three weeks until your presentation, and after that—"

"Can't you just leave me alone?" I hastened my pace, then spun and faced him. "She did that on purpose. You told her that my father and I met nightly. I want her gone. I want my own lady's maid. You influence my father. I'm begging you to do this for me."

Lord Dalry said nothing for a long moment, and I prayed he was considering my request. Finally he sighed. "Do not be angry with Miss Moray. Neither your father nor your lady's maid are as unfeeling as they appear. You weren't here before, so you cannot guess what it was like, how difficult life in this household was."

I laughed a mocking laugh. "Oh, I can guess, all right."

"No. You can't." His piercing gaze met mine. "Miss Moray's dislike of you has nothing to do with you and everything to do with your father. She was chosen by your father to help with the ruse, for everyone knows of her excessive dedication to Lady Pierson. I cannot grant your request, for she's necessary."

His face expressionless, he gave a slight bow, then turned back toward the library, leaving me at the foot of the stairs, wondering what his life had been.

⌒

Less than twelve hours later, my dislike for Miss Moray increased tenfold as I raced toward the breakfast chamber. I slid into my place and glanced at my father, trying to regulate my breathing. Kate gave me a shy smile.

"The warning bell sounded ten minutes ago." My father snapped his pocket watch shut and tucked it inside his coat. "There was plenty of time to arrive in a more ladylike manner. Next time you arrive breathless, you shall not eat. I will not tolerate uncouth manners."

I pressed against the back of my seat and gave him a nod. Miss Moray had taken an obscene amount of time dressing me and had been none too gentle, either. My scalp still tingled from her rigorous brush strokes.

"When I ask you a question, you verbally answer," my father said. "Is that understood?"

"Yes, sir."

Across the table, Lord Dalry met my eyes. No cultured veil hung over his features now. His sympathy was palpable. The difference between his polished and natural expression was so evident, I looked down. Who would believe that this was the same detached-looking gentleman, who at best lifted an eyebrow or frowned slightly?

"What hour is Lady Beatrice expecting Miss Pierson?" He held out his book for James to take, then faced my father. "With your permission, sir, I'd like to escort her."

My father's eyes skimmed the top of his paper. "That's hardly necessary, Isaac. She's not going."

"But, sir, that—"

"Isaac, not one word."

Lord Dalry looked ready to disobey the order, but before he could, a door slammed, followed by a clattering noise. Hard-soled shoes clunked on the floor in the hall. Someone must have been shoved or fallen, for something thumped against the wall, causing the dishes stacked on the sideboard to rattle.

"James, what on earth?" My father lowered the *Gazette*.

"I'll go check, sir." James hastened toward the door, but it swung open and a disheveled Mr. Forrester stormed into the room.

"Never mind, James." My father picked up his coffee and resumed reading his paper. "I think we have found the cause of our disturbance."

Mr. Forrester sneered at me, loosening his drooping cravat. "You would still be here."

Without so much as a flicker of his eye, my father continued to read. "As much as I value your theatrics, Robert, would you mind telling me why you are disturbing my breakfast?"

Mr. Forrester produced a worn copy of the *Times*, which had been tucked beneath his arm. He thumped it on the table. "Is this some sort of a sick challenge to Macy, flaunting your worth?"

"Do not speak that name in my house." Anger finally flushed my father's voice, and he sat forward, folding his paper in half.

Mr. Forrester's expression grew savage as he turned to view me. "What, are we worried about the Jezebel hearing me? She—"

"Now, see here." Lord Dalry rose, his eyes blazing.

Before Lord Dalry could take a step, my father reached forward and grabbed his sleeve. "Honestly, Robert. Isn't there some other household you can go and insult this morning? We've enough headaches with her presentation in three weeks."

Mr. Forrester unclasped his cape and, with a snort, flung it on the floor in a sodden heap. "Do you have any idea how widespread this problem has now become? Everyone is inquiring for more news of the Emerald Heiress, and I mean everyone. Even the beggars on the street are clamoring for news of her. What were you thinking, announcing your wealth like that?"

"I didn't." My father gave Lord Dalry's sleeve a fierce tug and silently demanded that he retake his seat, but was ignored. "That was the work of Lady Beatrice."

"Somehow I doubt that." Mr. Forrester pulled a side chair from near the buffet and wedged it between Kate and Lord Dalry. He grabbed a yeast roll from the table, tore it, and shoved one half in his mouth as he flopped into a seat. "You've gambled more than you can handle. You've no choice but to either succeed or drown. You need me to carry her story and you know it."

"Need you?" My father placed his folded paper to the side of his plate and crossed his arms. "So now we come to the real reason for your visit. Just how many papers have sold because of her story?"

"That has nothing to do with it." Mr. Forrester made a face of disgust as he swallowed. "I'm willing to help you for the sake of friendship."

"Tell me anyway."

Mr. Forrester shoved the rest of the roll into his mouth, then, with the serving fork, dug through the pork cutlets as if considering one. "The *Times* sold out by noon and had to run a second printing."

My father closed his eyes and pinched the bridge of his nose. When he opened his eyes, he glared at Mr. Forrester as if blaming him. "So much for wanting no part in this, heh?"

"Are you really going to sit there and insult me?" Mr. Forrester looked up. "As I see it, you have a choice: either allow the other papers to start poking around for more information, or give me the exclusive and they'll be forced to print what I do just to keep up with the demand. Within a month, I'll make her the darling of London, making it harder for him to reclaim her." Mr. Forrester ground his teeth as he looked toward me. "Speaking of which, we'll also need to do whatever it takes to keep her under lock and key." Lifting a dripping cutlet from the platter, he scanned the table for a plate to place it on. Dark-brown spots stained the tablecloth.

Lord Dalry shoved his plate to Mr. Forrester, eyeing him with aversion.

Mr. Forrester ignored him and shook his cutlet free, then made good use of my father's thought-filled silence by stabbing a forkful of Lord Dalry's breakfast as a sampling.

Silently, I prayed my father would refuse Mr. Forrester. But heaviness settled over my heart as I turned my gaze to the windows, for I knew my father wouldn't remain silent this long unless he was going to accept Mr. Forrester's offer. A thin mist wrapped the street in a chill. This entire situation had gone far beyond what I ever imagined when I sought sanctuary.

"All right," my father finally said, slowly leaning forward. "You have the exclusive, but only if Isaac becomes a household name alongside her. I want his name drummed into every article. Her protector. Her hero. Her ever-faithful guardian. I don't care how you do it, but make Isaac look like he walked straight out of Camelot in this story."

"No." Mr. Forrester's fork clanked on his plate as he threw it down. "Absolutely not!"

"Then you may leave my house, and while you're out, ask the *Times* to pay me a visit. I'm sure they'll be more than willing to accommodate."

Mr. Forrester stood, palms pressed against the table as he leaned toward Lord Dalry. "You don't have to do this, Isaac. You know that you have my full support in anything else. I'd move mountains to influence for you, but do not tie yourself to this jade. It will be the death of you. This goes far beyond what Roy should and can ask of you. She's a—"

"Sir." Lord Dalry looked expressionless, but his deadly tone commanded respect. "You would do well to remember the position this lady holds in my life."

I likewise stood and placed my napkin on the table, ready to leave. Before I could shove my chair out of the way, warm, strong fingers engulfed my left hand. I turned my gaze, surprised to find it was my father.

For the first time since we met, kindness filled his eyes. With a gentle nod, he directed me to retake my seat, to ignore Forrester, to trust him to handle this situation.

Across the table, a ghost of a smile played over Lord Dalry's mouth as he gave my father an almost-imperceptible nod.

My heart pounded as I wondered whether he was coaching my father too. Part of me wanted to reject my father's touch, for if Dalry suggested it, then it wasn't my father's true emotion, but something fabricated. Yet it was the first scrap of relationship I'd been fed from my father's hand, and even if it wasn't true, did I really want to discourage future attempts?

Barely able to keep tears of disappointment from my eyes, I retook my seat.

Who could have foreseen that in order for either of us to ever be whole again, our lives would need to be broken? And who but a master hand could have guided us safely along such a path?

My father swallowed twice after I took my seat, perhaps not certain what to do next. Keeping my hand firmly in his, he returned to Mr. Forrester. "Well? You heard Isaac. Are you for us or against us?"

A dampened Mr. Forrester answered, plopping back into his seat and retrieving his fork. "I'll do it. But she's duping you, Roy, and you're all falling prey to her manipulations."

My father stood and pulled out my chair. Strength coursed through his arm as he helped me stand. Drawing me close, he placed an arm around me and kissed my forehead. For the barest of seconds, my desire to feel cared for rendered me nearly useless. There was strength here, a barrier that not even Macy could break through. But I steeled my heart against full acceptance. He'd already wounded me too often. And besides, he did not own my ultimate allegiance. Only Edward did.

"Isaac, take my daughter." Clutching my elbow in an unrelenting grip, my father moved me toward Lord Dalry as if wishing to transfer my attempt to cling to safety.

"Surely there are some invitations she could work on. Forrester and I have matters to discuss."

Lord Dalry took my arm with a gentleness that could have been a caress. "Sir, if I may request it, I think she should go to Lady Beatrice's."

My father's jawline tightened. "For the last time, Isaac, no."

⁓

About the hour when the sun fell in rich, gold slants throughout the west side of the house, my father's angry voice tore me from the heavy pages of the book I'd been examining.

Outside, a thrush flitted on a nearby branch and chirped. I closed the book, feeling venturesome enough to take a peek.

"You have no understanding of the man." My father's voice

was harsh as I cracked open the door. "It's not safe to allow her outside the house."

"You have to trust her," Lord Dalry said.

My father attempted a laugh, but it was full of anguish. "It's not her that I don't trust." He rubbed his hand over his retreating hairline. "While I fear she'll embarrass herself—we both know she will—I believe her sincere about playing her part. It's him. You don't understand, Isaac. It's as though he can crawl through keyholes or emerge from the shadows at will. I know it in my very marrow; he's just waiting for me to allow her to step outdoors."

"I gave my word that she'd be there tomorrow."

"You shouldn't have, Isaac. It was rash of you to go and see her. I'm not allowing it. My daughter is not setting foot outdoors."

"What has changed since the morning you promised Lady Beatrice could have her throughout the week? You told her she could shape your daughter. You're going to lose Lady Beatrice's support. I've been working with Julia, sir, but she needs a woman's hand. It is evident that no one has taken pains to teach her. There's only so much I can do."

My father huffed and looked at his feet. "Give me time."

I drew a deep breath, wanting neither to be trained by Lady Beatrice nor to remain here.

"I gave my word, sir. Please, do not make me a liar."

"You only gave your word to force me, Isaac. Why shouldn't I make you eat that promise?"

"Why do you think you can wait, sir? Lady Beatrice has already announced her. There's so little time to prepare. Besides, I can't court someone who's not even out."

My father gave him a sour look. "This isn't a joking matter."

"Am I laughing?"

"All right." My father straightened and brushed off his sleeves. "You will follow the carriage to her house and back with my revolver."

"You can't be serious!"

"It's the only way I'll allow it."

Lord Dalry threw his hands in the air. "I don't even know what Macy looks like."

"You'd feel his evil before he was within a hundred feet of you."

"Sir, you're sounding as paranoid as Forrester. Your revolver?"

"She's not leaving this house unless I know you're armed and protecting her."

I hugged my book against my stomach, disliking the reminder of Macy's long reach and recalling that someone here worked for him and I still hadn't a clue who.

"Do you know how ludicrous you sound?"

"Isaac, this is the last time I'm offering this."

"All right, I'll do it, then, but this is absolutely silly."

"You've gotten your way. Now leave me in peace." My father turned to walk away, and I flew back to the couch.

Twelve

THE FOLLOWING MORNING, Lord Dalry's finger traced the sentences in his book. As I sipped my tea, I wondered how he managed to look so mild when I knew in less than an hour he'd be following my carriage with a revolver.

Kate half stood and fluffed her skirt.

"Kate, for the last time, sit down." Lord Dalry didn't even lift his eyes from the page. His voice, at least, sounded strained. "Look at Miss Pierson. Act like her."

"I hate London." Kate threw herself against the back of her chair. "Yesterday I spent the entire day doing nothing."

I gave her a sympathetic smile. Who wouldn't hate being here?

"There are plenty of books," Lord Dalry said. "You brought your sewing. If you're bored, it's your own fault."

Kate fiddled with the cross around her neck. "You promised that this morning you'd show me the neighborhood."

"I promised no such thing. I said I hoped to. Something more important has come up."

"What?" Kate stopped squirming in her chair.

Lord Dalry closed his book and set it on the table. "Kate, your manners are absolutely horrid. Sit and remain silent."

The door opened and we all straightened, expecting my father. Instead, Lady Beatrice entered, followed by Kinsley. Lord Dalry and I rose.

"Come kiss your grandmother." She stretched her skeletal fingers toward us.

I slowly realized she was speaking to me, not Lord Dalry. I obeyed and pressed my lips against her gaunt cheek. Kissing Mama's corpse had felt similar. "Good morning, La—Grandmamma."

Her eyes were depths of cold. She brushed me aside and went to Lord Dalry. "I know if Isaac says something will happen, it happens. So I'm here to retrieve my granddaughter for myself. How are you this morning?" She patted his cheek.

"Well, as always," he said with a smile. "Allow me to find you a seat. We've not eaten breakfast yet. Lord Pierson will arrive in less than two minutes. Will you join us?"

"Seat me across from Lord Pierson, but tell the footman not to set my place."

Though James was standing right there, Lord Dalry relayed the message as he placed her at the table. When my father stalked in, his mouth puckered in dislike before he bowed to Lady Beatrice.

"You've kept me waiting two days, Roy." Her knuckles looked swollen as she gripped the top of her walking cane. "That's hardly like you. You've never allowed Isaac to be late for one appointment. I hope you aren't setting a different standard for your daughter."

"I could not spare my daughter until today." My father shook out his napkin. "James, set her place."

A flick of Lady Beatrice's finger told James to remain where he was. "I have no need to wait upon invitation in this house. Had I wanted to join you, I'd have done so."

Sausage, kippers, tomatoes, eggs scrambled with ham, and marmalade rolls were placed before us. Juice, tea, and coffee were poured.

Lady Beatrice turned to me. "You may drink tea, but no coffee. No sugar. No milk." She turned to James. "Tell Pierrick that Miss Pierson needs to have an egg poached and plain toast. Under no circumstances is she to have butter."

"My daughter will eat what she likes and as much as she likes," my father said. "Go on, Julia, dish anything you like."

Lady Beatrice's laugh was more like a cackle. "Not if I'm sponsoring her, Roy."

They glared across the table at each other. My father yanked his napkin from his collar. "Then don't spons—"

"Sir." Lord Dalry placed a warning hand on my father's arm.

Lady Beatrice smirked, making me wonder how long she'd waited to have power over my father. I wrinkled my brow, wondering anew what this household had been like beforehand. My father gnashed his teeth, looking ready to throw Lady Beatrice on the street, so I laid my hand over his.

"Papa, I'm not even hungry. Please."

Lord Dalry's head snapped in my direction. A smile played on his lips as his eyes shone.

I felt myself blush under his approval even as annoyance prickled through me.

My father turned toward me, and his face evidenced that I'd struck a raw chord. He gripped my hand and swallowed, taking several seconds before he spoke, and even then his voice was gruff with emotion. "Where are you taking her today?"

"She needs new clothing." Lady Beatrice seemed almost pleased by the leverage my father's emotions gave her. "I've made an appointment for a fitting with Quill's. Perhaps you remember them? They made two of your wife's favorite dresses, or at least they were before you threw them into the fire as punishment." Lady Beatrice drummed her fingers on the table, making each click of her nails distinctive. "They'll be making all my grand-daughter's gowns. Then we're going to milliners and accessory shops. I want her to have new shoes, stockings, undergarments." She narrowed her eyes. "I fear this will cost you a small fortune, Roy, even if I have to have real jewels sewn into her clothing."

My father surprised me by laughing. "Spend as much as you like. At least she's more deserving than your daughter."

What emotion is one to feel during such discussion? My heart soared that my father had openly stated I was deserving, yet lamented the pain that crossed Lady Beatrice's face. All at once the borrowed clothing I'd existed in since my arrival felt stuffy and irritating.

"Please, may I come?" Kate asked in a squeaky voice, watching Lady Beatrice with awe.

Lady Beatrice turned her gaze to new prey. "Who are you?"

Kate stood and curtsied. "My name is Katherine Mary Jane Dalry."

"Dalry?" Lady Beatrice turned toward Lord Dalry. "Your sister, I presume?"

"Yes, forgive me." Lord Dalry acknowledged his lapse of manners with a nod. "My sister and Miss Pierson's travelling companion."

"Does your sister meet with your approval, Isaac?"

Lord Dalry frowned. "Her manners need improvement, but she's a happy soul."

Lady Beatrice twisted her mouth. "For your sake, then, I'll take her."

The poached egg and toast were placed before me, but I'd lost my appetite long ago; besides, my father had not yet released my hand, making it impossible to eat. He sat staring at Lady Beatrice as though trying to send a warning that he would not tolerate anything happening to me. It was selfish, but I felt pleased.

Eventually, he noticed my hand still in his and retrieved the *Times*.

⟿

"I expect her back at five." My father's voice echoed through the hall as he followed us. "Not one minute late!"

Lady Beatrice maintained a glib expression as Kinsley placed her cape about her shoulders. A sticky silence filled the air, during which I resisted the urge to wipe my damp hands over my skirt.

"I make no promises," Lady Beatrice eventually said, sweeping her long skirt from her way. She fastened her gaze on me. "Come, London awaits."

My father gripped my arm, holding me in place. His face had grown ashen.

"Sir." Lord Dalry took my arm from his. "She'll be fine."

When he released me, I hastened to catch up to Lady Beatrice's retreating form. Keeping my chin tucked, I stepped outside. The heavy air reminded me at once that I was in London. The ash was so thick I had to cover my mouth to keep from breathing it in. Beyond the wrought-iron fence, Lady Beatrice's carriage stood with plumed horses.

Miss Moray and Kate huddled next to a carriage behind ours. Miss Moray was speaking tenderly to Kate, brushing off the flakes of soot that landed on her cape. James caught my eye as he helped me step into the barouche. Relief flooded me. I'd all but forgotten he was to accompany us. He gave me a slight nod.

With dignity, Lady Beatrice joined me and waited until our carriage jolted before speaking. "Now that we're alone, care to tell me who you really are?"

I felt sullen and decided to mimic her manner. "I have no desire for further acquaintance."

She turned toward the window. "Please yourself."

A few naked tree branches shook overhead as our carriage crawled through the residential street. A haze swallowed all but the towers and spires of the house nearest us. When we reached Park Lane, we turned, putting Hyde Park on our left. I forgot my companion, enchanted by the early morning crowd. Where but in London would there already be so many people in the street at this hour?

Gentlemen rode on horses. Merry faces with ruby cheeks stuck out from beneath tall hats. Walking parties strolled along the sidewalks. I leaned forward, catching sight of a beggar child being jostled in the crowd. The gentry strode past her almost as if the poor child weren't there at all. The barouche rounded another corner, and I twisted to catch one last glimpse.

"You're acting positively common," Lady Beatrice snapped. "Have you never been in a city before?"

"No."

She huffed and primped her skirts. "What is your age?"

Keeping my eyes downcast, I pressed my mouth in a fine line.

"My daughter married your father nearly seventeen years ago. Say you are seventeen. No one would believe you are sixteen."

Our carriage stopped before a building with a black awning that read *Quill's*. Rows of display windows were streaked with London grime, though I had little doubt they'd been washed only hours ago. It was impossible to see the wares between the parasols and bonnets that crowded about the windows.

James opened the door and handed Lady Beatrice down first.

"Come along, dear." With hauteur, Lady Beatrice turned and offered me her black-gloved hand. "It's time we make Roy pay his dues."

Without waiting for Miss Moray or Kate, she walked in a straight line to the store. Many nodded and curtsied, but she acknowledged none.

Before I ducked my head inside, I caught sight of Simmons mounted upon a steed. My brow furrowed. Had my father also armed him and given him instructions to follow me?

Inside, a tinkling bell announced us, and warmth tingled my cheeks. A stout woman turned slightly. Her promenade dress was a magnificent fawn silk gown trimmed with stiff lace and

velvet. She gave us a grave nod, but her eyes twinkled upon rec-
ognizing Lady Beatrice, who placed her card on the counter and
rang the bell. A shopgirl with tired eyes stepped from the back,
snatched the card, and disappeared behind a curtain.

"I'll not be kept waiting," Lady Beatrice murmured to Miss
Moray.

While they were distracted, I observed a group of girls giggling behind fans. I shifted my weight, wondering if they'd
guessed I didn't truly belong amongst their class. Kate slipped
her hand into mine, flooding me with comfort.

A flushed woman swept from the back room. "Lady Beatrice
Kelsey." She gushed her words as she gave a deep curtsy. "I am
honored." She turned toward me, hand over heart, eyes glowing.
"Miss Pierson, I am humbled to be of service to you."

The girls squealed, and whispers of *the Emerald Heiress*
tittered about the room. My mouth dried as I peeked again,
causing more giggles. One young lady bit her lip, then took two
steps forward as if to shyly introduce herself.

"I wish for my granddaughter to be removed from the common room." Lady Beatrice's voice was able to freeze marrow as
she eyed the girl.

The shop woman pushed back a wisp of brown hair, nodding vigorously. "Yes, yes, of course. Please, come this way." She
parted the curtain.

"Proceed." Lady Beatrice nudged me forward, still glaring at
the girls.

My hands were ice but my cheeks felt on fire as we followed
the shopkeeper.

"How dare she," Lady Beatrice whispered to Miss Moray. Her
hand shook as she clutched my arm. "A mere daughter of a knight,
nothing more. Such audacity to approach us! This isn't the first
time that girl has tried to sidle up to the elite. I saw Eramus talking
with her once. I now believe she started the conversation. I have
it in mind to make certain her entire family pays for the insult."

"She ought to be ashamed of herself," Miss Moray agreed. "A jade if I've ever seen one."

Kate's brow rumpled with displeasure before she stuck her tongue out at her ladyship. It was quick; I doubted anyone but myself saw.

Having been an outcast many times, it warmed my heart toward Kate. I gave her a look of approval and received an abashed grin in response. At least I would have one ally this day.

⌒

For the next hour ladies unrolled bolts of material, creating rivers of spilled silks, taffeta, and satins. Miss Moray lingered over the table, fingering each selection. She set aside the most expensive, turning away the rest. Trims such as I'd never imagined were spread in display over every available space—lace beaded with pearls, embroidery more delicate than a child's fingers seemed capable of sewing. After the majority of the selections had been made, Lady Beatrice argued over the length of time required.

"We are not a slop shop." The shopkeeper frowned, clearly unmoved by Lady Beatrice's imperious threats. "It's not as if I keep bodice shells on hand. My gowns are unlike any others in London. They require extra time for the detail we give them."

"Do not mistake me. I expect no less than your very best—and I do mean your *very* best." Lady Beatrice swatted away Miss Moray, who'd brought a sample of Brussels lace for approval. "When my granddaughter comes out, would you prefer her to be wearing a gown from Quill's or from Smythe and Tippler?"

The woman bit her lip and eyed me standing quietly to the side.

"Lord Pierson will pay double your normal fees, triple if necessary. In addition, he'll also be happy to pay for all the gowns that are delayed as an apology to your other customers' inconvenience."

I eyed Lady Beatrice, understanding for the first time why

she'd gone along with this plan. She hadn't been in jest when she stated it would cost my father. Beneath my bodice, I felt perspiration rise as I wondered if my father could actually afford this.

The woman wiped her palms on her oversized apron. "There is one client about her size. For thrice my normal fare, I'll alter three of her dresses immediately, but her replacement gowns shall be very expensive. You'll wait on all the others."

"Agreed, with the exception of her coronation gown. I want better than you've ever produced, and I expect it finished within a fortnight."

A glint of excitement filled the shopkeeper's eye. She made an effort to smother the hope in her voice but failed. "There is one dress worthy. I had fashioned a gown for Her Majesty, but thus far the royal dressmaker refuses to meet my price."

Lady Beatrice tapped her elongated fingers on the table. "Is it white?"

"Yes, yes, and made of a very rare silk that was gifted to an MP, purchased at a very high price."

"And for my granddaughter's train?"

The woman signalled with her finger to follow her. Miss Moray looked up as we left, but chose to stay and sift through more fabrics. In a back area, four girls bent over satin material with a beaded silver passementerie. It shimmered unlike any-thing I'd ever seen.

"Yes." A slow smile stretched over Lady Beatrice's lips. "That one will be fine. We'll pay double to make certain no one else attempts to buy it. Send the first bill to Lord Pierson today."

⁓

By the time we returned to London House, thick darkness lay between the houses. Our street's lamplighter walked our lane, spreading pools of saffron light as he touched his pole to each lamp's wick. The clopping hooves of Lady Beatrice's horses accompanied Kate's and my ascent up the stairs. My legs trembled with each step. Not once had I eaten that day.

With shaking fingers, I searched for the hatpins stuck amongst the damp ribbons and feathers in my bonnet. Blisters had developed on the backs of my feet where my shoes had rubbed them. We'd visited milliners, accessory boutiques, and hidden specialty shops known only to the elite. Everywhere I went, I'd cost my father a treasury.

With a sense of sadness, my thoughts returned to the beggar girl I'd seen at the start of my journey. It was hard to justify how much we'd spent in the name of extravagance when there were so many hungry just outside the doors.

I pressed my hand against my heart as memory of Edward at that awful dinner with Lady Foxmore came to mind. No wonder that when forced to speak, he'd chosen the topic of starving cottagers.

"Who knew there were so many shops in London?" Kate said, her voice sounding as weary as I felt. She sank to a bench. "I didn't know it would be like that, or I never would have gone." She leaned forward and surveyed the hall while Miss Moray took my cape. "Where do you suppose everyone is?"

As if to answer her question, the library door swung open and Lord Dalry entered the hall, the pages of a book fluttering in his hand. His piercing gaze assessed me first. Before he stepped toward us, the sound of heavy boots stopped him.

"Where is Lady Beatrice?" My father stormed from a back room. Wisps of smoke escaped his mouth, and the scent of cigar filled the hall. His dusky face mottled redder as he swore and sent a small table sailing to the floor.

I folded my arms and clamped them over my stomach as I took a seat on the bench. I had not the energy to tell him Lady Beatrice had already left.

"She just departed for home, sir," James offered.

"Sir, I know you're upset," Lord Dalry began, "but if I may advise—"

My father ignored him and turned, bellowing, "James, have my horse saddled this instant! I'm going to pay her ladyship a visit she'll never forget."

I lifted my head in time to see him yank a riding crop from the umbrella stand, his chest rising and falling rapidly.

"Sir." Lord Dalry's voice sounded a willed calm. "I really think—"

"Isaac, my mind is made up." My father grabbed his cape from a closet. "And no amount of argument will dissuade me."

Lord Dalry frowned slightly as my father flung open the door. "James, bring Miss Pierson tea in the library. She looks famished."

Halfway down the concrete steps, my father spun around. "If she was hungry, then she bleeding well could have returned at five!" A flock of wood pigeons took flight from the front yard, crying out as they departed. Passersby stopped and gaped. My father lowered his voice to a gnarled whisper. "If she wishes to eat, then let her obey my schedule."

Lord Dalry crossed his arms, facing him. "Sir, you know as well as I do, she's had no say in her schedule today. Like it or not, I intend on seeing your daughter take tea."

My father looked at me and opened his mouth as if to question me but then suddenly snapped it shut again. "Fine! I'll deal with you when I return." He waved for James to shut the front door.

"Here." Lord Dalry placed a hand under my elbow, helping me rise. "Never mind your father's mood. James, please fetch us tea. Kate, I need to speak to Miss Pierson alone."

Even Kate was too fatigued to protest much. "I'm famished too."

"Miss Moray, will you oversee her tea?"

Steel-blue eyes bored into Lord Dalry. She neither dipped nor nodded. "As you wish."

"Come with me." With a gentle touch, Lord Dalry gathered my arm. "I have news."

Kate's eyes drooped as she leaned against Miss Moray and

started up the first flight of steps. Obediently, I stood, too weary to resist even Lord Dalry at that moment.

In the library, however, I paused at the threshold, unable to endure my shoes. I slipped them off and started anew on the hatpins.

"Here." Lord Dalry's fingers brushed against mine. The next second I felt the pins slide out of my hair. He came around the front of the settee, holding my bonnet with its pins lying atop it. "Rest. My news will save until you've had something to eat."

I sank into the luxurious chair and nudged my toes into the plush, mossy carpet. Cold seemed to seep from the dark corners of the room. Marble busts stared blankly at me. I shifted my feet and looked down. Had I ever attended a country dance at the Gardners' or run down a hill in the rain with Elizabeth? I closed my eyes, remembering how Edward and I had walked over sun-washed fields ripe with wild strawberries. Thinking of him brought heartache, which almost felt good. I'd grown adept at steeling my emotions of late, becoming a silent watcher as I was pulled in every direction, little more than a prop in this stage play.

Before long, the faint rattle of china announced tea, and I realized I'd nearly fallen asleep. I opened my eyes to find Lord Dalry sitting across from me, studying me intently. The aroma of roast fowl, baked apples, and fresh bread tantalized. Smirking, James entered the library burdened with a tray, opening and closing the door with his foot. "Pierrick is downstairs ranting as loud as Lord Pierson because I stole tomorrow's lunch." James set the tray on an ottoman, the only uncluttered space large enough to hold it. "You should see him. He's throwing copper pans and everything."

Like a soldier worn from battle, Lord Dalry placed his forehead against the heels of his hands. "I'll go smooth it over with him once I finish here. James, I'm supposed to keep a chaperone; will you stand guard outside the door? If anyone comes, step into the room and 'chaperone' us."

James grinned, then obediently slipped outside the door.

Lord Dalry poured tea and stirred sugar and milk into the steaming brew. "Sip this slowly." When I accepted the cup, he sat back in his chair again, studying me, keeping one leg crossed over his knee.

The flickering light cast shadows over his thoughtful expression. Wax candles added to the ever-moving, ever-changing light that danced along the walls and gilded the volumes burdening every shelf. I sipped my tea, waiting for him to reveal his purpose in remaining with me.

Rubbing his chin, he finally said, "I'm leaving on the morrow for nearly a fortnight, and I need to—"

"Leaving?" My blood ran cold as I sat forward. "You're not actually going to leave!"

The hope that rose in his eyes told me he drank in my response, taking it as a signal of progress in our relationship.

I turned my teacup in its saucer, frustrated at myself for giving him a reason to continue his relentless attempts at friendship.

"There's a slight problem with a group of your father's supporters. It seems that someone brought pamphlets on a hunting trip, and, according to Mr. Forrester, someone has been making arguments in favor of a radical movement and—"

"Forrester?" Was there nothing redemptive about that man?

"Yes, I fear he thinks—"

"Spare me what he thinks." I placed my tea aside, resisting the urge to dash it against the wall. I rubbed my temples instead. "I know perfectly well what that man thinks."

There was no reading Lord Dalry's expression, but his voice lowered. "While I'm sorry Forrester's opinion of you is skewed, I would rather you ignore him. Regardless of the source, I must go. Our party survives solely on the good graces of the Whigs at this moment. Any weakening might be the collapse of the Conservatives once and for all. Years of your father's work—our father's work—could be ruined in a matter of days. It happens constantly in politics."

I met his eyes, surprised. "That's right. Your own father died before you came to Maplecroft."

A curious expression knit Lord Dalry's brow before his color rose. "Someone told you?"

"Not exactly, but Mrs. Coleman mentioned it."

Lord Dalry swallowed and glanced at his hands. "May I ask exactly what she said? Would it break a confidence?"

"She said I should be glad my homecoming wasn't yours . . . and . . ."

Lord Dalry looked stricken as he met my eyes, waiting. All at once, I had the sharp realization that he truly had suffered. Only he'd dealt with it far differently than I. He kept trying to heal others, whereas I spurned them.

It was the first time we were on level ground and he was as exposed as I was.

"She said . . . ?" he prompted.

I shifted in my seat, trying to cover the fact that I'd lapsed into silence as I thought out how to handle him. "If you must know, she said you were too old to be sucking your thumb."

His eyes widened; then he laughed that amazing, clear laugh of his. "She would remember that detail." His entire body relaxed as he leaned back in his chair. "I'd nearly forgotten. Good gracious, she used to dip my thumb in cod-liver oil before tucking me in." He shook his head and chuckled.

Rather than give room for a friendship to spring up between us, I fixed my cold gaze on the flames. "If you'll excuse me, I'm tired and wish to retire now."

Lord Dalry quickly stood as I started to retreat. "Miss Pierson, wait, please. There's something very important I need to say—"

"Good night, Lord Dalry." It hurt to dismiss him so unkindly, but it was necessary. I gave him a stiff nod, then shut the door.

Thirteen

❦

A LETTER EMBOSSED with a *D* sat atop my breakfast plate the next morning. Though I'd arrived five minutes late, my father beamed and waved me to enter.

While he resurrected a wall of paper and ink, I picked up the linen stationery and frowned. It was completely improper for Lord Dalry to write when we had no formal understanding. Twiddling her fork, Kate feigned disinterest, but her gaze flitted to the note between my fingers. Even James rose up and down on his tiptoes.

I peeked at my father, who watched me from the side of his newspaper, his eyes twinkling, too overjoyed at the prospect that Lord Dalry and I were exchanging notes. I bit the inside of my cheek. It would serve him right if I ordered James to burn it. Yet my curiosity was too piqued for that extreme measure. With all his propriety, it was unlikely Lord Dalry would write unless driven by need.

The seal crumbled easily, and I unfolded the letter, aware of everyone's scrutiny.

Miss Pierson,

Forgive this letter, yet I feel remiss leaving without finishing what I intended to say last night.

Should something greatly distress you at Lady Beatrice's house, you have my permission to refuse to attend her. Tell your father that you are acting upon my direct instruction. He will honor my wishes until I can arrive home to defend them for myself.

Please take no such measure unless circumstances merit a drastic action. I trust your judgment on this matter, despite your Pierson temperament.

Until next we meet,
Isaac

I read his letter twice, puzzled over its entire tone. He'd ended with his Christian name. A hint that he wished me to use it? The paper crinkled as I folded the note. What on earth could he mean about refusing to attend Lady Beatrice and trusting my judgment on the matter? I found it insufferable. Pierson temperament, indeed! I'd never suffered from ill temper a day in my life.

James stepped forward to serve me, but I shooed away the steaming teapot he held. Looking up, I found my father waiting for comment. Did he actually hope I was pleased? Or did he think my moods were as fickle as his? I shivered, realizing how cold it was this morning, then beckoned the footman back. "James, I think I will take that tea."

Kate's lower lip protruded in a pout. "You mustn't be too hard on Isaac. Perhaps he's not very good at writing love letters yet. Practice might help him. I'm sure his next one will be better."

James's mouth contorted like an acrobat as he poured my tea. He turned the second he could.

"I can assure you, it's no love letter," I said, placing it aside.

My father laughed aloud. "I would have hoped that with as much money as he squandered on those woeful poetry volumes, he could have produced something better than that scowl. James, is there a problem?"

A red-faced, watery-eyed James turned and with a closed fist pounded his chest. "No, sir. Just a bit of dust caught in my throat." He squeezed his eyes shut and with great effort resumed a normal stance.

"May I be excused?" I asked.

"No. If I allow you to stay after you have the audacity to arrive late—you eat." My father nodded at the letter, and his voice softened. "What did Isaac say?"

I pushed the note farther under my plate. What if it had been a love letter? Did my father assume the right to monitor every aspect of our relationship? "It was a personal note to me . . . which . . . which I'd rather not share."

Crow's-feet crinkled around my father's eyes as he smiled and turned a page. "Fine. A little intrigue might lighten the mood around here."

Frowning, I glanced over the table, but my stomach was tied in knots. It was bad enough knowing I had to go face Lady Beatrice without the addition of Lord Dalry's strange instructions.

Fifteen minutes before the o'clock, my father exchanged newspapers. "You'd best leave now, Julia. The last thing I want today is Lady Beatrice on my doorstep."

I gave a nod and stood, suddenly wishing I never had to leave the walls of London House.

～⌒～

The distance to Lady Beatrice's residence was scarcely worth the climb in and out of my father's barouche. Little distinguished her street. The houses mimicked one another, patterned after their owners' attempts to mimic each other. The street's only distinction was a row of mossy elms that stood sentry. I eyed them, fearing for their lives. All it would take was a stray comment from a countess, a note that their existence differentiated the street, and down they would go.

Elaborate scrolled handrails flanked both sides of the wide stoop. From there, I plunged into Lady Beatrice's world, leaving James and daylight behind.

Her drawing room was a cerise nightmare, and though my only memory of it is from those weeks, I recall it with clarity. Drapes of that shade adorned with gold tassels matched the exact color of the stripes that alternated over the wallpaper. Red carpets stretched beneath the clawed feet of scarlet upholstered furniture. The only relief was an immense gilded crystal chandelier—yet even that was so disproportioned, it squatted upon the room like a giant toad amidst a faerie gathering.

Lady Beatrice sat near the window, taking the only shaft of light that managed to penetrate that chamber. Bitter lines etched her face, particularly around her mouth, as I entered the room. Though her knuckles looked rheumatic, she plied a large embroidery hoop that was situated near her.

"You will sit there," she instructed me, nodding toward a chair at the opposite end of the chamber beneath an arrangement of brown wax roses. "Study the book on the seat, and do not speak. Today is the day I receive callers. Expect to be removed from sight at a moment's notice."

I picked up the mildewed book and to my dismay found it was in French.

The look of pleasure on her face told me all I needed to know. I opened the useless book, knowing it was pointless to argue. This was part of her revenge on my father—to spend his money and then watch us flounder.

It made me feel defensive of my father. Her desire to see me fail became my fuel to succeed. She gave me a far greater gift than that, however.

Though it was her day for callers, no voice hailed in her hall, no footstep sounded at her door. She speculated that the rain or weather must be keeping everyone away, but we both knew better.

Dreadfully long hours passed, hours during which I looked at meaningless pages, my back ached, my neck cricked, and my feet alternately fell asleep. Whenever I dared to circle my head to stretch it, Lady Beatrice glared over her embroidery. Occasionally, she'd question me in French and then berate me for not knowing the answer.

By the time the sun cast long shadows over the room, I'd memorized the flaking crown molding, the art on the wall, the Bohemian glass collection, and the dying plants. When the clock chimed five, I rose, not caring if she commanded me to sit back down. I wouldn't.

Nonetheless, I felt pity for her. I'd witnessed firsthand the cost of bitterness on a life.

It was no wonder to me that Lord Dalry chose to continually forgive offenses. He, too, must have spent time there.

～

The windows of my father's house were aglow with welcoming light. During my absence, rain had washed the streets, so that as James helped me alight from the carriage, the wet brick shimmered like glass beneath my feet. Leaves, gathered along the cement stiles at the bottom of the wrought-iron gate, offered their dying fragrance—a respite from the city air.

"Careful, now." James supported my arm as I stepped firmly onto the ground. His kind tone alleviated the painful hours of her ladyship's scissored tongue.

London House once more displayed her enchantment. Inside, the ornate staircase and spindles shone and gave off the fragrance of beeswax. The polished floors looked wet with puddles of hazy light beneath the sconces. Two suits of armor glinted near the door, brave knights guarding the house during its slumber. I paused to view them as Kinsley approached, wondering if men had ever really worn them in combat.

"Did you enjoy tea with the duchess, Miss Josephine?" Kinsley's eyes creased in a kindly smile as he removed my fur mantle.

I could have kissed his wrinkled cheek as I breathed in his peppermint smell. Though I wanted to savor the moment, I reminded myself not to grow attached to this life.

He bundled my cape in his arms. "Come and warm your feet before the fire. You'd best pray your mother doesn't learn you've snuck out again."

"I'm quite certain she'll never learn of it," I replied.

"You always claim that right before you're caught." His cloudy eyes lit in expectation of a familiar retort.

Only I did not know my grandmother's reply. I gave a heavy-hearted smile. At least the world Kinsley wandered in seemed pleasant. The idea that my grandmother used to sneak out of the house was both shocking and satisfying. Perhaps I wasn't the first who risked scandal.

"Oh, thank goodness you're home." Kate's plaintive voice carried from the parlor. Before I turned, she'd raced to me and flung her arms around my waist.

I pressed my cheek against her glossy curls, gladsome for her presence.

"Goodness! I can hear your stomach growling. You must be starving." Kate stepped back and grinned. "I'm so glad!"

I wrinkled my nose at her as I peeled off my gloves.

In a trice, Kate bounced on her toes and clapped her hands with delight. "Isaac made certain tea would be waiting for you the moment you returned from Lady Beatrice's. Come see!"

Confused, I picked up my skirts and allowed Kate to tow me toward the parlor.

The sight that awaited me, however, caused me to pause at the threshold, amazed.

A full tea with shimmering crystal and sparkling teacups was set before a roaring fire. A three-tiered stand was adorned with a fully poached pineapple perched atop a glistening display of candied oranges, plums, grapefruits, and even a bowl of rubied cherries. Sugarcoated leaves nestled between the glazed fruit, adding to the glittery display. Lemon-curd tarts and pound cake sat alongside roasted chicken and herbed asparagus. Candles glimmered at varying heights, their flames adding luminosity to pink tulips that spilled from their vases.

"What on earth," I finally managed.

Kate plopped onto a settee, knocking a tapestry pillow to the floor. "Last night before he left, Isaac instructed the staff to have this prepared today. You should have seen it. It took hours! Your father's chef was here, screaming in French, calling everyone *imbéciles*, demanding this tea be perfect because it's part of Isaac's courtship."

From my side vision I saw the brown of James's eyes flick in my direction.

Tightness gathered in my chest. To refuse to laud the effort behind this tea would hurt the staff, yet neither could I afford to encourage Lord Dalry.

Thankfully, before I could speak, Kate turned toward me with shining eyes. "Shall I serve?"

I nodded, then turned to James. "I know you've had a long day too. Please extend my thanks to the staff for this lovely surprise. I am beyond amazement."

James's disappointment was evident as he bowed and ducked from the room.

While Kate warmed the pot, I took the settee across from her, trying to pinpoint the source of James's disappointment. Did it mean the staff was caught up in the possibility of a love story happening beneath their roof? This entire situation was growing more ludicrous by the moment.

The air was redolent with the scent of lavender as Kate poured.

"Isaac told James he wished you to try this tea." Kate licked a dollop of plum jam from her finger, then pointed to my teapot. "James asked your father for permission, and your father told him to charge it to the household account."

I frowned. "Your brother wanted me to drink this blend of tea? Why?"

Kate radiated with too much happiness to notice the sharpness of my tone or my question. "When your father left this morning, James pulled on his cape and left too. He came back from Exchange Alley not just with this blend but with this teapot too!" She leaned over the table, her eyes shining with delight. "It caused the most horrific row. The housekeeper said he had no business spending the master's money without his say-so. That's when Miss Moray joined in and said *she* wouldn't go out in the rain and risk her position on the likes of you—"

I struggled to maintain a composed expression, lest Kate leave out a detail. "She dared to say that in front of you?"

Kate's curls danced as she gave her tinkling laugh. "No, I was hiding in Isaac's snuggery. You can hear all sorts of servants' talk if you crouch near the door."

I gave her a disapproving look, which she discarded.

"James insisted that this teapot be used today. Can you imagine such audacity? Mama would be shocked and advise Isaac not to be so free with him, but I like James."

I stared at the yellow teapot with hand-painted roses. Poor James. No wonder he'd waited. And I hadn't so much as glanced at it.

"The teapot cost over thirty pounds! Mrs. King says Lord Pierson is going to be fit to be tied, but James threatened to expose all the secrets he knew about them if anyone tattles before he can give Isaac the bill to add to his monthly expenses."

Kate had dumped so much information on me, I scarcely knew which piece to consider first. I touched the teapot, and despite myself, my spirits lifted. A tiny piece of me finally existed here. There was no portrait of me amongst the hundreds of ancestors. I had not chosen the color of my room, the materials for my dresses, the style of my hair, nor any other of myriad details, but I had a teapot.

I turned it so that I could watch steam pipe from the spout.

No, I realized, James and Lord Dalry had a teapot. And a rather girlish one at that.

I sank against the pillow and focused on the rings of lights that rippled along the ceiling from the candles as the frightening realization overcame me of how quickly one could become lost in this sphere. I had nearly delighted over a teapot, forgetting that my entire life had been snatched from me.

All at once, I missed Edward so much I grew homesick. He would never do this to me. He would never, under any circumstances, take away my freedom, my choices.

A vision of Am Meer with its smoking chimneys and annoying chickens clucking beneath my bedchamber window rose in memory. There one didn't pass hours in silence. One could always hear Mrs. Windham or the clack of Elizabeth's knitting needles. There the rooms weren't so huge that they always felt freezing no matter how the fire blazed. Who wanted a tea such as this when the alternative was walking side by side with Edward beneath billowing clouds in a sparkling-sapphire sky?

Tears I hadn't had time to cry welled, but I took deep breaths to abate them. I needed to keep my head. To remain steady, I faced Kate.

The picture she created would have warmed even Lady Beatrice's heart. Kate held her saucer exactly twelve inches from her chin and kept her head perfectly straight.

What if I never found a way to escape this? I thought. What if Lord Dalry was right? There was only duty now. The dainty china cup in my hand suddenly felt too heavy to lift.

I eyed the august tea that testified to my father's distinction, wondering why everyone sought so hard for wealth, fame, position, and power. It was all a trap.

"Julia?" Kate's use of my name startled me. "Are you listening?"

"Forgive me." I retrieved my cup. "You were saying?"

"May I go with you to Lady Beatrice's tomorrow?"

I had to struggle to shift my thoughts. "I don't think your brother would allow it."

"Isaac?" Her nose wrinkled like a hare's. "What has he to do with it?"

"I don't know, but it seemed to me he feared something at her house. Have you any idea what he meant?"

Kate's brow crumpled in thought; then all at once horror lit her face. "Oh!" She touched her lips. "You don't suppose . . . ?"

"Suppose what?"

She set her cup down and placed her hands over her stomach. With gravity she said, "Eramus Calvin."

I angled my head, recalling the name from the newspaper article. "Her ladyship's nephew? What about him?"

There was a long silence, and then Kate turned toward me. "I overheard Isaac tell Mama one night. She cried, and he kept saying he shouldn't have told her."

"What did he say?"

Kate shook her head. "When Isaac found out I heard . . . If I told you what I learned, he would never trust me again." She shook her head. "Isaac never talks about his past to anyone except Mama, not even Ben."

"Ben?" I repeated softly. If I couldn't solve one mystery, perhaps I could solve another.

Kate's look was solemn. "Our missing brother. He disappeared one night, trying to help Mr. Forrester keep someone safe from a dangerous man."

I sat, too stunned to speak, though my gaze swept to the portrait of my grandmother that occupied the chamber. In this painting, she looked over her shoulder as her loosed black hair cascaded down her back. She wore her ever-present coy smile.

"Your brother disappeared helping Forrester?" I heard my voice as if through a fog. "How long ago was that?"

"Three years ago."

I felt as if my stays had been tightened to the point of my being unable to breathe. For I suspected the dangerous man was Mr. Macy. And if my father and these men had tangled with him before, yet he still roamed free, then it was highly possible my current situation would not soon be over.

Fourteen

KEEPING MY CHIN LIFTED and the book atop my head balanced, I turned in a slow, refined manner and glanced out the rain-speckled window, where I caught sight of a horse that had not been there the moment before. Behind it, fog curled over murky carriage tracks crisscrossing the cobblestone. The far streetlamps appeared as little more than glowing orbs, lost amidst swirling mists.

"A lady of good breeding does not shift her eyes. Keep them fixed straight ahead." Lady Beatrice tugged fiercely on her thread, puckering her embroidery, then allowed her work to fall to her lap. "Come, come. Now is not the time to dawdle. We've scarcely a fortnight and you cannot even walk right. Start anew. Step, pause. Step, pause. Now with a grand sweep, turn. No, not like that; your shoulders are slouched. You look positively common."

Taking care to keep all expression from my face, I adjusted my posture. Too many times during the past week, she'd slapped the back of my hand with a ruler just because I'd given her unladylike looks.

"Pretend I just said something witty." Lady Beatrice returned to her work, squinting to see in the gloom. "Laugh."

I drew a deep breath, hating this exercise. I'd yet to laugh in a fashion that met her approval. It was always too forced, too vulgar, or not airy enough.

When no laugh issued forth, Lady Beatrice paused, thread in air, thimble glinting in the lamplight. Her eyes hardened. "A peer who outranks you just said something witty. Now laugh."

The jangle of a bell caught both of us by surprise. She scowled, moving her embroidery to her basket. "Go take that chair. Do not speak unless I indicate my permission. Let's hope my guest is in no clever mood tonight."

Grateful for the respite, I took the chair, adjusted my skirts, then retrieved my own embroidery reserved for such an emergency. With a huff, I viewed the dismal room imprisoned within its red-striped papered walls and cerise curtains before jabbing my needle in and out of the linen. At least here was one area of my life her ladyship could not fault, though she tried. Mama had spent hours of her day embroidering and had taught me well.

The door opened and her butler, Taggart, stepped inside. "Lord Isaac Dalry."

Astonished, I looked up. Lord Dalry wasn't due back for nearly a week. Nevertheless, he strode through the door, dressed in a full riding cape and spurs. Half-hidden by the gloom, his unshaven face highlighted his unique chin, strangely making him look wilder. He bowed and removed his hat, revealing damp hair.

His eyes traveled in my direction. I couldn't help but question him with a look, despite my intentions to keep him distant.

He did not linger on me. Instead he turned toward Lady Beatrice, looking ready to tear down the house brick by brick.

"Grandmamma, Lord Pierson made it perfectly clear she was to be returned by teatime. Why is Miss Pierson still here?"

Lady Beatrice waited until she finished her knot. The creases in her face multiplied. "Honestly, Isaac. How do you expect me to teach that piece of work manners when you discard them yourself? How dare you barge into my drawing room making demands?" Her mouth twisted as she snipped thread. "It's not my fault the girl is nothing short of stupid. I've spent hours coaching her, yet she cannot manage even simple tasks."

"Then allow me to relieve you of her presence." In three steps Lord Dalry was at my side, lifting me from my seat.

I rose, astounded at the intensity of his grip, and dropped my sewing. It hit the floor.

"I want a word with Eramus before I leave too." Lord Dalry's angry gaze darted about the room as though he expected someone to emerge from the shadows. He slapped his hat against his leg. "Now!"

"Eramus?" Lady Beatrice's hands fell to her lap. "Isaac, of all things. Have you lost your wits along with your manners? His visit is not scheduled until Christmas. You know that."

Lord Dalry cut a quick look about the room. Barely visible, his Adam's apple bobbed above his cravat before his face reddened. He closed his eyes, whether from relief or embarrassment or both, I could not tell. "By your leave, then," was all he said, and he ushered me toward the hall.

∽

"Where's Kate?" Lord Dalry shook free of his cape, then held out his hands for mine.

"Sir?" Kinsley asked.

"Kate! My sister, Kate." Lord Dalry swept a riled gaze about the hall. "Where is she hiding?"

"Your sister, sir?" With a confused glance, Kinsley looked to me. "Miss Josephine, don't tell me you approve of this rapscallion?"

A look of surprise came over Lord Dalry, yet before he could respond, my father opened the library door. Scents of cigars drifted into the main hall.

He removed the cigar from his mouth. "Isaac, why the devil are you here? You're supposed to be at Crawl—" His eyes narrowed. "Why is Julia with you?"

Two gentlemen appeared on either side of my father. Their eyes laughed as they looked over Isaac's rumpled appearance and my blushing form. Behind my father's back, they seemed to congratulate themselves with their eyes, before the tallest one cast Isaac a smug, suggestive look.

I bit my lower lip, wishing myself far from them.

"I daresay, Dalry looks equally surprised to find you home, sir," the tall one said, then smiled a crooked grin at Lord Dalry. "Eh, old boy?"

The other chuckled and stuck his hands in his trouser pockets.

Lord Dalry gave them a look that would have withered most and took my upper arm, moving me behind him, from view. "Where is Kate, sir? She wrote me that your daughter was in danger. I removed her from Lady Beatrice's as a precaution."

"Kate did what? What does she know of—?" Suddenly my father remembered the men behind him and turned. "Excuse me, gentlemen." He shut the door and then traversed to a private room.

Lord Dalry ushered me inside with him. "It has nothing to do with Macy, sir."

Telltale red blotched my father's neck. "Well, you'd best be prepared to tell me what merits direct disobedience."

"It's nothing."

"Nothing!" My father screamed the word, then lowered his tone, glancing in the direction of the library. "You dare to leave Crawlsley's party when we're in the middle of a crisis, for nothing?"

"There's no crisis." Lord Dalry stripped off his gloves and

tossed them on a round table, evidently not caring that my father appeared on the verge of exploding. "Forrester had it all wrong. No one even possessed a pamphlet. But they all took merriment in the fact that I'd ridden two days to sway them to their own views. The trip was all for naught."

"Go get dressed and join me, then." My father's nostrils flared as he considered me. "Julia, order tea. My guests have done nothing except make inquiries about you since their arrival. Tea cakes and small talk will cure their curiosity."

Lord Dalry's eyes widened. "Sir, your daughter is nowhere near ready for such—"

"Do not argue!" my father commanded, heading toward the door. "I've spent the last hour trying to talk politics with them; if their curiosity over meeting the sensational Emerald Heiress will make them more reasonable, we're using it. Now go get ready."

A silence fell over our room after he left. Lord Dalry rubbed his hand along his stubbled cheek. He cast a glance at the clock, at me, then tugged the bellpull three times, an indication he wanted one of the higher staff members.

A moment later, a breathless James appeared. Though I felt certain he was surprised at seeing Lord Dalry, he managed to keep a bored expression.

"Lord Pierson has ordered tea for his guests. Miss Pierson and I will join them, so there'll be five. Send Pierrick my apology, but tell him to make it dazzle. If Kate returns home, make certain she does not know I have arrived. I want to catch her by surprise. I need to change, and quickly. If you can act as my valet within five minutes, then do so; otherwise send me anyone available."

"Yes, sir." James bowed and raced away.

"Come with me." Lord Dalry cupped my elbow and lowered his voice. "We'll settle with Kate later. Meantime, summon your lady's maid and change. Remain in your room until you hear me go downstairs. As I lack proof, I have not yet voiced my suspicions, but neither will I risk having you alone with those two."

∽

My every muscle stiffened as I approached the drawing room. Strange how an hour ago I wanted to be free of Lady Beatrice, but now I wished myself back with her.

From within, male voices, all polite, all with perfect inflections, laughed. Had I not known that tension was steeped into this tea, I would have thought everyone to be sworn friends.

"Ah." My father rose and extended his hand when I opened the door. "Here she is."

The remaining gentlemen rose. China and silver clinked; linen napkins fluttered to the floor. With my father present, no one wore expression except Lord Dalry, who gave me one brief smile, then became a polished mask of good breeding.

"Julia," my father said, "may I present to you Lord Alexander Kensington and Mr. Jonathan Billingsby."

The tall one was Lord Alexander and the stout one Mr. Billingsby. They both dipped their heads.

"How do you do?" Billingsby asked.

"May I find your seat, Miss Pierson?" Lord Alexander pulled an armchair nearer the table, situating me between him and his friend.

My fingers twitched, but to hide my growing dismay, I started toward the chair. My father and Lord Dalry cut each other panic-stricken looks.

Was it because I'd not returned any greeting? "I meant to s-say, I am well." My tongue felt twice its normal size, making it difficult to speak. I stopped halfway across the room and stepped on my overlong skirt. The sound of lace rending from the hem filled the space.

My father stared as though I had flounced into the room,

flopped in a chair, and spoken with a thick brogue. Both of the gentlemen's smiles drained.

"If you don't mind . . ." Lord Dalry's easygoing voice sounded behind me. "I would rather Miss Pierson remain with me." He took my arm, and never had I been more thankful for him. "I fear our Miss Pierson becomes terribly shy around gentlemen—a fault of having been constantly surrounded by female companions at her school. Lord Pierson and I have been working with her to cure it."

Somehow, I managed to find my way to the chair Lord Dalry directed me to and collapsed.

Ashen, my father took his seat, staring at me, horrified.

"May I inquire after the health of your sister?" Lord Dalry asked Lord Alexander, pouring tea. He pressed the hot cup into my hand. "I have every hope that Miss Pierson and Miss Kensington will form an attachment."

"She is fine, thank you." Lord Alexander did not return the desire for his sister to befriend me. Instead he fingered his teacup, his gaze flitting between Lord Dalry and me as though he was trying to decide which guise was true.

"And your father?" Lord Dalry sat back and looked at Billingsby. "When I left, a slight cold kept him from attending our club. Has he recovered?"

Billingsby nearly jumped when addressed but stopped eyeing me. "Yes, quite."

"Miss Pierson, wait until you meet Billingsby senior." Lord Dalry turned and spoke to me as though we were on the best footing. "He is exactly the type of person which delights you the most. Friendly and gruff rolled into one."

I smiled, though it felt strained. I saw by Lord Dalry's face that he wanted me to speak, but what on earth could he expect me to say with an opening like that? *"How lovely! I always hoped to meet someone friendly yet gruff"*?

"Perhaps your father will be so kind as to take tea with

Miss Pierson and me tomorrow," Lord Dalry said. "I think he would be the very type of person she should practice with. Your father always has the young ladies laughing within the first five minutes."

Mr. Billingsby cast Lord Dalry a doubtful look. No one spoke. Beads of perspiration formed on my father's forehead. My heart pounded so hard that the sound filled my ears. I was in over my head. This ruse would be a dismal failure. My father had just ruined his life. Macy would come and collect me. I turned to Lord Dalry, realizing he was the only person still trying, tears filling my eyes. Yet he had never looked so calm or collected.

"It's all right," he murmured, almost lovingly. "I quite prefer a wife who won't barge into my men's club." He turned to Lord Alexander. "Do you remember last season when Mrs. Lowry stormed through the doors because she suspected Mr. Lowry was playing cards?"

Lord Alexander laughed, placing his hand over his stomach. "I should say I do. Lowry still won't speak to me for laughing as hard as I did."

Billingsby chuckled and selected another tart from the tray. "I think that was the highlight of last season, and to my complete advantage. He was staged to rob me of over a hundred sovereigns when his good lady showed."

"Gentlemen." My father roused himself from his stupor and rubbed his temple. "Surely you can find better topics to discuss in front of my daughter."

Lord Alexander smiled directly at me, yet there was something rapacious about it. He considered me at leisure before saying, "Sir, I see the advantage in hiding your child from treasure seekers, and I congratulate you on an unspoiled daughter. It is rare to find such wealth attached to such meekness. I should be quite pleased for my sister to be introduced to her. Shall we make the arrangements?" He shifted his gaze to Lord

Dalry. "Dalry, I will align myself with you during her first few public appearances to help ease her into society."

"Thank you, but Miss Pierson shall not require *your* aid."

Lord Alexander tapped his fingers, glaring at Lord Dalry, then smiled anew. "You've scarcely considered it; therefore my vanity demands you do not realize the value." Lord Alexander selected a few dainties from the tray and passed the plate to me. "Even you have to admit she's going to need familiar faces until she adjusts."

Lord Dalry gave him a warning look, which no one could mistake.

"Perhaps you agree with me, sir." Lord Alexander lifted a brow in my father's direction. "My public support will only bolster confidence."

A charged silence followed, during which my father appeared to be weighing his words. In the hallway, footsteps approached, accompanied by Kate's cry. "Oh, Mrs. King, wait till I tell you what I heard today."

A second later, she burst into the room, obliging the gentlemen to rise. She gasped, the hem of her skirt muddy. Wisps of red hair stuck up from where she'd presumably snatched off her bonnet. She gasped anew viewing her brother. "Isaac!"

"Gentlemen, my sister." Lord Dalry stepped around me, making his way toward her. "Kate."

"Oh, now, don't be cross." She picked up her skirt and tiptoed away from him, toward the party, tracking mud over the floor. "I never actually said that Eramus arrived at Lady Beatrice's, so you can't blame me that you came home. I only said—"

"Kate! Not another word."

Mr. Billingsby guffawed and looked up from his teacup. "What! You mean to tell me that Dalry rode home because of the rumor about Lady Beatrice trying to attach Miss Pierson to that rotund nephew of hers?"

Lord Dalry gave Kate a look that demanded silence.

"I think we found the imminent danger that your daughter was in." Lord Alexander grinned and sat back. "Isaac, I concur with you: it was absolutely necessary to remove Miss Pierson from Lady Beatrice's immediately. I congratulate you on saving her from an unwanted wooing."

Mr. Billingsby laughed and dunked a biscuit in his tea. "Were I you, Miss Pierson, I would feel my intelligence insulted."

"Honestly, Isaac, don't tell me you plan on playing the part of a jealous lover," Lord Alexander said. "You're going to have to grow accustomed to the thought that more than one person will be seeking Miss Pierson's favor this season."

"Well, it won't make any difference," Kate retorted, sidling toward me. "Isaac is already in love with Julia, and the marriage contract has been drawn. So there!"

"Kate!" Lord Dalry lunged at her, grabbed her wrist, and pulled her from the room.

Heat flamed my face as the gentlemen burst into hearty laughter. From the corner of my view I saw my father look to the ceiling as though suppressing his temper. I wanted to crawl into a cupboard and die of humiliation. Only there was nowhere to hide, so I fixed my gaze out the window.

"Gentlemen," I heard my father say, "this tea is over."

"Don't be too hard on them, Roy." The voice was Lord Alexander's. Though he couldn't have been any older than Lord Dalry, he addressed my father as an equal. As he passed, he placed his hand on the back of my chair, his fingers brushing against my bare shoulder. "I'll write my sister and instruct her to make acquaintance with your daughter. I am most anxious for their attachment to begin."

"Yes, yes, I'm sure my daughter will be most pleased . . ." My father's voice faded, as did the scuffling noise of the gentlemen's departure.

I shifted in my chair, feeling too unworthy to even speak.

A moment later, my father returned to the chamber.

I tensed, waiting for his censure, but instead he took measure of me and softened before he sank into his chair. There he leaned his head back and pinched his nose.

"It wasn't all that bad, sir," Lord Dalry offered as he entered and took a seat.

My father opened one eye and stared as if to ask if he'd even been present. "What was that between you and Lord Alexander? That was a challenge if I ever saw one! Must you continually provoke him? If we lose his support, we lose every one of his cronies, and we can't afford it."

I listened, stunned that my father hadn't yet scolded me.

"I didn't provoke him," Lord Dalry said. "He provoked me. You saw it yourself. But I can't see why you're bothered. You know him and a challenge. If anything, now he's going to work hard at winning your favor. I wager he'll back your every argument for the next six months."

To my surprise, my father chuckled. "There's always a proverbial sliver lining with you, son. Is there not?" He lifted his head with a sigh and noted that I stared at him, before giving me a nod. "It's all right; you did your best, which is all anyone can ask. Thankfully, I've seen you navigate better. No repeat performance of tonight. Agreed?"

I felt as though I had swallowed my tongue but managed, "Yes, sir."

I finally looked to Lord Dalry for explanation. He, however, stared blankly at the wall, looking weary and deep in thought. He didn't seem to think my father was acting radically different. Was it possible that this was how my father acted when not stressed?

"Isaac, I'm sorry," my father said, returning his head to the back of the chair, "but after that display, Kate is returning home. I know you wanted to finally spend time with her, but she's a liability at this stage. Write your mother and arrange it."

Long after the house was silent, I sat before my hearth, staring at the embers, unable to reconcile the side of my father I'd witnessed tonight. I buried my fingers in my hair as I rocked silently. Somehow it awakened more pain, though I couldn't comprehend why. I pressed my hands against my heart, not sure I wanted to think or feel anymore.

Hearing my door open, I leaned forward and peeked around my bed. A young girl with a pale face and pink eyes blinked back, before nervously dipping. "Oh, do excuse me! I beg your pardon, miss!" She bobbed, showing her muslin cap, which ranked her no higher than a laundry maid. "I-I didn't know you were here."

I pressed my lips together. Here at least was a soul I understood, a salt-of-the-earth sort of person. Here was the type of folk Edward was lucky enough to be surrounded with, while I, on the other hand, was stuck with people who might face a debacle with resignation or burst like a thunderclap without warning.

My eyes trailed down to the copper pan she clutched. "Are you here to warm my bed? Where's Betsy?"

The girl fell to her knees like a prisoner before a queen. "I meant no 'arm, miss. I swear it. Betsy has fever and tried to rise, but I told her, sleep. We share a room, so I told her I'd do it."

I rose, imagining Lady Beatrice and Miss Moray dying of shock to see me addressing a laundry maid, but visions of Edward filled my mind. Surely he wouldn't allow someone to cower before him. "If you share a room," I asked, "aren't you feeling ill?"

"Not enough to affect my work, miss."

I crouched and touched her chin, causing her to flinch. Sadness filled me, for my own status barred any hope of knowing her. It made me long for Nancy with intensity. She wouldn't have been put off by pretenses.

I touched the girl's cheek and forehead with the backs of my fingers. She burned with fever as she watched me with glassy eyes. "I'll warm my own bed," I said. "You are dismissed."

Her face scrunched. "I can work, miss; I swear it. Please!"

"I'm not relieving you of your duties," I said, rising, tugging her up with me. "If you're sick, I want you to rest." The crocheted lace on her cap dropped over her forehead, as she looked unable to comprehend me.

"Go to bed." I pointed toward the door. "That's an order!"

She swallowed; then finally sensing that I was in earnest, she dropped the warming pan and ran from the room, arms stiff at her sides. I pulled on a woollen robe, intending to locate the housekeeper and communicate my orders that the girl be given bed rest, but in the hall, muffled sobs carrying from Kate's chamber stopped me.

I touched my forehead against the door, trying to use logic instead of emotion. These were not my people; this was not where I belonged. Entering to comfort her would be one more step away from my old life, embracing this new life.

All at once Kate's keen became so heartfelt it was impossible to resist going. I would untangle this later.

"Kate?" I rapped on her door. "It's me, Julia. Open the door."

Clumsy movement sounded behind the wood, and a moment later the lock clicked open.

Kate stood in her nightgown, tears streaming down her cheeks. "I'm being sent home!" Her mouth gaped with an ugliness that would have been comical were her grief not so apparent. "I . . . I wanted to spend time with youuuu and Isaac. You have no idea how little I see him."

My heart bade me to reach out and hold her, while my head warned me to stay detached from the Dalry family. "You're not leaving straightaway." I took her hand to lead her back to bed. "Isaac said your mother had gone north to visit family. You'll be here a little while longer yet."

"Yes, but your father says . . . he says . . ." New tears welled. "I can't go to the ball or anything! Isaac is supposed to find cousins for me to stayeeee—" Her words turned into a wail.

"Hush." I pulled her inside the room toward the bed. Our bare feet left impressions on the thick carpet. I pulled down her counterpane and nodded for her to climb in. "Sleep. Things will look brighter in the morning."

I shifted, not comfortable with my own lie. I couldn't remember the last time something had looked better the next day.

"Sleep beside me?" Kate rested her head on my shoulder, and I felt dampness. "Please."

I looked toward the door but then considered there was already so much sadness in this house. Could I truly leave her here crying alone? "All right, just for a bit."

Twenty minutes later, Kate's steady breathing filled the room. I snuggled beside her under the warm covers, staring at the fire, wondering how I was ever going to manage this household without the snippets of sunshine that Kate gave me.

I shut my eyes and conjured Edward's face to mind. *"You can do this,"* he'd assured me. But how? Without losing him, how? I curled my fingers into the pillow, determined I'd find a way, for his sake, if for no other reason.

Fifteen

ONCE, A TROUPE of performers traveled through our village, and I had the privilege of watching a tightrope walker suspended between heaven and earth, with nothing more than an open fan in each hand to assist him. Unlike the crowd, who marveled at his balance, I was most awestruck by his first four steps. I knew once he took those fateful steps away from his platform, his only choice was to finish. The wire was too high for him to jump.

The next two weeks of my life were much like that performance. My focus was narrow, my aid nothing more than social props. I did my best not to think of Edward, Am Meer, Mr. Macy, or even Mama. Mornings were spent in numerous fittings at Quill's. Afternoons took place at Lady Beatrice's house, where I practiced every imaginable social situation. I quickly learned my best defense was to act devoid of emotion, like a marble statue, pale and cold. When I spoke, no matter how much passion churned beneath my breast, I responded only in the most bored tone.

Hours were spent on my walk and my curtsy for my

presentation. Kate had stayed with me those days, always watching from the pin-striped chair under the ugly wax flowers while Lady Beatrice played the role of the queen. I wondered with each failed attempt if I'd ever have another image of a monarch other than that of an old woman, scowling.

It took two days just to balance with my knee near the floor, and another three to bow in that position. Nothing I did pleased Lady Beatrice when it came to my retreat. In the end, it was Lord Dalry's tireless work late into the evenings that helped me to manage my exit. He had me walk backwards with a tablecloth pinned to my shoulders, looking him in the eyes as he held my hands, matching his forward steps to my backwards ones.

When the dreaded day arrived, ice tipped the bare branches and made rooflines glitter as our carriage pulled in front of St. James. My breath came in vapors as I studied London's towers rising into the cloudy sky.

In the seat across from me, my father stirred and unfolded the newspaper he'd brought. He gave me a curt nod. "You'd best remove your cape now."

"She'll freeze." Lady Beatrice pulled our mink robe higher. "Whoever heard of arranging for a private presentation?"

My father disappeared behind Forrester's *Morning Gazette*, displaying headlines that anticipated my coming-out. Just staring at the print brought a new wave of unease. "Ah, well," my father said. "I've better things to do than sit around waiting for Her Majesty."

Lady Beatrice clutched her heart, horror-struck. "Of all the audacity. Someday you will regret your bulldog personality."

My father scowled and turned the page.

Wind caught Lady Beatrice's crepe veil and outlined her puckering face as she climbed from the carriage. With difficulty, I followed. My beaded train weighed nearly forty pounds, and black patches of ice spotted the ground. I felt so nervous, I scarcely noticed the cold as I gathered my skirts. It was probably the most expensive dress I've ever worn, yet my anxiety that day has erased almost any memory of wearing it. I was minutes away from deceiving my sovereign. Divorced people were forbidden from being presented. Nor were women of scandal or illegitimate children allowed. I eyed the imposing building, wondering if I'd be thrown into prison if they knew I was Julia Macy. My slippers crushed frozen leaves, making my steps sound like a dry rustling. Somewhere Edward walked under billowing clouds on his way to attend the needs of his poor.

Edward.

A familiar lump formed in my throat. Surely *he* would advise me not to lie to the queen. Yet, like that tightrope walker, what choice had I now except to continue on? Court attendants opened massive, creaking doors. The palace offered us relief from the biting wind, but a strange malodor filled the hall.

"For goodness' sake, hold still." Lady Beatrice dropped my train and fussed with the veil of my headdress.

I did my best to appear emotionless as an attendant waved for me to follow.

～

My steps faltered as I approached the grand drawing room. My walk was nothing like the glide I'd practiced for hours before Lady Beatrice; my legs felt too much like India rubber.

When I entered, Her Majesty watched me at a distance from her dais, surrounded by lords and ladies. I handed my card to the lord chamberlain but scarcely heard my name announced. For an eternity, I approached.

Only a year older than myself, Queen Victoria gave me an encouraging smile. I curtsied, managing to keep my balance, and waited for her to present her hand for me to press to my lips. Instead, cool fingers lifted my face, and I found that she had stood.

"I am well aware of your father's loyalty and dedication to

me," she said in a lilting voice. She kissed my forehead. "For that, I honor him by honoring you."

Dread that she had kissed me, the same as she would a daughter of an earl or duke, filled me. "Your Royal Highness," I managed.

Her eyes widened before I remembered the correct form of address was *Your Majesty*, then twinkled as she nodded permission for me to leave.

Remembering my last brief curtsy, I dipped, and the lord-in-waiting gathered my heavy train and draped it over my arm. Step by step, I backed away. My last glimpse of the queen was of her still watching me with amusement.

Outside, my world caught up with me again. Blood rushed to my ears, and I braced myself against a wall. There was no turning back now. I'd been presented to the queen. A uniformed man clutched my arm.

"You looked ready to faint," he said in a chuckling voice. "For a moment, I feared I'd have to carry you out."

I touched my gloved finger to my forehead. "She . . . she kissed me."

The man chuckled and led me toward the gallery, where Lady Beatrice waited with an arch expression.

"Well?" my father asked five minutes later, as I climbed into the carriage.

"She kissed me. She said it was to honor your service."

My father sat back with an uncomfortable expression, and I wondered if, like mine, his conscience bothered him. With a deep breath, he turned to the window and didn't speak on the way home.

❧

"My word!" Miss Moray stepped away from the coffin-size box, lid still in hand. "This dress will make headlines."

Kate, who had insisted on being on the bed, leaned over and

crinkled the tissue paper as she examined it. "Oh, Julia! Oh, oh. They've sewn real pearls in a diamond pattern over the skirt, and the neck is lined with—" she paused to count, her fingers trembling with excitement—"seven rows!"

Miss Moray lifted the soft Indian silk dress from the box, and the maids in the room gasped in unison. "It's a shame such a gown will be crushed at the ball." Miss Moray cradled it as a mother might a newborn. Her long fingers brushed over the pearl trim. "Are you ready, Miss Pierson?"

I stood and lifted my hands above my head as my only response. Miss Moray and I made it a point to talk to each other as little as possible. Layers of perfumed silk, a lime-blossom scent Lady Beatrice had chosen as my signature, cascaded over my head.

"To think there's still a whole wardrobe yet to come," Kate said from the direction of my bed. It squeaked as though she bounced on it.

Hands hurried to button my back and adjust my hair. Heavy, cold jewelry was laid over my neck and looped through my ears. When they finally stepped away, I turned to view Julia Pierson for the first time. The girl in the mirror certainly looked the part of the wealthiest heiress in London. Miss Moray's treatments had left my skin as flawless and white as porcelain. My coal-black hair was loosely braided down my back, then entwined with roses and pearls. Lady Beatrice insisted I wear diamonds tonight, despite my age, to distinguish my position. I touched the hollow of my throat as I turned my head, unable to believe it was I and not Lady Josephine returned from the dead.

Murmurs of approval issued from the maids before a rap on the door interrupted.

"For Miss Pierson," I heard James say when one maid opened the door.

With a toothy smile, the elderly maid waddled back to me and presented a silver tray with a white orchid. I unfolded the note next to it.

You will perform marvelously tonight. Have no fear. You are ready.

                                                              Isaac

Irritation surged through me that he dared to use his Christian name again, but I forced a smile for the benefit of everyone else, then slipped the note into my sash. Now that I had been presented, the hour was at hand when I needed to show that I had a will as strong as my father's and Lord Dalry's.

⟿

Hooves echoed over the courtyard, and torchlight filled our carriage as we arrived. I chanced a glance at my father. He sat rock solid, hand atop his walking stick. His face bore a new determination. Next to him, Lord Dalry gave me a slight nod.

When our carriage halted, my father held his finger up to the approaching attendant. "I've taken the liberty of arranging your dance card," he said, eyeing me. "Those of the highest precedence are first. Make sure you cause no offense. You'll be attending acquaintances within the Tory party, allowing Forrester opportunity to place their names in his paper. There are also gem merchants, whom we cannot afford a falling-out with."

The door opened and an attendant waited expectantly, but I did not move. "You arranged my dance card? But how? I've never heard of such a thing."

My father nodded for Lord Dalry to exit. "I've been receiving requests since the day I announced your return."

"Miss Pierson." Cold air filled the carriage as Lord Dalry offered his hand.

Just before my fingertips touched his, my father grasped my forearm and gave me a gruff nod.

I returned the gesture, understanding his communication to do my best. Heaviness constricted my chest as I climbed from the carriage. A magnificent, pillared building rose in gleaming white, scraping the starry sky. In the flickering torchlight it looked as authoritarian as my father. The false confidence I'd donned along with the gown now fled. How could I not fail? I was not born to this. This ruse was beyond my ability. The horses whinnied, rearing their heads as if confirming my doubts.

My father climbed out of the carriage after me.

"Where is everyone?" I asked, pulling my cape closed to hide my nervousness.

"We are amongst the first to arrive." The gold of my father's lion-head walking stick flashed as he adjusted his cape. "I'll not wade through crowds and horse manure to be fashionable."

Taking my arm, Lord Dalry chuckled. He leaned so close, his warm breath stirred the hair by my ear. "He's been this stubborn since the day I met him." Camaraderie filled his eyes as he secured my arm tightly under his own. "Perhaps now that there's two of us, we'll finally tame him and arrive so fashionably late, all we'll have to do is say our good-byes."

Wordlessly, I stared back. This was scarcely the Lord Dalry I knew. He completely disregarded the cold wall I'd been building, taking me behind that aloof image he wore. All at once, realization struck me. Now that I'd been presented to the queen, there was no turning back, and he knew our mutual fates were irrevocably tied.

Lord Dalry lifted his gaze up the long row of steps we had to climb. As we ascended, I glanced up. Far above, in a sphere of their own, a sprinkling of stars infused me with courage as memory of another fete tumbled to mind.

Mama and I had been at Am Meer the year the Gardners held a grand lawn party, which all notable families had been invited to.

When we arrived, Elizabeth was soon whisked away, but no one approached me. I scanned the crowd for Edward, but neither he nor Henry were anywhere to be found. Dance after dance I was overlooked, until it dawned on me that the women weren't visiting with Mama either.

Later I learned it was the same summer William published

his most notorious pamphlet that argued why reform-minded individuals should be free to have relations outside the constrains of marriage. Mama must have known it, and had she shed tears and declared herself much abused over the work—as she was wont to do when necessary—we might have been gathered into their fold and fussed over. But for reasons known only to herself, Mama grew haughty and refused to decry William.

I waited hours with the hot sun beating down upon me before leaving.

Toward gloaming, Edward hunted the woods near Am Meer until he found me crying amongst the roots of our ancient oak.

His smile was apologetic as he knelt and showed the scarlet welt across the back of his hand—proof his tutor wouldn't release him until his Greek translation was perfect.

"Jameson told me," he said. "Had I known, I would have risked my father's wrath earlier."

"I hate him," I said, meaning the tutor. That particular one was new and had cost me many an afternoon with Edward. "I wish he'd die or quit."

Edward grinned. "Henry's not idly waiting for either of those options. I warrant before the day ends, he'll be considering leaving his post."

I gave a teary laugh, hoping Henry had planted bees in the man's bed again. "Good."

Edward rose, extended his hand. "Come back and dance with me."

Even at that tender age I felt a dart of pride that, despite my being ostracized, Lord Auburn's youngest son sought me out to dance.

There was a slight hush when Edward led me to the center of the dance area. From the corner of my eye, I caught Mama standing, her face white as chalk.

Edward and I took our places, not caring a whit what anyone thought. The sound of violin and quiet hum of chatter carried through the thick summer air as he moved us through the dancers. Bright, twinkling stars proclaimed their joy above us. No one wore pride like Edward. It was as if he'd chosen me for his peculiar treasure and nothing pleased him more than my delight.

When the final strains finished, he grinned. "If my tutor discovers me gone, he'll whip me certain." He pointed to a hole in his trouser leg. "Besides, I should be on hand when my father discovers I set loose several shingles."

"Julia?" Mama's voice sounded from the fringes of the party.

I looked askance at her, taking a fortifying breath. Edward gave me a grin before dipping his head and disappearing into the blackness outside the glow of paper lanterns.

As Lord Dalry and I reached the grand staircase, my steps faltered and a great sadness engulfed me. I didn't want to be Julia Pierson.

"You'll do perfectly fine," Lord Dalry said, mistaking the reason for my hesitation. Then, surprising me with his boldness, he lifted my chin. "I'll stay near you the entire evening. If you need help, you've but to look at me, and I'll come. I promise."

I attempted a smile, for he truly believed I would someday become as polished and refined as he was. But to me he was like a chained man, weathering the storms of life, beckoning me to come and take shelter beneath his silk umbrella. Yet how could I, when someone like Edward still waited, hand outstretched, drenched but unconstrained?

I shifted my gaze to the group of gentlemen staggered near the top of the stairs. Discordant strains of music carried through the wintry air as musicians tuned instruments. Tall and distinguished, my father rapped his stick on each step, announcing his presence. The men turned. A few hid cigars behind their backs out of courtesy to me. Lord Melbourne broke from their group and pattered down the distance between us.

"Pierson, welcome." He bowed and took my hand, kissing it. "Miss Pierson, I hear the queen was rather pleased with you."

I dipped, borrowing Lord Dalry's serene expression. "Thank you for arranging it."

He gave me a perfunctory nod, then turned to my father. "Have you taken my suggestion and arranged her dance card?"

Nodding, my father reached into his waistcoat and produced a gold book, which he rendered to the prime minister.

Lord Melbourne opened it and scanned the names, his breath rising in puffs. "The first two dances? On the night she comes out. Are you certain?"

My father tapped his shining shoes against the concrete step, looking down. "Yes, I've had two more offers since we last spoke, both members of my party. There's only going to be ill will spread amongst them if we don't establish their upcoming union tonight."

Lord Melbourne handed me my dance card. His sideburns shone in the torchlight as he winked. "Yes, I heard about Barnes. Somehow I don't fancy your daughter would relish a marriage with someone twice her age."

I choked and began coughing.

"Allow me to escort you inside, Miss Pierson." Lord Dalry's face was bland, but his eyes shone with disapproval toward the prime minister.

"By all means, Dalry, take her." Lord Melbourne wrapped his arm around my father's shoulders, moving him toward the gentlemen. "Join us, Roy. Dalry will care for her. We were just beginning to discuss India."

I could tell by my father's face he had no desire to leave, but he went. Leading me inside, Lord Dalry lowered his head near mine. "There is the ladies' dressing room." He pointed to my left. "Go ready yourself. I'll meet you here in a minute."

Trying to walk as Lady Beatrice had taught me, I entered the indicated room. Scents of talc filled the space. Instead of the froths of tulle, silks, and satins I expected, the room was empty except for a row of maids, all of whom looked eager to assist.

They removed my cape, and wonderment filled their faces as they viewed my gown.

"Shall I check your dress for loose—" the maid plumping my dress licked her lips as though trying to decide whether they were real or not—"pearls?"

I touched my neckline, feeling their coolness. Every pearl on this dress was exactly the size of every other pearl, making me wonder how much my father paid. I imagined an individual white jewel coming loose and rolling over the dance floor. A fortune lost. "Yes, please."

When she determined everything was in place, I stepped out of the dressing room and found Lord Dalry waiting where he promised. An elegant smile curved his lips as he looked in the direction of the ballroom. His ivory waistcoat offset his gleaming white shirt, which notched over his jawline. When he spotted me, his expression changed to relief.

"Look at ease," he whispered, taking my arm, "and they'll think you are at ease. After paying our respects to our host, we'll address the highest-ranking peers first. I'll make certain to use their titles so you can't make a mistake. Hold your head high. You're the distinguished daughter of Lord Pierson."

A long gallery stretched before me. The walls were gilded, so that every flicker of the candles made them ripple like golden water. Heavily waxed parquet floors reflected glittering chandeliers. Screens of ivy, holly, and roses hid musicians still adjusting their instruments.

Scattered groups of people looked in our direction. Most, seeing who we were, inclined their heads in acknowledgment. Lord Dalry urged me in their direction.

"It's roped off for the elite," he explained as a servant unhooked a scarlet cord, allowing us to pass. "This space will be filled to capacity. On the other side, we'll still be able to move about at ease." Under his breath he added, "God help us if there's ever a fire."

A group of elegant ladies with large headdresses swanned themselves with ostrich-feather fans in slow, hypnotic movements. Their jewels glistened and shimmered with every graceful turn of their necks. Lord Dalry headed straight toward them. At our approach, the middle-aged woman in the center stepped forward.

"Isaac." She kissed his cheek, then turned to kiss mine. The tulle of her gown rustled and the sweet scent of hyssop filled the air. "So this is Lady Pierson's daughter. How do you do? Your mother was one of my dearest acquaintances. I quite see you as one of my own." She took my hands and spread them. "Isaac, I'm hosting a small gathering at my house tomorrow afternoon. I insist she be there. I will not take no for an answer. The poor child has been in London nearly a month, and no one outside of Lady Beatrice has even seen her."

"I fear I am already engaged tomorrow," Lord Dalry replied. "Perhaps another day?"

She slipped her hand to my back and gave a beautiful, lilting laugh. "Have Lady Beatrice accompany her, or Miss Moray. For I already told you, I shall not take no for an answer. Lord Pierson owes it to me for turning my first ball of the season into her debut. It's the very least he can do."

Lord Dalry bowed. "No one could refute that argument. Lord Pierson shall personally escort her there himself."

A sprinkling of delighted claps came from the ladies. The circle of men who had their backs turned to the conversation looked over their shoulders. "I say, Dalry, did I hear that right? You volunteered Pierson to one of my wife's parties? You're in for it tonight. However will he survive the chattering females?"

The men laughed, and the ladies within reach batted the speaker with their fans, one exclaiming, "Oh, hush, or Lord Pierson will learn of it."

The man turned completely from the group and made his way to us. "I hope he does. Miss Pierson, you have my permission to repeat this word for word." He bowed. "Tell your father I shall attend the party myself, just to see him playing tea with the debutantes."

This declaration was met with a hearty roar of approval from the men, and two more swore to attend as well.

I dipped slightly, wishing for the life of me I had managed to free both my father and myself.

The woman smiled at me and gave my hand a light squeeze. "Go and enjoy yourself, my dear. Tomorrow we shall become acquainted at leisure."

"Lady Northrum." Lord Dalry bowed, and I took his lead and curtsied. "Lord Northrum."

For the next hour, Lord Dalry kept his promise and never left me. I learned a new side to Lord Dalry. He was universally loved.

Matrons affectionately patted his cheek and sought compliments. Husbands whispered assurances they would support him next year and asked which side of a political matter they should take. Young men invited him to join them at their clubs and tried to persuade him to ask their sisters to dance. Young ladies switched their fans to their left hands, a sign they desired his attention. One girl even boldly pressed her fan over her heart, declaring her love.

Amongst the other guests, he wore a highbred mask, nodding and making necessary replies. With me, however, he whispered details about each person we'd just met and congratulated me for my performance. Each compliment was like a spun-sugar dainty, for I knew his aim. He hoped to bolster my confidence and, by so doing, convince me that I was capable. Yet like candy floss, his compliments offered no true substance.

However, even the sharp pangs of hunger can be staved off temporarily with delicacies. Time and again, I found myself pausing, waiting to see if my previous action, too, met his approval and then berating myself for caring.

"Thank you, son." My father touched Lord Dalry's shoulder,

breaking us from the conversation we were in. Crowds of people now filled the space, and the loud hum of voices made it difficult to hear. "It's almost time for the grand march. I'm going to accompany my daughter. How was she?"

"Splendid, sir." Lord Dalry transferred my arm to my father's. "You've reason to be highly pleased."

While my father spoke in low tones to one of his friends, I quickly swept my eyes over the ballroom. Amongst the elite, matrons and daughters cast furtive looks in my direction. Outside our area, girls pressed together, relishing every detail of my dress and hair, squealing with delight when I glanced in their direction.

To move from rejection to acceptance is far more difficult than one can imagine. There was a marked difference between me and the other girls that night. They had not faced my earlier struggles and therefore wore a different persona. It was in the arch of their brows, the angle of their heads. I studied them, baffled, amazed that they too needed to obey protocol, but they scarcely seemed cognizant of it.

As they strove to catch my attention, I couldn't help but recall how it felt being shunned as Julia Elliston. I eyed them, wondering how cold they'd grow if they knew the truth.

Yet the most curious emotion of all was the rush of pain I felt upon realizing I was adored as Julia Pierson. For she didn't exist.

"Ready?"

I returned my attention to my father, glad he couldn't read my thoughts. "Yes. Ready."

Pride shone over his face as we stepped into the open area. As we made our grand promenade, he stared at the sea of faces, declaring to all of Britain that I was his daughter and that we had nothing to hide. When the march ended, he remained on the dance floor while everyone else emptied.

In the gap of silence, while violinists raised bows and cellists bent over their instruments, he rapped his walking stick on the floor. The musicians paused, and patrons turned their heads. Expressionless, Lord Dalry negotiated his way through the press of people and stood just on the edge of the crowd.

"Lord Dalry," my father declared in a voice so bold even the outermost had to hear it, "tonight, I give to you my daughter."

Fans snapped open and whispers of *"shocking"* and *"scandalous"* undulated over the ballroom. Girls' mouths dropped and matrons cut each other looks. As my father led me to Lord Dalry, a hush settled over the room and society waited to see how we would respond.

"May I have the honor of your first dance, Miss Pierson?" Lord Dalry bowed, thankfully not twitching a muscle.

I curtsied, having little choice but to accept. In the next moment, my hand was in his.

∽

I avoided my father's gaze as I slid into my seat at the breakfast table the next morning. Neither did I acknowledge Lord Dalry, but I did give Kate's outstretched hand a squeeze. Once settled, I shuffled my feet. Blisters had developed over my heels, and the soles of my feet felt as though they'd been rubbed by carpenter's paper.

"It's about time," my father said. "We've been waiting for you to read the headlines."

I rubbed the back of my neck. Every muscle ached. Given the choice, I would have slept another hour or two. Why should anyone care whether I was present when they read the paper? My father's moods tended to be mercurial, but I sensed this morning he was jovial as he thought he was finally getting his own way. It irritated me enough to speak plainly. "You could have started without me."

I winced, waiting. But my father merely gave Lord Dalry an indignant look, then, with a huff, dug through the stack of newspapers.

Realizing that Lord Dalry had forced them to wait, I glanced at him. He appeared disappointed by my cold reception. I lowered my gaze, knowing he deserved better. The previous night he alone had been my saving grace.

Selecting the *Times*, my father unfolded it. James stepped forward, craning his neck, ready to refill my already-full water goblet. My father scanned the front page. His lower lip pushed out and his nose wrinkled.

"What? Is it bad, sir?" Lord Dalry asked.

"No. Kinsley forgot to iron the papers." He displayed ink-smudged fingertips. "He didn't cut them either. James, henceforth this is your duty."

"Yes, sir."

Instead of waiting for the problem to be amended, my father pulled out his penknife and slit the pages. He flipped to the society section and never changed expression as he read. I watched Lord Dalry to see if he could read Lord Pierson's mood, but he only stared, waiting.

"She did well. Here." He shoved the paper to Lord Dalry, who devoured the article. "You're mentioned several times too. We'll need you to make rounds at the club to further bolster your career."

I drew an offended breath. My father might have protected me from Macy, but in reality this was becoming all about what suited him and his ambitions. I was of no consequence, provided I obey. Without asking to be excused, I pushed back my chair and stalked from the room.

∼

"Open the top of the barouche," my father commanded four hours later, tapping the carriage with his stick.

Eyeing the branches rattling in the wind, I tucked my hands farther into my muff. It was too brisk to ride in the open.

"It will give you some color," my father said as the top was clipped down. "Your cheeks haven't had any bloom since you arrived home."

Wordlessly, I slid in. James's face remained neutral, but his eyes evinced his disapproval as he handed me an additional robe. Miss Moray must have been spying from the window, for she ran from the house with an armful of tulle. While my father glared, she stood tiptoe on the rung and draped the gauze around my bonnet and face.

"Enough of this nonsense. A little cold won't kill her." My father thwacked his coachman. "Drive on."

We lurched into motion, and I settled into my seat, sensing that his mood had turned dangerous. Whether because I'd left breakfast early, or because Lord Dalry had failed to inform him until a half hour ago that he needed to escort me to a gathering, I wasn't certain, but I had learned enough about Lord Pierson to know to keep silent.

"You were rude to Isaac at breakfast this morning," my father said. "Last night should have spelled out my intentions for the both of you well enough. I'll not have you treating your future husband as you have been."

I fixed my eyes on my father's. "I can assure you, Lord Dalry is not my future husband." There, I thought. I'd finally locked horns with him. Well, let him rant and rave. I was ready to battle.

"He is risking as much as we are. Is that really the best you're going to offer him? A spoiled brat for a wife?"

"No." I felt as contrary as the first night I met my father. "I can offer him emerald mines and whatever inheritance I'm set up to receive." My voice caught, making me sound near tears, although I was far too angry to cry. "And you can offer him a daughter, though she loves another. You can announce to your peers your intentions, all the while never once asking me for my thoughts on the matter. However, if you think I'm going to marry him or pretend to be in love with him for the sake of the papers—"

The driver turned enough that I could see the tip of his red nose, so I ceased.

My father's stare bored into me, with that same silent wrath I'd encountered before. Only now I lacked Lord Dalry's protection. Pedestrians noted my father's coat of arms painted on our carriage and waved to me. I was too upset to respond and didn't care if they thought me uppish.

Our carriage pulled before a large residence with a round-pebbled path. My father exited and offered his hand. When I'd found the ground, he backed me against the carriage. His arm, pressed over my shoulders, shook with anger. "I know you think you love that other boy. You are young and have proven that you are very foolish. Whom you marry is now my choice. If you drive away Isaac, then I'll only choose another husband for you. One who, unlike Isaac, will make no request that I give you time to grow accustomed to him. Learn to accept my choices, or I'll place you with a husband you deserve."

He released me, his words worse than a physical blow. With a tight grip he forced me toward the house, his anger kindled and his face red.

At the door, he handed the butler his card and never glanced at me while we waited.

"Lady Northrum is expecting you," the butler said, returning with a smile. "If you'll follow me please."

Palms filled the narrow gallery. Branches and leaves whipped my face and body as my father strode through them first. Happy murmurs of conversation drifted from the chamber ahead. I blinked to hold back tears.

"The Lord and Miss Pierson," the butler announced to the room.

We'd taken no more than two steps inside before my father halted so suddenly, I nearly lost my balance. In the nearest corner, flipping through a book, sat Mr. Macy.

Sixteen

I WATCHED my father's neck turn from flushed to pallid before he reached behind him and pulled me to his side. Keeping a tight grip on my wrist, he bowed to our hostess, who had risen. "Lady Northrum, thank you for your invitation."

I followed his example, trying not to look at Mr. Macy, but I tasted fear regardless.

"Roy!" At the far end of the gallery, Lord Northrum rose from his card game and waved. "Here I feared you weren't going to show, and after we all made a point to join you. We're having a beastly discussion about the Reform Bill, of all things. It's amazing how after all these years no one is tired of blathering about it. You had best come here, though, for if you remain there, they'll force you to discuss last night's ball."

"Coming." My father's voice sounded weak compared to his normal confidence.

I grasped his sleeve, wanting to cling and beg him not to leave me mere feet away from Mr. Macy. Taking my hand and giving it a tight squeeze, my father kissed my cheek and looked me square in the eyes before leaving.

"Come along, dear." Lady Northrum took my arm. Her hyssop perfume gathered around me along with her skirts. "We were all discussing your lovely gown last night. Weren't we, Mildred?"

"Indeed, indeed," the young lady cried. "Was it from Quill's?"

I sat on the tufted couch. A short distance from me, Mr. Macy crossed his legs. "Yes, Quill's." My voice sounded foreign. "That is correct."

"Did the queen really kiss you?" another girl asked.

"Yes, she did." I tightened my fist over my fan as Mr. Macy propped his foot against the rung of his chair and bit his thumb, still considering the passage he read. It was maddening. How could I keep my composure with him ignoring me?

"I say, Chance," said a gentleman sitting amongst our group. "Your frightful behavior is disturbing Miss Pierson. She's not stopped staring at you since she's entered the room. Don't sit there all morose. Come greet the girl."

"Am I disturbing you, Miss Pierson?" Mr. Macy looked over the pages of his book, then shut it with an irritated sigh. "I forget my manners as well as the rule that gentlemen are expected to keep the young ladies entertained." He held up his book. "Very well. Shall I read you the poem I am looking at?"

I stared, mesmerized, afraid to voice a word. I'd not seen his face since the night of Churchill's murder. He was more captivating than I'd remembered—more dangerous, more fierce.

Dark eyes met mine as he stopped before me. A small twist of a smile registered over his lips before he attempted to dismiss Lady Northrum with a wave. "If I'm going to be forced to amuse a child like a paid jester, the least you can do is lend me your seat."

"Oh, stop." She batted his leg with her fan. "You're alarming Miss Pierson with your odd manner."

"Then I'll kneel at her feet to read to her." He did, leaning so close his elbows sank into the cushion on both sides of my legs, pinning my dress. As he leaned near with a provocative gaze, scents of sandalwood and fine cigars brought a rush of memories.

"Good gracious, Chance." The voice of the gentleman who'd started this squeaked. "You're going to cause a scandal."

"Nonsense." If it were possible for words to caress, Mr. Macy's did. "She's the exact age as my wife, and I want her opinion of this poem. Now do I have your full attention, Miss Pierson?"

Like one fighting a trance, I slowly turned my head toward my father for help. He stared, his hand halfway over the table, holding the card he'd been about to play. The men at his table fidgeted, shifting their eyes between my father's hard, angry face and Mr. Macy's scandalous proximity to his daughter.

"I begin to see my problem," Mr. Macy said, teasing high in his voice. "It's no wonder I failed to keep my wife at my side, if my best charms are incapable of holding Miss Pierson's attention more than a few fleeting seconds."

"Chance, please stop," Lady Northrum whispered, then tittered in my father's direction. "I fear our friend's humor isn't understood by many."

"Then allow me to read my poem," Mr. Macy said. "Now pay attention, Miss Pierson. I'm thinking of sending this message to my wife. I desire your honest opinion.

"Can a maid that is well bred,
Hath a blush so lovely red,
Modest looks, wise, mild, discreet,
And a nature passing sweet,
Break her promise, untrue prove,
On a sudden change her love,
Or be won e'er to neglect
Him to whom she vow'd respect?"

"Really now, Chance." The gentleman pulled his cup of tea closer to his chest. "You'll have to forgive him, Miss Pierson. He's had a bad spell of love and has been in this humor for some time. I had not a thought he would act in this manner when I engaged him."

"I'm not finished." Mr. Macy gave him a silencing look. Then closing the book, he recited,

"Such a maid, alas, I know.
Oh that weeds 'mongst corn should grow,
Or a rose should prickles have,
Wounding where she ought to save!
I that did her parts extol,
Will my lavish tongue control.
Outward parts do blind the eyes,
Gall in golden pills oft lies.

"Reason wake, and sleep no more,
Land upon some safer shore;
Think on her and be afraid
Of a faithless fickle maid."

He paused, adding emphasis.

"Of a faithless fickle maid
Thus true love is still betray'd.
Yet it is some ease to sing
That a maid is light of wing."

Mr. Macy retreated slightly. "Your cheeks grow scarlet, Miss Pierson. Either you've read the gossip of my unfortunate marriage in the papers, or perhaps, like my wife, you've broken a solemn promise to someone who loves you dearly."

"Never mind him, dear." Lady Northrum patted my hand, causing me to jump. She laughed in a choking manner when my father stood. "My apologies to you, Lord Pierson. Our friend has been rather morose lately. We hoped to cheer him." With a pleading look at Mr. Macy, she frantically signalled him to rise.

"Oh, but I am cheered," Mr. Macy said. "Perhaps this room thinks me rude. We'll have to tell them our little secret, won't we, Miss Pierson?" His eyes twinkled at my sharp intake of breath. "Our families are well acquainted. Her father and I have a very long history." He turned and smiled at my father. "Is that not so, Roy? Miss Pierson is rather used to my strange manner too, I daresay. You see, I am Pierson's closest neighbor and probably the only person aware that Roy had a daughter he'd hidden. I've not seen her since she was a mere slip of a girl." Mr. Macy took my hand and brought it to his lips. "Did you think I'd forgotten about you? Were you offended when you entered the room and I ignored you? Nay, I have not, nor will I ever. It does my heart good to see you well."

I thought of Lord Dalry and tried to borrow one of his political faces. With a slight nod and a refined smile, I attempted to withdraw my hand as he caressed my fingers between his. His touch still heightened every sense in my body.

"What's this?" Mr. Macy chided. "You used to sit on my lap and speak to me quite openly. And now you sit there, so sober."

"So you've known her since her childhood?" Lady Northrum recovered speech first and placed a hand over her heart.

"I'm closer to this girl than an uncle."

The gentleman replaced his teacup in the saucer with a clank. His laughter filled the room. "I say, Chance, that wasn't very sportsmanlike of you. Here I feared Lord Pierson's wrath was about to fall on me." He turned and looked at my father, who gave a tight smile.

The gentlemen around my father laughed and resumed their

card game. My father excused himself, laying his cards on the table to join us.

"Where did you attend school, sweetheart?" Mr. Macy asked, taking the empty chair next to mine. "It's been a long time since I've been able to practice one of my languages. I wager I can speak the native tongue without accent."

"Without accent?" The gentleman snorted. "How would that be possible?"

Mr. Macy smiled and lifted his hand in a gesture toward me. "I assure you, it's completely possible. We'll test my experiment on Miss Pierson. I assume you speak the language since you've been there most of your life."

All eyes including my father's turned on me. My heart beat hard. "I went to school in America."

Mr. Macy laughed. "Since when is it fashionable to send our elite to that barbarous country? You show me how out of touch I am with young ladies. I would have guessed France or Germany. My curiosity is highly aroused. Roy, where in America is a school worthy of one of our heiresses?"

"Boston." The anger in my father's voice made everyone shift. From his stance behind me, he laid a hand on my shoulder.

Mr. Macy reclined with a catlike smile. "I'd love to hear her imitate a Bostonian accent."

"I'll not allow my daughter to muddle the Queen's English for amusement."

Mr. Macy twisted the black onyx ring on his finger. "What was the name of your school, sweetheart? I have an acquaintance who wishes to find a reputable place to send her daughter. Your father's tastes are impeccable. I'll recommend yours."

I swallowed and said the first name that came to mind. "The Boston Ladies' Finishing School."

Mr. Macy shook his head with amusement at my father. "How original." Then to me, "I fear I've not played the part of gentleman by questioning you for my own entertainment. We all know that every young lady wishes to display her skill at music." He turned to Lady Northrum. "I don't see your pianoforte. Where is it? It has been far too long since I've had the pleasure of hearing an accomplished pianist."

"Against the bay window." She turned and pointed at the instrument behind her.

I looked up at my father, pleading.

"Will you grant me the honor, Miss Pierson?" Mr. Macy stood and extended his arm. "I'll turn the pages for you."

"Some other day, perhaps." My father opened his pocket watch. "Chance, since we both seem to be free, there's some business I've been waiting to discuss with you." He turned to Lady Northrum. "I fear our visit must be cut short. Mr. Macy and I have been trying for ages to find a time to meet."

Seeing an escape, I rose, seized my skirts, and hoped my legs would carry me as far as the carriage. While my father assured Lady Northrum he'd not been offended, Mr. Macy acquired my arm and pulled me from the room. "Darling," he said, gathering me in his arms. "There's no need to shake. I am not angry with you, I swear it." He halted, then touched his forehead to mine as tears rose in my eyes. "You've nothing to fear from me. I'm too overjoyed to find you safe and well."

It was so absurd that I laughed, only it came out a sob. "Please."

With his right hand, he cradled one side of my face. "Don't cry, dearest. I'm not going to expose you yet. I've been trying to send your father a message for some time now." He chuckled, glancing toward the room we'd been in. "I think he finally received it." Then to me, "While I'm not angry, we do need to have a little talk. I'm arranging a private rendezvous for us."

I looked toward the doorway that my father should storm from any second.

"Why this intense look of fear?" Mr. Macy whispered gently.

My stomach hollowing, I lifted my gaze to where his white,

square-cut shirt framed his face. A knowing smile graced his lips as his mesmerizing eyes claimed me.

"I'll not even punish you," he said, hooking my chin and tilting it up, "though you probably shaved ten years off my life, running away from me like that. Have you any idea what Bradshawl's men would have done to you had they found you?" With closed eyes, he leaned toward me.

My father grabbed his wrist. His knuckles were white. "Do not ever touch my daughter again."

Mr. Macy raised his brows. "Won't producing an heir become difficult? Come now, Roy, at least try to keep your demands reasonable, or we're already off to a bad start."

"Give her to me."

I kept my chin tucked as my father pulled me from Mr. Macy's embrace. With the jumble of collecting our outer wrappings, my father managed to keep me separated from Mr. Macy. Sunlight blinded me as he opened the door and trundled me down the steps.

"Take my daughter home," he said to James, placing me in the care of our footman. "Fetch Isaac. Tell him I need him to return to the house immediately. Tell him what I've been fearing just happened."

"Yes, sir."

"Coming, Roy?" Mr. Macy's voice sounded a short distance away.

Gritting his teeth, my father left me. James escorted me into the barouche, giving me only a fleeting glimpse of my father climbing inside Macy's black landau.

‿

Again and again, I wrung my hands as I paced the foyer. For at least an hour, neither my father nor Lord Dalry returned. My eyes stung from the tears I'd shed while pacing. I wanted to know what Mr. Macy was telling my father, or what my father was agreeing to.

I was pressing the palms of my hands against my forehead, as though I could prevent the fearful thoughts, when a series of raps sounded outside. I spun, facing the door.

My father stepped into the hall looking like a lion deprived of its mane. He scarcely noticed me as Kinsley removed his silk-lined cape. Pinching the bridge of his nose, my father said, "Bring me laudanum. One of my headaches is upon me."

"Yes, sir." Kinsley retreated.

"Where's Isaac?" My father winced as he looked in my direction, then shielded his eyes.

"He hasn't arrived yet." My insides soured as I imagined how much money my father must have paid to make him look this stricken. Or did he plan to return me? I sank to the bench. "What did Mr. Macy say?"

My father's jaw clenched. "You're not allowed to speak of that man. Why do you continue to test me? So help me, the next time his name crosses your—"

The front door opened. Lord Dalry rushed into the hall with Forrester at his heels. A swirl of London's stale air accompanied them. While Mr. Forrester shed his coat, Lord Dalry rushed to me and inspected me from head to toe. Relaxing, he pulled off his gloves and whispered, "What's happening?"

"Macy was at the Northrums'." My father rubbed his eyes. "We had a talk."

Kinsley entered with a small glass on a tray. My father drank the milky liquid, then waved the butler away. "Robert, Isaac, join me in the smoking room."

"May I stay with your daughter instead?" Lord Dalry set his cape and gloves on a chair.

My father glowered at me. "Actually, bring her. I have some questions for her."

I placed my hands over my churning stomach, feeling shamed. Doubtlessly, my father's questions had to do with the things Mr. Macy revealed to him about our time together.

"Are you all right?" Lord Dalry grasped my hands and helped me to my feet.

I nodded, allowing him to take my arm.

"All I want to know is how much he asked to keep silent about the matter," Mr. Forrester said as he stomped after my father.

"He didn't." My father lowered his voice, but I still heard what he said as they turned down a passage. "He offered to buy her from me."

Mr. Forrester didn't try to stifle his bark. "What?"

"Blast it, man, not so loud."

"Surely you jest! How much did he offer?"

I returned my gaze to Lord Dalry, but he likewise followed their conversation.

"More than I thought he could afford." My father unlocked and opened a door I'd never seen before. Stale tobacco and smoky scents drifted into the hall. Tall windows lit the space. Brown leather chairs and couches were spread throughout the room, set at odd angles. Different ports and spirits lined the tables between the settings, ready to be served. On the far wall, there were several mounted heads—boar, lion, and bear, amongst others.

While my father poured a huge tumblerful of whiskey, Lord Dalry led me to a couch. "That's the last time she leaves this house." My father took a swig from his tumbler. "It's too dangerous."

"Honestly, sir!" Lord Dalry placed a hand on his hip. "She just came out. Aren't you overreacting a bit? You can't remove her from society because of one man."

"We'll have an occasional dinner. She can invite some of her young lady friends for tea."

"What young friends? She hasn't even had a chance to form attachments."

My father shook his head. "Isaac, I'm sorry. I know you were looking forward to advancing her. Not now. Not yet."

"Sir, you must at least hear me out. You're going to make her seem odd, draw suspicion that there's something wrong—"

My father held up a hand to him and turned to me. "What did Macy say to you while you were alone?"

"How delightful!" Mr. Forrester poured himself a drink. "Now she has her next set of orders. How could you have left her alone with him?"

I hesitated. What if my father considered it an option to give me back to Mr. Macy? What if I answered incorrectly?

"It's all right," Lord Dalry said as if reading my thoughts. "You have nothing to fear. No one is going to become upset."

Mr. Forrester laughed. "You're wrong there, Isaac. She'll have us all screaming at each other before the interview is finished, but do go on, Julia. Do tell."

My father cocked his head, showing that he was waiting, so I smoothed my skirt. "H-he said he was arranging a private rendezvous for us." Heat rose through my face as I realized how it sounded. "To talk, I mean."

Mr. Forrester chuffed. "Yes, I'm sure that's all the two of you ever do."

"Where?" my father asked, struggling to sit straight.

I could feel my color heightening. "He didn't say."

"When?"

"I—I don't know."

With a growl, my father set his drink aside. "I expect a direct answer to my next question. Were you about to kiss him when I entered the hall?"

"Of course she was." Forrester snorted. "Why are you so shocked? This is what I've been telling you all along. She's his lover."

"Quiet. I want to hear my daughter."

I avoided Lord Dalry's questioning gaze, praying he had been truthful when he'd said he always knew whether someone was lying or not. "No, I wasn't about to kiss him."

"How boldly you sit there and fib." My father rose. "I saw. I saw how he leaned over you. Are you denying it now?"

"No." My voice caught. "I'm not denying it. I wasn't about to kiss him. He was about to kiss me."

"Same difference," Mr. Forrester said, "unless you were poised to slap him."

My father cocked an eyebrow at me, so I felt obliged to say something. How could I explain the mastery Macy held over me when he was near? "I—I—"

"Say nothing," Lord Dalry instructed, briefly resting his fingers on my arm. Then he rose. "Whose opinion matters here more than mine? I take issue with him for trying to kiss her, not with Julia. I'll not allow either of you to question her in this manner."

"The issue here isn't whether Macy tried to kiss her or she him," Mr. Forrester said. "The issue is whether she's lying about seeking protection. Macy girls are the cleverest liars you'll ever meet. She's duping us and especially you, Isaac."

My father groaned and again pinched his nose as he sank back into his seat. "Then she's no Macy girl. She's the worst liar I've ever seen. Macy challenged her story before a group of people and she couldn't even fabricate believable answers."

"Unless she was trying to fail."

"Why? So that he can offer me a mint to take her off my hands? That makes even less sense. If you're so convinced she's his spy, then give me a reasonable answer as to why he sent her."

Mr. Forrester gestured toward me, his drink sloshing over his cup. "Why would someone pay for her? She's not even pretty."

"Lord Pierson." Lord Dalry's voice exuded anger. "This man is your guest, but do not ask me to bear this insult any longer. If you refuse to address this, I will cut all association with him. Newspaper or no newspaper—"

"Isaac!" The tremor in my father's voice made us all stare.

It sounded a command and a plea. He rubbed the heels of his hands into his eyes. He fell from his chair to one knee. Grey tinged his face. "Isaac."

Uncertain what was happening, I stood to rush to his side, but Lord Dalry caught my wrist. "No. Find Simmons or James. Hurry. Tell them your father's malady is upon him."

My father grimaced with pain as he pressed his forehead into the seat cushion of his chair.

Several things happened at once. Lord Dalry knelt next to my father, and as he braced him, my father's eyes rolled and he slumped, unconscious. Mr. Forrester grabbed my wrist and shoved me out the door and shut it.

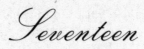

Seventeen

MY FATHER and I never spoke about those following weeks. Our supposed nightly meetings never took place. It was as if Mr. Macy's reentrance into our lives cut off all hope for kindling a relationship. Later in life, perhaps, we could have discussed his decision to yank me from society. But after the great scandal and its heavy toll, we never were able to bring ourselves to discuss that period.

I was like an actress shoved on stage and greeted with thunderous applause, only to have a hand reach out from behind the curtain and snatch me from sight again.

The effect was devastating. I went from being too busy to confront the sadness at having lost Mama and Edward to renewed hours of empty silence. While waiting for Lady Dalry's arrangements, Kate spent days at a time at her cousins' houses—and the Dalrys had many spread across London. My father camped at his clubs, it seemed to me, shunning all sight of me. He likewise kept Lord Dalry busy night and day, worried that without his continued influence, they'd lose alliances.

Midway through December, I penned the last acceptance and stared moodily at it. My handwriting was tight and drops of ink smudged it. If my father were to see it, he'd make me rewrite it, but I didn't care. He and Lord Dalry were accepting invitation after invitation while I never went anywhere.

The first week of my seclusion, I felt relief and was glad for the chance to slow down and recuperate. Thoughts of Edward carried me. While I answered the morning correspondences, I envisioned that somewhere Edward was also at work in his parish. By tea, I ignored the windy shrieks that rattled the panes by recalling our childish romps through the woods. At nightfall, after partaking of an empty dinner and sewing in an empty room, I lulled myself to sleep by picturing the life we would build when this was over.

Yet no soul can endure continual solitude, not even mine, which had been trained for it.

As the week turned into a fortnight, the isolation became unbearable and I hungered for human companionship. Even my resistance to Lord Dalry weakened, though I rarely saw him either. Thus, nearly two weeks before Christmas, when footsteps unexpectedly rang in the hall, headed in my direction, I roused from my stupor, set aside my pen, and stared at the door.

Lord Dalry appeared, his cheeks red with excitement. "Oh, good! I feared I wouldn't find you in time."

I was so desirous for companionship, I nearly welcomed him with the enthusiasm I felt. Just in time I remembered myself and borrowed his polished expression. "I fear I do not understand you. Time for what?"

He laughed. "We're going out!"

"Out!" I rose so quickly, I knocked my knee against the wooden desk leg, scattering the slew of Christmas invitations I'd just sorted. "Out? Truly? Where? A Christmas tea?"

His face fell slightly. "Your father is about to make his charitable Christmas donations. You're to join us."

"Donations? What does that entail?"

"Well . . ." He spread his hands apologetically. "We sit in the carriage while your father walks banknotes into the institutions."

I tried to hide my disappointment by folding the smudged letter and pouring wax over it, filling the air with an acrid scent. "Oh."

He ventured one step into the room. "Has it been that lonely, then?"

I made no reply as I added the letter to the basket of outgoing mail. It really wasn't his concern.

Dressed in his fur-lined cape, my father appeared behind him. "Have you told her, then?"

"Yes, sir. She's most pleased."

My father studied me as he pulled on a glove. He looked as though he doubted that fact. "All right; go summon Miss Moray and get ready."

〜〜〜

In the carriage, my father and Lord Dalry settled across from me. Lord Dalry watched my hungry glances at London with an air of satisfaction. But the first time I tilted my head to complete my study of a Gypsy woman telling fortunes, my father pulled the black curtain across the window. "A young lady doesn't look upon anything unseemly. The streets of London are filled with such things, and that includes Gypsies."

"Oh, honestly!" Lord Dalry said, directing anger at my father. "So she's to go from an empty house to a dark carriage? You can hardly call that much of a change."

"You're the one who insisted she come, not I."

"Yes, but I had assumed you'd at least allow sunlight in the vehicle."

My father's jaw firmed. "Isaac, enough."

Lord Dalry huffed. "Can I not at least point out the sights to her? What if she ever needs to find her way around London?"

My father thumped his walking stick, filling the carriage with a hollow thunk. "I said *enough*."

Lord Dalry crossed his arms, and I slouched back in my seat and stared at the drape-covered window. My resolve to escape this life strengthened. I felt like a wild bird, sitting caged in a parlor. I eyed my father, wondering if he still bothered attempting to apprehend Macy, or was he content now that he'd secured my place in society?

When the carriage reached its first destination, my father climbed out. "Stay here."

Lord Dalry waited fifteen seconds, then drew aside the curtain and pointed. "Look to your right. That's Westminster Bridge." I turned to view the brown stone structure and its arches over water. A cloudy sky stretched above it. "It was built in 1750. Behind it, do you see the old Abbey?"

I had no desire to look at old bridges and buildings. "Is Hyde Park visible from here?"

Lord Dalry gave a soft sigh. "No. We're closer to St. James, but your father plans on going to Cheapside hereafter, so we shall not see that park either."

I sat back, unwilling to reward him with a word. Did he truly believe he could make me happy?

He closed the curtain with a sober expression. "I promise you, I'll take you to Hyde Park, to the gardens, London Bridge, and anywhere else you wish to go when we're married."

His words brought a chill, but before I could argue, my father's gruff voice sounded outside the carriage. Lord Dalry turned his head, giving my father no greeting as he reentered.

Eventually, even my father grew tired of the dark and opened the view again.

London teemed with life, though I took care not to be caught noticing. Crowded streets became narrower and filled with beggars. Some were missing limbs; others hobbled about holding tin cups. Empty, soulless eyes occasionally met mine. My face grew warm as I considered how we must look, sitting in our carriage wrapped in furs and silks.

At various institutions, my father left us to duck into depressing buildings.

"You've grown very grave," Lord Dalry said on one such stop.

"Did you see all the beggars we passed?" I paused to see if he'd chide me, but he only waited for me to finish. "The cost of one of my dresses would feed so many of them."

His eyes shone and he tilted his head as if seeing me anew, but he made no reply.

Next, our carriage pulled before an iron gate pockmarked by age and rust. Beyond a barren courtyard stood a building with brown stains seeping from its windows. Girls in rags marched under the supervision of three teachers. One little girl, no older than five, stopped marching upon catching sight of me. Loneliness and hopelessness, which I understood, radiated from her eyes.

"Oh, let me out, let me out." I stood and moved toward the door, burying my father and Lord Dalry in my full skirts. "I must go to her."

"What are you talking about?" My father batted the material from his face. "Sit down, right now!"

"I can't. I can't. There's something wrong here. I know it. I have to go to her. I have to. I must."

"You will *sit*." My father's neck grew red.

The sensation I felt was intense and burned like molten metal. Once, when I was ten, I'd experienced a similar sensation when I came across a group of older boys tormenting a nest of baby birds they'd found. Though much smaller than they, I was so angry I drove them away.

My own acquaintance with loneliness made it impossible to obey my father now. Tears rose and I saw the monstrosity of witnessing such a vast ache and not being able to address it.

I glanced at the girl and then at Lord Dalry, who studied me with his fingers curled in a fist.

"Please." I knelt before him as best I could and placed my clasped hands on his knees. Then, knowing my use of his given name would motivate him, I added, "I'm begging you, Isaac."

His eyes widened as he wrapped my hands tightly in his. "Sir, I wish to give this to her."

"What? No! Have you gone insane too?"

"I'll go with her. I give you my solemn word, no harm will befall her."

I closed my eyes, hoping my father would relent.

"Allow us to walk in your gift," Lord Dalry said. "Can you not see how much this would mean to your daughter?"

"This is the last time I will allow you to talk me into bringing her on an outing." My father leaned over and opened the carriage door, then his billfold. The gold stamped and embedded in the calfskin flashed before he handed Lord Dalry a check. "My daughter is to return without a scratch."

Because I had knelt to beg my case, we were so tightly wedged, it was impossible to exit gracefully. My father set his teeth as Lord Dalry had to crawl on his seat, using his hands and knees to reach the door. When he finally managed his escape, he lifted me from the carriage.

Unable to wait for Lord Dalry, I rushed toward the gate. Teachers looked up, surprised, as I reached through the bars and unlatched the gate for myself, then headed straight toward the girl who had captured my heart.

Behind me, I heard Lord Dalry's footfall, hurrying to catch up.

The formation of girls broke, and suddenly I became surrounded by grasping hands. They whispered in awe, bringing to mind what a lady stood for in their minds. The sour scent of unwashed children met my nose. I scooped up the girl whose sorrowful eyes had arrested mine. The girl was scarcely more than flesh stretched over bones. I felt the jut of her sharp shoulder against mine. With Lord Dalry's help, I stood.

One of the teachers approached. "Are you . . . uh, are you considering taking a child?"

"No," Lord Dalry said. "We are here for charitable reasons only."

The girl in my arms shivered, and I moved her inside my cape. "They need coats," I whispered to him. "They need food too. I will not leave until I see them warm and fed."

"Will you please excuse us?" Lord Dalry bowed to the teachers' shocked expressions and steered me a few steps away. "Put that child down, now. Had I known you were going to make a commotion, I never would have advocated this."

I clutched the girl even tighter, wondering how the girl's mother must have felt on her deathbed, knowing she was leaving a child orphaned in London. Surely she would want me to fight. "No! She is near starving. I can feel her bones, and her dress is barely a rag." I looked toward my father's carriage, choking on my outrage. "I despise him. What he spends in a day would feed this whole school for a month. I'm not leaving until he at least feeds them."

Lord Dalry's face grew stern. He unfolded the check my father had given him. When he spoke, he sounded strict. "Take better care how you speak and form your opinions. Your father has given quite generously, enough that this orphanage could survive on his donation alone. The board must be stealing funds. I know of several others who make handsome donations here as well." He folded the check and placed it in his pocket. "We need to leave."

"You would do nothing?" I stepped away, clutching the child tighter. "You would just leave her here in this pitiful condition? How can you call yourself a gentleman? Edward wouldn't leave them, and neither will I."

His chest rose and fell rapidly as I evaded his attempt to gather my arm. "I intend on doing plenty, but not standing here in a courtyard arguing with you."

"Well, I intend on refusing to leave until something is done."

Lord Dalry made one more attempt to catch my arm, but I sidestepped him. I would dodge him all day or wrap my fingers around the bars of the gate and refuse to let go. His breath puffed in the air, and we stared each other down. As quickly as it appeared, his stern look faded and he nodded. "You're determined to be the death of me, aren't you?" He frowned and tugged at his gloves. "Well, tell me your demands."

"I want to see them warm, fed, and clothed."

His brows lifted and he rubbed the side of his face, looking over the building. Then, placing his hand protectively on the small of my back, he led me to the teachers. "Miss Pierson wishes to order food and material for your institution. Do your girls know how to sew?"

One of the teachers clung to the other, relief and tears filling her eyes.

"Lord Pierson shall oversee the bill." Lord Dalry glanced at my father's carriage and then at the small crowd gathering at the gate. He beckoned a grinning boy, who instantly slipped into the courtyard.

"Sir?" he asked, approaching.

Lord Dalry withdrew a card and a coin. "Here's a shilling. Find a cab and go to this address. Ask for a Master Simmons. He'll scowl at you, but tell him Master Isaac sent you. Tell him to have gruel, flour, cheeses . . ." He turned to me. "What other foods do they need?"

I shook my head. The girl in my arms grew heavy. Lord Dalry turned to the teachers. "Best go fetch your cook. Bring a pencil and paper."

For the next ten minutes, the teachers and cook named their needs, which Lord Dalry recorded. The boy took the note, but when he reached the gate, the crowd moved toward him, asking questions. All at once, everyone erupted in cheers and people began to run down the street, shouting for others to come see the Emerald Heiress.

"We are leaving now." Lord Dalry took my arm.

I cradled the child, who'd not said one word. "I can't leave all these children."

"She stays. Put her down. I've managed what you asked."

I closed my eyes, not wanting to release her. With all that was unfair in the world, I desired to see one person protected, one person provided for and happy.

When I looked at the child again, solemn brown eyes locked onto mine. Though she was young, it was clear to me she had followed our conversation with the uncanny intelligence that is born out of necessity for survival. She remained stock-still, so hopeful she seemed paralyzed.

I tightened my grip on her, unable to imagine walking away. I cast a look over the bleak courtyard. I knew what it felt like when I believed myself orphaned and penniless. How could I knowingly leave anyone to face the fear of the future alone? My next words came with difficulty. "Isaac, what about when we marry?"

Lord Dalry visibly started as I finally admitted such a possibility. Even so, instead of becoming indulgent, he remained as austere as my father. "No, we shall not repeat the mistakes of the past. You might think you want this child now, but it is a selfish desire. Her life would be miserable. I know; trust me. I'll give you anything in my power to make you happy, but I cannot and will not watch my history repeated. Set her down, now."

Praying that the girl would understand I had no other choice, I placed the child on her feet, compelled to obey without further argument.

"More people have gathered." He replaced his hand against the small of my back. "Stay near me."

At the gate, everyone crowded us. Dirty, frozen hands begged for alms. Wares were shoved in our faces. One man stepped suddenly into our path. "Who are you?"

Lord Dalry drew me closer and craned his neck to see my father's carriage across the street. "Do not delay me, sir. Move."

"Please." The man looked at me. "Just your name, then?"

"You do not address her, do you understand!" Lord Dalry sounded fiercer than I'd ever imagined he could.

The man's eyes flicked in his direction with fear, but he addressed me again. "Please, miss. All I need to learn is your name. Please."

"I'm Julia Pierson, Lord Pierson's daughter," I said, sensing he was not dangerous.

"Miss Pierson!" Lord Dalry sounded dismayed and angry at once.

"Then you must be Lord Isaac Dalry?" Excitement threaded the man's voice.

Lord Dalry shoved me behind him. "I am. Now that you know our names, who are you?"

I doubted the man heard, as he began laughing so hard. "Merry Christmas," he cried, clapping and running down the street. "A merry Christmas to the both of you."

I stared after him, amazed.

"You are under my care," Lord Dalry said in a displeased voice as he retrieved me. "Do not remove yourself from it by taking charge of a situation yourself. You have no idea how much you're worth. By confirming who you are, you've just placed us both in considerable danger."

He shielded me as we crossed the street and refused to allow the coachman to help me into the carriage, instructing him to keep away the crowd pressing us.

"What is happening?" my father asked, pulling me inside.

Isaac collapsed next to my father and glanced out the window at the growing crowd. "Do you remember telling me that if I saw something I thought your daughter would want for Christmas, to purchase it and send the bill to you?"

My father made no reply as thunder gathered over his face.

Isaac looked bland as he adjusted his cape. "Well, sir, you've just increased your donation to the orphanage considerably."

Joy lit my father's face as he peered at the front page of the *Times* the next morning. First his eyes widened, then he smiled, and lastly he threw back his head and laughed long and hard. "Good show, Isaac, good show."

Isaac blinked, having been lost in one of his books. "Sir?"

My father laughed again but handed the newspaper to me with a twinkle in his eye. "Julia reads it first."

I touched my fingertips together; they were syrupy from my sweet roll. But fearing my father's impatience, I took the article. Instead of waiting, Isaac rose and crossed his arms over the back of my chair. The headline read:

CHRISTMAS ANGEL VISITS ORPHANAGE

The article embellished the story of how Lord Dalry and I secretly went to a girls' home and lavished time and money. It reported how I moved about the children, keeping a little girl in my arms. The story made me sound saintly, beautiful, and it painted a picture of Lord Dalry as my protector and moral guardian. His political views were mentioned, along with the country's eager anticipation for him to take his seat. It steered the reader to believe that my father's wealth combined with Isaac's sound views would lead to a marriage rich with humanitarian efforts.

I took a slow breath, my emotions varied. How would Edward feel reading about Lord Dalry being painted as my protector when it was Edward who had ruined himself to preserve me? Moral guardian indeed! Yet another part of me swelled with hope that Edward would see I hadn't hardened while here, but I was becoming more like him. Charity was becoming as dear to my heart as it was to his.

"That man must have been a reporter for the *Times*," Isaac

said softly over my shoulder. "No wonder he was so pleased to learn our names."

"What man?" my father said. "You never spoke of a man."

"I meant to." Isaac returned to his seat and retrieved his book. "My only complaint is his descriptions of Julia. It's shameful a man of words didn't manage better compliments."

I looked up from the print. It was the boldest compliment he'd ever paid me. I gave him no smile. My father grinned, pretending not to hear, and dug through the other papers. I passed the paper to Isaac, wishing I'd never mentioned the possibility of our marrying.

The door swung open and Mr. Forrester entered, holding aloft a copy of the *Times*. "I thought we agreed she was to remain indoors at all times." He threw the paper on a chair and unclasped his mud-spattered cloak. "Not only did you risk her making contact with one of his spies, but you took her to an orphanage and gave someone else the story! The public is eating this up, and I don't even have a mention of it."

He threw his muddied cloak on my father's upholstered chair. My eyes widened in horror.

"What are you staring at?" he challenged me. "Do you have a problem with where I lay my capes?"

"Only your muddy ones," I said.

"I think you'd be happy for a glimpse of nature, for it's more than you're going to see for a while." He grabbed the last sticky bun, and his words became garbled as he chewed. "Of all the nasty things to do to me, Roy. There hasn't been one story of the heiress in ages. The next one is mine. What are you giving her for Christmas?" He swallowed. "I'll cover that."

"You can have the exclusive on her betrothal to Isaac." My father turned a page of the *Penny Post*. "Now remove your cape from my daughter's sight since it disturbs her."

"Gladly." Mr. Forrester yanked his cape from the chair and threw it at my feet. Grime splattered the hem of my dress. He smirked.

Before I could object, my father asked, "Did you receive my request?"

"I did." Mr. Forrester flopped in a chair. "But there's no chance you'll gain Moore's support."

"Just deliver what I asked and keep your opinions to yourself." My father gave him an angry glance, then turned another page.

"Sir, may we be excused?" Isaac rose, giving Mr. Forrester a nasty look. "I prefer for Julia not to hear the conversation."

"Wait." My father set his paper down. "Daniels is in from Africa. I'm planning a visit today. Be ready to join me in an hour."

Isaac shook his head. "I won't go, unless Julia does."

I shifted, uncomfortable that Isaac had used my given name for the second, third, fourth time this morning. My father must have noticed too, for instead of flushing red, he considered the idea. Thankfully, Mr. Forrester had shoved a serving spoon of baked eggs into his mouth and couldn't object.

"All right, we'll take her," my father said.

Mr. Forrester spat out the food. "Well, don't expect me to stay behind, then. I'd hate to miss a story if they stop at an alms-house along the way."

～

Trying to appear prim and dignified, I studied Mr. Daniels as he shivered before a roaring fire. He must have adjusted to the climate of Africa because he'd spread a wool blanket over his legs, and a plaid shawl covered his shoulders. Firelight flickered off his gold-rimmed spectacles. With curiosity, I eyed the top of his balding head, which was tan, making me wonder if they wore hats in Africa.

"What is this?" My father's angry tone shocked me as he held up a page and flapped it. "Tell me you did not sell gems of that quality for that price?"

Mr. Daniels wiped his nose on a handkerchief. "I sent word twice she could do better if she waited until I met with buyers from Dartmoor, but she insisted I sell them." He took off his glasses and polished them. "Who is Miss Elliston?"

I nearly choked on my astonishment. They were speaking of me?

"She doesn't exist as far as I'm concerned," my father said. "From this point forward, I'll handle her mine. Send the paperwork back to me."

"Eh?" Mr. Daniels gave a leering grin. "Tired of her bed already? She must not have—"

"My daughter is present."

"Eh?" Mr. Daniels looked in my direction. "Oh yes. Sorry." He certainly didn't sound apologetic. His eyes took on a vacant look as they roamed over the wrong parts of my body. I felt so uncomfortable I inched closer to Mr. Forrester.

"You've about fallen out of my graces," my father said to Mr. Daniels. "I prefer to finish the paperwork without your presence. Go to the back room."

Mr. Daniels looked both startled and annoyed to have been ordered by my father. He eyed his fire as though regretting losing its warmth, then rose, taking his blanket with him.

"Sir, I propose we cut ties with Daniels." Isaac placed a hand on my shoulder.

"When you run the mines, you can find your own dealer," my father growled. "In the meantime, he outperforms the rest combined."

"But did you not see the way he just looked at Julia?"

"I have to agree with Isaac here," Mr. Forrester said, giving me a snide look. "He just proved he's not much of a connoisseur."

"That's it." Isaac grabbed the back of Mr. Forrester's collar and tried to force him to stand.

"Are you witnessing this, Roy?" Mr. Forrester rasped, his face growing empurpled.

"Will you all be quiet?" my father roared, slamming his hand onto the table. "You're worse than a pack of monkeys. Julia, where are those papers I gave you? Why did you send word to sell gems for that price?" He threw a paper at me. It fluttered to the floor, and Lord Dalry released Mr. Forrester to retrieve it for me.

I remembered how my father handed me papers for an emerald mine the night I married Mr. Macy. I felt my brow wrinkle as I tried to remember what exactly had happened to the papers. The last memory I had of them was right before Edward and I visited Churchill.

"It's my name, but not my hand. I don't understand."

"Where are the papers?" My father's voice increased in volume.

I swallowed, trying to recall. "I think Henry's carriage is the last place I saw them."

"Henry?"

"Henry Auburn—Edward's brother."

My father's face contorted. "Well, apparently your vicar has decided to make himself quite a profit on your misfortunes. I have half a mind to sue him for this."

I found my feet. "How dare you accuse him!"

Mr. Forrester snickered, rubbing his neck. "Don't tell me a Macy girl had the wool pulled over her eyes."

"Shut up already," Isaac snapped, spinning to face him.

My father grew red, but not at Mr. Forrester. He leafed through more papers. "They've hit a vein in your mine, and the stones have been sold for a tenth of their value, and uncut, so you've lost potentially more!" He was near screaming. "How could you have allowed this to happen?"

"Do I have to defend her from you as well?" Isaac stepped in front of me. "Who gave her the mine in the first place?" His voice rose. "If you want to scream at someone, then scream at me!"

"Isaac, she's allowed an entire fortune to be lost." My father stood. "There must be at least twenty thousand pounds lining someone else's pocket."

Mr. Forrester chuckled. "Can I have that story?"

My father shook a fistful of paper in my direction. "Did you never even notice it was missing?"

I felt like crying and yelling too but refused to answer him.

"Did you even once check on your daughter!" Isaac matched his volume. "Have you considered that? Or were you so anxious to cover your sin that you tossed her to Macy or any other wolf, leaving her to fend for herself? Don't you dare shout at her! If you're mad about a lost fortune, then you take it out on me. Not her!"

Mr. Daniels stuck out his balding head from the back room. "Is everything all right in here?"

My father's nostrils flared. "Robert, take Julia to the carriage and wait there with her."

"Gladly." Mr. Forrester's fingers hurt my wrist as he yanked me from my chair. "Come on, dearie."

❧

Outdoors, I attempted to twist my arm free from Forrester's rough grasp. Anger and humiliation followed me from Mr. Daniels's office. I would not tolerate more today. "Release me," I demanded.

Across the street, my father's coachman spotted us and extended his neck to see around the passing vehicles. With a sudden yank, I managed to wrench myself from Forrester but stumbled into a jaunty-looking young gentleman. "Beg your pardon, miss." He stooped to pick up his tumbled hat. "I am quite sorry."

"Don't be. It's entirely her fault." Forrester dove forward in an attempt to grab my arm. "Stop misbehaving, Julia."

I evaded his grasp, hitting the back of my head against the cold iron of a streetlamp. For a second I only saw light, as if I'd looked directly at the sun. When my vision cleared, perspiration streaked down Forrester's brow as his mouth twisted in anger. It was satisfying to see him flustered for once.

"May I be of any service?" The young man dusted his hat on his sleeve, sounding puzzled by our strange behavior.

"No, we're fine, thank you." Forrester gritted his teeth. "Julia, you will come here this instant."

A throng of pedestrians, carriages, and street sellers separated me from my father's barouche, which shone in the morning sun. Everyone else seemed to thread their way through the busy streets. "I will not." I lifted my skirt, stepping over a pile of manure, intending to make a dash for my father's carriage.

I took two steps before feeling Forrester's fingers grab the neck of my collar. He yanked me backwards so hard, I fell against him. A curricle, whose path I'd almost stepped into, sped by. In the bombilation of London, I'd not even heard the hooves.

"Are you trying to kill yourself?" Forrester shouted.

The young man tugged his hat into place and gave us both an indignant stare as punishment for our uncouth behavior.

"Take my arm and stop acting like a Macy girl," Forrester hissed in a low voice. "Or at the very least, use some intelligence."

I elbowed him hard in the ribs and pulled away again. All this time I'd tried to please my father, remaining locked indoors, only to be yelled at about the emerald mines. I was finished cooperating. I felt a storm of tears rising.

"You!" A Gypsy woman appeared out of nowhere, putting me in mind of a mother hen as she flapped her arms. She brought her leering face near Forrester's. "You stole my amulet. You are trying to curse me." In a loud banshee voice, she wailed, "You put a curse on me!"

It drew a circle of hard stares.

I stepped backwards, away from her. Dirt crusted the bottom of her orange skirt, and she wore a stained green chemise. A sapphire-colored shawl cast a blue tinge upon her wrinkled face. "You curse my family; you curse my children and their children's children."

Two Gypsy men, wearing blue jerkins and red boots, stepped on either side of her, glowering at Forrester.

"Here now." A man whose armband and embroidered collar identified him as a bobby stepped into the midst of us, sticking his baton between the woman and Forrester. "Back away from the gentleman."

"He has stolen my amulet, forever cursing my family!"

"I said step away," the bobby commanded.

"Our family line will dry up if it's taken. He snatched it from my neck and placed it in his waistcoat. He's a thief, no gentleman."

"It's true," I cried out. The idea formed, and I took action before determining whether I should. "I saw him place his hand in his waistcoat; then he tried to force me to come with him, but I don't even know him."

"I saw her struggling with him, sir," the young gentleman offered, giving Forrester an angry stare.

Forrester looked ready to kill me, but I didn't care. Let him for once suffer being misunderstood. I glanced at Mr. Daniels's office, where I knew my father was screaming at Isaac. "My name is Julia Pierson," I said, then blushed at the response it drew from the crowd. I pointed to my carriage. "See, there's my father's crest. This man is no gentleman, I assure you."

If Forrester distrusted me before, he hated me now. "I'll show you," he said with decided calmness, glaring in my direction. He unbuttoned his frock coat and opened it.

A silver necklace with an amethyst-colored stone fell to the pavement. Even in the din of London I heard its clink.

For half a second, nothing happened.

Then Gypsies pressed about me, yelling and furiously waving their hands. Gentlemen hastened their ladies into buildings; commoners pressed toward the fray, jostling me away.

"Here you are." A dry voice sounded behind me, and I felt a death grip on my shoulder. "Come easily, because I assure you, whether you struggle or not, I'm not leaving without you."

Eighteen

CLUTCHING MY PURSE, I turned to view a lanky gentleman I'd not seen since the night I wed Macy. Mr. Rooke's cheeks appeared gaunter, and his face tan, as though he'd recently spent many hours outdoors. Two men stepped in front of me and another two stepped on either side, closing me in a circle.

"He said you knew better than to go with someone unfamiliar to you," Rooke said, not looking directly at me, but at Forrester surrounded by a screaming crowd. "Come along now. Macy requires an audience."

Fear snaked through my limbs, but with prodding from one of the men, my feet managed to shuffle behind Rooke's steps. Daylight deepened into cold shadow as I was directed into an alley, where Macy's black landau was lodged. I stopped, balking at the thought of being forced into the carriage.

"Relax," Rooke said in a bored tone. "He's not there. He's not even aware we've made contact."

I turned to glance at the mouth of the alley. Boys in rags ran by, doubtlessly joining the fray surrounding Forrester.

Behind me, a man with a black eye patch and a thin scar streaming over his cheek studied me with unabashed curiosity.

"They're going to start a riot," one of the men said to Rooke.

"Get inside," Rooke said to me, then withdrew a silver flask and turned to the man who had spoken. "They're smarter than that. Just make sure you pay them well for their assistance." He returned his gaze to me and stared as he took a swig. "Send a street runner to tell him I've picked her up and she's on her way. Make sure he's fully aware our carriage is going to be stuck in the aggregation of this row. I don't need him impatient with me when we arrive."

The man with the scar gave me a shove. "Move."

"Mind yourself," Rooke warned. "That's his wife you're handling."

"Wife?" The man stepped away, fear rising in his eyes.

"Best hope she don't complain," was Rooke's response.

My body felt like ice as I climbed inside the landau. The black velvet seats and polished nickel interior looked unused. Rooke joined me, and the man with the scar shut the door, enclosing us in a dark prison.

Rooke extended his flask.

I shook my head. "What does he want?"

Rooke shrugged while screwing the cap back on. "Orders were to bring you. I never ask why."

He closed his eyes and leaned back, propping his feet on the seat next to me, as if assured I'd make no attempt to jump from the carriage. I stared at the door. Or perhaps he knew we were locked inside and I couldn't escape.

As our carriage made one mysterious turn after another, my fear tingled into anxiety, and then anxiety into a manageable numbness. I removed my bonnet and gloves as the carriage grew warmer and mixed with the strong ale scent of Rooke's flask.

Occasionally, Rooke opened an eye and peered at me, but for the most part he looked asleep. I closed my eyes, thinking of Isaac and my father. By then, they must have discovered I was missing. I felt like crying. They wouldn't know if I was just lost, kidnapped, or had orchestrated my break from them. Doubtless Forrester would rant and scream that I'd slipped away on purpose to be with Macy.

To my estimation, it was well over an hour before our carriage halted and the coachman jumped down, signalling we'd reached our destination. Rooke stretched, opened the door, and then slid out. Wind tousled my hair as I accepted his hand and exited.

Neoclassic houses lined the street, and I could have laughed with relief. The architecture looked very much like the stately homes near London House. Rooke took my arm and, keeping it in a firm grasp, opened the gate leading to the house before us. As I stumbled alongside him, I finally had my first glimpse of the outskirts of Hyde Park.

Rooke opened the door and pushed me inside. I expected something dark and sinister. Instead, we entered a foyer that felt more like a cathedral than a house. A shaft of sunlight fell from the high window, lighting trompe l'oeil walls and a ceiling painted to look as though columns and Gothic stonework surrounded us.

Hands reached around my shoulders and unfastened my cape. The scent of Mr. Macy's cigars surrounded me. "Don't grow attached to the house, dearest, for I'm not keeping it longer than it takes us to resolve our differences." He lifted the curls that trailed beneath my chignon. "You needn't stand so stiffly," he whispered in his alluring, amused voice. "I'll only tempt—not force—you to my bed."

Heat rushed through my cheeks, for I'd forgotten how direct he was and how seductive his touch could be. A strange medley of haunting sensations, a twisting of all emotions, spiralled through me. I stood breathless as his fingers probed through my hair, finding the pins that held it. It wasn't longing that held me in a trance, but survival. He had collected me; there might be no recourse. Only a fool would stir the wasps' nest of his anger at the onset.

I swallowed, knowing I needed to keep my wits. My stomach grew tremulous as he kissed along the nape of my neck slowly and sensuously. I lifted my gaze to the trompe l'oeil ceiling. It wasn't a prayer, but it was a thought directed toward God. I wanted to believe someone cared that I was here.

"How your heart flutters," Mr. Macy murmured, nuzzling his raspy chin along the slope of my shoulders. He slowly started circling me, studying me.

I could only steal tiny glances, but I saw enough. His hair was unkempt, and instead of formal attire he wore an untucked shirt with the top buttons open. His feet were bare. Dark eyes watched me with their usual amusement. Every time I lost sight of him, it heightened how sensitive my skin felt as I anticipated his touch.

"Well," he finally concluded, "there's no bloom in your cheeks, but at least you're not as thin as before. A little fresh air will cure your paleness. Forgive me, dearest." He drew my right palm to his mouth and kissed it. "I had no intentions of driving you permanently indoors with that demonstration at Lady Northrum's. Come."

I glanced at the door, dreading to follow him. Intuition told me that obedience would serve me better than attempting to run. To my surprise, I was able to move my feet though I felt no sensation in my legs. Step after step, I padded behind him, my heart hammering.

Deep within the house, he slid open a pair of pocket doors, revealing a parlor stuffed with dark leather furniture, an oversized desk, and a low fire, reminding me of his private study in Eastbourne.

"Now isn't the time to lie to me," Mr. Macy said. I smelled his brandy-laced breath as the warmth of his body neared mine. "I want honest answers from my wife, starting with why you fled from me that night."

I glanced at the closet, wondering if he'd planted witnesses to spy on this conversation, to prove I wasn't Julia Pierson. "Sir," I managed in a whisper, prepared to play my alias at all cost, "I have no knowledge of why you brought me here. I am not your wife. Please, I beg you to contact my father, Lord Pierson. He'll confirm my identity."

Unbeknownst to me, I'd stared at the closet door the entire time I spoke. Macy's brows rose with amusement before he sauntered to the door and opened it, revealing an empty space. "Allow me to assure you . . ." He then proceeded to open every door in the chamber, proving them harmless. "There is no need to perform. Our conversation is private. Should I persuade you quickly, I daresay, neither one of us would desire an audience for what follows."

I felt my cheeks burn. "Why must you always mock me?"

"Mock you?" He stepped away and spread his hands in a gesture of helplessness. "Here I thought I was being rather direct. Sit, dearest, and no more games. You have an exceedingly tolerant husband, one who is more interested in resolving why you keep fleeing him, rather than lording over you."

As I sat on the leather sofa, I studied the layout of the room. When he'd opened the doors, I'd noted they only led deeper into the house. Heavy velvet curtains hung over the windows, but it was ridiculous to hope for escape through one of them.

Macy crouched at my feet, sitting on his heels, managing to make his odd position look dignified. "Now tell me. Why did you flee?"

My stomach tightened as I recalled that night.

"Be very careful," Macy warned. "I shall not be angry as long as you speak truth."

"We both know why." I lowered my chin. "You . . . you . . ." I forced myself to say the words aloud again. "You killed Mama."

"Look at me!"

I flinched at his ruthless expression as I obeyed.

"Someday I intend to see John Greenham writhing at your feet, ready to suffer the consequences of murdering your mother. On that day I shall also have the satisfaction of hearing him confess to you that I am innocent in this matter. But until then, give me one acceptable reason why you refuse to believe I had no involvement in her death."

I pressed my hand over my mouth and squeezed my eyes

shut to hold back the sobs. I couldn't do this much longer. When in his presence, I felt tempted to believe differently than when I was away from him. How did he always manage to intoxicate my surroundings and infect my thoughts? I wouldn't bend again. I wouldn't. Wanting something he couldn't escape, I cried, "You killed Churchill then!"

"Churchill? The solicitor?"

My fingers felt frozen as I waited to see how he would react to my knowing about that murder too. The look on his face was nothing short of incredulous.

He rubbed his forehead as if uncertain how to address this matter. "Does it make any sense for me to finance a deeper investigation into his murder, if I had done it? Especially when I could have been rid of an additional problem at the same time."

I crinkled my brow to show him I didn't understand.

"Forgive me, but I wouldn't have wept to see your lover dangle. Yet for your sake, I spared no expense to free him."

His words were incomprehensible at first, but then as I considered how long Isaac had remained at Am Meer, my father's expression as he read my letters, and the news that was so devastating Elizabeth wished to be the one to tell me, I slowly understood. "They accused Edward of killing Churchill!"

"Did your father not tell you?"

That my father and Isaac would choose to keep something of that magnitude from me infuriated me. I rose, needing space. "What happened? Tell me! I need to know."

With maddening calmness, Mr. Macy inclined against the back of the couch. "Edward was seen running from the scene of the crime, right before he disappeared for several days. Shall we say that certain conclusions were drawn?"

I felt so enraged I could have flown at him. "You mean you led people to believe he did it."

He frowned with displeasure. "*I* wasn't on hand either. Something rather dear to my heart disappeared that night.

I thought Bradshawl's men had taken you. You have no idea what I underwent fearing for your life." He looked askance, and his face was molded with an expression of pain. He shook off his thought and returned his attention to me. "When I realized Bradshawl's men didn't have you, I rode as hard as I could back to Adelia's. Edward had returned by then, but despite the numerous beatings, he refused to talk about his whereabouts."

I wanted to cry, envisioning Edward jailed, unable to defend himself as he was questioned. Of course Edward would never have confessed the truth. It would have betrayed me.

I spun toward Mr. Macy. "How badly was he injured?"

An expression I couldn't read crossed his face as he withdrew and lit a cigarette. "How wonderfully female you are. Here, your husband informs you he was nearly butchered trying to save you, and your response is to plead for information about your lover." He closed his eyes and puffed on his cig. "He was less bruised than I was."

"What happened?"

A lazy wreath of smoke wafted above him as he leaned back, eyes still closed. "I told you. I paid for his legal fees, I paid for a more thorough investigation, and I paid with a black eye, when Edward finally was free."

"Why?"

He grinned, then chuckled. "Apparently he didn't take it well when I asked him if he enjoyed my wife. Ironic, isn't it? The cuckolded husband being the one punched."

I felt so frustrated I could have screamed. Instead, I cried.

He released a deep breath, streaming smoke. When he spoke again, his voice chuckled. "No weeping, sweetheart. I forget how serious the romantic notions of the young are. It's bad enough my men wonder why I must kidnap my own wife to hold a conversation with her, without having her leave my house with streaked eyes. Forgive me. Sit."

My anger swept from me, for I'd not missed his hint that I

would leave. Rather than occupy the sofa with him, I edged to the chair. "Why did you pay to help Edward?"

"Had I known your father would advertise your whereabouts, I wouldn't have bothered. As it was, I couldn't allow the only person who knew my wife's whereabouts to be hanged."

"How did you convince them he was innocent?"

"Darling, the evidence was everywhere. Didn't you read about the case in the papers?"

The papers. I folded my arms over my stomach, deciding that I despised the publications. "No. I don't read them."

He laughed. "All those coded messages, and you haven't read even one?"

I said nothing.

"How on earth are you spending your days, then?"

This I had no wish to answer, nor did I wish for him to know that life with my father pained me. Mimicking Isaac, I adapted an aloof look, one of complete boredom, then shrugged.

The muscles around his mouth twitched. "Is it truly that bad, darling?"

His question brought on sadness, a sensation that I was estranged from any sense of home or family. I took care to display no hint of desolation, yet he saw it anyway.

His eyes sharpened as gravity replaced his facetiousness. Cursing, he leaned forward and stamped out his cigarette. "I have half a mind to punish Roy for his role in creating that expression. It borders on absurd that my wife sits here near tears, subjecting herself to a temper like his, because of a series of misunderstandings."

My voice would have betrayed me further, so I did not state that it wasn't a series of misunderstandings. Instead I studied him. He watched me with the amusement I'd often seen while at Eastbourne.

"We have quite a problem that we need to tackle. The last time you ran away, you blamed me for the gossip that engulfed us. I have no desire to lose your goodwill twice in such a manner. Your past scandal is insignificant compared to your current one. Rather than heighten your fall from grace, I'd prefer to extend my offer of protection and a chance to avoid the coming flood."

"I saw your offered protection at Lady Northrum's. No thank you. You tried your best to expose me."

The corners of his mouth tugged upwards. "Had I wanted you exposed, darling, all of London would be astir with the gossip that you are none other than the elusive Mrs. Macy. That demonstration was strictly to catch your father's attention. He turns away every inquiry and request for contact. He refuses to acknowledge me. Which brings me to why you are here. I know you will listen." He stood and sauntered to the decanters. "Brandy?"

I shook my head. "It's unladylike."

He roared with laughter as he poured two drinks. "I'm glad your father has taken it upon himself to coerce some manners into you, for you were rather lacking. However, let's not overcompensate. Besides—" he slid onto the sofa—"my wife is allowed to drink whatever she pleases."

I accepted the snifter, but for some unfathomable reason, I pictured Isaac giving me a quick shake of his head.

Mr. Macy rested against the arm of the sofa and sipped, waiting. He said nothing while the clock ticked and the fire crackled. Gradually I understood that he had no intentions of finishing our discourse until I partook with him. But why?

I stared at the decanter and the snifters lined upside down on the tray next to it. Memory of Forrester running his finger along the bottom of a tumbler in Eastbourne's dining room came to mind. I also considered the first night I met with Mr. Macy. He'd pressed me to drink that night as well.

"You still wear your thoughts plainly upon your face." Mr. Macy spoke in a sleek and unapologetic tone. "The very way you're sitting ought to give you a clue."

I realized my elbows were clutched close to my side, and

I hunched over my knees as if I were trying to make myself as small as possible. Every muscle in my body felt stiff. I met his dark eyes, understanding. He wished me to relax.

I sniffed the brandy. If, as in a faerie tale, I must drink a magic potion to go home, I would. Warmth slipped into my stomach. Little by little my fingers lost their hollow feeling, and I finally sank back into my seat.

"Do you feel capable of a business conversation yet?" Mr. Macy rose and poured himself another drink, then settled into the nook of the couch across from me.

"Business?"

His mouth slanted in a wry smile. "Yes, dear. No more kisses. You've gotten yourself rather entangled. Since your father refuses to acknowledge this, I have no choice but to talk legalities with my wife, whom I'd rather be seducing. How well do you understand the law surrounding our marriage?" From a nearby table he lifted a document and handed it to me.

I feared to touch it. "What is it?"

"For a politician, your father isn't as brilliant as his reputation. He never should have outlined his arguments against the legality of our union to me. I've taken the issue of our marriage to the Doctors' Commons. Here is the irrefutable proof that you are mine."

Ice ran through my veins as I took the papers. There was no need to read it. I believed him.

"Tell your father. The discourse is documented, so he can find it easily enough to read for himself, should he disbelieve you."

"You are mine." Macy's statement continued to cycle through my thoughts.

"You needn't look so forlorn." Mr. Macy switched seats, so that he now perched on the edge of a nearby table. I felt his fingers caressing my cheek. "Have I not proven myself a trustworthy husband? Even now I am proving it by attempting to hold back the scandal that is sure to break."

"My father will dispute this marriage at all cost."

"Really? Do you think he'll expose himself to do so? Even if he would, let him try. He believes his influence would sway the outcome, but I know the dirty, well-hidden secrets of every member amongst the gentry. This, however, is a discussion for your father and me, whereas you and I have different problems to solve. Consider this my fair warning to you, dearest. I'll not have you accuse me of ruining your life. I would very much like to structure your return without further damage to your reputation."

I stared at the document in my hands, feeling chills spread over my body. Deep within, I sensed he wasn't making idle threats. My longing for Edward crested and grew so sharp I could scarcely think. I wanted guidance and didn't trust anyone except him.

Holding back tears, I glanced at the clock, wondering if enough time had passed to satisfy Macy and whether he would release me. "May I go and discuss this with my father?"

A weary look replaced his studying expression. Sighing, he rubbed his eyes. "You have no idea how much it pains me to return you. If you knew half of what I know about R—" He bit off his own statement, looking vexed.

"How long do I have to consider your offer?"

"Not my offer, darling; my warning. There's no time limit. I'd rather you return of your own volition. I need to know you trust me and will stay put. Had one of Bradshawl's men intercepted you that night, you'd have been tortured and killed, just for the honor of being my wife. At least now, you're safe in your nest, with my enemies having no idea where my most precious possession is tucked. Stay until you're weary of being bullied and want freedom." He kissed my cheek. "Yet be advised, my tolerance has limits. I've already tolerated one lover while we're newlyweds. Don't ask me to stomach another."

"I have no interest in Lord Dalry, thank you."

He laughed. "Remain here. I'm going to dress so I can take you home."

Nineteen

❧

AN EASTERLY WIND whipped my skirts and skittered leaves as we retired from Mr. Macy's residence. The brisk air served to revive me, lifting Macy's spell, waking sensibilities.

Rooke scowled, turning up his collar. To Mr. Macy's great amusement, I'd requested a chaperone, lest a rumor spread that I was out alone with a gentleman.

I scrutinized his terraced row house. It matched every other house lining the street, betraying nothing of the corruptness inside.

"I've added lions to differentiate mine," Mr. Macy said.

Beneath windows reflecting the turbid sky, engraved lion faces emerged from the stone window boxes and roared around the rings in their mouths. I stared at their teeth, dismayed, until Macy's hand directed me toward his landau.

Rooke entered the carriage behind me, then pulled his hat over his eyes.

"You must not believe the things your father says about me." Mr. Macy shut the drapes, ensconcing us in shadow.

I held the top of my cape, trying to expunge the cold, but my teeth chattered. "Your name isn't permitted to be spoken aloud in his house."

"Really?" Mr. Macy's brows elevated. "Then he must know he'll eventually be forced to surrender you. But come now, doesn't Forrester at least mention me?"

"Yes," I replied moodily. "Continually. He accuses me of being your spy."

Mr. Macy laughed, leaning back in his seat. "He must think me desperate if I'm recruiting the likes of you. You're scarcely the type of girl I'd use to accomplish my purposes."

I bent my head. Humiliation mingled with indignation as I glanced at Rooke for his reaction.

"Julia, sweetheart." Macy turned me by the chin to face him. "I meant no wound. You know I regard you as my most valued treasure."

I made no reply. All I wanted was for this ordeal to be finished; I would do whatever I must to get back to London House. I would not argue; I would not speak.

Though the houses had suggested we were near my father's residence, we travelled for the better part of an hour before halting. Macy disembarked, ordering Rooke to stay, and then extended his hand. I knew we were at London House the moment I saw the curb and the unique pattern of brick corbels that extended from our house.

I stood, taking in the changes wrought since morning. No longer did London House appear well regulated and business-like. The open gate creaked in the wind. Muddy footprints were layered from street to door, evidence that a throng of people had trundled up and down the stairs since morning.

"Shall we?" Mr. Macy stilled the swinging gate.

I finally acknowledged him with a startled glance. "You're not going in, are you?"

With gloved fingers, he brushed the tendrils of my hair that blew freely in the wind. His features became so loving, my stomach twisted. "You think me the type of man to send my wife where I wouldn't dare tread myself? Of course I'm accompanying you. I wish to deem whether I desire to leave you in this milieu any longer."

Dismayed, I followed him up the steps. The door was locked, so I clanged the bell for James. He answered, his wig slightly askew. Seeing me, he gasped, but his words died upon spotting Mr. Macy.

Adopting a formal look, James bowed. "Miss Pierson, welcome home. I believe you will find your father in the library. He has been most anxious about you."

I entered and unbuttoned my cape. Angry voices carried from the library, my father's shout prominent. Mr. Macy removed my cape and handed it to James. Then, tugging off his gloves, Mr. Macy scoured my father's residence with his all-consuming eyes. His hand came to rest on my shoulder, squeezing as if convincing himself of ownership. "I have no objections to the house, but are you certain you wish to remain here, darling? Your father sounds rather brutish. Come home with me instead."

I tucked my chin, avoiding James's appalled expression. "James, you're dismissed. I'm famished. Have Pierrick send me up a tray." I placed my hands over my churning stomach as if to emphasize my manufactured appetite. "Hurry now. Go."

James's mouth pursed and he squinted at Mr. Macy, but he withdrew.

"That was almost convincing, darling." Mr. Macy slid his hand to the small of my back. "When he presents you with tea, I want you to eat. You've had a trying day, and while you may not feel hunger, victuals will benefit you."

I yearned to shrink away from his touch but feared to upset him. I fastened my eyes on the library door, just wanting to make it into the next chamber. At the threshold, I paused, listening to my father's shouts. If he was already this angry, how would he react at finding Mr. Macy in his house? Taking a deep breath, I entered on wobbly legs.

Four men I did not recognize stood alongside Mr. Forrester, Isaac, and my father, poring over a yellowed map of London, so large it engulfed the reading table. Their faces were bright red as tempers boiled over. They pointed at pins concentrated in one location over the map, arguing. Isaac alone sensed my presence. He straightened and dropped his compass. Blue eyes met mine, somehow calming me.

"Gentlemen," Mr. Macy announced in a loud voice, "I believe I found what you seek."

My hands began to quake, but Isaac managed to hold my gaze, exempting me from witnessing my father's reaction.

"I found the poor child wandering the streets of London unprotected." Mr. Macy laid his hand on my bare head. "She's slightly dazed by the experience, but I have no doubt in a few hours, when the shock wears off, you'll find her satisfactory."

Silence engulfed the room, and I shifted beneath Mr. Macy's touch, breaking Isaac's gaze.

"Ha-ha. Well, then, all's well that ends well." A man with thinning hair removed steamy spectacles and wiped them. His voice trembled as he polished condensation from the lenses. "Shall you . . . uh, I mean . . . Are there any instructions, sir?"

"No, Inspector." My father straightened and placed a weight over a corner of the map. "Take your men. You're dismissed."

The inspector shot Mr. Macy a panicked expression, betraying that his question had been aimed at Mr. Macy, not my father. The weight of Macy's hand increased as I realized that even here, he held power.

"Ah, well, ah, yes . . . I suppose I have your permission to leave." The inspector fumbled with a leather bag, attempting to shove loose papers inside. As many papers fell to the floor as inside the bag. "I do have your permission, do I not?"

"Leave," my father growled.

Mr. Forrester strode to the door and held it open. "Gentlemen, thank you."

Only Isaac dared to approach Macy. As if unaware of anyone but me, he crossed the chamber and took my trembling arm. He quietly assessed me from head to toe. I felt tension in his fingers, but he gave no visible evidence of his thoughts.

Three men slunk from the room. The inspector inched his way, taking shuffling steps. "If my presence was required, you know I would stay. I should hope that you would state whether you desired me to remain? You have only to say the word." He paused near the door, receiving no answer from anyone. Then, turning a sick, pasty color, he ducked from the room.

"Were I a politician, Roy—" Macy removed his hand from my head and sauntered to the mantel—"I'd address the problems with the corruption within the police force. Really, one must wonder what the world is coming to."

"State your business, then leave," my father said.

With a careless gesture, Macy lifted the lid of the cigar box on the mantel. He withdrew one, sniffed, and wrinkled his nose. "I'll gift you from my private stock. You'll thank me later."

"State your business."

Macy tossed the cigar into the case and shut the lid. "My wife appears wan; thus I'm displeased with your care. Had I known she'd be punished for my demonstration at Lady Northrum's, I would have spared her. Allow her to make the rounds in society again. I promise to behave."

"Is that all you came to say?" My father crossed his arms, glaring like a military commander wearing down an insubordinate. "State your true business."

"My true business? Surely you cannot think I approve of my wife's being held hostage." At the nearest bookshelf, Macy tilted back the leather and gilded volumes, looking behind them. "One would hope, as her father, you'd share my concern." He dropped the books back into place. His probing gaze swung around to the windows. "You have my word, Roy. I will leave Julia alone in public. I swear it." His attention travelled to Isaac and his mouth twisted. "That is, unless your lordling tests my patience too far."

"You've said your piece. Now leave."

"I'm serious, Roy. I expect to see my wife enjoying life. I'll not allow her to grow ill because she frets all day behind these walls." Macy frowned as he tested the windows. "You might want to have this lock secured." He tapped the right windowpane. "It would be easy to bypass, and I'd hate to keep one of my men continually occupied guarding these windows." He released the heavy draperies and made his way back to me. With a tender expression, he lifted my chin. "Sweetheart, are you absolutely certain you wish to remain?"

I swallowed, waiting for my father to cry out that it wasn't my decision, but he uttered no sound. I stared at my father, wondering if Macy had more power than he pretended. Perspiration prickled over my palms. Or did my father think I'd sought out Macy on purpose? I twisted my skirt into my dampened palms, wondering if he still wanted me.

"Having qualms?" Macy asked, his amusement evident.

Biting my bottom lip, I shook my head.

"As you wish, then." Macy drew near. His breath warmed my ear as he whispered, "I keep my men posted nearby. When you're ready to leave, you need only to step outdoors." He placed the gentlest kiss near my ear, then sauntered from the room.

I counted twenty seconds before I heard the heavy front door close. I covered my mouth, gasped a sob, and sank to my knees. I was safe. He'd actually left.

"Isaac, Robert, leave." My father stepped from behind the library table.

Lord Dalry knelt at my side, gathering me. "No, sir, not until I know for myself what happened to Julia—"

"*Leave!*"

"Come on." Forrester grabbed Lord Dalry's sleeve. "Just

because the door shut doesn't mean he actually left the house. We need to secure the grounds."

Isaac looked distraught, but when I refused to acknowledge him, he allowed Forrester to pull him from the room.

As I wiped my palms against my skirt, terror replaced relief. I faced my father. "Papa . . . I . . . I . . ."

His mouth twisted in odd directions, his jaw clenching. He took two furious steps toward me. I cringed, squeezing my eyes shut. Strong arms engulfed me and breath was crushed from my body. Anguished, choking noises followed, as I realized my father had fallen to his knees. He wept, clutching me tighter and tighter, as if fearing to let go. He wept harsh words, too garbled to understand but full of pain. I buried my face in his shoulder.

❦

An hour later, my father's bottle of port clinked against a crystal tumbler as he poured his second helping. Before drinking, he paused and rubbed his brow. When he looked up at my tearstained face, he grimaced. "Julia, for the last time, you're not married to that man."

"But I saw proof." I clasped my hands and placed them on the table, imploring him. "He was earnest when he said he carried as much weight as you."

My father gave a dark chuckle, downed the port, then chuckled some more. "He is a liar. He has always been a liar. Place no faith in anything he says."

Frustrated, I flung myself into a chair. Nothing I'd said convinced my father. I'd been arguing since my arrival that Macy still considered me his wife and wouldn't relent. "If you would only go and look at the discourse. He said you'd find it easily enough."

He slammed his tumbler down. "That proves what, exactly? That he is married to a Julia Elliston? Someone I've never met, never heard of? Consider the suspicious light it would cast upon us. I announce I have a sequestered daughter—whom no one knew existed—and then suddenly I take interest in the legalities of Mr. Macy's marriage. Can you not see the bait? See what he hopes will happen?"

"That's not his intention. If only you had seen his face."

"Name his intentions then." All patience left my father's eyes.

Exasperated, I dropped my hands. There was no way he'd believe me. "To spare me from another scandal?"

My father exhaled heavily through his nose. "Remind me why you wed him in the first place."

I turned my face toward the window, hating that he thought me the naive one. "He was protecting me from you."

"Was he?"

I waited until my voice would sound normal. "He swears so."

"You've lived with me now. Is there anything in my nature that would make you imagine I am such a brute?"

I frowned, deciding not to answer honestly.

"Macy has known me for nigh thirty years. He had full knowledge you were in no peril. Have you forgotten that Macy housed you under the same roof as your mother's murderer? Think upon that. Really consider it. This man never had a shred of concern about you."

My eyes drifted to Mama's vibrant sunflower painting behind him on the wall. I didn't know all the answers. No one understood Macy. Not even his closest friends. "And what if he really is trying to spare me?"

My father scoffed, pouring his third helping. "Julia, he cares nothing for you. Nothing. Why would he?"

Bruised, I lifted my gaze. Some words are a death knell. They become furies digging their talons into the soul, ripping and shredding all that they find. Another soul, another person might not have felt the sting, but something vital within me died.

And yet, though he was temperamental and difficult, I loved my father. At that time, it felt like a brute instinct, that some perverse rule of the universe forced a child to love her parent, even at cost to self.

I cannot tell you what my father said next. I saw the knit of his brow, the forcefulness of his opinion, but I ceased hearing him. It was as though he were miles away.

There is no hope for us, I thought. If he didn't see anything about me worthy enough to capture Macy's attention, then he saw no value in me. And if I was valueless to him, then it was time to take my fate back into my own hands.

My father stood, breaking my deep concentration so I could hear him again. "If Macy wanted to spare you a scandal," he ranted, "then why not just leave you completely alone?"

"Because," I said, feeling dead, "only the worst sort of rake actually abandons his wife."

I could not know it then, but my words struck the rawest chord in my father's heart. His bottom lip curled as he raised the back of his hand as if to strike. I had no fear of being struck, however. I looked up, waiting. The blow would only justify my decision.

No more would I hope to win my father's love. My only goal now was to find my way back to Edward, back to the only man who had truly accepted me and loved me.

My father did not strike. Instead, awareness seized him. He dropped his hand and, paling, stared at it as though it were foreign to his body. He set down his drink, stumbled a step or two backwards. Then with grief, pure and undefiled upon his face, he fled toward the door, where the visible outline of feet paced beneath the crack.

When he opened it, Lord Dalry and Forrester turned with anticipation.

"May I question her now?" Forrester unbuttoned his frock coat and started to shed it.

"No one is to question her!" my father roared. "I will not tolerate his lies circulating in this house!" My father spun, pointing his ringed index finger at me and, with spittle on the edges of his mouth, shouted, "You will not repeat one syllable of one word that Macy said."

Banishing emotion, I folded my hands over my lap, trying to appear dispassionate. Let him think I felt no regret for my words. Let them all think me wicked. I no longer cared.

"Roy, I need to know where Macy took her. Where—?"

"I forbid it! Now move from my path!" My father gave the door a forceful shove, bashing it against the wall, then stomped down the hall.

Forrester tugged on the bottom of his waistcoat, seemingly uncertain whether to follow him or attempt to question me. With a scowl, he turned and followed my father.

I bent over the map of London. My head throbbed as I took in a ragged breath.

My chair shifted suddenly to the right, and I lifted my gaze to find Isaac beside me.

"Julia?" His tone comforted and inquired.

I shook my head to show him I couldn't yet speak.

It seemed to me he held his breath, battling his next course of action. "Whatever took place between you and your father can be mended. I promise. His temper has been out of sorts all day." He rose and offered his arm. "Come, join me before the fire. I'll read to you."

I cupped my forehead in my hand, looking at the winding image of the Thames on the map below me. "Isaac, none of this is going to work. You've been kind to me, and I don't want to deceive you. But this isn't . . ." Tears choked me.

Questions plagued his eyes, but with an otherwise-emotionless expression, he took my arm and urged me to stand. I knew, even as I gathered my skirts to take the couch, he at least wasn't going to question me.

❦

I leaned my head against the arm of my father's tufted sofa, unable to sleep, as Lord Dalry read poetry, his tranquil voice calming the atmosphere. Seeing wisdom in Mr. Macy's suggestion, I'd forced myself to partake of tea and seedcake when James presented me with a tray. Warmth from the fire cocooned me, down pillows cushioned and velvet blankets covered me, yet for the last hour, disturbing thoughts had clung with deep hooks. I desired to go pace in my cold bedchamber, wringing my hands, yet the comforting presence of Isaac was so strong, I continued to lie still, feigning sleep.

"'That this the meed of all my toils might be.'" Isaac paused and a page rustled. "'To have a home, an English home, and thee! Vain repetition! Home and Thou are one—'"

The sound of creaking filled the chamber, before James said, "Sir."

"Shh. Don't wake her. What is it?"

"Lord Alexander and Mr. Jonathan Billingsby have arrived." James must have stepped inside and closed the door. His voice lowered to a whisper. "Lord Alexander claims he rushed over the moment he heard of Miss Pierson's ordeal. He insists on seeing her or he will be unable to sleep or eat."

"Just brilliant," Lord Dalry muttered, and I heard the book close. "Does he actually think she's going to believe that fodder? If it's not one wolf, it's another."

"Beg your pardon, sir?"

"Oh, don't play deaf and dumb with me. I suspect you've pieced together quite a bit more than we would like."

The fire crackled and I heard James shift. "Aye. I know well enough what's scaring Lord Pierson into stormy tempers." He cleared his throat. "If I may be so bold, it also seems to me the sooner you wed Miss Pierson, the better."

Lord Dalry gave a rueful laugh, and his chair creaked. "I tend to agree, but as it turns out, she can hardly stand my presence. I must be England's worst suitor. What am I doing wrong?"

"You, sir? Absolutely nothing!" James's voice grew light. "'Tis nothing more than woman's wiles. She's madly in love with you and just playing shy. Try waking her with a kiss."

This was met with Lord Dalry's golden laugh. "All right, enough. Step aside. Remain with her while I deal with yet another suitor. How many marriage offers have there been? Five?"

"Six, sir. The last one arrived yesterday, from Lord Alexander himself. But at least he's seen her in person, which accounts for more than the others. I had the pleasure of hearing Master Pierson informing Mr. Forrester of the offer as they partook brandy. 'Tis a pity you weren't present. Mr. Forrester contended for an hour this was the exact course of action that should be taken. By the end of the argument, Master Pierson agreed he would at least consider the future Earl of Kensington. Even went so far as to send an inquiry as to what sort of dowry would be expected."

"To that lout? Are you serious? I'll have Forrester's head on a platter for that."

"A better action would be to rid the house of the unwanted gents before his lordship learns they're here."

"All right, move aside."

I heard the door close, followed by the rattle of coal sliding down a scuttle. Alarmed by this new information, I slit my eyes open and watched James jab the fire.

"It isn't any of my business," he said, his white wig looking orange in the light, "if my young mistress wishes to feign sleep, but I hope she will at least consider what she overheard. I would never be permitted to tell my mistress that her father is becoming tempted by other offers of marriage." He started to rise, and I closed my eyes again. "Nor would I tell her that I've served as Master Isaac's personal valet for three years and can swear he's never been in love before now. It would be a smarmy shame if my mistress ended up with the likes of Lord

Alexander or Mr. Eramus Calvin when Master Isaac is willing to marry her."

Some moments passed in silence before the door clicked again.

"Are they gone then, sir?" James asked. I heard the ring of the poker being slid back into place.

"Yes, and you have my direct orders to receive no visitors tonight. No matter who."

"Very well, sir. Shall I prepare your evening wear?"

"No," Lord Dalry said. "Our plans are cancelled. I'll remain here with Miss Pierson while she sleeps."

"Very well, sir." James withdrew, leaving me far more agitated than he'd found me.

Twenty

❦

THREE NIGHTS LATER, I paused, pen suspended over paper. A drop of ebony splattered over the snow-white page. With a sigh, I tried to blot the ink but smudged my hand. Tears gathered, but I refused them. Since my encounter with Macy, they spilled too easily.

I shoved the post aside, wanting not to care that I hadn't seen my father since that night, or that I was still being tucked out of existence. I glared at the post. My penmanship was so horrid, society probably gossiped I'd grown slipshod.

"Miss Josephine?" Kinsley's kind voice rasped from the hall before he gently tapped on the door. "Are you in here?"

I set down my gold-and-tortoiseshell pen. Light from the sconce behind him shone through his sparse hair. "There are gentlemen callers who insisted on seeing the lady of the house."

I felt myself pale as I pictured Macy standing in the foyer with his sardonic grin and black cape. Gooseflesh rose over my arms. James and Isaac had gone to a club earlier, and William

252

and my father left an hour after them. Simmons hadn't been seen all day.

Rain pounded on the window as I debated how to handle the situation. "Please tell them I am not at home."

He bowed, backing into the hall. "Very well, miss."

Careful to keep my ink-stained hands from the silk material of my dress, I rose. After a count of twenty, hoping it gave Kinsley enough time, I tiptoed after him, my rustling dress scarcely more than a whisper.

The first voice I heard stirred life back into me, though I couldn't quite place its owner.

"I do *not* have the wrong house, and I will *not* leave until I see Miss Julia Pierson!"

Kinsley's reply was inaudible.

"No. *You* will march back down that hall, if it takes you another hour, and make certain she sees my card."

"Honestly, Henry," someone else said, "maybe we should just leave."

For a second, I feared I wouldn't be able to make my legs move. Henry—my Henry!—stood feet away, and my feet were glued to the floor. Then in the next instant, I rushed down the hall, holding my skirts.

Just past the entrance, Henry and Mr. Addams stood, dripping.

"Henry!" I shrieked.

He looked over and a huge grin spread across his face. With a laugh he opened wide his arms, and I flung myself into them.

He embraced me, lifting me off my feet. Not caring about the rain that ruined the silk fabric of my dress, I clung to him and breathed deeply of the scent of his coat and nearly wept. He used the same bay rum Edward did. There were also traces of the scent that clung to Auburn Manor. My homesickness crested such that I thought I'd never recover. I inhaled until I wept.

"Miss Josephine Anna Parkhurst, you will release that gentleman this instant." Kinsley's voice boomed behind me.

Henry gently set me on my feet. Still clinging to his lapels, I turned and found a master servant every bit as formidable as Reynolds was at Eastbourne. It was my first and only glimpse of the man lost to my father and Lord Dalry. "Imagine if your husband were to see you acting such. Shame on you! And you, young man." He shook a finger at Henry. "You ought to be ashamed of yourself."

Henry grinned, nodding good-naturedly. "Forgive me."

"I'll have no more hooliganism under my watch. Is that clear?"

Ever the leader of our foursome, Henry indulged him properly, as only the eldest son of a peer can. Kinsley left, promising that he would be keeping his eye on us.

"Honestly," Mr. Addams said as Kinsley pattered down the hall. "Henry, you're lucky that's the worst you received. How could you not know better than to lift her like that?"

"Oh, hush," Henry said. "Must you spoil everything?" Then to me, "Is it that beastly?"

"It's horrific. You've no idea!"

Henry looked me over with a critical eye and became serious before his gaze swept the hall, carefully viewing my surroundings. "Where's your father, then? I desire a word with him."

Alarmed, I shook my head. "He's out. And be glad for it."

Henry frowned. "Well, I'm not leaving until I've seen him myself."

"Henry, you mustn't!" I began.

"I say now, there's no need to make such a rash decision!" Mr. Addams removed his hat and shook out the water before replacing it over his red hair. "You said we'd leave London as soon as you checked on her. Well, there she is. She's perfectly fine. My mother's going to disown me if I'm not back by Christmas. I promised her!"

"I've changed my mind." Henry slipped from his cape. "Edward would want me to stay a few days."

"He would want nothing of the sort!"

"Yes, he would."

"No, he would not."

Henry frowned. "I ought to know my own brother better than you."

"My father won't allow you to stay, regardless," I managed between their bickering.

"There, you see." Mr. Addams thanked me with a nod. "We've no choice but to leave."

"It's not my fault you refuse to pay for your own passage home." Henry either refused to acknowledge what I'd said or hadn't heard me. "If you're going to take the charity of my carriage, you'll have to obey my schedule."

Mr. Addams took off his hat and squeezed water from it. "My word, Henry! Sometimes I wish you were the youngest of nine. A bit of poverty would straighten you rather well."

⌒〰⌒

When the library curtains had been opened and the fire built to a blaze, I had a better look at my visitors. Dark rings beneath their eyes suggested they were travel-weary. Both were thinner, likely due to a rigorous studying schedule.

A moment passed, during which I tried to collect and order the list of things I desired to learn. It wasn't likely my father would return home until bedtime, and I was famished for information about Edward.

"We've been following your story in the papers." Mr. Addams spoke before I could. "Your being the Emerald Heiress and such."

My smile fell. Last week there'd been an article predicting that my engagement to Lord Dalry would be announced at Christmas. "Well, don't believe the rumors."

Henry tilted his head as if perceiving my thoughts. "This

Dalry chap, is he the one who was with Edward during the investigation?"

I blinked, never having considered that Isaac had been Edward's companion during his ordeal. "Yes, I suppose he is."

"You suppose?"

It hurt to admit that I still knew next to nothing about Churchill's murder and the subsequent events. "I wasn't even told that Edward was accused until last week."

Henry's face contorted. "You weren't told?"

"It's complicated," I began. "They're protective—my father and Lord Dalry, that is."

"Protective!" Mashing his hat between his fingers, Henry found his feet. "Of what?"

I swallowed, surprised that my fingers were cold. "Well, of . . . me."

He thwacked his hat against his leg. "I'm sorry, Juls, but I doubt it is of you. It's their own reputation and prowess. How dare they! How dare they keep from you that Edward was nearly hanged!" He started to pace. "Would they have kept it secret if he had been?"

I shut my eyes, feeling too fragile to be yelled at. "I don't know, Henry. I don't know. Why are you placing the blame for this on me?"

"Oh, dash it all." I heard Henry flop back down to the sofa and opened my eyes in time to see him wrestling with his coattails. "This all just keeps getting worse by the day. I don't like that they would decide what knowledge you're allowed or not allowed to have."

I gave a bitter laugh, acknowledging the irony of it. "Isn't that what you and Elizabeth did when you kept Edward's ordination from me?"

He scowled. "It was for your own good, and you know it."

"And as you can see—" tears coated my voice as I swept a hand over the room—"your plan worked just brilliantly!"

"My plan! You're the one who married someone else. And you didn't do this to just yourself; you did it to us! All of us!"

I turned my face and worked to compose myself.

"Aw, Juls." Henry's voice softened. "I'm sorry. I don't mean it. This whole affair has us all out of sorts. It's not like us to be at a loss."

I pressed my knuckles against my mouth, but not because he'd upset me. His continual references to "us" were like water on parched ground.

"Satisfy me this much: The speculations about you and this Dalry chap are pure rubbish, yes? He doesn't actually think you're going to marry him, does he?"

"Oh, he thinks it, all right," I said, wiping my eyes with the backs of my hands. "It's complicated."

Surprise filled Henry's expression. "Have you made your position clear?"

"It's not like you think."

"Have you made your position clear?"

I nodded but sank against the back of the chair. How was it we were speaking of Isaac, when all I really wanted was news of Edward? I cast Henry a look that begged him to release me from this subject. He had no idea what it was like to be continually dismissed. He was the eldest son of a lord.

"Well, I, for one," Mr. Addams said, "am for the idea."

Henry's head snapped in his direction. "Who asked you? Keep out of this!"

Mr. Addams adjusted himself in his seat. "Well, if you're forcing me to miss Christmas, I'm going to dip my oar in as well." He faced me. "If you recall, my first advice to you was to move past your indiscretion and pretend it never happened. Edward was a fool not to go to Scotland when he had the chance. But look at this place." He gave a laugh of incredulity. "We're all missing the fact that you've become the daughter—*the daughter*—of Lord Pierson. It's either sheer madness or a miracle, and

I personally don't believe coincidences happen without a divine hand."

Sadness stirred in my breast, for part of me longed to believe as he did, to be comforted that there was more, some better hand at work. Yet I wondered how his theology would stand up under full knowledge of the truth. Seeing that I studied him, his smile widened with hope that perhaps he could be the one to reach the girl William Elliston had raised.

For the first time in my life, I didn't despise the simplicity of faith; I envied it.

"If only that were so," I said. "It's grown a bit more complicated than that. Only my father refuses to see it. I'm not allowed to speak of it. I'm not allowed to believe what my intuition tells me." Tears broke through my voice. "Mr. Macy will expose me if matters change beyond what they are now and will seek restitution of his conjugal rights. And he is earnest. I am certain of it."

Fear delineated Henry's face. "You've seen Macy?"

My face contorted as I tried to control my emotion; thus I could only mouth, *"Twice."*

"But your father knows?" Mr. Addams leaned forward.

I nodded, wiping my cheeks again. "He claims it's a bluff."

"He's right. Macy hasn't a shred of a chance. Not against Lord Pierson. If Lord Dalry marries you, Macy will have even less of a claim."

Henry swore. "What sort of asinine advice is that? Are you insane too? Either she's married to Macy or she's not. There's no such thing as less of a claim."

A throat cleared near the door, and the atmosphere intensified. I knew who it was before I looked; therefore I quickly rose and faced him.

It was the first time I had seen my father since our argument. Firelight flickered over the heavy gold chain clasping his cloak. His black boots glistened from beneath his woollen cape. His hands curled into fists, but he eyed our trio in a calm manner that increased my dread. I cringed, waiting for him to unleash his full fury.

As if finally understanding for himself that the benevolent image of my father painted in the papers was only half the picture, Mr. Addams, too, found his feet. He grew so pasty, I could mark every imperfection on his face.

Only Henry managed to forgo dread. He rose and gave a flippant bow. "Well, good. At least someone is here to give me answers. You must be Lord Pierson. As you can see, your daughter is too cowed to give us a proper introduction. I'm Henry Auburn, the brother of Reverend Auburn, but more importantly, heir to my father's title. Depending on what transpires during the next quarter of an hour, I will also forever be either your political friend or foe."

I winced, seeing that Henry's speech increased my father's ire. His eyes flashed as his jaw tightened. Isaac entered the chamber, loosing his cravat. Stunned, he stopped just behind my father.

"Isaac." My father's voice shook. "Take Julia to the back parlor. I'll deal with her later."

The blue of Lord Dalry's eyes fairly danced between Henry, Mr. Addams, and me as though trying to construct what was happening. His countenance held pity as he crossed the chamber to me.

He bowed slightly, extending his arm. Meeting my gaze, his eyes demanded, *Hurry.* Isaac faced my father. "Sir, I feel I'm owed an explanation too. Will you wait for my return before questioning these men?"

My father's jaw flexed as he eyed Henry, but he nodded.

The moment Isaac and I entered the hall, he pulled me away from the door. "Quickly, what happened?"

"My father found me with Edward's brother and Mr. Addams."

"What were you discussing?"

I hesitated, then confessed, "The legality of my marriage to Macy."

Isaac closed his eyes, and when they opened, he commanded, "Go directly to the parlor and remain there."

I grabbed his sleeve before he could leave. "Isaac, please." I allowed tears to gather, for I still hadn't learned anything about Edward. "*Please*, I still need an audience with Henry."

The pain in his eyes hurt me as well. He sighed, looking miserable. "I'll try."

∾

I sat in the parlor, eyes closed, listening with all my might, hoping to catch one last strain of Henry's voice. I was a prisoner awaiting the jailor to bring me news of whether I was to be exonerated or executed. The thought of Henry leaving before I had news of Edward nearly undid me. At the sound of the door, I nervously jumped from my chair.

I blinked, astonished to find Kate with her arms full of small parcels. Under normal circumstances I'd have hastened to greet her and felt gladsome for her presence. As it was, her sudden reappearance only made everything seem more dreamlike, so that I only managed to give her a stiff, confused nod.

"Goodness!" Kate entered and nudged the door shut with her foot. "You look like you've just returned from Lady Beatrice's. What's wrong?" She threw herself on the largest settee. Packages tied with ribbon spilled onto the floor as she pulled off her bonnet. Finding that the seat sprang back, she giggled and bounced a few times. With her eyes shining she asked, "Shall we take off our shoes and jump on it?"

My head felt as though it weighed a stone as I lifted it to acknowledge her. "Where have you been?"

Her mouth tipped up in a playful manner. "Did Isaac not tell you? He managed to find another of our cousins, though distantly removed, and sent me to spend the night with her." She wrinkled her nose. "It was horrid. She's half-blind and keeps twenty cats. Do I smell?" She sashayed to me, held her sleeve under her nose, and took a whiff. "I detect nothing offensive. Do you?"

After the stress of this morning, the simplicity of Kate's question made me laugh. Not a happy sound, but a laugh that relieved my tension more than tears could have.

Concern puckered her brow. "Don't let your father hear you laugh like that. He'll think it unladylike." With an impish grin, she pulled the pins from her Quaker-like bun and shook her head. Curls of reddish hair tumbled about her shoulders and down her back. "I thought I would never be free. She insisted that curls were of the devil and made me wear my hair like this. If she could see better, I have no doubt she'd write Mother encouraging her to wax my hair straight. Where is Isaac, anyway?"

I dropped to a chair and hugged a pillow. "With guests."

"And your father?"

I sighed, wondering anew what could possibly be taking them this long. I hadn't heard a sound from the library. "Oh, he's visiting with them too, I suppose."

She dimpled and placed her foot on the couch to remove her slipper. "Good. Then just once, I'm going to jump on this settee. You watch the door. I've wanted to since the first time I sat on it. Have you noticed that all the other furniture here is softer, yet your father always chooses to sit on this couch?"

I looked up at her. "Kate, don't you dare."

She only grinned, and before I could protest again, she stood and jumped. She went higher than I would have guessed she'd be able to. Her tresses fell about her shoulders and bounced with her. She laughed and jumped again, this time turning in the air.

"Oh, you must try this." With a flop, she landed in a sitting position and laughed.

The idea that Kate was jumping on my father's settee while he visited with Henry was more than I could take. I gave a hysterical giggle at the absurdity of it.

"Try it," she urged.

I shook my head, still holding back tears.

"Try it." She tossed her curls. "I don't know why you feel gloomy, but this will cure it. I promise!" She bounced a few more times.

It brought back a memory of jumping atop a haystack with Elizabeth. I'd been frightened we'd be caught, but Elizabeth insisted I hadn't lived until I'd stood on top of the world. Shyly, I'd climbed the straw embankment. Wind rushed through my hair as I spread my arms. It became one of those epic moments in childhood where I felt invincible. Edward, who had chosen to remain stretched out on our picnic blanket, had turned on his back to watch me. I recalled the pleasure on his face as he observed my transformation.

"Watch this!" Kate twirled in the air and landed with a peal of laughter. "Just try it once, please." She stood and extended her hand.

I swallowed, remembering that sensation and longing for it. I glanced toward the door as I slipped off my shoes. It was irrational. Unreasonable. But once more, I wanted to do something forbidden. Taking one giant step, I hoisted myself to the settee. Holding hands, we alternated jumps. Kate's hair floated in the air, while my braided loops hit my ears. For a moment, I was free. Free from society, free from my father's expectation to remarry.

Kate suddenly gasped and plopped to a sitting position. Still standing, I turned to see my father with Isaac, Henry, Mr. Addams, and James all standing wide-eyed in the doorway.

As soon as I slid down the back of the settee, Kate buried her face on my shoulder, giggling.

"Julia." My father entered, smiling, but it was stiff. "Mr. Auburn and Mr. Addams wish to bid you good-bye." He looked over his shoulder at Henry and, in a cold voice, said, "As you can attest for yourself, my daughter is happy. Isaac, see these men removed from my home, then finalize the arrangements

for Katherine. She returns home today as well." My father nodded to Kate. "Give your mother my greetings."

I slid my arm through hers and held her close. Kate looked
horrified but had enough sense not to protest with my father
present.

I swallowed my anguish, already feeling her loss.

Henry perceived my thoughts. As my father exited, Henry
gave him an indignant stare from across the room. With both
hands, Kate clasped my arm and turned to Isaac. Panic coated
her voice. "I can't return home. Mama's not home yet."

Lord Dalry extended his arm, gesturing for her to come with
him. "Lord Pierson sent his messenger. Our mother is expecting you tonight." Looking over his shoulder, he said to James,
"Hudson and Brown are occupied. Is there a stable hand who
might take her?"

"You can't send me home." Kate pounded fisted hands into
her lap. "I won't go. I won't. Julia needs me. Nobody else pays
any attention to her! Or loves her! I'm not leaving."

Again, Henry's eyes met mine.

Isaac colored. "Kate, you are not to say another word. If you
do not come this instant, I'll withhold your allowance for two
months."

With tears welling in her eyes, Kate glanced at Henry and Mr.
Addams, then raced from the room, followed by her brother.

Henry stepped toward the door to close it. "Devon, give me
a minute alone with Julia. Rap on the door if someone comes."

Mr. Addams gasped. "Henry, don't risk it! He'll be furious."

"Oh, hush! Are you my nursemaid now too? If you don't
leave, I can promise you, I'll remain in London for the entire
holiday, just to spite you."

Mr. Addams shoved his hat on his head with a frown but
thankfully stomped from the chamber. Henry faced me and
indicated James with a roll of his eyes.

"James, you may leave," I ordered.

"Your father—"

I clenched my teeth. "Now, James!"

He gave a cold bow. "Yes, Miss Pierson, but the door remains open." Then in a stiff manner, he likewise withdrew.

Alone, Henry wasted no time. He stepped close and gathered me. "Your father is difficult. As I know no one else will tell you what transpired, here's the gist. So long as your father is your protection, he'll have you play your role to the end. So in essence, you've traded one cage for another, and by golly, I'll not stand for it. What does any of this matter to us? Come with me. I'll oversee you and Edward to Scotland, and we'll figure this out amongst ourselves."

My longing was so sharp, I pressed against Henry's shoulder, scarcely able to contain it. I could be in Edward's arms in two days' time, and this ordeal would be over. Yet it would be moving backwards. Hiding solved nothing. Henry was generous, but did we want to live in a fashion where we continuously drained his purse? I pictured dark winters, living in poor quarters and constant fear.

"I can't," I said. "It's still trading this cage for yet another. Macy has got to be dealt with first. This is the only sphere in which we have a ghost of a chance of winning."

"Let them sort it out amongst themselves, Juls. You didn't create this. They did. It's not your responsibility. If you don't come now, he's going to force you to wed Dalry."

"If my only recourse is to be Julia Pierson, then I do what every other daughter does. I refuse to budge. I wear my father down and force him to accept my choice." I gave a derisive laugh, forming my plan as I spoke. "To think, after all this time, I actually have something worth offering Edward."

"Dash the money," Henry whispered. "You know as well as I do it would never suit him anyway."

"Yes, but neither does living on his brother's charity. Since we've gambled everything already, we may as well complete it."

"Henry." Mr. Addams's nervous voice carried through the door.

Henry's mouth twisted with indecision.

"Go." I shoved him a step toward the door. "Before we get caught."

He reached into his pocket and retrieved a small brown package and a book with a frayed cover. He shoved them into my hands. "They're from Edward. It's his personal Bible, Julia, filled with his notations. It took him weeks to convince me to bring it to you. He's consumed most of his waking life studying it. He insisted. He's afraid his good work will be lost on you if you have no instruction."

I averted my gaze, for my tears were private. Mr. Addams rapped on the door.

Henry kissed my cheek. "If you like, I can go find Lord Dalry and flatten him for you."

I gave a weak laugh, knowing he wanted one, then hugged his neck. "Give Elizabeth my love. Tell Edward I am ever his."

But Henry did not leave. "I don't like this, Juls. It feels wrong leaving you here."

"It's only until something is done with Macy; then we force my father to accept Edward. If he won't, I'll allow you to steal me."

Mr. Addams rapped again.

"Go!" I kissed his cheek and clutched Edward's presents against my body for strength as Henry's footsteps receded.

❧

"Good night, Daughter." My father leaned down and kissed my head. He smelled of the softened cloves he chewed for his breath before social engagements. "We'll be out late. Do not wait up."

It was the first time he'd bidden me farewell since my encounter with Mr. Macy. Suspecting it had something to do with Henry's visit that afternoon, I paused in my sewing to consider him. His best cloak was layered over formal attire. He wore low but elegant boots and colored silk cravats pinned by a diamond. Behind him, Isaac waited in the doorway, just as elaborately dressed. Looking that dapper, they had to be going to a ball.

Wistfulness gathered as I envisioned a London Christmas ball. As a young girl, I'd dreamed of attending a ball here at yuletide. I ducked my head. "May I go?"

Though my father's words were soft, his tone brooked no arguments. "I think not."

"Please?"

My father censured me with a look before he turned. "No dallying, Isaac. I promised the Cavendars you'd persuade the Whites to our side beforehand."

Isaac acknowledged him but knelt at my side. "Are you all right being alone, after seeing Henry?"

Not wanting to foster closeness, I returned to my chain stitches. "I'm fine."

"I'll try to schedule time with you tomorrow." Lord Dalry rose and left. His footsteps rang as he hurried after my father.

Kinsley, who had been standing by the hearth, harrumphed. "Stuffy old party, if you ask me," he said. "Nothing of interest for a young lady, all dancing and staying up."

His words brought a smile to my lips.

"Shall I fetch tea?"

"No. I'll be fine. Go enjoy your evening." When he left, I set aside my sewing and pulled Edward's gifts from the sewing basket.

On the velvet couch, I gingerly removed the gift and Bible from Edward. Part of me longed to sit in the firelight and savor this moment, but I couldn't forget my father burning my letters at Maplecroft. If I were to be caught, I knew I could not bear losing this. My hands shook as I removed a hairpin to slit open his letter.

Juls,

I've but a moment to pen this, as Henry—ever himself—is impatient. How can I speak even a fraction of my heart? I long to give advice, assurances of love, and bits of news. Close your eyes, Juls, and know them. Our souls have ever been one.

I pray these gifts please you. With Henry and Elizabeth's upcoming nuptials, Mother retrieved my grandmother's jewelry, giving us the task of dividing it. Considering you have an emerald mine, I wanted nothing to do with it. I knew your heart and my own would be the same—that Elizabeth should have them. Henry, of course, was adamant the matter be fair. It wasn't until I saw this item that we could reach any sort of an agreement. I took this for you. Elizabeth is to have the rest. I believe you will find it useful, living with your father.

I also am sending my Bible. If it insults rather than ministers, I beg you not burn it, but preserve it until we next meet. As you'll see, it contains my thoughts as well as any journal could. I pray for you every day; I likewise search the papers for news. I am proud to think of my Julia succeeding in that circle. I am well. Do not fret for me. I wish you the best Christmas with a deeper understanding than of previous ones. You know my unspoken thoughts. I need not say more.

Merry Christmas,
Edward

Four times I read the letter. While tears wet my cheeks, I treasured each word. It was the courage I needed. Thankfully, there was no hint he gave merit to the rumors about Isaac.

I turned over the package wrapped in simple brown paper that was so much like Edward those days. Plain, with nothing to mark him a gentleman, yet containing a heart that was a treasure.

Gently, I pulled loose the paper, which had been fitted perfectly around the box. Inside, nestled in a plain muslin handkerchief, lay an heirloom timepiece made of white gold and elaborately etched with flowers and filigree. Small diamonds encrusted the center of each flower. It was attached to a bar pin that supported four sizable pearls. I cupped it in my hand, feeling the weight. It was beautiful. So exquisite. I could have cried, wishing he had sold it. He lived in need, whereas I lacked nothing. I wound the watch and held it to my ear. It ticked as gently as fine rain.

I pinned the watch to my dress, then touched the frayed cover of the Bible. I'd sworn so faithfully never to open a Bible in my lifetime. Not even Isaac had been able to persuade me to look inside one as we drilled for my presentation.

I gave a weepy laugh. It was perhaps the lowest thing Edward had ever done to me. He knew I wouldn't be able to resist *this* Bible.

"Who or what are you," I whispered in a prayer to its author, "that makes everyone think I should heed this?"

I regretted the prayer almost instantly, for the same sensation that I'd felt in Eastbourne's chapel swept over me. An almost-palpable sense that something unapproachable and unlimited turned its full attention to my prayer. The impression was so real that chills spread over my body.

I chose not to attend it, like those who hear noises in the dead of night and refuse to speculate further, lest their thoughts take unwelcome directions.

Instead, I opened the Bible and was surprised and delighted to find Edward's scrawl. The first pages were a marriage index, filled out in various ink colors. As I read, I realized they were records of those he'd married. My eyes landed on the last entry: *Mr. and Mrs. Chance Macy.* Compared to the other names, his handwriting was erratic and the ink blotched.

I turned the page. It was filled with burials. The list was filled and carried over to the blank pages. I scanned through the names, hoping no one I knew had died, but one entry made my heart still.

Stillborn from workhouse—no one but myself attended the grave

I touched the words, seeing his face knit with grief as he stood alone, tending sheep no one else would. All at once, I became one with Edward. I felt his grief and joined him in it.

My fingers hovered over the book as though the pages were holy and not mere words. When I dared, I flipped through sections. Everywhere, Edward had scrawled notes, revealing his thoughts and heart.

I laughed softly as I grew teary. How could he have sent this to me? It was apparent he'd kept it since his Oxford days. This had to be his dearest possession. I clutched it against my chest, aching at the overwhelming feeling of love.

What if Mr. Addams was right that a divine hand was at work? What if, like Oedipus, no matter what Edward and I did, we would never overcome our fate? I sank against the back of the couch, tucked in my knees, and clutched the Bible against myself as I pondered the earlier sensation. William Elliston's teaching writhed against the notion of praying, but Mama always had. What if it was possible to be heard? What would I say? It took several minutes to compose my first thought-out prayer, which now amuses me.

"I'll serve you," I eventually whispered, "but only if you give me Edward."

It was at that moment I felt it.

An unease filled me—one that went against all rationale, all prior experiences. It was as if every fiber within my body rose up with a strong cry that far more was at work than I could understand and that I shouldn't presume to bargain my soul in such a manner—that to do so violated principles whose existence I had not yet fathomed.

The conviction was so heavy, I marveled that the entire world was not crushed beneath the weight of it, and yet so full of mourning and grief that no wail or requiem could ever capture the full dolor of it.

I'd heard stories of revivals and awakenings, where mankind touched the untouchable and birthed a resurgence of religious zeal. But those, I knew, depended upon the charisma of the speaker and the contagious fervor of the crowd.

But this! What could explain this?

It was.

I had to take a deep breath to contain the rush of the knowledge of the gravity that surrounded my situation. Mine was a different story, with a different purpose, and therefore woven in darker colors. There was no gradual revelation. It was stark and plain before me. Nothing less than a full surrender would suffice. If that meant losing Edward, marrying Isaac, or even returning to Mr. Macy—the choice wouldn't be mine.

Twenty-One

⁂

THE NEXT SEVERAL DAYS found me agitated. While servants hung mistletoe and holly, I paced London House in silence, my thoughts burdensome. The scent of fir filled the air as I mentally wrestled with the phenomenon I'd experienced.

I disliked that I couldn't prove it; it annoyed me that had someone told me he'd experienced such an anomaly, I would have dismissed him; and it chafed me that I had felt it and knew it was real.

I paid no heed to my father and Isaac as they hastened to engagements with empty promises that perhaps later they'd visit me. I only pulled my shawl tighter and watched them leave, feeling out of sorts. It was easier to accept the unnameable sensation I'd felt in Eastbourne—that, at least, was almost marvelous, like a dream one wanted to walk into.

But this?

Who wanted this? Too much exposure would drive any soul to wearing camel's hair and eating locusts. How easily I now pictured Edward tearing down pews and rending his garments.

Foolish was it to mock him, and wise to join him. But who had joined him? Elizabeth and Henry despaired, while Lady Foxmore taunted. How could anyone join him without experiencing what I had?

And that, too, agitated me.

The fact that the experience was personal, and not transferrable, galled me. If this was how the universe worked, and we were going to be held accountable to *that*, then how dare the rest of humanity be left in blindness for lack of experience!

I longed to reject God on that idea alone.

I longed for Edward to explain. It seemed such a monstrosity. Yet he had managed to bridge it, while I still couldn't. How could I? Here was a God who forced prophets to marry prostitutes, and the only terms of my acceptance involved a full surrender to him and his plan?

I was in such a state of mind when my father summoned me to join him in the library.

I'd been in the parlor, sitting in the window seat, staring outdoors. When James fetched me, I stood, trying to remember when my father and Isaac had returned home, for I had not heard them.

I entered the library and found Isaac and Mr. Forrester taking leave of my father. Looking grave, Isaac tried to catch my eye, but I avoided him.

He lingered, placing his hand on the doorjamb. "Please, sir, with your permission, I'd prefer to be here for this talk."

My father released a long sigh, staring at the papers. "Thank you, but no, Isaac."

Lord Dalry shifted. "All right, then I object. I think I have as much right to hear what's said—"

"Thank you, Isaac. Your request is noted but denied." My father straightened the papers by tapping them on the chair arm. "You're dismissed. I'll fetch you when we're finished."

"Sir—"

"No arguments. She is not your wife but my daughter, and I'll do as I see fit."

Isaac briefly frowned but left, softly shutting the door.

Alarmed by that introduction, I pulled my shawl tight.

Settled in a high-backed chair, my father thumbed through a sheaf of parchment. He thumped the papers in his hand twice with his thumb and set them down. Looking as though his arms were weighted, he poured himself a drink, then acknowledged me.

"Here." He blew out the candle on the desk, stood, and retreated to the window with his drink in hand. Once there, he motioned me to join him. When I reached him, he tapped the glass. "Now watch. These are the people who are affected by the choices Parliament makes."

I looked at the befogged streets, but there wasn't anyone there. I glanced back, but his gaze was fixed on the emptiness. I pulled my shawl as tight as it would stretch and tucked in my arms, uncertain how to act. A few carriages rattled past, stirring the mist. Still he said nothing but sipped brandy and waited. Eventually, a young girl carrying a broom ran by. She clutched a ragged shawl to her chin.

"She's the new street sweeper for the corner of Audley and Chap," my father said, watching her. "It's extraordinary that she hasn't been chased away by the stronger lads. She's had three black eyes, but thus far she manages to keep her post. I instruct James to pay her an extra penny when we pass. Never forget how lucky you truly are to be amongst the privileged. There are far worse things than having to follow protocol."

I felt pulled down by heaviness as I watched. The temperature was low tonight. The girl looked scarcely eleven. Too young to be out in a city in the dead of night. Yet I didn't understand why my father had me here.

My father took a piece of touchwood from the fire and returned to the desk, where he relit the candle, set down his drink, and rubbed tired eyes. "You're here because Isaac insists that you agree to the terms set forth for your betrothal before he signs it."

Trepidation swept over my body, turning my extremities to ice. "What?"

My father strummed his fingers. "It's high time this matter was settled, and tonight I intend to see it through. Are you going to accept Isaac as your husband, or should I look for another?"

Astonished, I raised my gaze. "Is that why Forrester is here? So you can announce it to the papers? What about Mr. Macy?"

"Unless that is your way of asking me to consider Macy's offer seriously, he does not figure into our plans."

I bent my head, feeling sick. "Our plans? What about what I want? What about Reverend Auburn?"

My father removed his gold pocket watch and opened the face. "Privilege comes at a price. You are my heir, my continuation. This is your last chance to have any say in the matter. You have one minute to decide if you will marry Isaac. When I leave this room, I will either announce your willingness to become engaged to Isaac or seal a marriage contract to another."

I coughed to cover my shock. "And I have no say in the matter?"

My father stopped strumming and consulted the clock. "You still have fifty-five seconds left of it."

"What if I refuse to marry anyone except Reverend Auburn?"

"I am not going to quibble about the finer points, but do you seriously doubt this matter will end to my satisfaction?"

The idea had seemed so certain when I spoke it aloud to Henry, but as I stood before my father, it appeared almost naive. I felt ready to fragment. If I agreed to marry Isaac, there would be no easy way to back out. Ten precious seconds passed. A tear strayed down my cheek, and I folded my hands over my stomach. "Tell Isaac I will marry him."

"Do you wish to see the terms?" He slid the papers on his left toward me.

I shook my head, despising him.

My father rose, the rich scent of cloves surrounding him. "Then endeavor to make him a good wife. Do not make him regret his willingness to marry you, despite your circumstances."

I fixed my gaze on my father's boots, wishing I'd never met him. Behind him, Mama's sunflower painting reminded me that I still didn't know their story, but I knew he'd managed to douse the fire that once burned in her too.

A white silk handkerchief appeared in my view. "Wipe your nose and eyes. Smile when Isaac asks you."

"He'll know it's not genuine."

"Just obey. He'll respect your attempt. It will serve to assure him you'll play your part."

I crumpled the handkerchief in my hand; then when he left, I tossed it into the crackling flames. Desperate to feel removed from this situation, I flung myself into a nearby chair.

Everything had happened so quickly. I scarcely understood life anymore. My beliefs had just been toppled, and I was no longer sure what I should or shouldn't do.

I hadn't even surrendered myself to God. If I had, would I have known what to say to my father?

"Julia?" Isaac's voice sounded from the door.

Crumbling, I buried my face in my hands.

He must have grabbed the blanket slung over a nearby chair and brought it with him. For he gently wrapped it about my shoulders, then knelt before me. He took my hands in his and kissed the backs of them.

"Your father tells me you accepted the engagement. Speak truthfully. Were you coerced?"

I sobbed a desperate, wild sob.

He sighed, stroking the back of my hand with his thumb. "Be honest with me, Julia. Have I any hope of ever gaining your love?"

Tears welled as I clutched his hand. "If I refuse you tonight, one way or another, my father will see me engaged."

"Have I any chance of winning your heart?"

I spread my hands. I no longer understood the universe or life. Everything was off course. "I don't know. How can I possibly know under these circumstances?"

Lord Dalry's thoughts were his own as he considered my words. "No true gentleman could accept an engagement under these conditions. Allow me to court you, Julia. All I ask is a chance to win your love."

I could scarcely read his face between the blur of my tears. "But my father—"

"I'll handle your father. I have my ways. If the situation grows dire, we'll discuss changing our agreement. Meantime, at least allow me the chance to gain your trust and devotion."

Prior to Henry's visit, I would have refused. But nothing made sense anymore. I had been wrong in my beliefs. What if I was wrong about everything? What if this was what was supposed to happen?

"Do you agree?" he asked.

Sniffling, I nodded.

He reached out and touched Edward's pin. "Is this a gift from Reverend Auburn?"

My eyes widened as I wondered how he knew. "Yes."

"The first morning I see you without this pin, I'll know that you are truly ready to accept a betrothal. On that day, I will ask you to marry me. Agreed?"

How could I not agree? It was more time. I nodded.

The blanket fell from my shoulder and he replaced it. He rose, kissed the top of my head. "I'll go speak with your father now."

⁓

"Miss Pierson." Miss Moray shook me.

In the grey of dawn, she looked like an angular shadow holding a beeswax candle. The draperies of my bed parted around her, allowing a draft of cold air. My head felt thrice its usual weight. "Yes?"

"Master Isaac bids me to dress you and have you downstairs. I have ten minutes."

I sat, groggy. "Ten minutes? Why?"

She made no reply as she withdrew a woollen dress from my armoire. I frowned at her but threw off my coverlets and stepped into the freezing air. I owed Isaac anything he wanted for his kindness toward me. Near the hearth, I shivered as Miss Moray exchanged my nightgown for the dress. Keeping her eye on the clock, she managed to button me quickly for once, then twisted my hair into a simple bun.

"Go without jewelry," she stated, draping a cashmere scarf over my head. "Now hurry. There's no time for more."

"No!" I opened my jewelry box and started to sort through its contents for Edward's pin. The last thing I needed was for Isaac to think I wished an engagement on Christmas Day.

The sound of servants scurrying about their duties filled the house as I exited my bedchamber. Lord Dalry stood in the foyer, dressed in a cape so long it brushed the floor. It made him look like a prince in a faerie tale. It was Isaac as I rarely saw him. Natural and at ease. It was impossible not to smile, especially as I'd promised to make an attempt. I leaned over the banister. "Sir, why have you awakened me?"

He grinned up. "You look as beautiful as the Madonna herself with that scarf over your head. No, don't remove it. I like it. Hurry downstairs, for we haven't much time."

Lifting my long skirt, so as not to trip, I obeyed. When I reached him, his eyes fastened on Edward's watch and his smile tightened. "Here." He held my white cape open for me. "We're going outdoors."

"Outside?" I slid my arms through the satin-lined cape. "My father is allowing it?"

Isaac laughed, wrapping his arms about me as he buttoned my cape. Near my ear he whispered, "He doesn't know."

I did my best not to stiffen. "And our chaperone?"

"We're not going far." His warm fingers took mine, and he drew me toward the front door. "I want it to be just us."

Even the air smelled different as he opened the entrance. I tightened my fingers around his. A new London glittered under a milky sky. It had snowed during the night. Snow softened every roofline, every cobblestone, harmonizing the city, concealing the drab browns of London. The white blanket had muffled the sounds of the city so that only faint bells and gentle noises greeted us.

"You won't often see snow in London, so take a good look," Isaac said, but his eyes were on me. "Soon servants will tend fires and horses will stir up the streets and our world will be brown again. Since it's going to be marred, let's be the first to make tracks."

"What a scandal we could make," I said, glancing at the windows of residences as we walked down the street, holding hands. "The Emerald Heiress and Lord Dalry playing in the snow."

He laughed outright, his breath frosting the air. "My uncle lives in the north. Ben, Kate, and I used to take sleds up his hills and fly down. We were too old last visit, so Kate and I snuck out and went sledding after dark."

"You! I'm surprised you allowed her to act so unladylike."

His eyes sparkled. "Don't think I'm not going to insist my wife join me next time. Yes, you may as well look that horrified because I'm perfectly serious. You need more merriment in your life." He turned toward me, placing his hands on my waist, under my cape. "I look forward to hearing your shrieks of laughter when we spill into a snowbank. I've not forgotten the way you jumped on that settee with Kate. I know merriment is still inside you, and I intend to find the key."

He leaned near, his eyes closing, about to kiss me. My heart pounded, but not with adoration. Since that unutterable experience, my world had turned chaotic, but to kiss Isaac would still be to betray Edward. All at once, I recalled Macy's last words to me. I had only to step outdoors when I was finished with my father, and his men would find me. My breath curled in the air as I panicked.

"Take me back. Take me back, please." I clutched Isaac's cape at his chest, nearly crying. "Please. Do not delay."

Seemingly disappointed, he drew me close. "All right. We'll return right now."

Clumps of snow clung to the bottom of my skirt as we hastened homeward. As we neared, I caught sight of my father peering from his library window. His jaw dropped upon spying us, and from his angry expressions and the movements of his mouth, I deemed that he shouted.

Isaac laughed and waved, then tugged my hand. "Come on. We'll enter through the servants' door, giving him a chance to cool before dealing with him."

"He'll be livid."

"Have I ever led you wrong, even once?"

"No, but—"

Isaac removed his hat, leading me down to the lower entrance. "Believe me, your father will not lecture either one of us today. Tomorrow, though, is another story."

We stepped into a dank corridor. Linens and aprons dripped from a clothesline just over the door, making the first steps icy. Scents of oyster, poultry, parsley, and butter filled the narrow hall along with the clang of pots. Each step toward the noise increased the amount of grease built up over the floor. I clenched my skirt, holding it above the grime, casting Isaac anxious looks. It was unheard of for a lady of my station to enter the servants' world.

When we reached the kitchen, haze from the fires made me want to sweep an invisible veil from my eyes. The dense air became choking.

"I'm going to introduce you to Pierrick," Isaac said as we drew closer to the clatter of pots rattling and knives chopping.

We rounded the corner. My father's kitchen occupied at

least a quarter of the lowest level of the house. Bowls, pots, and cutting boards spread over long wooden tables. High-backed chairs were pushed against walls. The walls were lined with long shelves holding serving platters and plates. Copper measuring pitchers and utensils hung upon brass hooks. In the far corner, there were two beds with straw pushing through the ticking.

The scullery girl at the opposite end of the room spotted us first and stopped working, her hands still plunged into the wooden sink. Piled around her were dirty dishes. Her drenched dress clung to her bony body, and perspiration streaked her face.

On my right, upper and lower maids sat around a table set with bread, cheese, and what looked like a weak tea. They rose, wide-eyed, and bobbed, stumbling over various forms of greetings which equated to "Merry Christmas."

"And a merry Christmas to you." Isaac rested his fingers on his lips and signalled for them to sit back down. Then catching my eye, he pointed toward a burly man with his back toward us. He was cutting apart a lamb with a cleaver, leaving splatters of blood on the wall. Next to him, underchefs paused in their work, leaving the lids of copper pots to rattle, as steam and bubbling water lifted them.

"Pierrick, how dare you ignore me!" Isaac yelled to be heard over the cacophony of noise. "Did you make it?"

The chef turned, holding his cleaver. "Did I make it? Did I make it?" He threw his hands in the air. "No 'Merry Christmas'; just did I make it?"

"Yes, yes, merry Christmas, my good man. Now did you make it?"

I could only stare at Isaac. I'd never seen him act so ordinary.

"Of course." Pierrick studied me with a discriminating gaze. "So you managed to convince the princess to come down to our world. Does her father know?"

"I told you I would introduce you to her, and of course he doesn't know," Isaac said. "I don't see it. You did follow the directions, didn't you? I've not forgotten that you tried to switch recipes last year. Where is it?"

The chef threw down his cleaver and wiped his hands on his apron, smearing it red. "I sent James with it to the breakfast table." He nodded to me. "Is today the day?"

Isaac silenced him with a look. "No. Thank you for making my request."

"Au revoir, Miss Pierson," Pierrick said. "I made a lemon sauce to dish over the vile, dry food his mother calls ginger-bread. I make the recipe the way Master Isaac likes, but I am no responsible for such a common cake. My sauce will help."

"Did you have to ruin my surprise?" Isaac called over his shoulder.

"What? That you have no taste when it comes to the finer foods?"

"It's a tradition in my family," Isaac said under his breath to me as we left the kitchen. "We'll enjoy this every Christmas morning from this point forward, but I wanted to give you the chance to deem whether you liked it for yourself."

Each word pricked my conscience. He was so certain he would win my heart.

"You can know that, far away, Mother and Kate are partaking of it too," he said, entering the main hall. Then with a smile, "Shush. Here comes your father."

"Breakfast started ten minutes ago," my father said, strid-ing into the hall, wearing a deep frown. Traces of his anger still blotched his neck and forehead.

"Oh, well," Isaac said, removing my cape.

"Isaac, you shouldn't have taken her out—"

"If you please, spare me the lecture." Isaac gestured for me to start toward the breakfast table. "And call me Lord Dalry. You may call her Miss Pierson."

I paused, expecting my father's wrath to fall.

"Well, Lord Dalry," my father finally said, "at least you're wearing attire this year."

"It would hardly be suitable to wear my nightclothes in your daughter's presence, sir." When we entered the room, James stepped forward to pull out my chair, but Isaac stopped him. "No, James. Lord Pierson wishes to serve Julia this morning. He'll seat her."

"You're determined to make this day miserable for me, aren't you?" my father asked, yanking my chair from the table.

Isaac laughed. "Had you even attempted to act less severe when your daughter arrived, I might have had mercy on you today. Would you like your father to fetch you tea or coffee, Julia?"

I feared to answer.

"I don't believe Miss Pierson knows the Christmas rules," James said from the sideboard, grinning.

My mouth dropped. Surely he'd be ordered from the room for addressing us.

"No, it doesn't look as if she does." Isaac offered me a smile. "Shall we let her in on the fun, James? You see, on Christmas I run the household. Isn't that correct, Roy?"

My father bowed with a sigh. "Yes, Lord Dalry."

"Isaac is in charge?" I faced my father.

"Yes, Miss Pierson, but Lord Dalry is quite mistaken if he thinks I'm going to play footman to my daughter."

"Oh yes, you will." Isaac selected the *Times*, opened it, and propped his feet on a chair. "And you'll obey any request she makes this morning. And if you behave, I'll not make you serve Lady Beatrice when she arrives for dinner today."

My father scowled.

"So we don't have to be on time for breakfast?" I asked.

"We don't have to be anything." Isaac turned the page. "Go ahead, Julia. I'm dying to see what sort of footman your father makes."

I laughed nervously and looked at my father. Would he really serve me? "I would like tea this morning, Roy."

"Lord Dalry, I draw the line at my daughter calling me Roy."

"Footmen aren't allowed to address us," Isaac said in a sing-song voice, never looking up from the paper.

My father shook his head, then yanked the steaming rose teapot from the sideboard. "Will there be anything else, Miss Pierson?"

I bit my lip and looked at Isaac. How far could this game go? "So James would be allowed to sit at Father's place and join us."

Isaac acted like my father by not removing his gaze from the paper. "Do you wish it?"

My father shot me a warning look.

"Yes."

Isaac closed the paper. "Very well, then. James, will you be so kind as to join us? Roy, set another place at the table."

༄

That afternoon, I descended the stairs an overdressed doll—the green velvet gown a Christmas present from my father. It was so pompous I felt certain Lady Beatrice had overseen its making. Likely she was punishing me for never calling on her after my debut. I felt ridiculous as the hair that had been parted and piled in ringlets bounced with each step.

"Ah, I hear Julia now." My father's voice carried from the front parlor.

He entered the foyer, and I could tell by his grimace he'd already warred with Lady Beatrice. He gestured for me to hurry, then pulled me into the room by my arm. Lady Beatrice sat by the fire, looking as tart as ever.

"Grandmamma." I curtsied.

Her mouth twitched, and she tapped her finger against the chair arm as she turned her head, ignoring me.

"Julia will entertain." My father placed his hands on my

shoulders and pushed me into the center of the room. "I have work, but I look forward to seeing everyone at dinner."

"Work?" a male voice asked from a corner. "Work on Christmas, Cousin?"

"Do not presume to question me, Eramus," my father growled. "I said I have work to do. That means I have work." He shut the door with a bang.

My skin prickled. The name had terrified Kate and brought Isaac home early. Curious to finally see him for myself, I slowly turned.

A portly young man leaned against the window frame with a bored expression. A large mole sat between his eyebrows, and heavy-lidded eyes added to his snobbish expression. "So." He rolled a sovereign between his podgy fingers. "We're supposed to be long-lost cousins."

I drew myself to my full height. Except that I found him ugly, there was nothing fearsome about him. "Eramus Calvin?"

"At your service." He puckered his mouth, viewing me as if he found me equally as ugly. "Come kiss me, for we are related."

Lady Beatrice humphed from her chair.

He was testing me. But why? Something about Eramus brought out everything averse in me. He reminded me of a goblin prince Mama read about who only dined on fattened spiders and sour milk. Summoning courage, I kissed his fleshy cheek.

When I drew back, he rubbed off my kiss with his lace handkerchief. "Thank goodness, dear, old Pierson is pawning you off on Isaac," he muttered under his breath, and then louder, "Do you play chess?"

"The thought is mutual," I whispered back. Then, in my speaking voice, "No, I do not." Which was not entirely true. I'd been taught but never enjoyed it.

"Well, there's nothing else here that interests me." Eramus gestured to a set board. "Lose a few games."

"I need company," Lady Beatrice protested.

"Shall I sit with you instead?" I asked. "When Isaac arrives, he can play chess with Eramus."

She closed her eyes as if suddenly napping and unable to hear me.

Eramus collected my arm. "So you call the family leech by his given name already? How can you tolerate him?" Eramus sat at the chessboard and, with bloated fingers, touched the tops of the ivory pieces. "Tell me, which one of these pieces best suits you?"

I dropped into my seat, and my ostentatious dress billowed around me as high as my chest, forcing me to push it down. "I have not the pleasure of understanding you, sir."

"Please, no flowery language." Eramus rolled the king between his fingers. "It's bad enough we're forced to suffer one another's company without having to flatter and cajole each other. You know what I mean." He spread his hand over the board.

I studied the chessmen. Which piece was I? Between Mr. Macy and my father, the answer was clear. My eyes settled on the front row.

Footsteps swelled, running toward our door. Isaac burst into the room with a wild look. A glint of pleasure filled Eramus's eyes. "How do you stand living under the same roof with such an uncultured clod, Cousin?" Then turning, he said, "Temper, temper, Isaac. I've not touched your precious bride-to-be."

"Excuse me." I rose.

Eramus moved his pawn. "Oops. The game has already started. It's ill-bred to leave now."

I glanced at Isaac for direction, but he only yanked on his waistcoat and gave me a look that asked whether I wished to be rescued or play it out. I sighed, plopped down, and combated the billows of my dress again.

With his disciplined look, Isaac sat across from Lady Beatrice and made inquiries after her health. With the air of a victim, she sighed a long string of complaints.

"Pathetic, aren't they?" Eramus asked, looking at them.

I gave him my most sullen look and moved my pawn. "Merry Christmas to you too."

～

James touched the match to the plum pudding and jumped back as it burst into flames. Eramus leaned around the display and repeated his last request. "You still haven't granted me permission to take Julia out, Cousin."

My father waited until the pudding had been snuffed before replying. "I think not, Eramus. Julia doesn't care for the theatre."

"Then why did she look like a beggar eyeing a shilling?" Eramus reached out and patted my hand next to my plate, smirking at Isaac.

Isaac gritted his teeth and glared. All during dinner, Eramus had taken jabs at Isaac. When James presented me with a platter, Eramus would dish my food, selecting my cuts, licking his fingers between each presented dish so his saliva mingled with my food, taking away my appetite.

"Why are you debating me?" My father sank his knife deep into the pudding. "I told you, Julia despises the theatre. I'm not going to force her to go."

"Then where shall I take you, Cousin?" Eramus propped his elbow on the table. "Choose anywhere you'd like. The opera? A ball? A soiree?"

"As if I would allow Julia to go anywhere with the likes of you," Isaac finally said. The first words he'd spoken during dinner.

"You forget, as her blood relative, I don't require a chaperone. You needn't worry; I know Pierson intends her for you. But there's no reason why she must remain cooped indoors while you make the rounds to the clubs." Eramus smiled at me. "Besides, having the toast of the season at my side will help my standing considerably."

"And paying your debts would help even more," Isaac replied in a crisp tone.

Eramus blinked at him like a frog. "Well, Cousin, where shall I take you next time they abandon you? You are aware that Isaac dances with all the pretty girls while you're home . . ." He shrugged as if not being able to guess what I did.

My father curled his lip, warning him to stop.

"I would have thought you'd show Eramus more appreciation, Roy." Lady Beatrice spoke from her place near the hearth. "He's done nothing but dote on your daughter since he's arrived. And it's perfectly true what he says. Everyone is a-gossip about how she never leaves the house."

Eramus took a bite of pudding. "I haven't the slightest idea what to say when asked about it. At my club there are rumors that you keep bars on her window."

My father tapped his spoon against the table. "No one actually said that!"

Lady Beatrice laughed. "There are worse rumors tied to this strange situation. London is whispering, Roy. Do you think it's gone unnoticed that except for one ball, she hasn't been seen publicly?"

"James, bring me a Scotch." My father shoved his pudding away.

"Drinking won't amend the situation," Lady Beatrice mocked. "Her absence in society is commented on at every breakfast, tea, and card game I attend. I can scarcely take a stroll without an inquiry as to whether she'll attend an upcoming event."

"Sir." Isaac's calm voice caused us all to look at him. "It's true. She needs to come out again."

"All right," my father finally conceded, accepting the Scotch. "All right. She'll go to Lady Koop's soiree with us, Isaac."

"Well, it's a start," Eramus said. "As long as I get to show her off next." He raised his wineglass to me. "Cheers."

Twenty-Two

❦

VOICES MURMURED beyond the entry hall, where the butler gave greeting as his footmen relieved us of our wraps. Feeling all nerves, I faced Isaac. He stood with one hand behind his back—poised and detached. When he felt my gaze upon him, he gave me a brief, loving smile before returning to his trained demeanor.

Until that moment, I'd not realized how intimate we'd become in private.

"Julia." My father offered his arm and led me toward our hosts standing amongst palm branches just inside the reception room. The Koops looked nothing like their stationery, which was large and grand.

"Roy, what a lovely surprise!" Lady Koop's earrings and necklaces glittered as her chest swelled with pride. "You've brought your daughter."

My father grunted, but Isaac greeted her amicably, making up for my father's lack of social grace. I gave her a shy smile, clinging to my father's arm.

Before Isaac finished his inquiries, my father started toward the gathering but then halted.

Less than a yard away, Macy conversed with a gentleman. Three young ladies surrounded them, all trying to position themselves to catch Macy's attention.

Candlelight highlighted Macy's fetching appearance and deep-set eyes as he looked up and became aware of me. A seductive smile curved his lips before he disengaged himself. Keeping his gaze strictly on my father, he approached and bowed, then spoke quietly. "Roy." His handsome features filled with affection as he viewed me. "I'm glad to see my wife out. For her sake, I'll remove myself and find another soiree."

My father's hand tightened over my arm as I paled.

"Mr. Macy," Isaac greeted, stepping to my side and taking my arm. Macy looked at him, then clucked his tongue at me before stepping away.

Behind me, I overheard him approach Lord and Lady Koop, saying, "I fear I shall not remain."

"Why ever not?" Lady Koop sounded distressed. "Is something wrong?"

Isaac placed his hand on my shoulder and attempted to steer me out of hearing, but I refused to budge.

Mr. Macy laughed, haunting me with its sound. "Not a single thing, my dear. In fact, I'm most pleased. However, one of my strange whims has overtaken me, and I wish to depart."

"But Lord Pierson just arrived, and his daughter is with him. Aren't you interested in seeing the Emerald Heiress for yourself?"

Even Isaac ceased his attempts to remove me, curious to hear the response himself.

Macy laughed again, this time with a sardonic thread laced through his tone. "When I wish to better acquaint myself with her, I shall. In the meantime, I fear you shall not have the honor of two newspaper sensations at your little gathering. Now, if you'll excuse me."

I peered over my shoulder in time to see him touch his forehead in salute to me before he ducked out of sight.

"Are we all just going to stand here, transfixed by a liar?" My father flexed his hand, glaring at Isaac as if blaming him.

"Miss Pierson?"

We turned at the soft cry of feminine delight. Lady Northrum hastened toward us as fast as her rustling skirts allowed, her fan swinging from her wrist. "Lord Pierson." Her cheeks glowed pink as she gathered me to her for a kiss. "Will you allow me to take your daughter and make her introductions?"

A muted protest sounded behind us from Lady Koop, but etiquette demanded she remain by the door to greet guests.

"After all—" Lady Northrum lowered her voice, drawing me closer—"you are rather awkward when it comes to young ladies, sir."

Isaac broke the tension with his clear laugh. "She has a point, sir. Yes, by all means, take Miss Pierson."

My father gave her a stiff bow, making me suspect he was angry with Isaac.

"Come, my dear." Lady Northrum tugged me away, speaking to me but aiming her voice for my father to hear. "I have charges your age with me tonight. My nieces. I shall introduce you."

Traces of sandalwood occupied the atmosphere as we passed the spot where Macy had stood. I closed my eyes, feeling undone by the scent. Ever since I'd been forced to allow Isaac to court me, I never ceased to worry that I might still be married. Tonight when Macy called me his wife, no doubt had clouded his voice.

"Brava, Charlotte. Brava." A middle-aged woman stepped away from her husband. She held out shaking hands, evidencing her nervous agitation. "I felt on edge the entire time. Indeed, for half a moment, I feared I might faint. It worked just as you said it would. How did you find the nerve?"

"Hush," Lady Northrum whispered. "She doesn't know there

was a conspiracy to rescue her from her father." Then to me, "You mustn't feel alarmed. You're not being disloyal."

The other woman patted my cheek. Tears misted her eyes. "No, you mustn't feel divided about him, Miss Pierson. Your father is just horribly awkward when it comes to overseeing your introduction. We don't hold you to blame, my dear. Your penmanship alone tells us of your distress with every refusal you write. Matters of this nature do not come naturally to him. Your mother suffered under his rule too."

They stared anxiously, waiting for me to speak. I fiddled with my gloves, unwilling at first to respond. Our masks are our death, yet we don them at all cost. A good daughter, a good wife, must always show respect, whether it is deserved or not. No one knows better than a gentlewoman that during such moments her piety is judged. In such circumstances, not only is a lie the only appropriate answer, but the truth will condemn you. The faulty logic being that if one was quiet and biddable as is fitting to her gender, then naturally the other person would be benevolent and loving.

After hesitation, I gave the only socially acceptable answer. "My father is a very good man."

A man standing near us chuckled and raised his drink. "Good for you, my dear. It serves you two right, maligning Lord Pierson like that to his daughter. He'll be most pleased when I tell him how you stood up for him."

"Oh, you wouldn't," the woman I assumed to be his wife cried. "He never allows this poor lamb to go anywhere. If he thought we insulted him, she might be locked away until next season."

"Watch me," he said and departed in my father's direction.

"He's going." His wife fluttered her hand over her heart. "Oh, he's simply horrid and loves to torment me so. Hurry! Take Miss Pierson away. Do something!"

With a look of annoyance, Lady Northrum pulled me to the back of the room toward a group of young ladies who were observing us over their fans.

"Miss Pierson, may I have the pleasure of introducing you to my nieces, Miss Millicent Knight and her sister, Miss Anna Knight." Lady Northrum retreated with a nod.

The girls wore matching taffeta dresses and gave shy smiles. Anna Knight in particular met my eye with a look that reminded me of Elizabeth. They each took an arm, and more girls flocked to us.

Across the room, my father observed and visibly loosened for the first time in months. He smiled at me, then turned to conversation with the gentlemen.

"Did you see that Mr. Macy was here?" one of the girls whispered, joining our group.

"Yes." Anna Knight leaned into the group. "But he's already left. Have you ever seen anyone so handsome?"

A matron passed within hearing, and my party blushed and snapped open fans, constructing a wall of paper and lace about us.

"Did she hear?" one of the girls whispered with dread.

Millicent stood on tiptoe, looking over the tops of our heads. "I think not. Otherwise she would have gone straight to one of our mothers."

"Why?" I asked, growing cold. "Are you not allowed to speak of him?"

This was met with charged squeals. Uniformly, our group moved, a mass of tulle and satin, farther into the corner. Fans closed slightly as girls checked the location of their chaperones, then snapped open again.

"She doesn't know, does she?"

"Hush, you tell her."

"No, you!"

"Oh, you mustn't!" a girl squeaked in excitement. "What opinion will she form of us?"

A girl with a velvet headband pressed closer. "He's only recently rejoined society. He's come out of seclusion in search of his wife. She's our age and seduced Mr. Macy during the night, then on their wedding day left him for another lover!"

Blushes rose and fans fluttered.

"Dahlia, hush. Hush."

"Look, you've made her color."

"Oh, how could you say such a thing out loud, and with the Emerald—I mean, Miss Pierson present."

"Because it's true. That's why." Dahlia poked her head above the fans one more time before continuing. "But if you ask me, he deserved it. Nearly fifteen years ago, he used to be engaged to Phoebe Poole, who is now Lady Marcus. She nearly took her life in despair when one day he suddenly dropped their engagement."

I tried to mimic their pleased yet shocked expressions but felt suffocated.

"Her family tried to sue him, to force the marriage. In the end, he sent a large sum of money with a scathing letter naming her every fault, telling her he detested her and ordering her to stop writing."

Scandalized expressions succeeded squeals. My father looked over at our group, smiling.

"Mr. Macy said something about you." Dahlia hit my wrist with her fan, bringing me back to her. Mischief filled her eyes, so I deemed it was shocking.

"Stop teasing Miss Pierson." Anna Knight took my arm, defending me.

"But I'm not. Did you not see me standing near him while he spoke to Mr. McKinnett? He says he's half-considering divorcing his wife." She waited until that shock settled. "I heard him distinctly say he might marry the Emerald Heiress since she lived in a convent most of her life and wouldn't cause him problems. That's when you walked in the room. Did you not see the look he gave her? He was quite taken."

I felt as though I were falling from the highest building in

London. The advice Reynolds once gave me at Eastbourne on how to handle the rumors cycled back from memory. *"Act bothered that your time was wasted."* I forced what I intended to be a patronizing smile, but it felt strangled.

"You ladies look to be in such interesting conversation." Isaac's voice came from behind me, and I felt his warm touch on my elbow. "I thought I'd come and learn for myself what the ado is about."

Amorous eyes greeted him.

"We were telling Miss Pierson about Mr. Macy." Dahlia rested her fan over her heart, giving him a flirtatious look.

"Ah." Isaac never changed tone or expression. "The poor man's story has been splashed all over the country. Do you not think we could allow him some peace?"

Their heads drooped as though shamed, but I could see they were still admiring him.

"Miss Pierson, some of my friends from Cambridge are present. I should very much like to introduce you." Isaac addressed the girls. "If you'll excuse us, please."

With mixed feelings I left the circle.

"I saw your discomfort," Isaac said. "I'm sorry it took so long to rescue you. I was stopped along the way. There are the friends I spoke of." He pointed to three men, who immediately struck me as wellborn. From across the room, they bowed.

Pride shone over Isaac's face as we neared. A knowing look passed between the gentlemen as we were introduced. I gave them tight smiles, wondering how my life had gotten me here.

The gentlemen gave Isaac nods of approval when they thought I wouldn't notice. I looked toward the girls, who still tittered and whispered and giggled. I nodded to them, feeling trapped and unable to speak my own truths. I studied them, wondering if everyone in this room was caught up in a charade, and we were all only playing our parts.

"Miss Pierson, may I persuade you to play for us?" Lady Koop offered me a cup of tea.

I froze and looked at the instruments with dread. Then in my panic, I blurted out the worst possible thing. "Which instrument were you thinking of?"

Isaac reached out and accepted my teacup when I made no move to take it. "I fear Lord Pierson doesn't approve of his daughter being placed on public display. I must forbid it."

Eyebrows rose, and I stared at the delicate cup Isaac handed me. Did their shock stem from my father's undue strictness or Isaac's display of mastery over me? I felt heat flush my body. Or did they all suspect I couldn't play?

"Well, then perhaps you will entertain us, Miss Knight," Lady Koop managed, still giving Isaac and me a horrified look.

"Yes, ma'am. I'd be honored." Anna rose, smothering her delight.

I sat back, suddenly grateful Isaac had joined me. He insisted that cigar smoke gave him headaches, becoming the only male present here.

Anna chose a large harp. When she looked at Isaac, a deep blush filled her cheeks. Her fingers plucked out a lyrical song, which her vocals made achingly beautiful. No one whispered or fluttered a fan until she finished; then lavish praise poured forth. She tentatively looked at Isaac for his approval.

He continued to cool his tea until he realized she kept looking expectantly at him. "Oh, pardon me, Miss Knight," he finally said. "That was truly enchanting."

She floated to her seat and clung to her sister's hand, burying her head in her shoulder. Pity swelled in my heart. How long had she fancied Isaac? I stole a glance to judge his thoughts, but he'd already forgotten her and was staring at the clock, looking miserable.

Dahlia, however, glared at Anna with a shade of jealousy, then adjusted her skirts. "Miss Pierson, has your father set your wedding date? You are marrying Lord Dalry, are you not?"

No one looked in our direction, yet I read their secret pleasure that someone dared to ask the question out loud.

Sensing her intent was to wound Anna with her question, I scathed her with a look.

Isaac prodded me with his elbow, telling me to behave, but when he spoke, his voice was almost bored. "Soon we shall make our wedding date public, but not yet. Lady Koop, would you mind asking Miss Jameson to sing next? I've heard her voice is excellent but have not had the opportunity to judge for myself."

﹌

That evening, as Isaac settled into the carriage, he beamed at me. "I cannot tell you how delighted I was to have you at my side!" He handed me back my fan and gloves. "My friends adored you."

I smiled but could not accept his praise nor return his compliment. I disagreed with his assessment. And so I changed the conversation, mimicking what he'd done all night. "You are well received amongst the ladies."

He wrinkled his nose and removed his hat to comb his fingers through his hair. "Yes. It's rather strange, isn't it, and even more awkward when they act so silly with you there. I assumed their attention would end this season, when they realized there is no chance I might be your father's heir."

I spread my gloves over my lap, feeling weary. "Well, at least you know it's not your inheritance they're after. That much is nice."

He didn't warm to my compliment as I intended. Instead he gave me a sharp look. "Is that what you think of me?"

There wasn't time to answer, for my father climbed into the barouche and ordered the driver to start. As we passed the bonfires that dotted various streets, Isaac stared out the window with a perturbed expression. For a mile, I refused to speak as well. It wasn't as though I had asked for any of this. Yet when we passed from light to shadow, I couldn't bear the tension.

"No, Isaac," I said. "I don't think that of you."

"What's this?" My father roused, sounding angry.

"It's nothing, sir. She's just finishing a private conversation we were having before you entered the carriage."

Something must have unsettled my father at the party, because he snapped, "You dare disturb my peace for that? Julia, never again wait so long to answer a question. It's positively ill-bred." He turned his head. "Isaac, I didn't ask you to answer for her. You're acting just as uncouth as she is now."

⌒

It is no easy task to write about that time in London. Those were the weeks when I silently screamed and screamed, unheard by anyone. I was drowned out by the busy rattle of carriages, the never-ending cries of street vendors, the murmur of voices, but most of all, the clamor for prestige.

I danced on numbed toes, wearing paper-thin smiles, carefully observing the faces around me. Each bite of my life tasted bitterer than the last. I moved through crowds, stammered through chitchat at soirees, and waltzed through ballrooms, wondering how long it would be before I choked.

The girls continued to intrigue me the most. They all seemed so adapted, content to be in my exact position—resigned to remaining under their fathers' rule, happy to rely on the gentlemen for their fate. It was as though they'd forgotten how to run through meadows barefoot with blades of grass stuck to their legs, or lie outdoors at night beneath a star-filled sky with a friend like Elizabeth. It dawned on me once, as I stopped dancing and stood still amidst a swirling ballroom, that maybe they hadn't forgotten—maybe they'd never known.

I wanted to believe that my life would be rectified—that I

would find my way back to Edward. But as each day passed, that hope became a guttered candle, sitting in a draft.

For the first time, I searched the Scriptures. My belief was intact before I began, for I did not doubt my experience. It was my trust that needed won. Therefore, I scoured them to learn what would happen if I surrendered.

Edward must have been drawn to the paradoxes and hard truths in Scripture, for he'd underlined the passages that bade children to obey their parents and triple-underscored the verses about remaining where you are called. I found little comfort there, yet other passages brought unexpected emotion and yearning. The idea of never being forsaken or alone again held me transfixed. Thankfully, Edward had mapped out and correlated those verses too.

Isaac watched, bemused, as I struggled through Edward's Bible. The first time he saw me reading it, he studied its distinctive cover as if intuitively understanding it belonged to Edward. He spoke no word but gave a nod of approval and somehow seemed to relax at the sight.

Thereafter, he watched patiently from the outside as my brow knit in frustration. I noted that as I pored over those pages, Isaac would often pause his reading, his gaze lingering on me with a growing respect and admiration. To his credit, he never commented, though I am certain he longed to. I refused to ask him questions. By then, I relied on him for every area of my life—relationship with my father, connection to the staff, and support during our outings. Furthermore, our shared existence had only served to heighten our friendship and attachment. I grew to love him fiercely, but only as a brother. To make him my spiritual mentor, too, was more than I was willing to yield, for that was Edward's rightful role. Somehow I felt that seeking Isaac's aid on that subject would tip the last domino of my resistance to marrying him.

Those of you familiar with my story may wonder how Eramus

fit into that season of my life. He was there, on the fringes. My father disliked him, but not nearly as intensely as Isaac did.

Eramus might have set me loose into society, but he benefitted little from my popularity.

For several weeks, he'd turn up at the same functions, but Isaac always steered us clear of him or insisted we leave early. It wasn't until Lady Beatrice complained, in early February, that my father ordered me to write Eramus a note, telling him he might be my escort for the next fortnight.

"Are you sure you won't change your mind, son?" My father adjusted the hood of my velvet opera mantle around the ringlets Miss Moray had piled over my shoulder. "Eramus isn't taking her far, and I could use you tonight."

"I'm certain," Isaac said, pulling on his gloves.

My father nodded permission for Miss Moray to leave, then stepped back to view me. Though I tried to no longer seek his approval, my heart rebelled and soared when he chucked the bottom of my chin. "Enjoy yourself tonight."

I paused, tightening my mantle, before replying. "I will."

Behind my father, Isaac pinned me with his stare, telling me he sensed my untruth.

I gathered my purse and fan, avoiding his direct gaze, disliking the idea of a marriage where one could never lie.

My father placed my hand on Isaac's arm. "Son, take good care of her."

"I promise, sir."

"Are you sure you don't want to take our carriage?"

Isaac laughed, picking up his hat. "It would only offend Eramus. Since he thinks he's Julia's escort, he'd object to Lady Beatrice's carriage not being used."

"Are you armed?"

Isaac gave my father a sullen look, buttoning the top of his coat. "Yes. Against my better judgment."

Frowning, my father spoke gruffly. "Watch that she isn't exposed to Eramus's gambling."

"I'll try, sir, but I can't promise."

My father grew silent, glanced at the clock, and then rubbed his palms over the pockets of his dinner coat. "What if you took Julia there, then joined me halfway through?"

Isaac's jaw tightened. "Sir, I am determined in my plans. I ask that you not try to deter me."

My father growled, "Fine. But if Eramus brings her back early, I expect you to attend me!"

He swung open the door, bellowing for one of the footmen to tell the coachman he was ready to leave for his club and to fetch his walking stick and cloak.

On Isaac's arm, I stepped into the chilled air. A layer of fog bobbed over the street, no higher than James's calf. Lamplight cast hazy circles over the gently moving mist. Above, it was impossible to discern more than four dimly lit stars. Sewage tinged the night air, but I breathed deeply regardless.

Isaac turned ever so slightly, the streetlamp revealing a worried expression. "James," he suddenly announced, facing into darkness again, "walk a good distance ahead of us."

"Sir?" James looked up from the bottom of the stairs.

"Give us privacy."

"How can I chaperone her if I can't see her?"

"Precisely. Now walk."

James jammed his hands into his greatcoat, breathing heavier. "What if Lord Pierson learns of it?"

"Walk."

James gave one last pleading glance before stiffly marching down the pavement. He stopped at the gate.

"Keep going," Isaac called, holding me in place on the top step. "Go as far as the bend in the curb."

"But, sir—"

"Shall I tell Lord Pierson that you kissed one of the upper maids?"

James audibly gasped and spun around. "That's hardly fair, sir! I'd lose my post."

"Then march."

James squared his shoulders and turned. With arms rigid at his side, he announced to the mist-covered cobblestones, "Sir, under duress I will obey your order. But she is the daughter of my master, and therefore it is my duty to inform you that her father would highly disapprove. I think you're being very unfair to me."

He sounded so comical, I covered my mouth to suppress giggles.

"March," Isaac ordered, his tone warming as I giggled harder.

The gate clanged shut, and after a minute, Isaac pulled me close and we began our descent into the condensation.

"Julia, I apologize in advance," he said, slipping his gloved fingers between mine, the fog cradling about us as we passed, "but I need to ask you about your earlier hesitation."

"Hesitation?"

"When your father told you to have a good time, you hesitated. Answer me honestly: Has Eramus ever acted unseemly toward you?"

His question was so startling I stopped walking. Sharp, cold air stung my lungs as I wondered why Eramus so agitated Isaac.

My suspicions were confirmed when Isaac swallowed hard, his entire countenance changing. He clenched his free hand into a fist as if scarcely able to keep his composure. His words came out strained. "What has he done?"

"Nothing," I assured him.

Isaac's Adam's apple bobbed above his cravat.

"Why does he worry you?" I asked.

His eyes looked lost in some troubled world of his own. Something about his manner stirred pity within me. Here was a soul locked in a private torment. Another pilgrim on the path

I travelled. He peered over my shoulder as he acknowledged my question with a nod. "It's my burden. Forgive me for troubling you."

We heard a scuffing sound, and Isaac looked over. Mr. Billingsby and an elderly gentleman were staring at us, unsmiling. They tipped their hats.

"Surely this isn't our Lord Dalry out with a young woman and no chaperone?" the white-haired man said.

With a sheepish expression, Isaac released me and called, "James? Where are you?"

"Ahead of you." James's voice carried from a distance. "Exactly as you ordered."

Isaac deepened a shade, then with hands on hips, turned from the men. "Well, come back."

"May I inquire as to the identity of your companion? Her parents need to be made aware of this situation."

Mr. Billingsby laughed and leaned on his walking stick. "Can you not tell by looking at her, Grandfather? That's Miss Julia Pierson, Lord Pierson's daughter. She's also the girl that Lord Alexander is courting."

Thankfully, I felt too drained to blush and gave them a brief curtsy. "My father is perfectly aware that I'm with Isaa—Lord Dalry."

Isaac winced, hearing my use of his first name. James came running. He flushed with guilt, spotting the gentlemen, but then whipped off his hat.

"I feel it is my duty to oversee the lot of you back to your house." The elderly gentleman opened his arms like a mother herding her flock of children. "Turn about. I intend to see that Lord Pierson receives quite an earful."

Mr. Billingsby chuckled. "You'll have to wait until tomorrow during sessions, for I saw Lord Pierson's carriage not more than five minutes ago. Consider. If you take them home, you only give them privacy, and I'll have to send Lord Alexander to chaperone."

The elderly man pulled out his pocket watch and frowned. "Of all the hours for me to find such a shameful display." He glared at Isaac. "Where were you taking her?"

Isaac huffed and finally looked in their direction. "I'm escorting Miss Pierson to her cousin Master Eramus Calvin. He's staying with Lady Beatrice."

"Shall I go with them, Grandfather?"

"Have you learned your lesson, young man?" Lord Billingsby eyed Isaac from beneath his tufted eyebrows.

"Yes, sir."

Lord Billingsby tapped James in the chest with his walking stick. "A faithless servant never advances. Remember that."

"Yes, sir."

"Come, boy. We have guests to receive. Your parents are going to be furious at our late arrival as it is."

Mr. Billingsby gave Isaac a smirk. "I hope for your sake Lord Alexander doesn't challenge you to a duel to defend her honor." He looked at me, trying to appear sincere. "He speaks of nothing except you, milady."

"You're as undisciplined as the lot of them," his grandfather commented. "I hope Lord Alexander has more sense than to allow you to do his wooing for him."

They turned the corner, so I did not hear Mr. Billingsby's murmured response.

James pulled on his sleeves. "Imagine how furious his lordship is going to be when the Lord Alexander Kensington shows up expecting to take Miss Pierson for a stroll."

Isaac looked at me but, perhaps thankful that there was no hope of resurrecting our conversation, simply nodded. "All right. Let's go fetch Eramus and get this night over with."

At Lady Beatrice's house, James ran up the steps and pulled on the bell chain. With growing interest, I waited for Eramus to emerge from the blackness so I could study him anew.

When he finally did, he scarcely glanced at me. He surveyed

his servant, who continued to polish his black leather cape as he exited. Eramus craned his neck over his shoulder as if to ascertain it was spotless.

"Start readying my bed at midnight in case I come home early. Make sure new warming pans are inserted every half hour." He smacked the valet away and plodded down the stairs. "Cousin." With half-closed eyes, he kissed my cheek. "I'm pleased to see your father has finally come to his senses."

His hand closed around my forearm. "Look how the leech bristles when I touch you." Eramus laughed and opened the door to Lady Beatrice's carriage. "You may as well grow used to it, Isaac. Tonight Miss Pierson is under my care. Though I daresay we will be looking for our first chance to sneak away from you, shall we not, Cousin?"

Isaac gave him a bland look, seeming so disinterested that even I had a hard time discerning that he felt emotion. To honor him, I adopted the same bored expression, ignoring Eramus.

As we jostled down one street and then another, the feathers in my headdress vibrated against my neck. The outlandish quality of the evening increased as the carriage turned onto our street. I frowned at our nonsense. We had walked to Lady Beatrice's only to ride back the way we came? Why, I wondered, hadn't Eramus simply picked us up?

I turned slightly to study him. The dull-yellow light of a streetlamp flooded the carriage, emphasizing Eramus's grotesque features. Goblin-lidded eyes stared in my direction; fleshy cheeks sagged on either side of his overlong mouth. "Isaac, tell your future bride to stop her incessant flirting," Eramus said in a monotone. "She keeps giving me the most eliciting glances. If she keeps it up, I won't be responsible for my—"

Isaac had Eramus by the collar before I blinked. "I am not going to allow our war to resurface." Isaac twisted the wad of material in his fist. "You are finished tormenting me. If I have to—"

The carriage door opened, and Lady Beatrice's coachman shifted his gaze between Isaac and Eramus.

"Phillip," Isaac said in a calm voice, "escort Miss Pierson to the front door. Julia, go greet our hosts. Eramus and I will join you in a moment."

The coachman held out his hand for me and practically had to lift me over the two gentlemen in midfight. As soon as my feet touched the ground, Phillip hesitated, looking between the two men. Something about his stance, his hesitation to interfere, made me wonder if he hoped Eramus was about to receive his comeuppance.

Isaac met my eyes. "Julia, go inside."

For a moment, I stood, rising above the sea of fog—lost.

Music and laughter flooded from the house, and light cascaded down the stairs, stretching in a wide rectangle over the concrete. My dress felt heavier than normal, stealing my breath as I ascended the stairs. Reflecting over the last few months, I realized how hard Isaac had worked to learn even the minute details of my life—how I drank my tea, if my shoes pinched, what my varying expressions meant. Yet, I scarcely knew anything about him. Shame filled me. Here was another soul who surely suffered this life too.

"Whom should I announce?" The butler came down four steps to greet me.

"Miss Pierson," the coachman said and, after bowing, hastened back to the carriage.

"This way, please."

On the arm of a butler, I entered the home. The tinkle of glasses and laughter rang from the next room. Vases of honeysuckle and roses tangled with ivy clustered over tables and out of wall pockets, filling the air with their sweet scent. While the maid removed my cape, I braced myself for the shocked expressions I'd encounter when the other guests learned I had arrived alone. The butler opened the door and whispered my name to a waiting footman.

"Miss Beerson," the footman called into the room.

Only those playing whist nearby heard, but they did not bother to look up. Huddles of conversations dotted the room; strains of Mozart—played on violin, cello, and pianoforte—drifted from the archway leading into another large gallery.

I breathed easier. Etiquette demanded that I greet the hosts and correct my name without stressing my importance. With the refinement I'd learned at Lady Beatrice's hand, I turned about, praying I could spot them in this crowd. I wasn't even certain what our hosts looked like.

"Good heavens, it's that girl again," said a familiar gruff voice. I looked up to find Lord Billingsby's tufted brows narrowed at me. "Where is your escort? Where is young Dalry now?"

I weakly gestured to the window.

A woman sidled next to him and asked in a loud whisper, "Who is it, Harold?"

"Of all the nuisances. It's Lord Pierson's daughter, only now she has no escort."

Her hand fluttered to her heart. "Good merciful heavens."

I waved again in the direction of the window. "M-my escorts . . . have been detained."

"Oh, dear. Oh, my." The woman looked over the room, trying to ascertain who had seen me. "There's going to be scandal."

"Not in my house, there won't." Lord Billingsby thumped his walking stick. "Jonathan!"

Mr. Billingsby's large frame turned from a nearby group of people. A smug look fell over his face, and he immediately came. "Yes?"

"Well, you know the girl; now she's your problem."

He gave me a lopsided smile. "I fear I cannot understand your meaning, Grandfather. Are you saying you've arranged a marriage? That's rather unfair. You've just destroyed my political career before it even started."

"She needs an escort," the woman whispered, pulling me

near Mr. Billingsby. "She came without one. Keep anyone from learning it."

He bowed. "I'll place her under the care of Lord Alexander."

I held in my sigh.

As we left, the woman called for a servant to fan her, then weakly asked Lord Billingsby what I meant to accomplish by such recklessness, and at her soiree of all places.

Mr. Billingsby led me through the room, which was swelling with music. As we threaded toward the end of the gallery, people gave each other glances of significance, telling their acquaintances to look who had arrived.

Lord Alexander stood amongst a group of gentlemen, a half head taller than the rest. So deep were they in discussion, he failed to note our arrival.

Mr. Billingsby tapped Lord Alexander from behind. "You'll never guess who is with me."

Lord Alexander turned his head slightly, so as to be heard but not bothering to look. "It's bad form to introduce someone so awkwardly. Your friend will have to pay for your ill manners, for I am not going to greet him. Had you half a wit, you'd be participating in this conversation, instead of philandering about the room."

"Oh-ho-ho," laughed Mr. Billingsby. "Very well, then. Shall we leave, Miss Pierson?"

My name had the effect he desired. Lord Alexander spun, nearly dropping the sherry between his fingers. He cast Mr. Billingsby an incredulous look, then blurted, "What is she doing here?" He squinted at his friend. "And why are you escorting her?"

Mr. Billingsby's smirk increased. "Sheer luck. Dalry lost her and she stumbled in here."

The gentlemen surrounding Lord Alexander shifted with an odd reaction. No one pasted a smile and bowed as I'd grown accustomed to. Instead, their glances at Lord Alexander were pregnant with fear, contrasting with the jaunty atmosphere, making this group stand out like a sharp angle.

Lord Alexander viewed me with dismay but was the first of his friends to recover. "Miss Pierson, here; allow me to find you a glass of sherry." He looked at a well-dressed gentleman to his left and hesitated before saying, "Fred, go fetch her one."

The gentleman appeared jarred by the order but turned and headed toward a footman.

Lord Alexander bowed, finally managing a smile, though his eyes remained alert. "I'm glad you landed amongst us, Miss Pierson. Do you have any idea how dangerous it is for you to wander into the wrong house with your . . . past connections?"

Even had I been in a normal frame of mind, his statement would have disturbed me, but already troubled about Eramus, I stiffened, staring.

"Here, you're frightened. Forgive me, Miss Pierson." He placed a hand on my shoulder. "You've nothing to fear from this group. Let's just say that you've fallen amongst . . . *his* friends."

I stared, doing my best to appear nonchalant.

"There's Dalry," a man said, pointing. "She ought to be safe enough with him. Look at his expression. I wager tomorrow Lord Pierson is going to rip him to shreds for losing the girl, and he knows it."

"Pierson would be the least of his worries if something happened to her."

Isaac stood under the archway, frantically searching for me. When he spotted me, he adopted his high-cultured face and made his way toward us.

"Well, do we let him take her?" the blond gentleman asked.

"I'm thinking," Lord Alexander said between gritted teeth. "The fact he lost her once is evidence enough she needs another protector, but I doubt he'll take kindly to my assuming the role." He glanced sideways at me. "Yet it's not Dalry I fear offending."

Our eyes met. His manner, his expressions reminded me of Mr. Rooke or Mr. Greenham. Only Lord Alexander lacked the mastery Mr. Greenham commanded. It was almost as if Lord Alexander were a fledgling, stretching his wings for the first time.

"He would instruct you to take me back to Lord Dalry," I said with a cold pit in my stomach.

Without even considering whether I spoke truth, Lord Alexander took my right arm and guided me in Isaac's direction.

Isaac halted and waited with a face of stone. "Kensington," he said upon our approach.

"Billingsby brought the poor, terrified girl to me," Lord Alexander whispered in anger. "I have half a mind to keep her with me. I'd hate for Lord Pierson to learn his daughter was left in incompetent hands and I failed to assist her."

"Neither Lord Pierson nor I require your help, thank you."

Lord Alexander folded his arms. "Then why is she in my care and not yours?"

"I had a debt to settle with Eramus."

"Calvin? Don't tell me that toad is here as well."

"He's Miss Pierson's primary escort."

Lord Alexander snorted, then turned to me. "First your father guards you, and now he sends you out with a cad and an escort who loses you. Know that I shall remain at this party as long as you do. Feel free to call upon my services, for in good conscience I cannot leave you alone. Dalry."

Isaac and Lord Alexander gave each other stiff bows.

While Lord Alexander retreated, Isaac watched him with annoyance, then turned toward me. In a rare display of public affection, he drew my hand to his lips. "You look pale. What happened with Eramus had nothing to do with you. Had I known Alexander Kensington was inside waiting, I never would have sent you alone."

Behind Isaac, Eramus stormed into the room, anger boiling over, twisting his already-ugly features. I turned to find Lord Alexander's group all watching me with sharp and sober expressions. I slid my fan over my wrist, considering the dark irony. One side of the room was filled with Macy's men, and on the other was Isaac's tormentor. I slid my arm beneath Isaac's and leaned into him, realizing how unisonant we actually were. For all his polished manners, he was exactly like me, completely secluded in the crowded room, haunted by his past.

I resisted my desire to lay my head on his shoulder. With discomfort, I realized that if my father forced me to marry Isaac, I could grow to truly love him. He already was my teacher and comforter.

"Julia?" Isaac asked, and I felt his light touch at my elbow. "Did he offend you?"

Bitterly I laughed, avoiding looking at him. "No."

"Something has changed. What?"

"If I try to talk about it, I'll cry. Can we go home?"

Isaac glanced about the room, his polished expression gone. "Tell me."

The first tear trickled down my cheek. "Why? You won't tell me about Eramus. Why should I tell you what is disturbing me?"

With a gentle touch, Isaac moved me to an empty corner. "Sit." He withdrew an iris from a vase and held it up as if he were showing the bloom. "You mustn't cry. I won't ask another question tonight—I swear it—but you must pull yourself together. I can't take you home; I'm not your escort."

I concentrated on ignoring the rising sadness at our situation and nodded. "Will you tell me about Eramus?"

He gave a soft chuckle, then made a noise of distress. "Why that?"

"I want to know."

His chest filled with air, though I never heard him sigh. "If you wish, but not until this fortnight has ended and we are free of our obligation to him. But you'll tell me what disturbed you tonight, at home."

Understanding that I wouldn't get a better offer, I nodded.

"That's my girl." Isaac took my hand in his and gave it a

squeeze. "I'll tell you what. Look in that far corner. See those four men? We'll start by socializing with them. They are so enwrapped in their scientific pursuits, their conversation will revolve entirely around a new species of plant or some other tiresome topic. It will help you collect yourself. Do you think you can manage that?"

✦

Toward midnight, the dull buzz of the surrounding conversations reminded me of a drowsy afternoon at Am Meer by the beehives. Beneath my sweltering dress, my chemise clung to my body. I glanced at Isaac, still deep in conversation with a gentleman about the Corn Laws. We'd gone from science to England's financial concerns, then lastly to politics about an hour ago.

Isaac kept my arm in his, and the humid warmth of our bodies diffused through my limbs. I stifled a yawn. Like sticky honey, the desire to sleep coated my thoughts, causing my eyelids to grow heavy. For a second, I rested my head on Isaac's shoulder, just to close my eyes a moment.

"Miss Pierson tires," the gentleman said with a smile in his voice, and I blinked awake. "Why not take her home and come back to finish our talk. Miss Pierson, you've been most kind to tolerate us."

I tried to give him an elegant head bob, but even tired I knew it was clumsy.

Isaac smiled at the gentleman, but I knew it was placed. "Perhaps we should end our conversation now. Unfortunately, we have two more parties we need to make appearances at. It's best we move on."

The gentleman took a sudden step backwards. "Let us hope the night air revives her. Shall we finish our conversation at White's? I'll be there this Tuesday. I know Harrison would be interested in your thoughts about this as well."

"I fear I have no plans to attend the clubs this week. Miss

Pierson has been very tolerant of her father's and my work. It's her turn to attend functions."

"So? Why not come afterwards?" He nodded at me. "Take her to the balls and then join us for the night debates. If what you're saying is true, this changes my entire view."

"Perhaps." Isaac broke contact with the man. "Do you have your fan? Shall we?"

"Well, come on, my good man. What club will you attend tonight? I'll join you there, if I must."

"None. Good night." Isaac took my arm and we escaped by ducking under palm leaves and hastening past a matron surrounded by daughters. As the gentleman attempted to follow us, the mother bowed, obliging him to stop and acknowledge her. Leaning near, Isaac said, "I'm sorry, Julia. I should have realized we were talking too long."

"Are we really going elsewhere?"

"Eramus told your father he planned to visit three places at least." He wrinkled his nose. "It's up to him. Go wait by the door. I'll pull your escort from his card game. From the rumor I just heard, he's lost an inordinate amount tonight."

He elbowed his way back into the crowd. In the foyer, I fanned my neck, enjoying the thinner air. The night had been trying for more reasons than learning that members of the gentry knew I was Mr. Macy's wife. All those weeks of practice, and I'd forgotten the correct way to address a duke, which Isaac had quickly amended. Once a girl had leaned over and whispered something in French to me, nodding at Isaac, and all I could do was smile and hope she wasn't insulting him or inquiring if we were closer than we ought to be.

Feeling eyes upon me, I stiffened and looked about. Four doors down, in the night-filled hall, Lord Alexander stood astride a threshold. His expression was one of irritation, but he scarcely rested a glance on me. Instead, his eyes darted between the doors surrounding me.

Isaac returned with a drunk Eramus, who seemed too intoxicated to stand, much less notice me, and started to gather our outerwear. Eramus sank into a seat, nearly falling from its corner.

Lord Alexander lingered a second, watching us, then melted into the darkened room with a dissatisfied expression.

～⌒～

Moonlight glided across the smooth floors, adding luster to the marble busts and clock faces, as Isaac and I slipped into the hall. My cheeks hurt from smiling, my hands tingled from clapping at the musical performances, and my feet were so swollen they felt glued to my slippers. I dropped my fan and purse on the table to the sound of Eramus's carriage rattling away. I shut my eyes, realizing I'd never been so happy to be back in London House.

The gold brooch securing my cape felt cool to the touch as I unclasped it. Heavy velvet and satin slid from my shoulders and fell to the floor with a rustle. February's fingers pierced my skin as the warmth from the cape evaporated.

While Isaac gathered my fallen garment, I peeled off my beaded footwear. Though tempted to leave the slippers scattered over the foyer and force Miss Moray to trek down three stories to retrieve them, I hooked them around my fingers and stood to leave.

"Wait." Isaac shook off his own cape and uncharacteristically left it crumpled on the floor. He took two steps and reached for me but paused when I made no move to continue up the stairs.

"Julia." He touched his forehead with his fingertips as though trying to reason which thought to speak first. "I know you are weary, but what happened at Lord Billingsby's tonight?" The huskiness coating his voice clashed with the serene atmosphere of the hall.

I was so fatigued, it felt like I'd consumed too many glasses of claret as I slowly met his gaze. For the first time, I saw him as all the young ladies throughout London saw him—handsome as the Greek god Ares, only without violence. Moonlight sharpened his features as candlelight never had. For one second, I allowed myself to admire him.

His eyes widened, but in a refined movement, he slid one hand to my waist and cradled my face with the other. His lips touched mine, and for half a second, I considered exploring the kiss. But I thought of Edward, and all at once, a mere mortal pressed his lips against mine. Not a god, just a man. One whom I still did not love.

"Julia." His words were a sigh as he kissed my temple, then trailed along the side of my face.

By allowing one weak moment, I'd committed my cruelest act to date. As though an unravelling thread were being pulled, I had to stop this somewhere, lest everything come undone. Pulling away, I met his gaze. The love that filled his eyes was unbearable. He mistook my dismay for surrender, for he drew me against him, kissing my neck.

The front door rattled.

Wiping his bottom lip, Isaac spun. My father and Simmons gave us a disgruntled glance before entering.

"Honestly, Isaac." My father shoved his walking stick between the umbrellas in the blue-and-white porcelain stand. He yanked off the white silk scarf, then fumbled with his greatcoat buttons. "What if I had brought a guest back to the house with me?"

"I know how this must look, sir, but I assure you. It was . . . I—I—" Isaac wet his lips and took a deep breath. He extended one hand as if to speak, but it didn't appear as though words were coming.

I crossed my arms, pulling them to my stomach, knowing how much harder it would be the next time I needed to refuse a betrothal on the basis that I still didn't love Isaac.

My father gave a dismissive wave. "Not here. Go to the library. We'll discuss it there." Isaac bowed and retreated. Once he was gone, my father yanked at the fingers of his gloves, slowly considering me.

I resisted the urge to wipe my lips, though I still felt Isaac's kisses. My father narrowed his eyes. I lifted my chin and looked away, feeling contrary. Why had he so freely dismissed Isaac but censured me?

In a sudden burst of anger, I coldly met his eye. Let him see that I wasn't swooning over Isaac. "What?" I finally asked. "Is that not what you wanted?"

He shoved his gloves into his pockets. "Go to bed, Julia."

I started up the stairs, measuring each step to show him that I was not afraid, but then realized I needed to tell him about tonight.

"Lord Alexander knows that I'm Mr. Macy's wife."

Even in the semidarkness, I saw his features harden. "How many times are we going to discuss this? You are not that man's wife." He paused, allowing his rebuke to settle. "What makes you suspect that?"

I inhaled, resisting the urge to cite English law in argument toward my being married, but answered the question he meant. I explained what had happened, but my father was unmoved.

"He wasn't speaking of Macy," he decided. "When he said you'd fallen amongst 'his' friends, he meant me. Our political alliance is a known fact. Go to bed."

"You weren't there," I protested.

He gave a huff of annoyance. "No, and neither did I need to be to recognize female hysteria when I hear it."

I had to swallow twice before answering, and when I did, I took a stab in the dark. "I'm glad Mama left you."

He startled, giving me a queer look, but then ignored my remark and proceeded to the library.

On the second landing, I paused and glanced down. Simmons alone remained in the foyer, and he ignored me as he tended to my father's outer garments. Moonlight streaked across his back in a pale rectangle as he bent, retrieving the articles.

My stomach twisted as I realized he'd heard every word. I still didn't know who Macy's spies were, but if Simmons was one, Macy would know my father's weakness in not believing me.

Twenty-Three

EDWARD'S WATCH felt cold in the palm of my hand as it sparkled in the morning sun. In the mirror, Miss Moray observed me as she parted my hair into plaits and applied generous amounts of pomade. Tapping my thumb against the sharp end of the pin, I envisioned Isaac's dismay and felt loathsome.

"Hold still now." Miss Moray stepped onto a footstool so she could better position herself to coil my hair atop my head. "Don't bend at all, or it'll fall apart."

I closed my fingers around the watch. How could I have allowed myself to kiss Isaac? He would expect me not to wear the pin today, especially with my father breathing down his neck. Knots tied my stomach. If I joined breakfast wearing the watch, how would it not injure him?

The rays of sun moved, warming my skirt and back, yet I felt barren.

A lump rose in my throat. None of this situation was fair to Isaac. I opened my palm and stared at the glittering pin. This desperate hope for time was playing with fire. How long until it burned me?

"There, finished." Miss Moray dusted off her hands before using my shoulder to aid her balance as she stepped off the stool. "Best move on now."

෴

Arms folded tight over my stomach, I eased into the breakfast chamber, wondering how many more mornings to come would feel sickening.

Sunlight poured into the dark room, making the polished floors gleam. Isaac sat alone at the oversized table, staring at a book, yet he scarcely seemed to register the page. Rather, he gave me the impression of a man holding a book to keep occupied.

"Isaac." Fearing I'd spoken too softly to be heard, I pulled my shawl tight.

He jumped to his feet, casting aside the book. His gaze riveted on the pin. He wrinkled his brow, but as understanding dawned, his face paled.

Not realizing the unspoken tension, James smiled at me and pulled out my chair. I refused to meet Isaac's bruised gaze as I took my seat. Thankfully, Miss Moray had dressed me in a full skirt, and I made a show of tucking it beneath the table.

"Julia," Isaac said.

Heat rose through my cheeks and ears as I carefully unrolled my napkin. Then, unable to keep up the charade of indifference, I cast him a pleading look not to do this.

"Julia, please believe me, I never would have kissed you . . ." His voice failed, and ducking his head, he clenched his napkin. "I thought . . . I thought—"

James's eyes grew as round as shillings, but finding an excuse to leave the room, he bowed and shut us within.

"Tell me what I'm doing wrong."

There was a quality to Isaac's voice that nearly undid me. What could I say? The fault did not lie with him. I focused my gaze on a saltcellar. What if I was mistaken to hold out for Edward? I swallowed, wondering where I would be this morning if I had handed my life over to God. Would I be required to obey my father's wishes?

"Are you not speaking to me now?" Like a defendant awaiting his verdict, Isaac waited for me to say something, anything.

A single set of footsteps reverberated in the hall, saving me from having to answer. Surprised, I glanced over my shoulder. My father was supposed to be in session. The scent of cloves filled the chamber as my father stormed into my line of view. He motioned for Isaac not to rise. "Well? Should I announce it today?"

All pain left Isaac's countenance, though I noted his fingers tightened over his napkin. With an urbane expression, he lifted his eyes and looked at my father. "Sir?"

My father's brow furrowed as he placed his hands on the back of his chair. "Have you finished yet? Can I send Forrester the announcement?"

Isaac opened his mouth as if suddenly remembering an appointment. "No, sir. I've not asked her yet."

My father's knuckles turned white as he waited unsuccessfully for a better response. I shifted in my seat.

"She's sitting right there," my father finally growled.

Isaac turned and viewed me, his gaze flickering to the watch. "Yes. I can see her."

"Well?"

"Well, what, sir?"

I squeezed the edges of my chair as my father looked on the verge of having an apoplexy.

"I've had just about as much of this as I'm going to allow. I want whatever is holding up this engagement resolved."

Isaac picked up the book he'd been holding when I entered the room and stared at it. "Sir, we agreed from the very first day that I could do this my way. I'll ask her when I'm ready."

My father's upper lip curled as he turned to me. My face tightened as I strove not to cry.

"James!" My father shoved a chair against the table. "Bring me my coat and walking stick. I've already missed the opening session."

James clamored into the chamber, carrying my father's black woollen coat. My father yanked it from James's arms and glared at Isaac. "It didn't appear to me last night that you would be forcing anything on her." He shoved his arms into the coat, grabbed his walking stick, and gave Isaac one last fierce glance before stomping toward the door.

Suddenly he stopped and patted his chest. "Oh yes. Of all the bothersome nonsense, Lord Billingsby sent me a note this morning. Something urgent. Whatever it is, he thought it worth missing the morning session to talk privately." He pulled an open letter from his waistcoat and flung it on the table. "Make yourself useful today and attend him."

Isaac reached for the note and gingerly opened it. "Sir, I believe I know what is bothering Lord Billingsby, and it involves me. You see, last night—"

"Just fix the problem!" My father motioned for James to move from the doorway.

"But, sir—"

"Isaac, I haven't time to care what this is about. Just solve it."

"Yes, sir."

"I'll be out late. I'll see you both tomorrow."

Any appetite I might have had departed with my father. Isaac frowned as he read Lord Billingsby's note for himself. Then, with a sudden flush of temper, he stood, wadded the note into a ball, and tossed it into the fire. With the poker, he jabbed his frustration out in the embers.

Without glancing again at me, Isaac grabbed his frock coat from the back of his chair and left the room, his brow creased.

❧

"I said bloomin' move!" a man screamed a short distance away, causing Isaac to stir and look out the carriage window with disgust. There was little to be seen, for a thick fog choked our view, tangling traffic, embedding our carriage two streets from the opera house.

Eramus smirked and tapped his palm with the silver knob of his walking stick. "Are you ready to risk exposing your precious bride to the evils of London yet?"

Isaac curled his index finger over his lips, his countenance discomposed. Someone coughed nearby, choking on the thick fumes swirling in the fog.

Eramus sat back and spread his arm. "With traffic like this, we could sit here all night. What's your concern? It's hardly a distance and she'll be between us the entire time. Even Roy would approve of our arriving on foot."

I stretched my neck, which felt cricked, then attempted to yank my velvet cape out from beneath Eramus's boot. "I agree, Isaac. Anything would be better than sitting here."

"All right, fine." Isaac unfolded from his slouched position. "Since Julia desires it, we'll attempt to walk through this gloom. Eramus, stay here while I talk to Hudson, and keep your mouth shut for once. We're both tired of hearing your ugly voice."

The carriage swayed as Isaac alighted with a hop. Wintry air accompanied the brume. I nestled the Elizabethan collar of my opera cloak about my face, while Isaac tried to instruct our coachman on what to do once the congestion became disentangled. Out of nowhere, a canine raced to Isaac and snarled at his feet. Hudson tried to whip the hound, making Isaac's task all the more difficult.

"You know, Cousin." Eramus broke into my thoughts as he leaned into view. "I pity you, having to unite your life with the family leech. You do know that is the only reason your father allowed you into his household, don't you? He was in the process of seeing if there was any way around his entailment. Spent the last year fighting for the right to pass it on to Isaac. Rather convenient, having a bastard daughter around to wed the leech."

I glared at him, wondering how much truth was behind that statement. I shook my head, refusing to believe it. "You couldn't be more wrong."

He chuckled. "You don't fancy Isaac, do you? No, I can see by your face that I've hit a truth." Then, leaning forward, he called to Isaac, "Even the misbegotten family members would rather toss you back, Isaac."

It was only a flash of pain, but I saw that Eramus's jab had found its mark.

Fire lit through me, and a temper flared—one that only Sarah, my nursemaid, had ever beheld. I tackled Eramus and beat him with my fists as hard as I could. Before I managed to bloody his nose, however, Isaac gripped both of my upper arms and pulled me from the carriage backwards.

One look at his demanding face doused my temper. He'd probably never seen such an unladylike display in his entire life. My emotions still high, I hit the carriage until my palm hurt.

"What on—?" Isaac wrapped me in his arms, drawing me near. "What did you do to her?"

"How dare you!" Eramus's walking stick hit the hard ground. He pulled out a handkerchief, with which he mopped his face and checked for blood. "That, Isaac, was a display of her repulsion at the thought of marrying you."

I would have struck him again, had not Isaac grabbed my wrist. "You are the daughter of Lord Pierson." His harsh whisper sounded in my ear. "And as such, you represent him. Cease immediately."

Hudson's eyes were round, but they beamed with pride, and for some absurd reason, that calmed me. I nodded, smoothing my skirts.

"He isn't worth our time," Isaac continued in my ear as he placed one hand on the small of my back. Then, looking over his shoulder at Eramus, "You're not allowed to walk alongside us. You will follow."

Shielding me, Isaac guided me through the embankments of fog that enwrapped us in our own private world. Even Eramus, only a few paces behind, was indiscernible.

"Are you recovered?" Isaac placed a hand about my waist as if to ensure I could not misstep in our dense cloud.

I nodded. Though we were surrounded by coughing and coarse laughter, I saw only thick mist, which the light struggled to pierce. Behind us, Eramus bashed his walking stick in rhythm to his steps—a resounding *thwack*, *thwack*, *thwack*.

"Must you?" Isaac looked over his shoulder, his hand tightening.

"I rather like it," Eramus replied. "It's sort of like the ticking of a clock. A steady marking of time, toward revenge, toward something you can't stop, something that will eventually catch you, no matter how hard you try to hide."

Isaac gathered me closer and stumbled on toward the opera house. "This is the last outing we're taking with you. I can promise you that."

Eramus thwacked his stick harder. "What makes you think I've not grown bored of these excursions myself? They're not living up to my expectations either. It's far past time I tried something new."

Light spilled from the colonnaded theatre, defying the thick fog that swirled around us. Theatregoers alighted from carriages and arrived on foot, leaving behind the dank and rotted world of London. Cries of delight and laughter sparkled as the elite praised each other's fortitude for battling the "beastly atmosphere."

I gripped closed the velvet folds of my opera cape, hoping my color wasn't too high, longing to remain in the fog, in obscurity.

"Steady now," Isaac whispered, urging me forward.

Strains of an overture carried from deep within the building, but I scarcely noticed as the eyes of ambassadors and government officials turned to watch our approach. They offered Isaac smiles.

"I say," an elderly man with an ear trumpet announced to his companion as we passed, "who is that girl with the raven tresses? Why are we all looking at her?"

The young man gave Isaac an apologetic grimace before speaking into the silver horn rather loudly. "That's Lord Pierson's daughter, Lord Dalry's betrothed."

Isaac tightened the hand on my arm upon hearing the declaration. My cheeks grew warm and I made an attempt to turn my head into Isaac's shoulder.

"No, my dear." The delicate fragrance of hyssop and roses filled my senses before Lady Northrum kissed my cheek. She whispered so low, the rustle of her dress hid it. She tipped my chin up. "Let them see you blush and delight in your virtue. Tonight London is meant to celebrate you, will celebrate you." She touched Isaac's chin, her expression motherly. "I thought you would never arrive. What happened? Where is your escort?"

Isaac indicated behind us with a roll of his eyes.

Even Lady Northrum cooled with distaste as she took in Eramus. "Ah, well, do not allow Master Calvin to ruin tonight." She gathered my arm and rustled me down the gallery, but her words remained directed at Isaac. "The second program has started. I'd hoped you'd arrive during the promenade, but it can't be helped now. At least the papers printed that you were attending tonight, and my acquaintances are on the lookout for you."

Isaac nodded, unbuckling the gold clasp of his wool cape. Before he decided what to do with his outer garment, Lady Northrum motioned to one of her trailing servants. "Give your wraps to John."

Isaac gave her another nod of thanks. "And our escort? Will you keep him occupied as a precaution, at least until our appearance, I mean?"

"Yes, yes, but hurry while the music is still soft." Lady Northrum pressed her fan against his arm, urging him forward.

"What tier and box?" Isaac asked.

"The grand tier, next to the royal box."

Nearby a young lady gasped as Isaac removed my cape. Lady Northrum's eyes lit. She clasped her hands together with a lilting laugh. "I never would have thought Roy could manage the feat so well."

Eyes up and down the gallery admired my exterior. I wanted Mama's locket to hold, though I knew I looked faultless. Tonight, Miss Moray had spent hours ensuring that I looked regal for my first appearance at the opera. My father had surprised me with a gold moiré silk gown he'd had commissioned from Quill's. Rounded sleeves made of tulle scarcely veiled my bare arms, and the neckline was low. Large cut citrines glittered over my milky throat and were woven throughout the thick coils of my braided hair.

I placed my free hand on Isaac's arm, alarmed at the attention being paid us, realizing how legendary we'd become.

Lady Northrum chuckled. "The wonderment in her eyes alone shall make her the toast of London. Tonight will be the sensation we planned. Tomorrow every paper will carry the story."

Isaac gave her a quick shake of his head, indicating I wasn't aware of the plan. My marvel at being at the opera faded. Was this why my father paced the hall before we left, barking orders at the servants? This was nothing more than a ploy to keep our names in the papers?

I glanced behind me to deem whether Eramus knew. He eyed my stones with a hungry fascination but remained dressed in his cape. He twisted his mouth, ready to give me an ugly look, but before I could finish my observation, Isaac whisked me toward the wide staircase.

Step after marble step, we climbed to the backdrop of

percussionists knelling doom on their kettledrums. The intensity of the sound rose, until volumes of music crashed over us.

Outside one of the farthest boxes, we stopped. Isaac peeked through the heavy satin curtain, then allowed it to drop back into place. "We'll wait until the decrescendo before entering. Are you ready?"

I turned my head instead of answering. This morning during breakfast, Isaac and my father had passed the morning papers back and forth with looks of significance. I had assumed, until now, it was political matters, not an announcement for London to come and see me at the opera tonight.

All the tension crested at once. I felt an impending catastrophe, the same as I had before that fateful dinner that ended with my marriage to Mr. Macy. The feeling grew stronger with each rise and fall of the frenzied notes. Something was very wrong. Something worse than Eramus's vile temper. Something worse than making a fool of myself in front of everybody.

To my right, someone started down our passage, but I felt so stressed, I didn't care who it was. I bent over, placing my fingers on my temples.

"Julia?" Isaac asked.

The stranger halted so suddenly, I glanced in that direction and deemed him to be a servant, as the tips of his shoes were scuffed. Shadows veiled his face, but something in his manner tugged at me like a misplaced memory.

"Are you ill?" Isaac dropped on one knee and studied me.

I shook my head. "I don't want them to see me."

"Who?"

I squeezed my eyes shut, continuing to feel as though I were spinning. Disaster was creeping along, one spider leg at a time, but who would believe my premonition? "Everyone. I can't do this anymore."

"We've done this a hundred times, and have I ever let you fall? Tonight is no different than any other. Well, except perhaps for the fact that Lady Northrum has made it her pet project to oversee that you finally attended the opera."

My voice became strained, but I managed, "That's not what I mean. Take me home. Please. Take me away from here."

"Julia, of all the requests." Cupping my elbow, Isaac forced me to straighten, then buried the tip of his cold nose in my hair. "Whom would you rather face? Your father tomorrow morning when he learns we were on the verge of making our appearance but changed our mind, or a few busybodies viewing us through the lenses of their opera glasses?"

I crossed my arms, refusing to answer.

"One hour. That's all. We'll enter. We'll sit. We'll leave."

I surrendered with a slight nod. The ostrich feathers nestled in my headdress brushed my throat and shoulders.

"I wouldn't ask this of you if I didn't know you could do it," Isaac said softly. With the back of his finger, he traced the curve of my cheek, and I knew he was curbing his desire to kiss me, as I remained stone-faced. "You won't even have to speak. I swear it. Just leave this to me."

I nodded, taking a deep breath.

"That's my girl." Isaac released me and crept back to the curtain. Peering through the slit, he resumed waiting for the right moment.

Still feeling heavyhearted, I pressed my back against the cold marble wall. What was wrong with me? I unfurled my fan to circulate the air near my face. Why must it be so hot here? I glanced down the hall where Eramus would soon appear and bit my lip.

"Ready?" Isaac's voice pierced my melancholy thoughts.

I stirred and realized the music had softened. Isaac waited with his gloved hand extended. He looked handsome tonight. His white collar and white waistcoat brought out his blue eyes.

I filled my lungs, taking a deep breath, catching Isaac's distinct scent. If anyone were capable of carrying me through tonight, it would be he. Tilting my chin at the exact angle Lady Beatrice taught me, I gave him a slight nod, feeling the weight of my earrings sway with the dip of my head.

Isaac's eyes filled with pride, as though he sensed my willingness to trust him and continue regardless. He parted the satin curtain and led me into view. The warmth of his hand over the small of my back bled through to my skin, instilling me with a sense of calm.

In the dim light, I perceived a theatre superior to any other in the world. At least five tiers spread in a horseshoe, which rose into a large oval arch with sunken coffers. An immense chandelier hung from the archivolt, and from the center of every box dripped a miniature crystal chandelier, a jewel on the forehead of a queen.

I clutched Isaac's sleeve and looked up at him, stunned. It was unlike anything I'd ever experienced. A sea of sparkling, starry people clothed the house. Expensive French perfumes mixed with scents of talc powder and the hypnotic fragrance of flowers. Here were collected the powerful, the affluent, the beautiful, and they all welcomed us. Men stood and bowed to Isaac, while their ladies gave me their most affecting head nods. For one magnificent moment, I belonged amongst them.

Joy shone in Isaac's eyes as he watched me. This was his world. His arena. He looked as eager to introduce me to it as a child on Christmas morn. Keeping my hand in his, he slowly led me to my chair, then pressed my hand to his lips—giving London the show of affection they desired. Programs rustled as partners nudged one another, urging them to watch Lord Dalry's wooing of the Emerald Heiress.

Isaac held my fan and opera glasses, taking review of the floor and nearby tiers as I adjusted my skirts. After returning my accoutrements, he gave me a reassuring smile, then ensconced himself in his own chair.

It took several minutes until my heart stopped pounding, but the worst was over. I had succeeded, and nothing terrible had happened. Adopting Isaac's untroubled expression, I set my gaze toward the stage, but it took several more minutes until I'd settled enough to pay attention to the singers.

I squinted at the heavily made-up women who strutted up and down the stage, drowning the atmosphere with their magnificent voices. They sang in Italian, which I could not follow. Isaac did, however, and became fully absorbed. With an index finger curled over his mouth, he seemed to hang upon every word of the drama. I remained poised, granting even the most curious of onlookers enough time to have their fill of the Emerald Heiress.

Eventually, the curtain behind us rustled, and Eramus clomped into our box. The scent of cheap wine and tobacco accompanied him as he flopped into his seat. I hid my grimace of disgust and tried to stifle the reek by holding my hand under my nose. I frowned, wondering how he'd found a tavern and partaken in that short span.

He poked my shoulder. "Here, give me your opera glasses."

I glanced at Isaac, but he was so transfixed he hadn't noted Eramus's arrival. With a sigh of surrender, I handed over the gold and mother-of-pearl frames.

The music fell to silence, and a few people smothered their coughs. A new concertino began. The haunting lullaby of uilleann pipes warbled out a melody that hung suspended in the air before strings slowly undergirded its sad tune with their own heartsick cry. It brought to mind the night Edward crept over the wall at Am Meer and asked me to be his wife.

I pressed my hand against my collarbone, brushing my jeweled choker, feeling my sorrow tenfold. Had the composer read my heart and felt my anguish before penning the morose notes? It was the first time I'd heard music mimic my sentiments, and it unnerved me.

"That is one presumptuous fellow," Eramus muttered as he leaned over the box, looking over the audience instead of the stage. He prodded me with his elbow. "I caught him trying to spy on the leech and you earlier as I entered our booth. Now look. He's down there on the edge of the pit, still spying. Look."

Eramus returned the glasses and pointed his podgy fingers to an arched entrance below. My stomach soured as I recalled the man standing in the dark prior to our taking seats. I wet my lips and raised the glasses.

Right where Eramus had pointed, I saw an outline of a man who indeed seemed to be watching our box. As if waiting for me, he stepped from the shadows and allowed the dim light to highlight the curves of his face.

I blinked, scarcely believing my own eyes. My body hollowed as I stared, afraid to trust my senses, afraid the vision would vanish. I wiped my eyes before raising the glasses again to make certain.

Edward stood rooted amongst the tide of glittering jewels and feathered headdresses, looking straight at me. The sight of him held me spellbound. One sensation after another washed over me. My entire body trembled as I viewed him. I could have wept; I could have laughed. How was it possible?

My fingers tightened over the gold case as I gasped back a sob of joy. Never had Edward appeared more purified than here. The ground beneath his shoes was hallowed, unworthy to feel his tread, and yet the people around him had no knowledge of his existence. Edward was actually *here*, at the opera!

"By Jove, you know the fellow." Eramus nudged my shoulder. "Give those back."

I tightened my grip, preferring death to losing sight of Edward. He looked ragged and thin, making me suspect he'd been in London for some time. Had Henry convinced him he needed to come for me? That was so long ago. Surely, he couldn't have—I squeezed my eyes shut, lowering the glasses. How much had a ticket to the opera cost him?

They say I was a vision of elegance and refinement as I

watched from our box. The image everyone recalls is that I was so moved by my first opera that I sat spellbound with tears streaming down my cheeks. The truth is I wasn't at that opera.

My soul knew its mate and could scarcely contain its joy. It soared; it laughed; it screamed its delight, taking flight over that crowded auditorium, paying no mind to the stage. My love, *my only love*, had come. Unable to contain the fullness of it, I had little choice but to lean forward, pressing my hands against my heart as if enchanted, so I could weep with the joy.

My mind spun with possibilities. That Edward had come for me, there was no doubt. And though it was likely he had a plan, I devised one of my own, in case he'd overlooked an element. My thoughts were that when the opera finished, we would run, fleeing hand in hand through London's fog-enshrouded streets. If I could publicly disappear with Edward, it would give us bargaining power. I felt heartache for Isaac, knowing how torn he would feel returning to my father empty-handed. But the following morning, after it was too late not to marry, Edward could approach my father and negotiate with him. I would remain hidden until we had his support. It was so clear in that moment, I marveled that I'd not thought of it before. If my father could protect me as Isaac's wife, then surely, surely he could protect me as Edward's.

My hope was so apparent, that to this day my reputation as an opera enthusiast reigns. Dignitaries and nobility have ever hoped to court favor with me by including opera as entertainment. Yet here is the rub: I despise the opera. It has ever served as a reminder of this night.

Isaac was the opera enthusiast. When the last notes washed over the audience, he was on his feet and insisted on remaining until the last curtain descended. It took him another five minutes to gather our glasses and check beneath the seats. I could scarcely breathe with impatience.

By the time Isaac took my arm, the opera boxes surrounding

us had emptied and all tiers had drained. Heat radiated through the building as I tried to push through the mass of bodies.

Isaac tightened his grip on my arm and gave me a questioning look as he held me still. "Your father expects us to tarry a bit," he whispered. "Just stay with me and smile. I'll handle the small talk."

Because we were seated so close to the stage, everyone was in our path. Frantically, I stood on tiptoes but could catch no sight of Edward. Stiff satin skirts, heavy perfume, and dithering fans webbed us in. Gloved, feminine hands reached out to pat my cheek, and men slapped Isaac's back as we tried to thread through the mass.

"Yes, it was wonderful. As you can see, Miss Pierson was quite moved. If you'll please allow us to pass," Isaac said again and again, until he sounded like a trained parrot.

Instead, the crowd tightened around us, and more questions poured forth.

"How soon until the happy announcement?"

"Are you both free Friday?"

"Where's Pierson, old boy?"

I tightened my hold on Isaac's arm. In another minute, I would dissolve into tears. I'd read accounts of people being trampled in large gatherings, and for one desperate moment, I elt in danger of it.

"By jingo," Eramus said in a quiet voice next to me. "Isn't that Lord Melbourne approaching?"

I lifted my gaze to find the prime minister indeed making his way to us, spreading his gloved hands open as though he were about to gather Isaac and me into his fold. The crowd parted easily enough for him. Reporters trailed him, their eyes shining in anticipation as the prime minister approached. They scribbled furiously as they took in Isaac's and my attire.

It was then I finally caught sight of Edward.

Behind the reporters, he charged up the stairs, using his elbow to clip through the crowd, his face determined. When our eyes met, he paused, gripping the banister. His very countenance asked whether I still welcomed him.

My throat tightened that he would even consider such a thought. It took all my restraint not to fly to him that very second, but it wasn't possible. I couldn't even reassure him with a look, for Lord Melbourne inclined. I turned from Edward and gave the prime minister my most polished and welcoming smile. I comforted myself with the thought that a few minutes hence, Edward would know the depth of my love.

"Lord Dalry." Lord Melbourne extended his hand. "How delightful to see two of our brightest luminaries at Her Majesty's Opera House."

Two things happened at once. Unaware of our precarious position, Edward started toward me. Next to him, the tall form of Lord Alexander studied me with a knit expression before his gaze alighted on Edward, and he spoke the eleven words that crumbled my world.

"I say," he cried out, "isn't that the chap responsible for stealing Macy's bride?"

Stunned that he had possession of that knowledge, I gaped as his question burst like thunder over the crowd, rippling out in the form of shocked cries of delight.

Edward alone failed to notice. His intense gaze focused on me, he battled the crowd. A Highlander brandishing his sword could not have appeared more fearsome.

Like a gear clicking into place, Lord Melbourne's suspicion animated his features, and I could see he guessed that I could be Macy's missing bride. His entire body froze as he took in Edward's aggressive approach toward me. He bent, clutching his chest, before shooting me an accusing glare.

Thankfully, I'd seen his reaction, giving me time to compose my features. Months of Isaac's painstaking training saved me. Keeping my arm looped through his, I watched Edward's approach with the perfect urbane yet half-curious expression.

In my peripheral vision, I saw Lord Melbourne doubt his own suspicion and straighten again. He watched, fascinated, as Edward halted before me and stood panting.

Only then did Edward seem to realize the scandal he was creating. I saw the whites of his eyes as they slowly moved from right to left. All conversation died and everyone stared.

He tugged at his collar, then bowed—a public signal asking me to recognize him and grant the privilege of speaking with me.

Though we stood only feet apart, oceans and continents stretched between us. I could not acknowledge him without tipping over the first domino in a row. In less than an hour, society at large would guess I was Macy's bride. There was no possible way Edward and I could manage to run off and hide with the entire opera house watching and blocking the exits. Later, reporters and spectators would descend on London House, for I was not one, but two newspaper sensations. When the last domino fell, my father and Isaac would be ruined and I'd most likely be returned to Macy. I'd already lost Edward forever, and knew it, for if all of London knew who I truly was, there would be no chance of building a new life with Edward. The only thing I might still be able to salvage was Isaac's and my father's reputations.

Casting Edward a look of scorn, I leaned closer to Isaac. "Darling, I don't like this man's manner. My head hurts. May we leave soon?"

"Of course." Isaac's voice sounded pale as he bowed to Lord Melbourne. "By your leave. Shall I see you at the club tonight?"

Lord Melbourne carefully searched my face, his relief apparent at finding what appeared to be annoyance toward Edward. Smiling, he broke into a nod. "Yes, yes. By all means take her home and find me later. Jefferies is in town, and I wish to introduce you."

Gathering my skirts, I started to give my back to Edward.

"Wait, please!" Edward broke protocol and took a step closer. "I beg you!"

I froze and gave him a second glance, knowing if I shed so much as a tear, all was lost.

Edward ran his fingers through his curls, giving Isaac a heated look and leaving me in no doubt of the animosity between them. When Edward returned to me, his tone softened. "Please. Are you Miss Pierson, the Emerald Heiress? I've . . . I've read about your work with the orphans, and I have tried everything in my power to see you. If I could just have one moment of your time, please."

Lord Melbourne watched, as tense as a bowstring.

A lump rose in my throat, which I didn't dare to swallow. I gave Edward a look of disdain before turning my back to him. "Isaac, dear heart, give that man a shilling or two, will you?"

Isaac's horrified gaze swiveled my way, but I tightened my clutch on his arm, begging him to remove me. Seemingly bewildered, he fumbled around in his white waistcoat and withdrew two pound notes, which he crumpled into Edward's pocket.

How I managed to escape, I know not. Tears weren't enough. I wanted to run. I wanted to scream and rend my dress, but Isaac's firm grip on my elbow kept me from anything other than a graceful exit.

Outdoors, scalding tears refused to stop as we stepped into the blinding fog. Thankfully, Isaac gathered me to him and with swift steps hastened me toward the carriage, back into the swirling mist.

Twenty-Four

HEARING ISAAC'S RAP on the door, I buried my face in a pillow to muffle the sound of my harsh weeping. But it was of no use. My shoulders heaved as my sobs deepened.

"Julia." The door handle rattled; then Isaac rapped again. "Let me in."

I turned over, hugging the pillow to my stomach, reliving the stricken look on Edward's face as I turned my back toward him. It was worse than the one he wore the night I married Mr. Macy. I keened anew.

"Julia, please. Open the door," Isaac said. Then his voice lowered as he spoke to someone else.

I closed my eyes, which burned. It was past three in the morning. Why couldn't he leave me alone? I didn't want him. I never wanted him again.

The lock on my door clicked, and I buried my face in the pillow as the door groaned. Two seconds later, the mattress sank as Isaac crawled onto my massive bed. Wet, sticky strands of hair were brushed from my cheeks and tucked behind my ear. "You've not stopped weeping since we've come home. Enough."

I sobbed harder, turning my face into my curled fist.

He lifted me and tried to pull me to his chest, but I resisted. "Crying is not going to take it back; it's not helping. I *can* help you, however."

Trying to abate my tears, I finally looked at him. Earlier, after we'd left the opera, he'd refused to so much as glance at me as our carriage carried us home, whereas Eramus had openly gloated.

"Are you angry with me?"

Isaac rubbed his tired-looking eyes. "I was." He leaned forward and pulled a shawl from a nearby chair, reminding me I wore only a thick chemise. "I wondered what sort of woman I was marrying. But since you've been unable to cease your tears, I see you had no desire to hurt Edward like that. Not even Kate can cry five consecutive hours."

Empty, I looked over the chamber. The dress Miss Moray had spent hours primping lay on the floor, rent. In my haste to be removed from it, I had torn at it. One citrine and gold earring remained in my ear; the other I'd flung into the ashes, along with the choker.

The image of hurt gripping Edward's face as I uttered those dreadful words came back, and I began to cry anew. "I'm lost, Isaac. I am so lost."

"You are not lost." He drew me to him and cradled me against his chest. "I have you in my keeping, and I know where we're going."

I clung to his silk and velvet dressing gown, accepting the comfort of his embrace, if not his words. I'd seen the way Edward had glared at Isaac. They were enemies, and I was in the wrong arms. New sobs rose. What did any of it matter? I'd betrayed Edward in every way a person could.

"No!" Isaac gave me a small shake. "Collect yourself before

your father finds me unchaperoned in bed with you. Even my influence doesn't carry that far." Isaac produced a handkerchief. "Here."

I shook my head. I'd cried so long that even silk would irritate my eyes.

He opened his mouth to speak again, but the pounding of servants running down the hall alerted us. Isaac wasted no time disentangling himself from the covers and bed. My father's heavy voice carried from the foyer as Isaac opened the door and slipped from my bedchamber.

I shut my eyes, praying he wasn't spotted. Already the situation was more than I could endure. Was it possible for a person to become undone? Instead of my father's ranting, however, I heard Isaac greet him as he started down the steps.

Weary, I removed my remaining earring, then leaned against the headboard. Isaac had calmed me but had not extracted the deep ache. Nothing ever would.

On the landing, I heard my father say, "Is she still awake?"

"Yes, sir. I just checked on her."

The door opened and my father entered. His eyes narrowed as he took in my swollen nose and red-rimmed eyes. "What happened?"

Isaac shifted behind him. "Reverend Auburn was at the opera, sir."

My father drew to his full height. "Julia, how shameful. You're as good as married to Isaac. Control yourself."

Isaac wedged himself between my father and the threshold in order to gain entrance to my room. "It wasn't seeing Reverend Auburn, sir. He tried to speak with her, and she . . . she had to cut him."

My father yanked off his silk scarf, his scowl relaxing. "Well, if he was foolish enough to approach her, then he deserved it. He knew better, Julia. You only did what you had to."

Isaac frowned but didn't dispute my father.

My father gave my face another glance, then flushed red. "It's just a combination of nerves." He came to my bedside and drew back one corner of the covers. "Too many things all combined into one night. Sleep now, Julia. Tomorrow you'll stay home." He waited until I slipped my feet into the cool pockets of the sheets, then looked thoughtful. "For the next week or two, I'll keep you here."

I set my teeth and silently accused him with my gaze. His decision had nothing to do with my welfare. He feared I would meet Edward again. We both knew it. I had sacrificed my happiness for him, and this was the height of our relationship?

"It works out well," my father continued, ignoring my tacit assault and keying off my lamp. He backed toward the door. "With Eramus's brash actions, I'd rather not keep their names paired. Rumor has it, he lost a fortune tonight at the tables."

～

When I next opened my eyes, my room was filled with sun. I glanced at my gown, still crumpled on the floor, then realized that my father must have ordered Miss Moray to allow me to sleep without disturbances. Having no wish to see her either, I slid from the bed and saw to my own toilette.

Tears rose as I touched Edward's pin. Though there wasn't any hope for us now, I couldn't bear the thought of becoming betrothed to Isaac the morning after betraying Edward. Pinning it on, I started down the steps.

Mr. Forrester emerged from the library as soon as my shoes clacked against the wooden floor. "Oh, it's only you." He lowered the open book with a sneer. "Young ladies shouldn't wear hard-soled shoes. It's unbecoming."

"And old men shouldn't try to have wit, for it reveals the depth of their stupidity!"

Mr. Forrester's steps rang through the foyer. "If you had any sense, you'd confess your knowledge about what happened last night."

I spun, despising him for daring to talk to me about the opera.

Mr. Forrester wrinkled his face in disgust. "So you did know. I knew you weren't to be trusted. Get out of my sight." He threw his book at me, but it sailed over my left shoulder.

Rage boiled over. I might have ruined my life, but I was done putting up with this buffoon. I ran, snatched up the book, and hurled it back. The corner hit him just above the eye.

"I hate you!" I screamed, picking up the closest object—a rare vase. I hurled it at Forrester, but he stepped aside and it smashed against the wall.

He scrambled to use the library door as a shield. "Here now! There's no call for—"

I attempted to throw a bust of Caesar, but it was too heavy and landed with a thud near my feet. It cracked. I grabbed my father's walking stick from where it rested against the table.

"Give me that!" Mr. Forrester left his sanctuary and lunged for the stick.

I swung at his head and missed just before Isaac's face appeared over the second-floor banister. He took the stairs by threes and caught me from behind, wrapping strong arms about my waist, lifting me from my feet. "Julia. Stop this. Right now."

When my anger broke, there was only grief. I sobbed anew as Mr. Forrester plucked the cane, midswing, and towered over me.

"What did you do to her?" Isaac screamed, pulling me close.

Mr. Forrester touched the forming goose egg on his head. "You're taking her side? That banshee of yours tried to kill me. That's what's going on. I just proved once and for all she's working for Macy. Where's Roy? He's going to hear this."

"He's out." Isaac stepped away. His face burned with anger, and shaving lotion ran down his chin and neck. He lifted the front of his shirt, revealing a line of hair down his stomach as he wiped his face.

"Make him leave." I pointed to Mr. Forrester. "Make him leave this house."

Isaac wiped his eyes with his sleeve and repeated, "What did you do to her?"

"Has this entire household gone mad?" Mr. Forrester pointed at the shilling-size egg on his head with an exaggerated motion. "*I'm* the injured party here. Have I ever laid a hand on a woman? Do you really think that of me?"

"You threw the book at me."

Mr. Forrester leaned near. "And I'm beginning to wish I had aimed."

Isaac held up his hands for peace. "Julia, please. I cannot send Mr. Forrester away until I get to the bottom of this." He wiped his neck again, frowning. "I'm hardly dressed for this conversation." He turned and shouted, "James!"

"Sir?" He appeared so quickly it was clear he'd been eavesdropping.

"Take Julia to breakfast, please."

"Yes, sir."

In the dining room, James fussed over me, pouring tea, setting the fruit dish before me. He ignored Mr. Forrester's request for coffee.

"Just wait until your father arrives." Mr. Forrester shook out his napkin and grabbed a pear. "If he shies from beating you for that shameful display, I'll volunteer."

I stared at my plate, wondering where Edward was this morning and if he felt as heartbroken as I did.

Isaac entered wearing linens instead of silks, so I knew he had no plans to leave this morning. He took his seat and held his coffee cup between his hands. "James, tell Pierrick I want poached eggs with kippers and tomatoes. I'm not eating one of his blasted French breakfasts. Not this morning."

"Have him send the croissants, though." Mr. Forrester

continued to probe the bump over his eye. "Bring plenty of preserves with those too."

"I want both of your attention," Isaac said, watching his cup as James poured coffee. "I want to know what happened. Julia, I'm allowing Forrester to speak first. I'm asking you to remain silent until he finishes."

"I'll talk when he leaves." Mr. Forrester pointed to James, who took the hint and shut the doors. Mr. Forrester stood and leaned so far over the table, his frock coat touched our dishes. He selected the *Times*, the *Morning Gazette*, the *Penny Post*, and the *Daily Tidings*. "See the headlines? She knew Macy was going to set those fires but said nothing."

I gave him a shocked look. "You can't actually believe that."

Isaac snorted and scanned the front page of the *Times*. "Of all the stupidity! Of course she had no knowledge. And for that matter, how do you even know it was Macy? Do you have proof?"

"She's the proof. When I mentioned last night to her, you should have seen her face."

Isaac's expression suggested he found Mr. Forrester to be a half-wit. "I thought you were in the news business. How can you not know what's truly upsetting her?"

Mr. Forrester wasn't listening. "If it wasn't the fire, why should she have a violent reaction because I said I knew about last night?"

"Isaac, he threw a book at me," I cried, unable to sit silently.

"You deserve far worse."

"You're despicable and—"

"Julia, even if he refuses to, *you* will act genteel." Isaac looked at Forrester. "We are at Lord Pierson's table. We are not barbarians, we are not Americans, and every person here is capable of worthy conduct."

"Did she send or receive any messages last night?" Mr. Forrester asked. "Find out that much."

"She was at the opera with me." Isaac's voice was black.

James chose that moment to enter with a squeaky-wheeled cart.

"James, last night did Miss Pierson send or receive a message?" Mr. Forrester asked.

The pitying look James gave informed me he knew what had happened at the opera. He laid croissants on the table. "No, sir."

Mr. Forrester folded his arms over the table and leaned forward. "Well, did anything out of the ordinary happen last night, James?"

James paused, and I held my breath. "Yes, sir, but I've been waiting to tell Master Isaac about it in private."

"What is it?" Mr. Forrester demanded.

James nodded in my direction. "Sir, if I may request, I would rather not say with a lady present in the room."

Curiosity sparked in Isaac's eyes. "Go on, James."

James took a breath. "Well, sir, sometime near dawn, Bruno kept disturbing the neighborhood by barking. The coachman was with Simmons, and quite frankly, I've had problems managing the groom on duty, so I went to lock Bruno in the stable myself. By the time I got my trousers, robe, and slippers and arrived at the stable . . ." James licked his lips and again nodded in my direction.

"Go on. Finish the tale," Isaac said.

"Someone had beat the dog to death, sir."

I sucked in my breath and covered my mouth. Cold tingled up and down my body.

"Beat him?" Isaac asked. "What on earth? Who?"

"I don't rightly know, sir. The groom returned home and confessed to drinking in a part of London his mother would be ashamed of."

"Where is this groom?"

"Still retching, I should imagine. I've been waiting for you or Lord Pierson to have time to discuss the matter."

"Relieve the groom of his duties, without reference and no more pay than he's due."

"Yes, sir." James bowed. "Is there anything else?"

"No, leave. We wish to dine in private."

"Very well, sir."

While James rolled the cart from the room, Isaac addressed Mr. Forrester. "You don't suppose it was Macy, do you?"

"Give her lover more credit than that," Mr. Forrester said. "He only beats people to death, not canines. There were some vagrants in Hyde Park last night terrorizing this area. They didn't make front page because of the fire. It was most likely them."

Isaac made no response but started to dig through the stack of newspapers. He scanned the society pages of three and handed them over to Forrester. "If you wish to know about Julia's reaction, here are the stories covering last night. Why weren't you at the opera? I thought you were covering this."

Mr. Forrester scowled and displayed the headline covering the fires. "Something else came up that required my time. Besides, I told you, I think it's a bad idea to keep your names linked now that she's established. I beg you, Isaac, let her go."

As he read the articles, however, Forrester's face evidenced distress at having missed another newspaper sensation. I fastened my gaze outdoors, glad that if nothing else, Forrester wouldn't profit from Edward's slight.

～

My hand still trembling, I dipped my pen. After breakfast, I had declared my intention to work on correspondences. Isaac requested I remain with him by working in the library. I glanced at him sleeping on the couch, understanding why he'd chosen this chamber. It took him less than five minutes to fall asleep.

Mr. Forrester, who also refused to leave my side, sat playing solitaire in the room. Above his eye, his goose egg was turning purple, searing his forehead. As if sensing my gaze, he sneered at me.

"You know that I'm near exposing you, don't you?" He flipped over the king of spades. "When I finally expose you, will Macy be angry enough to punish you?"

I rolled my eyes and wrote: *Lord Pierson accepts with pleasure the invitation of—*

Then, unable to take his faulty logic, I said, "If you were to expose me, don't you think you'd be the one punished?"

Baroness Hamely for dinner on Sunday, tenth of February—

"Someday you are going to regret having met me." He finished a suit.

"I can assure you, I already do."

"Not like you will."

I dipped my pen and held it over the pot until the drips of ink stopped, then wrote, *at seven o'clock.*

"Who was here last night?" Mr. Forrester pulled an ace from the pile and set it aside. "Which one of his curs beats a dog?"

I bit the top of the pen, suddenly reminded of last night. Though determined not to cry, my face twisted. My vision blurred too much to bother finishing my reply, so I looped the nib several times on a fresh piece of paper—the expensive, pound-a-sheet, for-royalty-only paper.

"You forget I saw you at Eastbourne." Mr. Forrester sat back and crossed his legs as he shifted tactics. "You can fool your father and Isaac into thinking you fear him, but I watched the pair of you together."

I held the melting spoon over the candle, prepared to seal my scribble, wanting to conceal that he'd rattled me.

Mr. Forrester's chair creaked. "My manservant said that the very first night you met Macy, you spent the entire night with him. Is that true?"

I looked at Isaac. Even in his sleep he looked refined—no parted mouth, no jerks of movement, just the steady rise and fall of his chest. My skirts rustled as I went to him and gently tapped on his arm. He stirred and sat. "Are you finished?"

I folded my arms over the edge of his couch. "He won't stop asking me questions about Macy."

Isaac snapped his head in Forrester's direction. "What is wrong with you?"

"Don't be fooled." Mr. Forrester resumed his game of solitaire. "She played Reverend Auburn the same way, and betrayed him in the end."

Fresh pain seared me as I again saw Edward's face.

Isaac was on his feet, quivering. "You are speaking of my intended. You may be a guest of Lord Pierson, but if you open your fat, stupid mouth again, I'll box you. I swear it!" He knelt and gathered me to him. "Sweetheart, sit with me and I'll read while we wait for your father."

I settled on the settee, mournfully recalling how Edward had once dragged Mr. Forrester out of a room by the collar for insulting me.

Forrester shook his head in pity as Isaac selected the poems we'd been reading together in the evenings. I leaned closer to him, no longer caring about keeping Isaac distant. What did it matter now? Let Forrester see Isaac's protectiveness of me.

Isaac must have also wished for Forrester to understand his steadfastness, for he spread a blanket over me, then pressed a kiss into my hair. He opened one arm, an invitation to rest against him, which I accepted. Soon his soothing tones filled the room, and I closed my eyes.

The poem he read spoke of a freshly mounded grave under a lazuline, cloudless sky. In his lulling tone, mossy gravestones were described under gnarled rowan trees. It mingled with my dreams, so that a warm breeze caressed my cheek, carrying the fragrance of new dirt. Thunder rumbled in the distance as I stretched over a grave, refusing to be comforted, refusing to leave.

A door slammed, and with a gasp, I sat forward and blinked, surprised to find myself in the library. The imagery of the grave had been so realistic, the breeze so true, I felt disoriented.

"Did you dream?" Isaac asked.

Before I could answer, my father, followed by James, stumbled into the chamber.

Forrester jumped to his feet and, like a child anxious to tell on his siblings, pointed a finger at us.

My father held up his hand, grimacing. "No one speaks." He winced at the sound of his voice, pinching the bridge of his nose. "Isaac, dress; join me for lunch. Afterwards you're coming with me. I . . . won't be able to talk and need you to."

Isaac rose. "Sir, if you're in that much pain, what difference does one day make? We could all use a day of rest."

My father looked angered but couldn't respond. His face had grown ashen again, and he gripped either side of his head. Desperate to help him, I tugged Isaac's sleeve.

"Fetch Lord Pierson laudanum," Isaac directed James in a hushed tone. "Make no noise as you leave."

"No." My father rocked, holding his head. He sagged against the doorframe. "Go . . . go to our physician and get morphine. Tell him I need syringes with it."

A slight hitch in Isaac's breathing was the only suggestion of his dismay. "Sir, allow me to escort you to your chamber."

"No. I need to be there this afternoon. You're not ready to debate them alone. Take me to the dining chamber."

Isaac approached, but while my father winced in pain, Isaac mouthed the words *laudanum only* to James before bracing my father's arm.

They staggered into the dining chamber, where my father demanded the clock be stopped, the fire screened, the drapes drawn, and all lights extinguished.

My father clutched Isaac's arm like a feeble child. I scrambled to take his other side, but Isaac shook his head, telling me to keep a distance. My father stumbled as he sat, swatting his hand before his face, seeing insects I could not.

James brought a bottle of laudanum and gently set it before

my father. I eyed the liquid, feeling ill. Though I no longer believed Mama had killed herself with the drug, I hadn't seen such an amount since the night of her death. Instead of being angry his instructions weren't followed, my father poured and swallowed more than I would have thought safe.

James did a magnificent job of soundlessly setting the table. Even Forrester sat unusually quiet, studying my father with concern.

Nausea rose through me, so that I had to cup my hands over my mouth to keep from breathing the pungent smell of the haunch of venison. Why, I wondered, did my father get these headaches? He looked near death. Whenever I glanced at Isaac, however, it wasn't my father he fixed his concern upon. His gaze rested on me.

All at once, cold air and light lashed through the chamber. "Sir!" Miss Moray stood in the doorway. She held her head high, her gaze scathing. Behind her, Mrs. King, the London house-keeper, labored for breath.

Isaac and I were on our feet and out the door, pulling them from the threshold. Gently shutting the door, Isaac angrily whispered, "What on earth merits disturbing our lunch in such a manner?"

Miss Moray swallowed her surprise that we chose to eat our meal in such grotesque fashion. "I beg your pardon, sir, but the citrines we leased for Miss Pierson's opera costume last night are all missing. I've just discovered it."

Isaac rubbed his brow. "Are you certain you looked everywhere?"

Miss Moray stiffened. "I checked four times, sir."

Isaac's expression was pained as he looked at the ceiling. "All right. Lock up the servants' hall and search their rooms. Locate me when the jewels are found."

Mrs. King dipped. "And if they're not located?"

Isaac ran his fingers through his waxed hair. "If it comes to that, I'll question the staff myself. You're dismissed."

Miss Moray eyed me with displeasure as they left, as if believing I'd stolen them. I scowled at her, not caring a whit what she thought.

"Prepare for this evening," Isaac said after they were gone. "For once, I'm not looking forward to your father recovering from his headache. He's not going to take well your hitting Forrester with a book nor the missing jewels."

"Why didn't you call for the physician?" I demanded. "He's had more laudanum than is good for him."

"The last thing we're going to do is call in a physician!"

"How can you not? How can you do nothing?"

As if counting silently, Isaac shut his eyes. When he reopened them, he was his composed self. "Is he not a father to me as well?" He pressed his lips, then said, "If I call your father's physician, he'll only treat it with a supply of morphine."

He grew solemn and gave me a look that asked if I understood.

"And?"

He rubbed his brow. "I've sworn to your father never to disclose more. I've also sworn to never allow him near morphine again. Do you understand? Or do I need to break troth with him, lest I lose your trust next?"

I rubbed my neck, once more wondering about Isaac's unspoken childhood, but to show him I was finished, I nodded.

"Trust me," he said, gathering my arm. "Tomorrow, he won't even remember today. That much is a mercy. I'm going to accompany him to his club tonight. Will you be all right staying home alone?"

I gave a reluctant nod. "So long as Forrester's gone too."

～

I sat that night cross-legged on the library floor, cradling Edward's mementos. The pitiable items seemed laughable without their meanings attached. A dog-eared, stained Bible filled with notes scrawled in sloppy penmanship. A withered oak leaf found tucked in Psalms. The only item of value was the timepiece, but even that carried a curse. Each morning it represented Isaac's broken heart, and now it represented mine.

Nevertheless, I lovingly touched each one, knowing the time had come to tuck them into a hatbox, stored for a future day when the pain subsided. But that, too, was unacceptable. Becoming a person who could open this box without heartache would be the third and final betrayal of Edward.

I suddenly wanted reasons and answers. Why had any of this happened to me? Was I being punished because William had raised me with false ideas? Because I'd scorned the vicar in my village? Because I'd believed Mr. Macy's lies?

I did not cry out again to God. I already had his answer—my story was different and he wanted me to entrust myself to him. But I didn't care what he was doing, as he hadn't bothered to consult me before planning it.

All at once the door slammed open, and a dark form stepped up to the threshold. It is one thing to wander into the slough of despond, mourning one's role in the universe, but it is quite another to have Eramus Calvin disturb the elegy.

I rose, frowning. Before I could inform him that Isaac and my father were out, he stumbled into the chamber. One side of his face was scraped, and patches of blood smeared his cheek. He held his rib cage, wincing. "Fetch your father."

"Are you injured?"

"Your father, you daft idiot! Get. Your. Father!"

"He's not home."

To my amazement, Eramus's face grew monstrous with rage. He stormed to the mantel and retrieved the fire poker, which he beat mercilessly against the tiled hearth. Breathing heavily, he turned toward me with a look of murder. My blood ran cold.

"Now what!" he screamed and again struck the poker on the floor.

This time, he was so close I could smell the whiskey lacing his breath. I froze, recalling a string of terrors from my childhood when William was similarly volatile.

Eramus advanced. "He dared to cut my allowance, while he lavishes a fortune on a queer-gotten daughter! He gives Isaac everything and me nothing! Northfield is rather poor compensation for losing an heiress—"

He seized and crushed my finger. Pain sparked through me like wildfire. All thought and reason departed as I sank to the floor.

"We're going upstairs, Cousin, and this time you're going to find me something more valuable than *semiprecious* stones in exchange for my silence. Do you understand?"

I nodded, realizing that Eramus had taken the citrines. The idea of him sneaking about my bedchamber horrified me, but when I recalled James's story that morning about the stable dog, my eyes widened with fear and my breath came in hard pants.

"Not a sound!" Eramus warned. He snatched my wrist and tightened his hold, dragging me to the hearth, where he jabbed the poker into the hot coals. "So long as you stay quiet," he said, turning the poker, "there will be no need to hurt you."

I glanced at the door. Sober, there wasn't a chance of Eramus risking my father's wrath. But inebriated?

"Hullo. What's this?" Eramus bent and picked up Edward's Bible and watch. He pocketed the timepiece, but with an indifferent toss, he threw the Bible to the flames.

I shrieked and went after it. It had already caught fire, but I pulled it out and beat the flames with my skirt. When I finished, the pages were singed and the cover blackened.

"Rogue," I screamed, hugging the book to me.

"I said quiet!" Eramus shouted, then threw the watch on the carpet before him. As if testing me, he lifted his foot to crush it.

I dove for the timepiece. His foot crushed my wrist, holding me in place.

A grotesque snarl tangled his features before he ripped the poker from the coals. "You all think you're so much better than me! Everyone thinks Isaac is such a perfect example! Well, let's see how the leech likes having his precious bride's face marred."

Time slowed as I calculated how hard I'd have to yank my hand from underneath Eramus's foot in order to cause him to lose his balance. Closing my eyes, I managed to relax my arm before I wrenched it back with my full weight. My forearm screamed in pain, but Eramus stumbled backwards, hitting his head on the mantel.

I remember my absolute panic as I found my feet, for I recall that my underpinnings made standing difficult. I have no memory of leaving the chamber and running through the front hall, though I can remember the sensation of being pushed down the front stairs. My head struck the last step. Warmth trickled down my scalp. I blinked, trying to make sense of Eramus's silhouetted form standing in the doorway of London House.

Dazed, I struggled to my feet, grabbing a rock.

As if drunk on my fear, Eramus took each step one at a time.

Tottering, I grasped one of the fleurs-de-lis and opened the gate to the street. For once, the street was empty. No street sweepers or carriages were present. I ran, feeling dirt and snow on the cobblestone beneath my stocking feet. I barely made it to Chap Street before I was winded. My stays wouldn't allow me to breathe.

I doubled over, gasping, wondering where to go. My eyes followed the familiar route to Lady Beatrice's house, but what good could she do? Every window in the Billingsby house was dark.

Hyde Park.

The words formed in my thoughts. I glanced at the hazy glow of lamps in the near distance. Hadn't Forrester thought it possible the vagrants from last night might have wandered to our street? Surely there would be people there, or at least somewhere to hide. I wiped blood from my eyes, gathering the last of my strength, then dashed across the first street.

A hard wind picked up my hair, whipping it around my face, making it impossible to see. Having no choice, I turned temporarily, praying that Eramus couldn't walk against the gale.

It was then I saw it.

Only one more street over stood a house I'd seen before, distinguished by fearsome carved lions emerging from stone window boxes.

Without thought, I changed course. My lungs screamed for oxygen as I lunged toward my last hope. Behind me, metal clattered over cobblestone, making me wonder if Eramus had thrown aside the poker to help him gain speed. It gave me the last burst of energy I needed.

Seconds later, my free hand frantically grasped at the stairs as I tried to scramble up. Arms encircled me and yanked me from behind.

Eramus hissed in my ear, tightening his arms, taking away my ability to breathe.

I eyed the door, desperate, realizing I hadn't even managed to bang it. In a desperate attempt, I blindly threw the rock in my hand. The sound of smashing glass filled the air.

Warm yellow light flooded the features of Eramus's face. He looked up in surprise as the voices of men filled the air.

"What the dev—" I heard Mr. Macy's voice start to yell.

With a startled cry, Eramus dropped me and ran. I landed on the stone step.

"Julia!" Mr. Macy's shoes appeared in view before he lifted me and nestled me in his arms. He removed his hand from the back of my head and stared at the sticky red blood in amazement.

I buried my face into him and clung, gulping for air. I feared he'd leave me, but I couldn't speak to beg him not to.

"Snyder," he yelled, cradling me. "Get that man running down the street. If you value your life, you won't lose him. Shhh, darling." He carried me inside. "My word, what's happened?"

In the drawing room where we'd spoken before, he set me down on a couch and tried to back away, but I clung harder and, finally finding my breath, sobbed.

"Sweetheart." He pressed his lips against my forehead. "You've never been safer than you are at this moment. I need you to calm yourself. I need to examine you."

"D-don't l-l-leave."

"I swear it; I'm not going anywhere. Shhh." He wrapped me in his arms again. "All right. I'll hold you a bit, but you're injured and I need to assess how badly."

I cried until my breaths came in short gasps. Frightened at my inability to stop inhaling, I stared at him.

"It's all right." His sharp eyes slowly ran over my features. "This can happen when one panics. As you calm, your breathing will become regular. Now let me have a look at you."

He sat back, revealing that my blood was smeared over his silk shirt and his chin. My dress and his gold couch were also stained.

"Don't allow the sight of blood to unnerve you." His tone soothed. "Just focus on taking calm breaths." With an austere expression, he ran his tapered fingers over my head. He unwound my braid and gently felt the back of my skull, where my hair was matted. "How did this happen?"

"He—he—he—" I couldn't catch enough breath to finish. "Pushed . . . stairs."

His jaw hardened, but he nodded. "I think I understand. The good news, it's just a gash, not deep. Head wounds tend to look worse than they actually are. Now let me see your hands." He gingerly overturned them and stared at my burnt palms, encrusted with pebbles and dirt.

"He tried . . . to burn . . . ," I gasped, " Edward's Bible."

One brow elevated. "Did you dive in after it?"

I nodded, earning one of his sardonic chuckles.

"Yes, and beat out the fire with your skirts." He lifted a charred section of my dress. "Doesn't that rather defeat the purpose, darling? I thought the point of the book was to keep one from flames."

"Sir." A man entered the room. "He caught a cab, but I heard him say which opium house he was going to."

"I said not to lose him." Mr. Macy's tone chilled the air as he continued to examine my hand.

"I've got someone tailing him."

"Don't let him take drugs," Mr. Macy said as he pressed his fingers into my neck and made me move my head from side to side. "If he has, don't let him consume more. I want him sober. No one is to see him leaving the house, either. Understand?"

"Yes, sir."

"Send word to the Koops. Business detains me and I won't be joining their dinner."

The man's footsteps faded into the hall.

Through my sleeves, Mr. Macy felt my arms. I winced at the spot where Eramus had pinned me with his boot. After taking a penknife from his pocket, Mr. Macy cut my sleeve and ran his fingers over my developing bruise. "Did he have something to do with this?"

I nodded, feeling my face twist.

His jaw tightened in anger, but he met my eye with a reassuring gaze as he encircled my rib cage with his fingers and ran his hands over my bodice. When I stiffened, he gave a slight smile. "You'll have to forgive me, darling. I'm not trying to impose on your modesty. I want to make sure you don't have any more injuries." Next he peeled off my stockings and examined my feet. "You're bleeding here too. Where are your shoes?"

"Home."

"Be brave again, darling." Macy removed his coat and threw it in a chair, then loosened and pulled off his cravat. He sent a servant for a basin and pitcher of warm water, then dimmed the lamps around the room, leaving one fully lit, which he returned with.

Taking his knife, he held it over the flame a few seconds before dipping it in brandy. "I need to dig out the pebbles from your hands and feet. And I'm going to use brandy to clean your wounds before bandaging them. It will sting."

He swabbed my hand with the alcohol. My breathing had returned to normal, and the first tears of relief, instead of panic, filled my eyes. Mr. Macy looked tender as he carefully dug each piece of gravel from my hands. His face was a mixture of anger and softheartedness. Each time I gave a small cry of pain, he winced as though he'd injured himself.

After a while I studied him, scarcely able to believe this was the same man who burned businesses and blackmailed others.

His gaze lifted before it flickered with annoyance. "I see they've finally begun talking about me at your father's house. Otherwise you wouldn't look at me with such amazement. Tell me what you've heard."

"My father still forbids anyone to mention your name."

He kissed my palm, having removed the last of the dirt. "Well, perhaps I owe Roy at least one favor after all."

A knock interrupted us. Macy opened the door, retrieved the basin, whispered new orders, and then set the basin on a low table near the couch. Without asking permission, he dipped my hair into the warm water and soaped my hair and scalp with a sandalwood wash. He rinsed it, then carefully examined my wound after toweling my wet hair.

A maid returned with one of his satin dressing robes and socks.

"Undress to your chemise, darling," Mr. Macy said, then frowned when I blushed. "I won't look, for heaven's sake. Besides, I'm the last person to feel modest around."

I stood stiffly as he unbuttoned the back of my dress, but allowed him to disrobe me from the torn gown and wrap me in his robe. It smelled wonderfully of his cigar blend and scent. He sat me down and placed a pair of knit cashmere socks on my feet.

Like he used to do at Eastbourne, he took the couch across from me. "Now, tell me who that man was."

I stared at my bandaged hands. Now that the terror had passed, I didn't want Macy in my confidences. I glanced about me, wondering what on earth I did want anymore.

"Darling," Mr. Macy continued after a pause, "when you invite me into a situation, you waive the right to choose the degree to which I become invested. Now talk, for I am rather angry but prefer to make knowledgeable decisions over rash ones."

I eyed him and decided I would take no risks with his particular mood. "Eramus Calvin."

"Why was he chasing you? Leave out no details."

I chose my words carefully, trying to shield Isaac and my father. I told him about Edward's gifts and the missing citrines.

Mr. Macy leaned back and crossed his legs, looking pensive as I spoke. When I finished, he leaned forward. "You have my deepest promise, Julia. Eramus Calvin will never bother you again. Here." He withdrew a gold-and-black onyx ring from his pinkie finger. "Everyone in the underworld knows this ring; keep it on your personage. If you ever run into problems in the future, show it. If they know anything about me, they'll respect it."

I took his ring and studied it. The craftsmanship was extraordinary. It was a square-cut onyx; each corner was upheld by hooded cobras whose fangs served as prongs. Their four serpentine bodies twisted flawlessly into the ring's shape. I couldn't imagine how he thought I'd ever wear it. Rather than offend him, I slipped it into the pocket of his robe for him to find later. "May I return home now?"

Silence met my request. Feeling a cold pit in my stomach, I waited several seconds before peeking. He sat, finger curled upon his lips, his eyes penetrating. "Do you really think that's wise? Here I thought Roy's house was a safe enough place." He frowned as he rose and stalked to the hearth, where he finally withdrew a cigarette. "I'm not sure Roy suits you, darling. Think hard. Is that what you truly wish to do?"

"You—you mean I may leave?"

He snorted, then spoke around the cigarette as he lit it. "My wife can do whatever the blazes she wishes. If you haven't noticed yet—" he spread wide his arms—"I don't exactly lord over you."

I glanced at the door, wondering how to transition from that statement to be able to leave.

He flicked the match into the hearth, looking annoyed. "Fine. You may leave when I have Eramus in my keeping. In the meantime . . ." He crossed the room, set his cigarette aside, and stirred a packet of white powder into a glass of claret. "I want you to drink this. It will calm you enough to sleep. I won't push you further while you're in this state of mind. Drink."

I accepted the glass. Warmth stole over me almost instantly. My senses were also anesthetized; the idea of resisting him never occurred to me as he led me to the couch. "Sit," he said. "You'll be surprised how comforting it can be to be held, saying nothing."

He settled next to me, wrapping me in his arms. Within seconds I could hardly see the chamber, and my body felt twice as heavy. Exhausted, I leaned against him, vaguely aware of his scent. Each tick of the mantel clock stretched longer than the one before it.

At one point, I woke when Mr. Macy stirred and heard him say to someone, "The irony is too rich for words. My own wife assaulted." He laughed with dark humor. "She has two of the most powerful men in London at her disposal, and yet someone still dares to bully her."

"I wish you'd just let her go." It was Rooke.

"I couldn't even if I wanted to." Mr. Macy shifted as though trying to become comfortable. "My fate is bound up in this slip of a girl. Hard to believe, isn't it?"

"If you ask me, she's jinxed and is going to be the ruin of us."

"Keep your opinions. Who was watching her house tonight?

She should have had protection the moment that man pushed her outside."

"Adam. We found him playing dice."

"Where is he now?"

"With the one you sent us after. Who is he?"

Mr. Macy sighed and I felt him move. "Never mind his identity. I'll deal with him personally, later. Go send a note to her father's staff. I promised she could return when I had her assailant in custody."

"Why don't I just take her there?"

"No. Let him fetch his daughter for himself. I'm curious if he dares to."

❧

Strong arms and the scent of cloves pulled me from my dreams.

"Paaaaapa?" I asked.

"She sounds drugged." It was Forrester's obnoxious voice. I tried to tell him to go away, but the words got lost before they reached my mouth.

"Yes. She was rather hysterical when she reached me. I gave her something to calm her nerves." Mr. Macy's voice sounded as if it echoed from a sharp angle. "Really, Roy. The only reason I'm allowing her to go back is because she wished to, but my patience wears thin. This is your last chance to work things out with me. Why do you insist on your own ruination?"

"Help me get her to my carriage," my father said in a stern voice.

I opened my eyes, but the room looked filled with fog. A glass clinked, and through the blur I saw a form at the drink table. It was Macy. "Make a request, any request," he said, "and see if I won't trade for her."

"The Flanders documents," Mr. Forrester said.

"Done."

"And the letters from the Mallory affair?"

"I will give you every letter and document in my possession that you can ask for by name," Mr. Macy said. "In addition to what I promised for your protégé, Pierson."

"You'll return to Eastbourne," Forrester continued, "and abide by the rules my father placed on you."

There was a slight pause, followed by, "Yes . . . provided she's with me."

The support on my left side vanished as Mr. Forrester stepped away. "Do it, Roy. Look at her. She's safe here. He'll care for her."

"Paaapa," I said with effort. Surely he wouldn't leave me.

"Robert, are you out of your mind?" My father struggled to support me by himself, but his strong arm never stopped clutching me. "I want to know why she's here. Where is her clothing? What happened to her hands?"

Mr. Macy laughed. "I'm sorry, Roy, but I'll not betray your daughter's confidences. If she wants you to know about tonight, let her tell you." His voice took on humor. "I'll certainly not deny anything that she claims we've done."

"Leave her," Mr. Forrester said in a whisper. "She's not what you think. She's the one who gave me the injury above my eye."

"Either you help me get my daughter into my carriage," my father said with quiet fury, "or don't ever show your face to me again."

I felt someone take my left arm, none too gently.

"The offer stands," Macy said.

Twenty-Five

⁂

I AWOKE CALM. My head throbbed and my hands smarted. I wasn't in my bedroom, but a smaller room, downstairs in London House perhaps. The bed linens were white and the bed of a simple iron construction. The draperies over the window were closed, and black crepe covered the mirrors, making my stomach drop. Isaac sat in a chair at my bedside without expression.

"Who died?" I asked. Fear that it might be my father filled me.

"Eramus."

With a tingle of horror, I realized that Macy must have killed him. I covered my mouth with my hand.

"There are magistrates waiting to speak with you."

"Why?"

"The last person to see Eramus alive said that he intended on visiting you. Did he?"

All at once, I recalled Eramus leering and turning the poker over in the hot coals. I shivered and nodded.

"He hurt you, didn't he?"

I nodded, half-expecting Isaac to comfort me, but he remained silent, slumped in his chair, his eyes fixed on the floor.

"Is my father angry?"

This stirred Isaac for a moment, but he would not meet my eyes. "I'll find him."

A few moments later, my father, Forrester, Isaac, and two investigators stood beside the iron bedposts.

"Are you up to answering some questions, miss?" one of the investigators asked.

"Yes." My mouth felt dry and tasted bad.

"We'd like to speak to your daughter alone," the other said.

My father protested, but Forrester reasoned with him until he left the room.

"No need to look so frightened of us, miss." The tall one moved Isaac's chair near the window. "My name is Constable Laverock and this is Constable Noyes. Did you see your cousin Eramus last night?"

"He came to the house."

"What time?"

I tried to remember, but except for Edward's unwound watch, I hadn't glanced at a clock. "Around eleven, I think."

They nodded and looked as though that confirmed prior information.

"Just tell us what happened."

I licked my lips, wondering how to manage this. Constable Noyes poured me a glass of water. I took a sip. "I think he owed people money and intended to take some of my jewelry."

"Did you two have a heated argument?"

I felt my brow wrinkle. "Not exactly."

"Never mind; just continue with your story."

My voice was shaking now. "He threw my Bible in the fire, and I took it out of the flames; then he tried to destroy a piece of my jewelry."

"Go on."

"I jerked free of him and he fell, and—"

They gave each other sharp looks. "Where were you?"

"In the library."

Constable Noyes frowned. "Miss Pierson, Constable Laverock and I had the honor of waiting for you in the library. Are you aware that the servants are concerned over a missing poker?"

I didn't know whether I should answer yes or no. No, I had not been aware that the servants noticed it missing, but yes, I was aware it was misplaced.

"Do you know anything about it?" Laverock asked.

"Yes, Eramus chased me with it."

"Chased you? Where?"

"To Mr. Macy's residence."

My answer was met with a different response than I expected. They froze. Noyes finally asked, "Whose residence did you say?"

"Mr. Chance Macy. He took me inside and personally tended to my wounds."

"What wounds?"

I withdrew my hands from under the covers to show them, but the bandages were gone. I blinked at the change, bringing to mind how Macy's ring had contrasted against the white dressings. Wondering if I had dreamed that part, I slipped my hand into the gown's pocket and withdrew the ring.

The constables' gazes locked on the ring. Laverock broke out in a cold sweat, never taking his stare from the ring, except once to look at me in amazement. "I—I think I understand. You and your cousin were on a walk when you were attacked from behind." He turned to Noyes. "That explains the second body in the river. Their chaperone."

Noyes nodded agreement and took a step away from me. "She escaped and found shelter with Mr. Macy."

Laverock was a pasty color now and unbuttoned his collar. "What injuries did you sustain, Miss Pierson?"

I touched the back of my head and winced. It was swollen where it'd been gashed. "The back of my head mostly. My hands."

Noyes backed toward the door and placed his hand on the handle. "We'll file it in our report. I don't have any further questions. Do you?"

Laverock shook his head but looked at me with fear and amazement.

"How did Eramus die?" I asked. "Where was he found?"

"It's not something for a lady to know, miss," Noyes said.

"She's holding his ring," Laverock hissed in a whisper. "If she asks a question, you give her an answer." Then to me, "He was found floating in the Thames, facedown. The back of his head had been bashed in and . . ." He paused and looked at my hands. "His hands and feet looked as though they'd been held over a fire. His arms and legs were broken, and—"

Fearing I might be sick, I looked around for a basin. "And the other man?" I managed to say.

Laverock fished in his pocket for a piece of paper. "Adam Tanby."

Constable Noyes opened the door. Isaac and James waited in the hall. Without asking permission, Isaac entered and took a seat. James motioned for the constables to follow him.

I waited for Isaac to speak, but he didn't. Five, ten minutes passed in silence. James brought in tea and sweet rolls and set them at my bedside.

After several more minutes, Isaac rose, leaned over, and pulled a cigar box from the dresser in the room. I lifted the cover, and the scent of Macy filled the room. Inside, the missing citrine jewelry sat nestled in velvet.

"There was a note." Isaac's voice tightened. "Your father must not have wanted you to read it. Macy said he tracked down every piece Eramus stole except one. The necklace was stripped down, but Macy offered to buy you any necklace you desired to replace it."

I could only stare at the glittering stones.

"Is that his robe?" Isaac asked.

I looked down, though I already knew I still wore Macy's scarlet-and-gold dressing gown. Heat filled my face. "Yes."

He remained blank-looking, but his jaw tightened.

Misunderstanding his dismay, I thought him jealous, so I explained, "My dress was soaked with blood and scorched. My skirt was crusted with mud, and Macy cut the sleeve of my dress trying to assess whether I was hurt or not."

I pushed up the sleeve, surprised by the grisly marks Eramus had left on my arm. Looking at it made it painful, whereas previously it barely ached.

Isaac stared, horror-struck. Protection filled his eyes, but I could see he battled another emotion. When a pair of footsteps sounded outside the door, he rose.

My father, trailed by Forrester, appeared. "Is the story the constables told me true?"

"I didn't hear what they said," I replied, "but I told them the truth."

Isaac looked askance from his corner, as though he knew I was dissembling somehow but couldn't figure out where.

"Tell me what happened, then," my father said.

Isaac turned his back to me—I believed so I couldn't read the emotion on his face should he show any. Keeping my voice steady, I told about Eramus and my midnight chase to Macy's house.

Forrester addressed my father. "He's been right under our noses, which means she's been slipping in and out this entire time. Notice how she knew exactly where to run."

"I never should have taken you in! Robert's had you pegged from the beginning."

"Sir?" Isaac spun.

"I've known Eramus since he was born," my father said, collapsing in the chair. "He wouldn't terrorize my daughter.

I don't know how you ended up at Macy's, but that story is a falsehood if I ever heard one."

"She's not lying."

"Isaac, I know you had hopes . . ." My father placed his elbows on his lap. "I'm sorry."

"There are things I've never told you about Eramus," Isaac said. He spoke and stood as though he were separated from his emotions. "This is my fault. I—I thought I had the situation under control. May I speak to you privately in the smoking room? I don't want Julia hearing."

They were gone over an hour. Though Isaac had once agreed to share with me what he knew about Eramus Calvin, I never asked to learn what they spoke about. I couldn't bear to know Isaac's pain. I had my own terrifying memories of the man.

When they returned, my father boiled with anger. "We will mourn Eramus for two weeks, out of respect for Lady Beatrice. Then I never want his name spoken again!"

❧

The tranquillizer Mr. Macy stirred into my drink that night brimmed over into my life. Impassivity ruled London House. Even the lavish woodwork and polished surfaces seemed cold and uninviting. Isaac, the gentleman as always, tended to my needs but never allowed me to see past his mask. My father attended sessions, but when he came home, he looked at neither Isaac nor me. He spoke softly, walked softly, and spent many hours in his smoking room, the scent of Havana smoke strong outside the door.

Each morning, as I clad myself in crepe, I felt a grim sense of relief. There could be no betrothal during our seclusion of grief. The rules of mourning did not allow me to wear Edward's pin, which could have saved us from our daily ritual of tension, but Isaac no longer seemed to note me.

Surprisingly, it was Lady Beatrice who sought my company.

The magistrates told her that Eramus died protecting me, so she clung to me, hours a day, crying in my lap. Numbness still accompanied me as I stroked her back. I'd stare, wondering if she actually wept for Eramus or for herself. Many times as I held her frail, shaking shoulders, I looked over at Isaac in wonderment. He sat with a black mourning band wrapped about his arm, his eyes distant.

Mr. Macy haunted my dreams. The dreams repeated themselves over and again until I felt that I never slept but only shifted from the same incubus into reality. It started with Mr. Macy, taller than Mr. Greenham, picking me out from the mud or a crowd of jeering people. He'd take me home and coil around me like a snake, suffocating me. Just when I readied myself to die, he was replaced by Edward, who comforted me, telling me that it was all a nightmare. He'd never left me.

I woke one night, sobbing, the images of Edward receding.

As I had every night that week, I started to collect myself by lighting a candle. Sometimes, if I turned onto my side and stared long enough at the flickering light, sleep would overtake me. But then, all at once, I realized I couldn't do this anymore. Even if I fell asleep, I would only repeat the dream.

I wanted freedom. But how?

As I cast a desperate look about my bedchamber, I felt the nagging sensation that perhaps my freedom lay in surrender.

But surrender to what?

I kicked the covers off my feet, frustrated, eyeing Edward's charred Bible.

I've looked there, I silently screamed to God. I even believed the solution was there. But what was that to me? I couldn't make sense of it. There was no one to explain.

Yet even that thought rang false in my mind. For I'd not forgotten the way Isaac watched me read, patiently waiting for me to approach him.

Before I could change my mind, I grabbed my shawl, stole from my bed, and pattered down the hall.

When I reached his door, however, I couldn't knock. How could I disturb his sleep in the middle of the night with questions I didn't have the words to ask? Instead I leaned against the wood, wishing I could go back in time.

The door opened. Isaac, clad in a nightshirt, fastened on a pair of trousers as he gave me a questioning look.

I shrugged, telling him I didn't know why I was there either.

He sighed, then took my arm and led me to the staircase that was farthest from my father's chamber. "Sit," he said, and when I obeyed, he took the step above me and wrapped me in his arms.

"I killed Eramus," I whispered. "I killed him by going to Macy."

"Did you go to Macy with the intent to have him killed?"

"No."

"Then you didn't kill Eramus. You're not responsible for what Macy does."

It was the first conversation we'd had since the attack and the calmest I'd felt since that night.

"I can't take you not speaking to me anymore," I said. "It's more than I can bear. Why do you act as though I'm not in the room?"

Isaac said nothing.

"Is it because . . . because I still love Edward?"

"No." His voice was pained. Isaac shifted me closer against him, though somehow there wasn't anything provocative in it.

"Then why?"

He rested his chin against the crown of my head, so that I felt him speak. He paused for a long moment as if wrestling with his thoughts. "I failed to protect you from Eramus. I believed I was capable but risked your life." I felt his throat tighten before anger coated his voice. "And if I can't keep you safe from the likes of him, then how . . . how dare I presume . . ." He clutched me tight.

I said nothing, realizing how precarious my footing was. This was Isaac exposed.

"You should have seen your father's face," Isaac eventually continued, "when I had to confess that I knew Eramus was dangerous, that I exposed you, that I lost control of the situation."

I sighed, scarcely able to imagine how difficult it must have been for Isaac. He'd performed so flawlessly for so long that somewhere along the way he'd forgotten which part of him was real.

I rested my head against him, wondering if he even knew where his true feelings began and where duty and honor ended. He loved me sincerely—there was no doubt of that. But what I couldn't decide was whether it was because he thought we suited each other or because it was his nature to love. Who could tell if he followed duty or ardor? He might have loved anyone with equal devotion; it just happened to fall to me.

"Why are you here?" he eventually asked.

I allowed the back of my head to sag against his chest as I recalled my struggle. "I don't know. It feels foolish now."

"Tell me anyway. I could use something foolish."

I felt my cheeks warm as I pondered how to talk to Isaac about what I'd experienced. More than once I opened my mouth to speak before finally asking, "Have you ever . . . have you ever felt God?"

"Yes."

His frank answer stunned me. For a second, I wanted to be offended that he was so certain, so sure. But then, with a chuckle, I realized I felt the same way.

"Does this have anything to do with why you've been searching Scripture?"

It was all the invitation I needed. My words did not flow eloquently that night, but in the darkness of that stairway in

London House, I haltingly poured out my devastation and sorrow at Isaac's feet. I told him about what I'd experienced at Eastbourne, what I hoped to achieve by seeking my father's aid, and the time I'd finally prayed and then feared the depth of what I'd touched.

Each word cost, for they exposed years of hurt, potentially giving Isaac mastery over my forming beliefs. I tried to guard myself, waiting for him to begin defining what I should believe and then urge me to obey God by obeying my father and marrying him.

As I finished, I stole a glance at him and found his lips twisted.

"You dare to smile," I accused.

He sobered, looking rueful. "I meant no harm. It's just that you're asking me to assign meaning to loss, one of the most hindering aspects of faith." He waited several moments as if gathering his thoughts. "When considering surrender, I suppose, the primary question to ask is whether or not a person actually knows what's best for herself."

I stiffened at the ludicrousness of that thought.

"For example," Isaac continued, "most, given the chance, would choose discovering they'd been left a vast fortune over suffering a crippling disease. Yet I've seen the former cause utter ruination and grief, and the latter drastically bring healing to someone's relationships and outlook on life. Which is truly the blessing and which the curse?"

I sat stock-still in his arms, desiring to be open to new ideas, but still wanting to think through his argument.

"You're on the right path; I can say that much. It is no easy decision to lay down your life, especially without assurance of what that will entail. You fear being further broken, but consider that in the hands of Jesus, a broken loaf can feed thousands, while intact it will feed only one."

I hid my pain, feeling as though we were discussing my willingness to give up Edward.

"Maybe," Isaac continued, "he has a mighty plan. And maybe the reason he's not softened your approach is because he knows how difficult your steps toward him are, and it ravishes his heart that you proceed anyway."

I couldn't help but give a disbelieving laugh at the image of Julia Elliston captivating God. I shook my head, imagining how quickly my former vicar would rebuff that notion. "I don't think so, Isaac."

"Not many choose to die, and I know better than anyone how dear your former life is to you. If you hand over that, do you really believe such a sacrifice would go unnoticed?"

The idea of love won me. I could never follow the God of my vicar's making, but this—this made me yearn. The thought of a God who waited patiently, hand outstretched, eagerly anticipating me . . . that thought undid me. Perhaps it was because of Isaac too. His daily care and tender ministrations set another example, painted another image.

I would liken my first step toward faith like stepping up to the edge of the cliff, spreading arms wide, and falling backwards in trust that God wouldn't let me fall. I'd never felt so frightened, yet drawn. Like Abraham placing his son on the altar, I knew the conditions under which I approached. I had to release all.

That night I surrendered. I accepted that I could lay down the heavy weight of my burden in exchange for rest. The price was costly, but once exchanged, I found a deep well of peace that could coexist with grief. My only witness was Isaac, who laughed outright, a husky laugh that contained the very air of a father laying eyes on his newborn child.

⌇

The following morning as Miss Moray spread a rose-colored gown over my bed, I opened my vanity drawer and pulled out Edward's watch. Morning light caught its engravings as I considered it. It is one thing to decide to mentally take a step of faith, but quite another to live it out physically. I fisted the time-piece, knowing that no matter what transpired, Edward alone would be the longing of my heart. A glance in the mirror told me I appeared as frightened as I felt. Swallowing, I placed the watch back inside the vanity.

Isaac immediately noted the absence of Edward's pin as I slid into my chair. One unguarded look in his eyes gave me a glimpse of his soul, but his own brand of diplomacy quickly took over. He returned to his breakfast as if making an unspoken pledge that he wouldn't rush me. To anyone else he would have appeared leisurely, but I noted how he couldn't stop smiling.

I attempted to return his smile but suddenly felt shy and anxious to move the attention from me. My father, buried behind the *Times* of London, did not acknowledge me, so I gave Isaac a meaningful look, asking what in the papers occupied him. Still grinning, he shrugged.

When the morning correspondences arrived, a glint of purple—a royal envelope—peeked through amongst the ivory. With a growl, my father tore it open and scanned the contents.

"Write an acceptance this morning." He handed it to me. "You and Isaac shall attend."

Isaac lifted his eyebrows as he sipped his tea.

I held the invitation between my fingers, disliking that after so long, our first outing would be a court function. They were particularly nerve-racking, as the price of error was high.

I handed the purple page to Isaac. "It's a costume ball."

His face fell as he read it for himself. "I hate these. Every female asks me if I know who she is, and I never do. The horrid feeling intensifies with each wrong guess. Two years ago, I started a feud between two rivals." He handed the page back. "At least this year they know my heart is taken. Maybe that will help."

"Let's disguise ourselves," I suggested. "Make it impossible to guess who we are."

"No." My father's voice grumbled from behind the headlines. "Neither of you have been in the papers for weeks." He folded and lowered his paper before sagging against his chair, studying us. "Which means we need costumes London will talk about."

Isaac shot me a look of alarm before placidly buttering a scone.

My father nodded thoughtfully as though he weighed different ideas in his mind, eventually deciding on, "Tristan and Isolde. I'll arrange for the costumes."

"A tragedy, sir? Really?" Isaac protested. "Haven't we had enough of those lately?"

Instead of answering, my father stood and glowered. Isaac, however, didn't lower his chin or look askance. He stared back.

My father merely grabbed his stack of newspapers and left the chamber.

❧

A fortnight later, I stood before my mirror at evenfall, looking over the medieval-styled dress. It was red and fastened across the chest with a band of material that connected to a blue cape trimmed with cross-stitched Celtic lions. The dress's trim was stitched with thistles. A wispy veil, cut in the front and attached to my head with a gold circlet, fell down my back.

Another girl, from another era, stared back at me, making me think I would have fared well as a chieftain's daughter, centuries prior. The garb suited me.

Isaac paced at the bottom of the stairs in the foyer, giving me a chance to view him privately. Alone, he wasn't self-possessed. His normally placid face was filled with anxiety, and he chewed his thumbnail. His costume was thinly hammered armor that a smith had taken time to ornament. The silver plates weren't bulky and were connected with some stretchable fabric that allowed him to bend elbows, knees, and waist. It broadened his shoulders and made his legs appear muscular. I frowned, considering how handsomely my father had paid for our costumes.

"Sir Tristan." I leaned over the third-story balusters. "I thought you died. How glad I am to see you live!"

He looked up with a warm gaze, and had I not seen him a moment ago, I would have believed he was truly in full control of his emotions. "Let us hope we will have a better ending than that." He bowed deeply. "You look beautiful. Come down."

When I reached him, I spun to show him my costume.

"What age wouldn't have suited you?" he asked. "You could have played Helen of Troy, Cleopatra, or Esther. I wish Lord Pierson had chosen Penelope and Odysseus, so I could come and free you from all your suitors."

My father arrived, carrying an unlit pipe, and smiled at us. "You look nice without jewelry. Natural." He reached out and touched my hair, which lacked its normal elaborateness. "You are your grandmother's image. Did I ever tell you she was one of the noblest women I've ever known?"

Made self-conscious by his approval, I swept down my lashes. "Mama used to say I looked like her too, and that it was a comfort, given the family she lost."

My father's body tensed as he jerked his head toward Isaac, ignoring me. "Keep a good eye on her tonight. Do not disappoint me again."

Isaac's shoulders fell. "I promise, sir."

My father frowned, looking at us as if he felt uneasy, but then retreated, banging the bottom of his pipe against his open palm.

∽

"Watch out for pickpockets," Simmons warned as Isaac lifted me from the carriage. A throng stood between us and our destination.

Isaac slipped his arm through mine and took my hand, making it harder for us to be parted.

Sprinkled amongst the bootblacks, chandlers, chimney sweeps, tinkers, and hawkers were the elite, in historical or comical costumes. The bright silks, dyed feathers, sparkling jewels, and costly lace stood out. All at once, a beggar child jostled between two women whose panniers made them look as though they'd stepped out from the court of Louis XIV. Dirt-encrusted hands reached toward me. Simmons grabbed the child by his shirt as if to haul him away.

"Wait!" I ordered.

Isaac gave me a questioning glance.

"Can't we give him something?" I pleaded. "A sovereign?"

Isaac's laugh was good-natured. "Simmons, you heard your mistress. Hand that child a sovereign."

Simmons opened his mouth to protest but then, with a vinegary twist of his lips, decided better. He shoved a hand in his pocket and dispensed a coin. Five grubby hands extended in his direction, and three more beggars joined the fray, engulfing him.

"Quick," Isaac whispered. "Now's our chance to escape."

Laughing, we reached the steps. Isaac drew up my hand and kissed it as if celebrating.

Lord Melbourne approached. "A perfect political couple. The strength and wealth of Roy Pierson united with the sensibilities and honor of Isaac Dalry. Welcome." His mouth slanted. "Where is Pierson?"

Isaac bowed. "He regretfully couldn't attend."

"Who's your chaperone?"

"Lord Pierson sent his steward, Simmons."

Lord Melbourne smothered a smile. "Humph. Based on your arrival, I'm not sure he's suited for the task."

Isaac released my hand. "Forgive me. I had to guide Miss Pierson through the streets. It was crowded."

"Of course, of course." Lord Melbourne looked over our costumes. "You'll have my full support on the first bill you champion, if you would just tell me who you are instead of making me guess."

"Tristan and Isolde." Isaac sounded glum. "Lord Pierson's idea."

I suppressed my smile. I would have disclaimed the costumes too.

Lord Melbourne waved us inside. "Tell your father that I noted his absence with displeasure. Next time I'll word the invitation more carefully." He sounded offended, but his features told me we were carrying back a private joke.

When the first dance began, Isaac led me to the dance floor with his head high, and though I started the night shamed by our riches, it wasn't long until I was swept away in the delight. Lord Alexander surprised me from behind the bulky costume of Henry VIII. I met Millicent's and Anna's future husbands. Isaac and I mingled but were never far from each other. When no one was looking, I mouthed the names of the girls who approached Isaac, so he could guess correctly the first time who flirted with him.

That night I saw the first evidence that I could heal. The ache still throbbed, but I embraced it and gave it acceptance. I also learned there was a measure of pride in being escorted by Isaac. Instead of withering beneath my father's care, pain had mysteriously made him flourish. I'd never seen anyone as tenderhearted toward others. My heart swelled with pride as he asked the wallflowers to dance and made a point to acknowledge each servant by name. Even so, I was not allowed to forget he was my father's protégé.

"Here you are." Isaac arrived at my side when a set of girls left me. "Let us break etiquette this once and discourage anyone from disturbing us while we speak privately. Why did you snub Dahlia earlier?"

"You noticed?"

"Yes. Now answer me."

I looked up at Isaac's searching gaze, wondering if he noted everything I did. "Because she scorned some of the other girls' costumes."

"I don't care for her either, but I need you to befriend her. The man she's going to marry is very influential—"

"Excuse me."

Isaac and I both jumped, startled out of our talk by a young man, bowing. He stared with wide eyes. I wrinkled my nose. Something about the manner in which he was immaculately groomed, its style, put me in mind of somebody or something.

"Miss Pierson?" He swallowed. "*Please*, may I have this dance?"

Isaac stepped between us. "Have you been introduced?"

"Please," the gentleman begged me. "I've circumvented many obstacles to ask you for a dance."

Isaac took my upper arm and pulled me closer. "You don't belong in this sphere, do you?"

The gentleman started breathing rapidly but touched Isaac's arm as he lifted it to call the guards. "In that case, I must beg Miss *Elliston* for a dance." His pitch heightened as he used my former name.

There was a dangerous pause, in which we all stiffly eyed each other.

"Allow me to dance with him," I said to Isaac.

"No." Isaac's voice was iron.

"Look at him," I pleaded. "Do you really think him dangerous?"

"Who are you, sir?" Isaac demanded.

"I just wish to dance with Miss Pierson. Nothing more."

"Then why threaten us?"

"Did I?" The man flushed red. "I didn't mean to. I was told to ask Miss Pierson to dance and, if she refused, to ask under the name Miss Elliston."

People nearby began whispering and pointing. Lord

Melbourne also started backing out of his conversation with his eye on us.

Isaac's countenance suddenly became debonair, but his voice kept its dangerous quality. "Who instructed you?"

"Please, may I dance with Miss Pierson?"

"Yes." I extended my hand, making it impossible for Isaac to prevent me without causing a scene. The young man realized his opportunity and seized it.

Isaac looked furious with me but only said, "If you take her outside the dance floor, you'll regret meeting me."

"Sir, I swear to you, I won't harm Miss Pierson."

The young man and I joined the waltz, keeping near the perimeter for Isaac's sake. Isaac's face was set like flint as he watched us with crossed arms. Those around him looked happily scandalized that I had provoked him.

"Well, sir," I said, "I've granted your request. Explain yourself." Up close, I noticed the sun had highlighted his hair. His shoulders were brawny, and the hand encasing mine thick. "You're no gentleman, are you?"

He looked down. "No. I'm a farmer."

"How on earth does a farmer gain access to a court ball?"

"He said if I gave you enough time, you might guess who sent me." He waited for me to understand, then added, "I know him as Mr. Higgs."

I shook my head, confused. "I have no idea whom you mean."

"Then I'm to tell you that his first name is John."

My entire body refused to move for a second, throwing us off step as the man's identity dawned on me—Jonathan Alexander Greenham. The man Macy swore would writhe at my feet. The man who confessed to murdering Mama. I wanted to look to Isaac for reassurance but knew he'd storm the dance floor.

"Who are you?" I demanded.

"Call me Thomas. Mr. Higgs is offering you his assistance. He sent a letter, which is on my person."

Bitterness surged through me. "Tell him I've already experienced his brand of *assistance* when he murdered my mother."

Thomas's eyes widened, and it seemed to me that my statement gave him an understanding of some sort. "I'm sorry, Miss Pierson. I know nothing of your difficulties."

The music stopped, and Thomas pulled the letter from his pocket. I hesitated, then shoved it inside the embroidered sporran that came with my costume.

"Speak to no one of our conversation," Thomas whispered. "He tells me that he is placing his life in your hands by making contact."

I pinched my lips. This was so like a Macy trap, begging me to keep information secret.

Isaac approached and took my arm.

Thomas gave a nervous bow, looking uncertain, as though Mr. Greenham had given detailed instructions on what to do only until this point.

"Mingle," I whispered. "Keep your hands crossed behind you, in gentlemanly fashion. Leave when the next dance starts and no one is paying attention."

Thomas bowed, then melted into the crowded room.

"What did he want?" Isaac demanded.

I looked at those eyeing us, some with amusement, some with displeasure. "I can't tell you."

"Yes, you can and you will. Right now."

His mask was slipping, and I feared we were about to have our first fight here in front of everyone.

"All I know is that he is a commoner. A farmer. His name was Thomas."

"A farmer?" Isaac looked thunderstruck. "What did he want?"

Lord Melbourne approached us with a smile fastened on his face. He took Isaac's arm and mine, placing himself between us. "Dalry, Miss Pierson. You two look far too close to a disagreement for my liking. Whom were you dancing with, Miss Pierson? Where did he go?"

"I couldn't tell you, sir." I felt myself blushing.

He looked at me. "I've not forgotten that your father told me you suffered a disappointment. But do not forget all that your father—and Lord Dalry—have spent a lifetime building. I know a broken heart feels insurmountable, but I expect far better of you than that scene."

I wanted to refuse to look at or acknowledge him. My mother's murderer had just contacted me, and he stood lecturing me on broken hearts? Insurmountable indeed! I'd still not grown accustomed to life without Edward. It was a weight on my heart every day. And how many nights did I wake with the fear that I'd ruin my father's and Isaac's careers? Dread of my scandal hung over me every hour of the day, knowing at any moment Macy or a mistake would reveal my identity. Temptation to educate Lord Melbourne on the worthlessness of his statements fluttered through me.

I tamped down my indignation and dipped. "Forgive me, sir."

Lord Melbourne looked at me long and hard.

"Excuse me, sir," Isaac said in a firm voice, taking my arm from the prime minister. "Julia and I were about to dance the next set."

"Yes, go dance. Try to make up for the tension you just displayed. We are having a private dinner at midnight. I want you both there. Understood?"

"We are honored," Isaac said, inclining his head. "We'll leave no one in doubt of our mutual attachment."

Lord Melbourne nodded and retreated.

Isaac gently pulled me to the dance floor and drew me close as we waltzed. "Julia, I'm sorry you were lectured. He doesn't know. Just dance with me. We can settle this later, between ourselves."

I nodded, but my hand shook in Isaac's and I could hardly keep step with him. I swept my gaze over the crowd, looking for the farmer, for questions were now piling. I wondered where my mother's murderer was hiding and why he took concern over me.

"Juls?" Isaac's voice was soft.

I startled like a jackrabbit. Tears swam to my eyes as I faced Isaac, for he'd used Edward's nickname for me.

Something protective surged through Isaac; I felt it jolt through him. His face etched with concern, he maneuvered me from the dance floor. I thought him on the verge of questioning me again. Instead he tilted up my chin and pressed his lips against mine. When he finished, he searched my face.

"Can we go home?" I asked, holding back tears.

"That wasn't a request to join dinner. That was a command."

I gave a stiff nod, not certain how I'd manage to keep up a facade for several more hours. My heart felt like an open grave.

He kissed my hair through the veil I wore. "I'll not leave your side. Let them gossip. I'll also make certain the dinner is trouble free for you. I'll shield you from questions. It won't always be this way."

I shook my head twice, for he truly believed our future wouldn't be such, but I didn't. "You're wrong. I'll never fit here."

"You forget." His whisper scarcely stirred the veil near my ear. "I already know who you are capable of becoming."

At dinner, while the ladies compared their various experiences with housekeepers, I listened attentively to the men's debates, taking in far more than was deemed proper for the feminine mind. Isaac sat next to me with his arm along the back of my chair. More than once, in between the brilliant arguments he fashioned for the men, he answered questions the women tossed me, though he cast me confused looks.

The truth was, the ladies' questions fell on deaf ears. Who could note their idle chatter while the men debated weightier matters? And Isaac was nothing less than extraordinary. At home he was so meek and quiet I never would have believed the passion with which he now argued points with the men. Those I knew to be Conservatives watched him with shining eyes, anticipating his joining the House of Lords next year. As expected, I held my tongue, not wanting my father or Isaac to be embarrassed by a woman interjecting her opinions. Yet my gratitude for Isaac had never been more complete. I knew in private he'd listen to my thoughts in full. I paid keen attention, aware that I would always have audience with one of the most influential politicians in the country.

Twenty-Six

EVERY FIBER of my body recoiled as I turned Mr. Greenham's missive about in my hands. The paper was cheap and thin, but it was sealed with an excessive amount of wax. With the tip of my finger, I touched the waxen ridges. The impression itself was unlike any I'd ever seen before. It was a double cameo that featured two ancient Greeks. The Spartan in the forefront was bearded, helmeted for battle, while the Athenian's face was scholarly with a classical expression. They brought to mind the sharp contrast between my father and Isaac. Behind the sealing wax, ink as brown as mahogany bled through the folded page, showing the refined script of a gentleman.

Knowing I needed to hurry, I bit my lip. Somewhere three floors beneath, Isaac and my father partook of brandy. My father wanted a report on the evening the moment Isaac, Simmons, and I returned. Likely enough, when my father learned what had transpired, he'd burst into my chambers demanding explanation.

If I wanted to know what the letter contained, reading it now was my best chance.

Even so, the idea of opening a letter from Mama's murderer stretched me. I shut my eyes, trying to remember what it had felt like to be free, to breathe in a deep lungful of fresh air, to sit across from Edward's smiling face.

Willing all emotions to fade, I removed a pin from my hair. I knew, of course, the letter's content would shift my world yet again. I just never could have imagined how much.

J,

Chance is far from discontinuing his disturbances in your life. I wish to entrust information with the hope that knowledge will give you a greater measure of security than ignorance.

I have in my keeping the papers that Forrester's father once had. If you trust that Forrester will not betray me, tell him to meet me at the Margrove Tavern, Leadenhall Street, 23 March, Friday going into Saturday, midnight.

Take extreme precaution. Chance is far more dangerous than even your father perceives.

Burn this letter. Tell no one, as this information will endanger their life. Should you be unwilling to trust Forrester, send no one and I'll contact you another time.

May God protect and keep you. I pray for your safety.

Your humble servant,

J

I memorized the names, then held the corner of the page over the flame and watched it darken before igniting. When it curled to its death, I scattered the ashes until nothing legible remained.

ᴥ

Isaac met my gaze the following morning as he unfolded his napkin.

My stomach clenched, and I avoided his stare. The last thing I wanted to do was to place him in danger. I stiffened as my father entered the chamber, waiting for him to demand to know why I had disobeyed Isaac and danced with a farmer, but my father only gave a curt nod before grabbing his newspaper. A front-page article caught his attention straightaway, but Isaac's steadfast gaze pinned me.

He might have delayed telling my father, but judging by his expression, he hadn't forgotten the incident. I pretended to consider the dish of oysters and bacon that James lowered for me. I had not anticipated how to handle Isaac. I pressed my lips. Keeping him off the scent would be highly difficult while trying to arrange a private encounter with Forrester. Surely that alone would arouse Isaac's suspicion.

"Just tea, please," I finally told James.

"Why aren't you eating, Julia?" Isaac asked.

I flushed with guilt as I met his gaze.

With a loud thwack, the *Times* landed between us on the table. We both jumped and looked at my father, amazed. He handed me the paper with one of his withering stares.

It wasn't hard to locate the article that had upset him so. Skipping the description of the ball, I read only the part that mentioned Isaac and me.

Lord Dalry and Miss Pierson spent little time circulating, keeping to their own private tryst. Their engagement is expected post-haste, as their attachment was well evidenced by a public kiss.

I clasped my hand over my mouth as Isaac scrambled to find what upset us.

My father stood, his hands rooted on the table. "You dared to kiss her in public without an engagement?"

"What?" Isaac scanned the paper. "Oh no! Oh, Julia, I never imagined . . . I was only trying to lessen the speculation over our fight."

"Fight?" My father knocked the paper out of Isaac's hand in a sweeping motion. "You argued? What about?"

"I can't tell you, sir."

My father's face turned crimson. "If you kiss my daughter in public, then I'm entitled to demand answers. We are sending an announcement of your engagement to the papers today."

I gasped and rose also.

"Sir, you can't. I've not asked your daughter to marry me yet. We are not engaged."

"Enough!" My father's voice came out a roar. "Ask her, and ask her now!"

"Oh, be serious, sir! This is not the way I intend to ask for her hand, with you looming over us because of a newspaper article."

My father sent a frosty gaze his way. "Tomorrow, whether you've asked her or not, there's going to be an announcement in the paper!"

My father stormed from the chamber. Isaac signalled for me not to panic as he hurried after him.

I sank to my chair because my knees felt too weak to support me. Though I'd been telling myself that I hadn't entertained false hope, I realized it was a lie.

All I could picture was Edward reading the news, and how he would never learn or understand that my heart had never been for this. I felt positively ill.

～

"What's so urgent that your father can't wait?" Mr. Forrester asked as he burst through the doors of London House and found me sitting on the bench in the hall. He yanked off his cloak and shoved it into James's hands. "Where is he?"

Even though I sat there on the off chance that Forrester actually would visit today, I was so stunned I dutifully indicated the correct chamber. "They're both in the library, talking."

Mr. Forrester sneered and started down the hall without so much as a bow.

"Wait!" I jumped to my feet, recovering my wits. "I need to tell you something."

He knocked me aside, touching the spot where his goose egg had been. "Forgive me, but I don't fancy another dealing with you. Good day, Miss Pierson."

I grabbed his sleeve. "It's about Greenham."

He halted and half turned. "I swear I must be an idiot. What? What about Greenham?"

I wet my lips, looking at James, then lowered my voice. "He wishes to meet privately with you."

Mr. Forrester placed a hand on his hip. "Trust a Macy girl to have contact with her mother's murderer. I swear, I don't know how he finds them. How would you know?"

I gritted my teeth. "I'm not at liberty to tell."

"No, of course you're not. Stop wasting my time." He started toward the library.

"It was a letter!" I stepped behind him. "He claims he has the documentation that your father had, and he's willing to hand it over."

Mr. Forrester turned, looking as though he'd tasted something rotten. "Show me. I know his penmanship."

I wrung my hands, watching as James left. "I burned it. It was in the instructions."

He touched his forehead as if he were daft for not immediately understanding. "Oh, how foolish of me. Tell me more about this letter that can't be verified."

I allowed my hands to drop. "Never mind. I can see you don't believe me."

"No, no," he said, crossing his arms, broadening his smile. "Quite the contrary. I've never met a more honest girl in my life. Of course I believe you. You have my full attention."

I felt so frustrated I could have kicked him. I crossed my arms, thinking of all the insults I wanted to say. "If you would just listen! Greenham asked me to arrange for you to meet him tonight, at midnight."

"Oh, my, so soon? How utterly efficient. What would you have done had I not stopped by today?"

"He's risked his life to communicate with me. The least you could do is hear me out."

"I'm all ears. Please continue."

I could see this was useless, yet I delivered the message. "Leadenhall Street, Margrove Tavern. Do whatever you wish."

"Tell Macy that by now he ought to be able to set a better trap," he said, reaching for the library door handle.

"I half hope it is Macy," I said, "and you go and never return."

"There are your true colors." He tipped his hat. "Now, let's go see if this 'urgent' visit with your father was set up by you too. Thank you for today's entertainment."

He joined my father and Isaac, still laughing to himself.

I sank to the bench and cupped my forehead in my hands, waiting.

～

A half hour later an ashen-faced Mr. Forrester emerged, tucking a folded piece of paper inside his waistcoat. My father stepped to the threshold, his face black, revealing that they'd argued.

Forrester gave him a curt nod, no friendliness in it. "Roy, please, I'm telling you, this move will forever destroy Isaac."

"Do you want the announcement or not?" was my father's unyielding reply.

Forrester glared at me. It was immature, but I smirked. Let him stew on the fact I was marrying his precious Lord Dalry. At least someone else felt sickened over this too.

～

That evening Lady Northrum raised my chin and smiled at me. "Roy, your daughter doesn't look well. Perhaps a hiatus from London would put bloom back in her cheeks."

Her touch startled me from the private world I'd been wandering through. Realizing that she and her husband were taking their leave, I tottered to my feet, nearly losing my balance.

"Forgive me. I . . ." I blinked, unable to think of a suitable excuse for neglecting my duty. Being engrossed in memories of Edward was no proper excuse, particularly as her ladyship was there to consult on plans for the upcoming wedding.

My father stiffened but studied me with concern. "I may take your advice. Thank you."

She smiled and nodded before patting Isaac's cheek. As she stepped into the night, the feathers on her headdress danced in the north wind. Even though she counted Mr. Macy as one of her friends, I liked her, even trusted her.

"Aren't you well?" my father asked.

"Just a headache," I lied. It wouldn't do to hurt Isaac on the eve of our engagement.

"If I may . . ." Isaac moved me closer to him. "Why don't I go read to your daughter, sir?"

My father adjusted his cuff links. "No, I need both of you circulating with the others. If her head hurts, let her rest for a half hour and then join us."

There were other guests there that night; in fact, the dining room was filled to capacity, a rarity for London House. Outside of the Northrums and Forrester, however, the only other person I truly recall from that dinner is Isaac. He seemed particularly compassionate toward me, forgoing all questions about the farmer and making certain I didn't miss necessary cues, such as picking up my utensils first, allowing everyone to begin. Looking back, I understand why. He took great pains to cause no stir or even whisper that would threaten the stability of the house of cards so very near completion. He'd endured much, patiently waiting for the day when he could shape his own future.

Isaac kissed my temple, then whispered, "Shall I have James bring you laudanum?"

I gave him a slight shake of my head.

My father placed his hand on Isaac's arm and directed him from the chamber. "Do you think Lady Northrum's assessment of Julia correct? What say you to a week at Maplecroft? Be out of the city while the news breaks? Breathe some country air? Think it will suit her?"

"I think the idea's capital, sir!"

"Good, good. I'll alert the staff. We'll leave in the morning."

I held in my noise of disgust as they withdrew. Had they asked my opinion, they would have known I had no desire to visit the estate. I hated its empty halls and freezing silence. At least here in London everything was bustling, moving, going. Here, petty matters cropped up every hour, temporarily distracting me from the heartache of Edward.

I turned from their retreating forms and took refuge in the drawing room, where I'd first met Lady Beatrice. I took the settee near a window. At least there I could watch the streets for occupation.

❧

Past eleven, Mr. Forrester wandered in from the library, smoking a cigar. Though I registered him, I pretended I hadn't until a thick cloud of blue smoke filled the chamber. I turned. "It's impolite to smoke with a lady present."

"Which is why I would never dream of it," Mr. Forrester

replied. Then before I could rise, he plopped down in a chair and said, "Well, well, well, Macy's planted you nicely. Tell him he can be pleased. Your father and Isaac have settled your wedding date, which house you'll let, which servants will transfer with you. They're still in debate over the honeymoon."

I felt a stab of betrayal and closed my book, stunned. No one had consulted me.

"Six weeks away from wedded bliss and fulfilling the next stage of why Macy placed you here . . . that is, unless I can convince Isaac of your continuing affair with Macy." Mr. Forrester stretched out his feet and crossed them.

Mentally I did quick calculations. That would be May. I was stunned that Isaac would just make these plans without me. Outraged, even. It didn't seem possible, yet Mr. Forrester was too sure of himself to doubt it.

"If you notice . . ." Mr. Forrester raised his hands and spread out his fingers near his ear, managing to keep the cigar. "It's close to midnight, and I'm still here, not off on some wild-goose chase."

I stirred from my incredulity, not particularly caring about Mr. Greenham at that moment. I was too furious with Isaac. I threw my book aside as I charged toward the door. "James!"

He arrived within seconds.

"Tell Isaa—" *No,* I thought, cutting off my own words. I would not call him Isaac when I was this angry. "Tell *Lord Dalry* I wish to see him."

"You little wench," Mr. Forrester cried, springing from his chair. "The moment you learn the wedding is now upon you, you try to send your future bridegroom to his—" He stopped, pulled his revolver from his pocket, and checked the chamber. "Never mind, I'll spring the trap myself."

It wasn't until he stormed out the front door that I realized Forrester thought I intended to send Isaac to Mr. Greenham. James watched, goggle-eyed.

I was too furious to care. "Never mind, James. Go tell them both that I went to bed. I will not rejoin the guests, as my presence apparently isn't required for anything!"

❦

The next day, Isaac tried to catch my eye as he assisted me from the carriage, but I avoided his gaze, as I had since we'd left London. That entire day had been a disaster. It began at breakfast when my father discovered the engagement hadn't been announced in Forrester's paper. His mood wasn't lightened by the staff's harried attempt to get us out the door, nor by my utter refusal to speak to either him or Isaac. The entire carriage ride had been a silent standoff to see who could maintain a foul mood the longest—my father or myself.

"Julia," Isaac whispered as my feet touched the ground, "please, I don't know what's happening, but I must go see Mother and Kate. Will you be all right for a few hours?"

I gave a curt nod, focusing on the towering grey stone of Maplecroft.

"What is it?" he pressed.

"You set our wedding date?"

He glanced at my father, who brushed past us as though he hadn't heard and made his way to the house. Isaac waited until he was out of hearing. "May I ask who told you that?"

"Does it matter?"

Isaac took my hand in his. "It's not what you're thinking."

"Go home to your family." I broke free, then gathering my skirts, hastened toward Maplecroft.

He caught my arm, forcing me to stop. "You have no idea what I've been battling for the last twenty-four hours. If he'd had his way, we'd both be standing before an archbishop right this second with a special license. After the coverage of the ball, Lord Alexander attempted to make his offer for your hand more tantalizing. Your father nearly conceded, too!"

I attempted to shake him off. "You expect me to believe my father would choose someone over you?"

"Yes, because Lord Alexander offered me his sister in the arrangement." He pulled me behind the carriage, out of sight of Maplecroft. "Her dowry rivals yours, and everyone knows his older brother is near death from wasting disease. Your father would gain two empires instead of one."

My cape snapped in the wind as I considered this.

"Imagine the temptation your father felt. But I insisted I'd only marry you. And the only way to satisfy him was to finalize our plans. There wasn't time to consult you." Isaac shook his head. "And the way Alexander's been spending his time lately, he'd probably give you a disease."

"Disease?"

Isaac actually blushed, and deeply. "Do not repeat that!" He pulled me closer to him. "Now you understand. Who even told you about any of this? I expressly told your father I wanted to be the one to give you these tidings."

"Forrester," I admitted.

He made a noise of exasperation. "I cannot wait for the hour when I can finally free you of his presence! But until then, refuse to talk to him. Now, will you be all right for a few hours?"

I turned my head and viewed Maplecroft, recalling my first view of it beneath the moon. Little did I know then, by setting foot inside, I'd lose any means to control my life. The walls of my world were crumbling faster than I could repair them. As if sensing what was brewing, I suddenly wished Isaac didn't have to go and visit his mother. "Yes, but how long will you be gone?"

Isaac breathed relief and kissed my forehead. "That's my girl. I'll return as soon as I can."

∽

The following afternoon four gentlemen bashed on the front door of Maplecroft and demanded entrance. Once more the hall was filled with barking hounds and loud voices as the men made it clear their little women *would* celebrate Isaac's and my betrothal—dash that the newspapers hadn't carried the announcement yet. They'd heard it from the Dalrys themselves, which was good enough for them—besides, the neighborhood could use a good fete.

My father acquiesced, likely happy to have further proof Isaac and I had truly conceded to become engaged.

That night, Miss Moray added jeweled combs to my hair. My father had already gone to the home of Colonel Greenley, our host. The plan was that Isaac and I would appear together.

Though not in London, Miss Moray adorned me with an unusual amount of jewelry. I stared, dismayed. My every movement glittered, scattering prisms in an aura about me.

"Are you not pleased?" Her voice was testy.

"Shall I not appear too . . ." *Arrogant, haughty, conceited* all ran through my mind. "Sparkly?"

"You are genteel. This is your first appearance here after being a headliner for months. You must look your part."

I sat before the mirror as her angry footsteps receded. A glance at the clock told me there wasn't time regardless. With a sigh, I resolved to be a shimmering spectacle and grabbed my fan.

I envied Isaac as I descended the stairs. He looked smart—dashing, even—as he stood next to James, our chosen chaperone. The footman's eyes widened as he scanned my appearance. His mouth twisted as he struggled to gain composure. Isaac didn't lift an eyebrow, telling me how truly awful it was, for I knew his trained demeanor when I encountered it.

I spread my skirts. "I look ridiculous. They're going to think me vain."

"They're going to think you look lovely." Isaac took my hand and kissed it. "You're not nervous, are you? Not after all those court functions."

"It's not that. It's just . . ." I hesitated but then realized nothing except the full truth would satisfy him. I extended my arms, allowing the wall sconces to catch the facets, bouncing and scattering prisms of light. James placed his gloved fist over his mouth but choked out a laugh before he could help it.

Isaac shot him a deadly warning look. "You're fine. They'll assume it's the fashion in London." He took my arm and moved me toward the door. "There is something important I need to talk to you about before we arrive, though. There's going to be a girl in attendance tonight." He looked pained. "Evelyn Greenley, the colonel's daughter. I fear . . . I fear news of our betrothal may upset her greatly."

Here was news! I looked at him, shocked. "She was your sweetheart? Before me, I mean?"

"No." Isaac held open the carriage door. "She was engaged to Ben, my identical twin."

My astonishment couldn't have been more complete. "Your missing brother . . . he's your . . ."

Isaac's expression pleaded with me not to discuss this now. Yet as I settled into my seat, I felt stunned with amazement. An identical twin! I'd read of them in books, but never had I encountered a set. All at once, I wanted to know everything about Ben. How could I not have known? Once again, shame clutched my heart as Isaac settled next to me. What else had I not taken time to know about him?

"Evelyn took his disappearance very hard." Isaac rocked to one side and cleared out his cape. "She took it as awfully as—" His eyes widened as he suddenly stopped, but with a shake of his head, he pressed on. "Well, anyway, I don't know how to explain this, but there are times, actually quite often, she . . ." He leaned forward and pressed my hands between his. "She thinks I'm Ben. Or at least she pretends to."

I stared at him, alarmed. "Is she sane?"

He looked uncertain how to answer. "I don't know what to

think. It's a very difficult situation for me. Everyone says Ben is dead, but I know he's not. I also know he would want me to treat her tenderly. Will she bother you much?"

The carriage jounced over a few grassy spots while I tried to think of what to say. In the end, it was Ben I couldn't stop thinking about. I'd always had the impression that identical twins had a bond like no other. "Why did you never tell me about Ben?"

He sat quietly for a moment. "I liked being seen for me and not the other half of Ben. I valued being an individual in your eyes. And then, when I'd said nothing . . . well, it became awkward to bring it up."

I pressed my lips together, wondering if it had hurt Isaac to be away from his twin most of his life. Yet I knew better than to press him for details just yet. Later, when we didn't have a function to attend, I planned to gently probe for more information. Instead, I focused on the girl. "Well, we're not married yet. I would understand if this Evelyn were made aware by degrees."

Displeasure filled Isaac's face. "She knows how to read, Julia. This is our engagement party. When are you going to stop clinging to Edward? If he's so wonderful, why couldn't he keep you from Macy? Why did he leave you when you needed him the most?"

I yanked my hands from his. "What would you know of love?"

The stubborn jut of Isaac's chin was the only indication of his anger. He sat back and looked into the night. I wanted to stop the carriage and march home. I imagined a hundred different ways I could avoid Isaac tonight. When the carriage stopped, Isaac didn't alight.

"Julia, I'm sorry." His voice was weary. "Let's not be at odds. Especially tonight. Please."

"Another function where we have to play our public roles, Isaac?"

"No. I really am sorry."

Before I could form an answer, Hudson opened the door.

Isaac climbed out and offered his hand. I managed without his aid and then refused his arm.

The noise in the drawing room dimmed as we entered. This was far different from London. Here, they were shrewder. They were far better acquainted with Lady Pierson. The matrons carefully studied my features, shocked, before flapping their fans and giving each other disapproving stares. The men wore hints of a smile, as if the appearance of a love child secretly amused them.

From the corner of my eye, I saw Isaac tense with anger before making a show of offering me his arm. Never had I been more grateful for it in my entire life. His strength carried us through the doorway and into the thick of their knowing stares.

"Colonel Greenley," Isaac said, bowing. "We are honored."

"Miss Pierson, Dalry, how nice of you to finally join us." Colonel Greenley raised his wineglass and motioned for my father to step forward. "To our guests!"

My father paused the conversation he was having with two men and lifted his glass. A hesitant scattering of wineglasses joined him.

"How are you holding up, my dear?" Colonel Greenley asked me in a low voice.

"Wonderfully! How could I not?" I whispered back. "They simply adore me, as you can see."

Colonel Greenley and I apparently didn't share the same sense of humor, for his brow creased in confusion as he took a step backwards.

"She's perfectly fine, thank you," Isaac smoothed. "I hear Pierson is planning to hunt in the morning. Are you joining him?"

Colonel Greenley stared at me a second longer, then chuckled. "I wish I had your skill at turning a conversation, Isaac. Go on, mingle."

Isaac directed me toward a man his age near the windows,

as a young woman slipped into the room and edged behind a palm tree. Wistfulness tinged her features as she viewed us. She was slight with dark-blonde hair. Despite the hollowing of her cheeks, she was picturesque. More than one matron clucked with sympathy and turned to whisper. Though she never took her eyes off us, I detected no resentment. She seemed the type who would feel agony over every gesture between Isaac and me, saving them to lament over privately.

Isaac was aware too, for his arm stiffened, though his conversation did not lapse. Compassion forced me to break from Isaac. "I must go speak with her," I said.

Isaac didn't have time to stop me.

The girl's blue eyes looked over my dress and jewels, and a little sigh escaped her. I ached for her, for it was apparent she was nowhere near recovering from her grief.

"How do you do, Miss Greenley? My name is Julia Pierson, and I'm especially pleased to make your acquaintance."

Tears welled in her eyes. "Are you not afraid to associate with someone . . . someone addled?" Her eyes wandered to a group of women who watched us, horrified. "It's what they think and whisper, you know." Her mouth trembled as she turned her gaze back to me. "I'm so happy for you, Miss Pierson. Isaac is so wonderful, and so are the Dalrys. You'll both be so happy."

"Will you call me Julia?"

She looked taken aback. "You do not dislike me, then?"

"Why would I?"

"Have you not heard . . . that sometimes—" she stepped farther into the palm leaves—"I pretend Isaac is Ben?"

I debated my answer. She didn't *seem* mentally unbalanced, at least. "We all grieve differently. I think I can understand."

She grasped my hand. "I promise not to do it anymore."

"Will you show me the terrace?" I slipped my arm in hers, deciding the other guests didn't need to see this. "I would like a glimpse of the stars."

Outside, she leaned over the balcony and gave a strange laugh. "You must think me odd. But if only you saw what Ben and I were like. . . . He was wonderful, so wonderful! But why am I telling you? Being in love with Isaac must be equally glorious!"

"I do hope that I'll meet Ben someday," I said.

Her smile suggested she'd given up. Presently, she linked our arms.

The rest of the night we were inseparable, and she took it upon herself to make my introductions, which probably did more for my standing in the neighborhood than anything Isaac could have done.

As Isaac and I left with my father, Colonel Greenley hastened down the steps after us.

"I am deeply indebted to you." Colonel Greenley pumped my hand as if I were a Frenchman. "If it is ever in my power to grant you a favor, do not hesitate to ask."

When I stared at him, confused, he explained further, "Outside of Isaac, you are the first person my daughter has spoken to in over a year. Not only did she speak with you, but to everyone here tonight. I had all but given up hope. Thank you."

My father smiled and nodded as if he'd accomplished the feat. "Perhaps we should arrange for her to come and stay with Isaac and Julia after the wedding. See if we can bring her further out of her shell. I know the very room in their new house she can occupy."

I opened my mouth, ready to protest, but Isaac winked at me as if telling me to endure my father a little longer. The time to walk independently had not yet come.

Colonel Greenley shifted his weight, considering the idea. "Will you be keeping your busy schedule?"

"Rather, but we might arrange for Kate to be with Evelyn."

Colonel Greenley rubbed his hands against the cold, giving me a sharp look. "What say you to the idea?"

For a second, I was pure astonishment. My breath frosted

the air as it came in hard pants. I couldn't even remember the last time my opinion was taken into account. My father frowned, heightening my discomfort. His expression made it impossible to tell what he expected me to say. Because he'd just agreed to have her, I gave a hesitant nod.

Colonel Greenley crossed his arms as he huddled unprotected against the cold. His smile, however, couldn't have been warmer. "Good. Then I'll send her soon."

❧

That night, as I stepped from the carriage, the grass beneath my feet was hard with frost. Isaac had gone home to be with his mother and Kate, so I steadied myself on my father's arm, casting a quick glance at the stars. The cold air made them throb with a matchless brilliance that left me breathless. Each one was so luminous, each orb so alight with jubilation, that my heart ached. That night they diminished our significance with their infinite numbers. How tenuous all seemed when one thought that in a hundred years they would still dance in the same pattern, while I would be gone. Longing stirred, but I wasn't certain what I wanted anymore.

"What on earth!" my father exclaimed before releasing my arm and storming toward the estate's entrance.

A quick glance revealed the source of his alarm. Golden light poured from his library window, bathing the lawn.

I hastened after him, but the sheer weight and volume of my skirts prevented my catching up with him.

"Robert!" My father's shout reverberated from the library as I entered the hall. "What do you think you're doing!"

By the time I reached the library door, my father was loosening his cravat and glowering at Forrester, who stood at the desk. At his feet were stacked piles of my father's private documents. Every lamp in the chamber was lit. Sitting in their pools of light, ledgers and fragile record books sat open. Behind Forrester, every drawer had been opened, their contents now on the rugs. Bookshelves contained huge gaps.

Forrester laughed with near hysteria. "I have him, Roy! I finally have him!" He pounded the desk in his excitement. "It's so obvious! It's been staring us in the face the entire time!"

My father pocketed the long strip of silk, considering his chamber. His thoughts were unreadable; in all the months I'd lived with him, it was the first time I'd encountered this expression.

All at once, he noted my presence. "Remain here," he ordered Forrester, then turned and ushered me from the chamber. "Good night, Daughter." He kissed my cheek and moved me toward the stairs. "You'd best go to bed."

He walked me to the staircase. I considered trying to eavesdrop, but, as if reading my thoughts, my father waited at the foot of the stairs until I ascended.

⌣

The following morning, Isaac carried the scent of fresh air, and cold clung to him as he surprised me with a kiss on the cheek.

"Brava, darling, on your performance last night." He grinned, dropping into his seat, then piled eggs and ham on his plate and grabbed a sweet roll. "Glitter and all." He wiped his fingers on a napkin while gesturing for coffee. "Ben is going to be eternally grateful!"

I nodded my greeting. "Forrester's here."

Isaac threw down his pastry. "I solemnly swear that when we're married, I'll forbid him to visit so we can get a break." He slurped his coffee, then waggled his eyebrows as Forrester entered the chamber and collapsed into a chair.

Forrester held his face between his hands. "Where's Roy?"

"Couldn't you have at least tucked your shirt in?" Isaac asked.

"Why? It's only Julia." Mr. Forrester scowled at me. "I can assure you, she's not shocked."

Before anyone could respond, my father's footsteps approached. He snarled, catching sight of Forrester. "There you are! You said it'd be in this morning's paper! What are you up to?" He threw the *Morning Gazette* on the table.

"Not there?" Mr. Forrester picked up the sheaf and pretended to scan the pages before brushing them to the floor. "Hmmm. Odd. Probably tomorrow."

"If it's not in by Friday, I'm giving it to the *Times*."

Mr. Forrester's mouth looked like the food in it had suddenly soured. "You swore I could have the story!"

"Why should I wait when every paper is nipping at this opportunity?"

"Because you promised, that's why."

My father made a growling noise. "Friday, Robert. Friday!"

He knocked James from his path as he left the breakfast room.

Forrester picked up *The Standard* from the bottom of the pile. "What's using him up?"

"Excuse me," Isaac said to me, snagging another roll before hastening after my father.

I rose too, but Forrester pinned my dress with his foot.

"Are you drunk? Get your boots off my dress," I ordered.

He obeyed, keeping his gaze on the paper. "Greenham was at the tavern."

I dropped my heavy skirts. "And?"

Mr. Forrester propped his feet on the cushion of a chair next to him and continued to read. "It's his opinion, if you marry Isaac, he wouldn't live to see another month."

An eerie feeling, similar to a shiver, worked its way up my spine. "You think Macy would kill him?"

He turned a page. "Oh, I have no doubt about it now."

The room suddenly felt empty. I waited, but Mr. Forrester only discarded his paper and then took up *The Token* and started reading anew.

"That's it?" I demanded. "That's all you have to say?"

"Yes." He flipped a page. "Unless, that is, you agree to help me get rid of Macy."

"Kill him?" I backed away, remembering Macy's tender face as he tended my wounds.

"Only a true Macy girl would jump to a conclusion like that, though Greenham swears Macy took no pains to train you." He chuckled, shaking his head. "It's entirely possible you are the most unlucky person walking the earth. The moment you first drew breath, you became the most tempting bait on earth for Macy."

I paused, his words painting anew Mama's story of how the midwife nearly dropped me in my fury. Though I did not fully grasp Forrester's meaning, his tone communicated that perhaps it was with good reason I had kicked and screamed that day. "I don't understand."

In answer, he reached into his waistcoat and withdrew a velvet pouch, which he placed on the table. When he unrolled it, I nearly gasped in amazement.

Inside was a necklace consisting of five individual chains. The base was thin blue enamel, which looked almost like something only royalty would wear. A strand of pearls, a strand of rubies, a strand of opals, and a gold filigree chain all looped at varying lengths and were held in place by gold flowers with large pearls.

It was so delicate and beautiful that I reached out and touched it before I remembered my manners.

"Take it." He shoved it across the table. "It's yours."

"Mine?" I couldn't help but lift it.

"It's the replacement necklace Macy offered to buy you."

"I don't understand."

"He sent a note after murdering Eramus. He offered to replace the broken necklace. I spent half a day searching for something this costly, curious to see how much he'd pay.

I bribed the shop owner to send a note to his house, stating that you'd admired it and were inquiring to see if he was willing. I set it up so that if Macy was, it'd be sent to Lady Northrum's under the guise of a repaired piece."

"And he purchased it?" I looked at the beautiful necklace, stunned.

"Guess at its cost."

I tied the ribbon, sealing it back in its burgundy folds. "You shouldn't have done this."

"Thirty thousand pounds."

The knowledge I held an empire in my hands was even more breathtaking.

Mr. Forrester finally set aside the newspaper, turning his full attention on me. "He's never spent that much on anyone except himself before. He's serious about keeping his wife. You need me if you're ever going to be freed from him. I am one of the only people in the world who finally knows how to contain him."

"Why do you need me, then?"

"Need you? All I want from you is the satisfaction of check-mating him with his own queen."

I shook my head, backing from the chamber.

Mr. Forrester chose another newspaper. "Eventually, you're not going to have a choice. Macy will never relent. I can wait as long as you can."

Twenty-Seven

✛

THAT MORNING, not knowing what else to do with myself, I sat in the window seat of my bedchamber and stared at Eastbourne. Forrester's words kept echoing in my head: *"Eventually, you're not going to have a choice."*

When he'd spoken them, I almost shrieked with laughter. When, since joining my father's household, had I had a choice?

I was weary of intrigue, of my father's bullying temper, schedules that I had no say in, the endless parade of new faces. I'd been pushed step-by-step in a direction I never intended to take—pushed so gradually that I scarcely knew how it happened.

My heart beat in angry jerks. The idea that I had say in my life was an illusion. And what had the illusion won me? Was I any freer? I wasn't certain who I was anymore. I knew the smiling, masked version of myself. But she, too, was only an illusion.

What did I want?

My first thought steered toward the impossible—Edward and Mama. But knowing they were unattainable, I thought smaller. What if I decided whom I'd visit for once, or what I would wear that day? What would I have wanted to do right then, before I came here?

The answer was so obvious, I felt like a simpleton.

I hadn't breathed fresh air in ages, nor been warmed by the sun's rays on my skin. Each time I daydreamed about Edward, had I not also yearned for the outdoors? I needed to walk in the wind, to feel grass beneath my feet. To wander in solitude.

While in London, I'd become so conditioned to submit and obey that guilt enwrapped me as I made a decision without first consulting my father or Isaac. I would walk to the ancient oak tree that Edward had found our first morning here.

Deciding my impotency was the illusion, I donned a walking dress, the plainest dress I could locate, then wrapped myself in a shawl and hastened outdoors before anyone could stop me.

The frost that had glittered over the landscape this morning had dissolved, leaving behind piebald patches of mud. Mist enshrouded the fields like a distant wall providing me with longed-for isolation.

Mud caked the bottom of my skirts, and my legs burned as I climbed up the hill. I could have spread my arms and spun in circles. I felt freer than I had in months. My body felt a strange mixture of temperatures—cold in the nose, ears, and toes, but tingly warm everywhere else.

When I spotted the first spiralling branches of the golden oak, however, I hesitated and nearly lost my resolve to finish. The thought of sitting at the tree without Edward was painful. But then, determined to at least touch the trunk, I picked up my skirts.

I wiped my nose with my sleeve. I'd been so full of hope the last time I'd been here. I thought I'd win my father, see Macy defeated, and find my way back to Edward. Would I have come had I known my old life would be entirely stripped from me?

I'd nearly touched the trunk when a cold wind lifted something from the ground, a brown fabric, which flopped, then fell. My stomach lurched upon realizing a vagrant lay propped against the mossy bole. My first instinct was to flee, but the head turned, revealing Edward's distinctive locks curling around his boyish face.

It was so unexpected that for a moment I thought myself dreaming.

Twigs and leaves were intertwined in his mussed hair, much like the time when we'd played soldiers and crawled through Mrs. Hodges's thicket. Only this time, Edward's breathing was too rapid and his cheeks too flushed.

Dampness soaked through my skirts as I knelt by him.

He grinned, his wonderful lopsided grin, reserved just for me. "I read in the paper you'd left London." He attempted to sit forward but couldn't lift his head. He relaxed against the trunk again. "I think I have a fever."

I smiled, trying not to show my alarm. "You do look it."

He shut his eyes. "You can't tell by looking. You're supposed to kiss my forehead. If it feels heated, then it's a fever."

I laughed, managing to keep tears from my voice, then removed my glove and felt his brow with the backs of my fingers.

His skin scorched mine.

"How long have you been here?" I asked. Sparks of alarm rushed through me as I recalled that the temperature had plummeted during the night.

He swallowed instead of answering.

I pressed my lips against his forehead, brushing aside his curls. "Edward, darling, can you walk? With support, I mean?"

He opened his glazed eyes and studied me a long minute. "Am I too late?"

I looked down, not certain if he was asking about us or for him. Therefore, I was at a loss to answer.

"Have you married Lord Dalry?" he clarified.

"No." I could barely choke out the words. "But . . . but I'm engaged."

"Do you want to be?"

I shook my head.

He gave a weak chuckle. "This keeps happening to us, doesn't it?"

I sank fully to the ground, feeling as though a gentle rain refreshed my soul, feeling whole again. "Rather."

"Well, at least you haven't married this one yet. That much is in our favor. We'll have to trust God for the rest." He shut his eyes. "I'm sorry, Juls, but that's all the sermonizing I can manage."

"Well, I appreciate the effort. I've embraced Christianity now, you know."

A smile tugged over his lips. "Don't become alarmed, Juls, but I fear I'm now delusional. I'd like to tell you what I thought you said, but it might get me socked."

I kissed his brow again, then his temples, not caring about my duty to Macy, my father, or Isaac. "Don't worry, darling; there aren't any apples about."

He gave no response, seemingly asleep.

I drew a deep breath, worried. I picked crumpled leaves from his hair, surmising that while my engagement to Isaac was being celebrated by all but me, Edward slept in the cold and in the leaves, waiting, trusting. How could he have known I'd come? What if I hadn't?

I pressed my cheek against the top of his head, not certain how to fit Edward's arrival into my newfound faith. What would my surrender look like now? Was I supposed to do nothing, to fall blindly and trust, or was I supposed to rebel and fight my father with every ounce of energy? It was my first crisis of faith, albeit far more wonderful than I could have imagined. At least—at *least*—I had Edward during it.

"Ed." I kissed the crown of his head. "I need you to come with me. You have to stand. I'll support you. The house isn't far."

He opened his eyes and stared as if his thoughts came

slowly. Then he nodded and struggled to sit forward again. Wrapping his arm about my shoulder, I helped him stand. He shifted more of his weight to me than I expected, making us both wobbly.

I did not allow myself to feel emotion as we stumbled toward Maplecroft. Haltingly we made progress. Beads of perspiration dotted his brow, making fear clutch my heart. After what seemed like hours, Maplecroft, with her false offers of sanctum, loomed into view.

They must have noticed I was missing and had been searching, for the front door flew open and James raced toward me, his white periwig bobbing as he made haste.

"Help me carry him to a bed," I ordered. "Then send William for my father's surgeon."

"Your father—" he began.

I met his protests with a look that was feral. "I don't care what my father thinks. You will obey me! And if my father protests, fetch me and I'll handle him! Am I clear?"

Instead of hurt or anger, his eyes sparkled with pride as though he'd been waiting for this moment. The whites of his teeth flashed. "Perfectly!"

❧

It took about forty minutes before Edward was in bed and an apothecary was sent for. Once satisfied that Edward was in good hands, I went to my father.

Clutching my shawl against me, I knocked on the library door. Then, with annoyance, I realized my skirts were muddy and my hair stuck up in wisps.

"Enter," my father's stern voice called.

I tried to press down the freed hair that surrounded my face while I nudged the door open. My father sat sideways in his chair behind his desk, waiting for me with a dour expression. Seated nearby, Mr. Forrester watched with a wicked grin.

"Where have you been?" my father demanded. "I sent for you an hour ago!"

My fingers felt numb. "I went for a walk."

His eyes narrowed and his jaw tensed. "Isaac gave you permission?"

Heat replaced the cold numbness. "No, I gave it to myself."

My father met my eyes with surprise, but his frown was friendly as he picked up his pen and returned to his documents. "Honestly, Julia. You should know better than to scamper off alone. Next time, have James or William accompany you. Or better yet, Isaac."

I took a steadying breath. "I wasn't alone. Not exactly."

Both their heads swiveled in my direction, but before they could inquire further, the clatter of footsteps rang in the hall. Isaac swung open the library door; behind him, James doubled over, red-faced and panting.

"Sir," Isaac cried, "I pray you be calm."

My father dropped his pen. "What on earth! Isaac, I thought you were with your mother."

Breathless, Isaac shot me a look of wonderment.

I shook my head, communicating my father wasn't yet aware.

My father stood. "Isaac?"

I hugged my shawl tightly against me. "Reverend Auburn is here. I found him beneath the oak tree."

Isaac placed a supporting hand on my back. "I ask you be lenient. James explained the matter. Apparently Reverend Auburn is feverish. She's not disobeying you. It was an act of charity."

I expected my father to explode, but his eyes locked on Isaac's protective stance before he gave a nod. "Fine, but it's not wise for Julia to visit him. I'll not encourage his blatant disregard for her safety by continuing to make contact. When he recovers, Isaac, I want an audience with him."

"As you wish." Isaac grasped my upper arm, urging me toward the hall.

"No." I twisted free. "I'm sorry, but no!" Then, not knowing what else to do, I flung myself before my father's desk. "Please, you don't understand. I—"

"Isaac." My father motioned him to leave.

I kept my gaze on my father, so I could not judge how Isaac felt as he left. But when the door clicked, I said, "I beg you to reconsider."

"May I remind you that you are betrothed to Isaac."

"Then let me beg to be released."

My father's stare turned iron-cold. "If I were you, I'd choose my next words and actions very carefully. If Isaac suddenly comes to me, wishing to be free of your engagement, you'll find yourself wed to Lord Alexander before your friend wakes."

His threat aroused everything contrary in me. "You cannot make me marry someone else, not now! Not when Edward is here!"

My father's eyes constricted. "Shall we test that theory?"

Mr. Forrester yawned, then stood. "Should I leave?"

"No, remain." My father glared at me. "This conversation has ended. Julia, you are dismissed."

❧

Each step away from my father's chamber made me feel weightless, as if all were too nightmarish to be real. I slipped into the parlor where Isaac and I had first taken tea. There, I sank against the wall, then pounded it with my fists.

I wanted to scream, *Why me?*

I'd surrendered. It wasn't fair.

From the wall, Lady Josephine watched without sympathy, nothing more than a cold painting, immune to loss. The first sob broke through. She wasn't really family. She was just a painting. I had no family except a tyrannical father. I looked wildly about the room, unable to restrain the panic. Everything in my life was nothing more than a facade. Was I truly the

Emerald Heiress? Was my father the benevolent man everyone believed?

I slid down, then stretched facedown on the floor, no longer caring what was ladylike.

The door opened and to my dismay, Forrester's tall boots slipped inside. I gave a bitter laugh, turned on my side, and pressed the heels of my hands into my eyes. Of course *he* would come. "Go away."

Rather than hearing his footfalls die away, I felt the air move as he crouched beside me. When he spoke, his voice was low and near. "No matter how important your juvenile love affair seems, your real problem is down that hill. Within the last quarter hour, Macy took residence at Eastbourne."

Disquiet washed through me as I ceased crying and squinted at him.

His expression was that of a poacher finding game in his trap. One of his knees dug into the carpet while his arms were folded across each other. Excitement lit his eyes. "How far are you willing to go in order to wed this reverend of yours?"

I pushed against the floor to sit straight, then wiped my eyes, considering him.

For the space of a minute, his smile was wicked as he met my eyes with an unwavering stare. His meaning, however, was clear. If I helped him blackmail Macy, he'd help me wed Edward.

Elsewhere in the estate, the muffled laughter of two maids carried to us. In the stable yard, horses whinnied and a dog barked as grooms shouted to each other. They were all so alive. I glanced at the lifeless portrait of Lady Josephine, feeling as though my own life were on the verge of forever ebbing away from me.

I returned to Forrester's steadfast gaze, wondering what he meant when he asked how far I was willing to go. Yet my heart pounded hard within my chest.

Was ever such an apple held out before Eve? For as long as

I could remember, I had envisioned marrying Edward and pictured our life in London, where I had believed he would practice law. I'd envisioned a tight, narrow house—one where we'd smile and dote upon our children and fuss about the butcher's bill until we were able to join Henry and Elizabeth.

Tears blurred my vision as Forrester patiently waited. How long had I felt shoved underwater, waiting and hoping I'd soon achieve a gulp of air? How could I not take the only hand extended to me? For surely I would otherwise drown.

Yet hours spent reading Edward's Bible raised new thoughts. *"If any man will come after me, let him deny himself, and take up his cross, and follow me. For whosoever will save his life shall lose it."*

I pulled my shawl tighter against me. Was this a matter of surrendering to God or finally standing up for myself and not allowing my father to dictate my life?

My father's firm tread sounded at the end of the hall, each step like the last ticks of a dying clock, announcing the end of my time with Edward.

No further incentive was needed. I gave Forrester a curt nod, telling him to count me in. To say I was innocent in this matter would be a lie. Though I did not know what Forrester intended, I knew it would be drastic. Nor could Forrester have foreseen how dearly it would cost him too. I am convinced that had he known the manner of Pandora's box our partnership was about to open, he would have left me well alone.

Twenty-Eight

I WAITED HOURS that night for my father to retire. I perched in a chair, feeling queasy with each toll of the grandfather clock. The monotonous ticking of the mantel clock above drove me mad as I tried to mentally prepare for my task. Edward's presence must have unsettled my father, for he did not order James to key down the lights until near one in the morning.

I waited a quarter hour more before Forrester's soft knock sounded on the other side of my door. I rose on hollow legs and slipped out of my bedchamber, hoping I didn't look as sick as I felt.

At the bottom of the stairs, I refused to acknowledge Lady Josephine.

Taking long strides, Forrester led me to the drawing room, where he opened a floor-to-ceiling window and stuck out a leg. He turned, offering his hand. "You first."

I recall that only a few stars pierced the darkling sky that night, belying how illustrious their display had been just the night before.

Forrester jabbed my side.

"Tonight you must trust me completely," he said with a glance toward Eastbourne. "First, he'll test our unity. No matter what he says, do not lose faith in me. He must see our full confidence in each other. Do you understand?"

"Oh yes, we'll have no problem there," I commented snidely.

"He needs to know you can stand on your own. Show no weakness."

Beneath our feet, pine needles cushioned our steps, releasing a clean, woodsy fragrance into the air. I ducked beneath dark boughs, wanting to remind Forrester that Macy already knew my weaknesses, and that he was one of them. Instead, I placed one foot in front of the other.

"Don't look so pale," he demanded. "Be confident. Oh, and no matter what I say, show no surprise. He needs to think you are familiar with the information."

"Yes, well, on that point—"

"Quiet. Just listen. Don't eat or drink anything he offers. Once we are there, I can't help you. You have to speak for yourself. Don't attempt to help me either. Keep in mind, I have a pistol hidden on me."

I faced him, suddenly desirous of some form of protection. Somehow I doubted Forrester himself was an option. "May I have it?"

"Can you shoot?" He reached inside his vest as though considering handing it over.

"No."

He scowled, withdrawing his hand.

After a quarter hour of twigs snapping and an unsteady descent, we reached the stone lions, the entrance of Eastbourne. I hesitated, eyeing their silent warning growls as Forrester pounded up the steps and clattered the knocker.

Taking deep breaths, I glanced behind me at Maplecroft, glad that Edward was safe inside that thick fortress and not here. The large hinges groaned, and I turned in time to see Reynolds open the door.

A rush of affection filled me, and before I could help it, I stepped toward him.

"Mrs. Macy!" Delight filled his features. "Welcome home!"

Forrester chuckled as if finding humor in the greeting, then pulled me inside the golden, pillared hall. "Tell Macy we're here."

Once again the beauty of Eastbourne struck me. Dry-mouthed, I scanned the space, amazed that for the span of three or four hours I'd been its mistress. A flutter of doubt coursed through me. Why did Mr. Macy's home effuse warmth, while Maplecroft lay under hoarfrost?

"Steady," Forrester whispered, as if sensing my thoughts.

I felt despair. How very different were the two lives offered me. One full of freedoms untold, petted and pampered; the other harsh and strict—but respectable. I clenched my skirts, refusing to believe those were the only two options available to me. I hoped against hope I might still manage to open yet a third option—a life with Edward.

As if proving how different from my father he was, Macy emerged from the passage that led in the direction of his study, dressed in black silk lounging pants and a robe made of the same material.

Heat rose through my cheeks as I tried not to note his bare chest.

Barefoot, he crossed to me and kissed my cheek, then gave Forrester a confused glance before returning to me. "Darling, you know I don't care whom you take up with, but really, I must draw the line at Forrester."

"Ha!" Forrester crossed his arms. "And here I hadn't thought you capable of speaking truth."

Macy's eyes locked on him. I gave an involuntary shiver, for the very atmosphere snapped and sizzled as if lightning were about to strike. Slowly, Macy turned and gave me a questioning stare.

An awkward silence fell as I realized there was some sort of a hidden exchange happening; if I were to stay in this game, I needed to retort. Both men waited, but there was nothing I could say. I sensed much but knew little. Furthermore, though I had mentally prepared myself, I hadn't factored in the effect that standing inside Eastbourne would have on me.

Macy noticeably loosened, then caressed my cheek. "The problem, Robert, is that you don't understand Julia as well as I do. From that cocky expression on your face, you think she's supplied you with some bit of information. Whatever she told you, I warrant it can't be proved in court." He withdrew his touch. "Still, you've returned my bride, so I'll be lenient."

"Well, good." Forrester grinned. "Once we've had our say, we'll try to repay your generosity."

"We?" Macy shot me a shocked look. "Don't tell me this buffoon talked you into one of his mad schemes." His eyes mesmerized as he chuckled. "I can see caring for you will be a full-time job. If it's not someone stealing your jewelry, it's someone with a death wish asking you to join him. Come along, darling." He laced his fingers in mine. "Let's see how well you manage extortion. Shall we adjourn to the drawing room?"

I bent my head in a shy manner, allowing Macy to move and manipulate me. I instinctively felt the magnitude of our mistake by going there that night, and I wanted time to analyze, which meant claiming the safety of his amusement.

Sweat beaded Forrester's face, but he maintained his confident swagger.

Macy opened the door to a chamber that was more cathedral than drawing room. Though I'd seen it before, and though I'd lived with my father, it still impressed. Lacunar ceilings towered above shining floors decorated with zebra-skin rugs and plush velvet furniture. Within the hearth, tiles glistened as fire inhabited its logs. The chamber's crown was equally impressive. The fan-tracery vaulting was gilt, as were fanned ceiling bosses. I eyed the ceiling's recesses, lined with sky-blue paper overrun with golden vines.

Macy positioned me near a love seat and gestured for me to sit. Forrester plopped into the seat across from me, while Macy poured three brandies.

Balancing the snifters, Macy extended the first one to Forrester.

"Thank you, but no," Forrester said. "I hope you wouldn't use your botany skills until you've heard us out, but I don't feel like chancing it."

"Botany?" I asked.

Mr. Macy laughed as he perched on the arm of the love seat. "Yes, dear heart. I dabble in the poisons. Good heavens, Robert, if I decide to allow you to leave, I hope you'll choose better-informed partners." He planted a glass in my hands. "Surely you know I wouldn't poison you."

Mr. Forrester shot me a warning look.

All at once, Eastbourne's hothouse made sense, the plants he'd painstakingly journalled in his library and the powder he'd given me at his residence in London after tending my wounds. I recalled mornings at Eastbourne when he had managed to function despite having no sleep. I stared at the amber liquid, wondering if this was how Mama died—a combined effort of Macy and Greenham.

Macy planted his bare feet on the nearby seat cushion, then elbows on knees, waiting. His eyes glowed with expectancy as Forrester slowly shook his head.

I knew in my heart of hearts that Macy had the upper hand at this point. I needed to drink it, if only to make Macy think he held more control over me than he actually did. I lifted the glass, gave Macy a frightened look, and took a long sip.

Macy smirked at Forrester as he slid onto the love seat. Knee bent, he placed one leg behind me and dropped his other leg to the floor.

"Now tell me." He removed the ruby combs from my hair. "How did Robert convince you to take this measure?" Macy's fingers pulled loose and unbraided my tresses.

I glared at Forrester, silently demanding he protest. But he only watched, tight-lipped. My breath caught as I wondered what sort of imbecile would bring me to Eastbourne without sharing his plans.

"It's all right, darling." Macy tilted his head and touched a pulsing vein on my neck as if fascinated. "There's no need for fear. I already forgive you." He lifted his head toward the door and shouted, "Snyder!"

The door opened and two men entered.

Macy waved toward Forrester. "Lock him in a secure chamber. I'll decide what to do about him in the morning." His fingers strayed to the buttons along the back of my dress. "Tell Reynolds my wife and I wish to adjourn to her bedchambers. Tell him I won't be tolerating disturbances tonight."

Here, I finally found protest. "Not until you've heard me out." I wrenched from his touch. "Forrester stays until I've said what I've come to say."

This, too, amused Macy. He motioned his men to leave, then propped his chin on his hand. "All right, sweetheart. Tell me what you know and what you're demanding. I'll pay double your demands, if you like."

"I imagine her first request is to stop hearing your false endearments," Forrester said, color returning to his cheeks. "She's soon to marry Reverend Auburn, and I'm certain her future husband wouldn't approve her spending the night with you."

Macy chuckled and kissed my palm. "Is that what he promised you, dear heart? How does he think he'll convince Roy?"

"Oh, I don't know." Forrester laced his hands over his knee.

"I think I'll just point out to him that a poor man is better than a Gypsy. That should work, don't you think, Mr. Rainmayer?"

Macy had been tenderly tracing the side of my face, but his fingers instantly curled into a fist. All charm and all charisma vanished. There was a chilling silence, during which Macy probed my eyes, shooting tendrils of fear through me.

Forrester grinned, switching his laced hands to the back of his head. "Julia and I have both entrusted our information to confidential sources. Unlike my father, if something happens to us, your secret will be exposed in my newspaper immediately. So first, you can wish us long and happy lives."

I swallowed, amazed Forrester couldn't feel the murderous intent radiating from Macy.

"And just what exactly do you hope to get from me?" Macy's voice was guttural.

Forrester picked imaginary lint off his frock coat, crossing his feet. "I don't think you have anything worth offering. We have our own fortunes, making your ill-gotten gain of no interest. After that, she pretty much owns the rest, doesn't she?" Forrester leaned slightly forward, crossing an arm over his knee. "You will go back to the restrictions my father placed on you. For our silence, you will remove yourself from society. You will return to the reclusive life he imposed on you."

The vein in Mr. Macy's neck throbbed, though he kept a calm demeanor. He gave a slight tilt of his head, his eyes hard and glittering, like those of a raptor. His baleful gaze settled on me.

Having already pieced together that Macy's real name must be Rainmayer, I did my best to feign shock. I cast him a look that I hoped conveyed confusion and fear.

"You've tested my patience too far, dear," he said in a voice that rendered me cold from head to foot.

Mr. Forrester leaned forward and plucked the brandy glass from my hand. "Be glad she's not charging you rent."

Panic closed off my throat, making it difficult to breathe. How could he not see Macy aimed to murder us? It was so clear. He was a cornered animal, willing himself to be calm before the kill.

Macy's left hand came to rest on my shoulder, causing me to jump. His grip was tight. "Julia, I need you to go to your chambers. Even now I shall be lenient with you, but I have further business to discuss with Forrester."

Forrester ceased looking boastful, as though finally realizing our danger.

Macy placed a kiss at the base of my neck, rebuttoning the top of my dress. "Go. Have Reynolds wait with you. I shall be there shortly."

My hair stood on end as I looked at Mr. Forrester. He was a dead man the moment I set foot out that door. The calculated way Macy's eyes roamed over him confirmed he was already playing out the deed in his mind.

I rose as commanded but was unable to move. Mr. Macy stood, took my elbow, and guided me to the hall. At the threshold, I faced him. "Don't kill Forrester. Please. I beg you."

Macy signalled his men to approach.

"Please!" I clutched his robe, praying somehow there was a way out of this nightmare.

Macy's features offered no insight into his thoughts, but he said, "What did you hope to gain tonight, Julia?"

"Edward. Forrester promised to convince my father. I didn't even know what we held over you until now."

Macy angled his head to study my face, then held up a finger to his men. "Where did Forrester find his information?"

"Tell him nothing," Forrester demanded behind me.

"Watch him," Macy commanded his men, moving me farther down the hall.

I glanced toward the entrance doors, hugging myself. "Mr. Greenham."

Macy's eyes narrowed. "John! What the blazes does John have to do with this?"

"At a costume ball. He sent me a letter—"

"How?"

"He sent a farmer."

"How do you know his occupation?"

"I asked; he was tanned and his hair sunned."

Macy nodded agreement with my assessment. "What accent did he have? What part of the country?"

"The Midlands."

"Be more specific."

"I swear it, I don't know."

"His name?"

"He called himself Thomas. That's all I know."

Macy shut his eyes for a second, unclenching his fist before he moved me to a bench. "Tell me word for word what John said in his letter."

I swallowed, feeling wretched. Today so far, I'd betrayed my father's trust by agreeing to help Forrester, Isaac's by kissing Edward, Forrester's by confessing to Macy, and now it was Greenham's turn. "It said he had the papers that Forrester's father owned. He wanted Forrester to meet him."

"Where?"

"Margrove Tavern, Lea—"

"Leadenhall Street. I know it. How long ago?"

"Three days."

He was all astonishment. "What else did the note say?"

"That if I didn't trust Forrester, he'd make contact later."

Appearing incredulous, Macy rose and started pacing. "Contact you! That breaks the first rule. He knows better . . ." He placed one hand on his hip and covered his mouth in deep thought.

All at once, he turned and looked at me as if he'd never seen me before. Had I transformed into a shining goddess, he couldn't have stared at me with more amazement. Steepling his hands before his face, he paced anew. With brows drawn together, he looked menacing. His steps were planted as though he willed the floor to give way to his foot instead of being content to walk with permission like the rest of humanity.

The results of his thoughts carried such magnitude that he dropped to his seat and sat with legs spread, hands on knees, and mouth agape—as if too weighted by his own plan to move. He looked at me once, started to speak, but then covered his mouth and again thought deeply as if reviewing every detail anew.

"I'm sorry, sweetheart," he finally said. "To spare your feelings, I'm telling you this in advance. There is no longer an easy transition back to me. I fear it takes no ordinary bait to bag extraordinary game." He drew me into his arms and pressed kisses in my hair, but there was no affection in them, only excitement. "I fear you shan't enjoy being dangled, but know this: no matter how bad it becomes, when you're returned to me, you shall find me as doting as ever."

There was no proper response to those words. In them I heard the foreknowledge of my and my father's doom. Yet those fateful words also held a promise of escape—at least temporarily—and that was all I wanted.

Lacing his fingers in mine, Macy drew me back to the drawing room. Forrester waited, soaked in perspiration, pointing a revolver at the men guarding the door.

"They may both leave," Macy said to his men, gesturing toward the front door.

Shaking, Forrester edged the room, keeping his revolver trained on Macy's chest. I looked askance at Macy, not certain what to make of him. He nodded once, as if assuring that his permission to leave was genuine.

Forrester roughly grabbed my arm and yanked me toward the entrance. Fearing to take my gaze off Macy, I watched him all the way to the doors. He stood, impassive and expressionless.

When the door closed behind us, Forrester exploded. "What did you tell him?"

I twisted from his hand, then rubbed my arm. "Everything!"

"You almost killed us!"

"Don't yell at me!" I screamed back at him. "If it wasn't for me, right now you would be undergoing torture!"

"He was *testing* you! Seeing if you had the nerve to stand up! What do you do? You fawn all over him, making cow eyes!"

Furious, I ran ahead, scooped up pinecones, then turned and pelted them at Forrester. "And *you* just sat there! He would have killed you, if it—"

Forrester grabbed my arm midthrow, none too nicely. "Stop screaming. His house is always under surveillance. The last thing he needs to learn is that we aren't unified."

I dropped the pinecones and wiped my hands on my skirt, laughing with hysteria. "Yes, let's not let him guess that!" Then, feeling sick, "We've just made everything much, much worse. So, so much worse."

"He only wants you to think that. Now that he knows we can dislodge him from society, he wants you to think he's in control. I guarantee you, right now he's much more worried about how we found out our information."

"I told him."

"You told him!" Forrester's voice rose to a high pitch. "What did you say?"

"That a farmer from the Midlands was my contact."

"For months I've been trying to get information out of you! Months!" Forrester's feet slid over the steep hill. "Five minutes with Macy and you divulge everything you know. You've ruined us."

Instead of responding, I focused on my climb. My hands were raw from digging into the dirt and clutching at tree roots, trying to keep myself from sliding down. What did it matter what Forrester said? It was a miracle we'd made it out of Eastbourne. I couldn't even contemplate where I'd be if we hadn't.

At the top, Forrester paused and waited. I could make out

his dark form against the sky. Dirt and stones tumbled downhill whenever I lost my footing, but he never offered help.

"Let's get you to your bedchamber," he said when I managed to reach the top.

I sat, needing to catch my breath first. Beneath us, the lights of Eastbourne were extinguished one by one. "Explain to me," I said, steadying my breath, "who Mr. Rainmayer is."

"Shall I give you my documentation too? That way you can run down the hill and supply him with that next!"

I picked pine needles from my hair. "If you don't tell me, I'm marching upstairs and waking my father to tell him you dragged me to Eastbourne."

Forrester made a frustrated noise. "*That* is how you black-mail! Not whatever the dickens you were doing down there." Then, when I placed my hand on my hip, he dropped to the ground next to me.

"The late Mr. Macy lost his wife early in marriage and went abroad. He died on the voyage home, leaving only his son, Chance, from a second marriage as his heir. Or so we thought."

"Chance Macy wasn't his son?"

Forrester shook his head. "No. From what my father pieced together, Chance was a Gypsy hired on as a servant. But when he arrived in England, he walked off the boat as Macy's son. If you ask me, though I have no absolute proof, he probably killed his master in order to assume the role."

"He's . . . You mean Mr. Macy is a Gypsy!"

"If you consider, his complexion should have given it away years ago."

I remembered all of Macy's kisses, feeling amazed I'd been kissed by a Gypsy. Mama and Sarah wouldn't even allow me to wave to them in the marketplace. "Your father knew this?"

Forrester gave a curt nod. "Yes, all those years he was reclusive, that was my father's doing. It was his means of keeping Macy's blackmail in check."

"If he's an imposter, why didn't he discredit him years ago?"

"If you were Macy, a man without conscience, and someone learned you were an imposter, what would you do?"

I still hadn't been able to comprehend that Macy wasn't legitimately amongst the elite. It didn't seem possible. I gave a disbelieving laugh, recalling that I didn't belong there either.

"My father was wise enough not to take everything that matters from Macy. He left him his dignity. But my father hadn't comprehended Macy's next step."

I cocked my head. "Which was?"

"To find out who the real owner of Eastbourne is. Which, legally, upon the death of your father, is you."

"Me?"

"It's willed to Roy and, in the event of his death, his offspring."

"Yes, but I wasn't even seen as his daughter until this year."

Forrester breathed out a laugh. "You don't know Macy as well as I do. I guarantee you, locked away somewhere in that estate are papers, evidence—something that proves you're the daughter of Roy Pierson."

I was silent as I recalled the mass of papers in Mr. Macy's study and how he'd said he possessed his own copy of my parents' correspondences. I shook at the thought. "So what happens next?"

"Despite the fact you bungled it tonight, he knows we mean business. You watch; he'll remain tucked inside Eastbourne. We won!"

Nothing is rarer in life than a true idiot, and I take great pleasure in saying that Forrester was the chief stone in my collection.

I held in my exasperation. "What about Edward? How will you keep your end of the bargain?"

He snorted as he stood and brushed off his clothing. "Yes, yes. I took care of that as soon as you agreed to help me.

Tomorrow morning, at the breakfast table, I'll begin my campaign to aid your marriage to your vicar. Don't be late."

⌒

The following morning, my father surprised me by greeting me with a kiss before ensconcing himself in his chair. He even paused to study my tired eyes before spreading the napkin over his lap.

"Julia, I'm sorry about yesterday. When your friend awakens, I'll allow you to visit him. I'd like for you to properly thank him for his past service to you. I think, perhaps, it would ease you later in life, if we explain to him, too, why you must marry Isaac."

I stared at him, certain he'd see my guilt, but he gave no hint. I glanced at the clock, feeling sick, wondering where Forrester was. I couldn't begin my counterarguments without him. Isaac smiled at me as he took his seat, making me wonder if he'd helped my father reach his decision. I gave a faint nod of thanks as Isaac drizzled honey over his pears.

James entered with the tray of newspapers. Blanched, he gave me a horrified look before he set the stack beside my father. I narrowed my eyes, uncertain what he'd tried to communicate. Instead of remaining, James turned and left.

I stabbed a bite of melon as my father skipped the *Times* and selected the second paper. I did not raise my fork, however, for I feared the queen had died as I caught sight of his face.

He aged a decade in the span of a minute, then speechlessly laid down the newspaper and withdrew to the window.

Wide-eyed, Isaac and I leaned forward. The front page of the *Morning Gazette* had a likeness of Isaac and me. The artist had a good hand, for the images were true. The article that followed outlined how Isaac learned that I had a secret engagement to a vicar and had heroically stepped aside, sacrificing his happiness for mine. The story highlighted Isaac, praising and congratulating him on this act and on his political views. Edward's name wasn't mentioned.

My composure broke as I read it. I frantically shook my head, trying to communicate that I hadn't known about this. My father came back and laid a hand on Isaac's shoulder before I'd finished. My father looked broken. Isaac was worse. I'd never seen him so pulverized. He looked at me, and I knew then he had wanted me as his wife, not for my money, not because of my father, but because he loved me in his own way. Stunned, anguished, he met me with a look that asked how I could do that to him.

Forrester entered and scowled. "What is she sobbing about now?"

Instead of roaring and throwing Forrester from the house for the article, my father pointed at it as though he couldn't speak or move.

Forrester grabbed the pages from Isaac and read. Anger contorted his face before he screamed, "You little hussy! You switched the articles in my saddlebag, didn't you!"

I stared at Forrester, absolutely flabbergasted. "You know I didn't! Tell them! Tell them the truth!"

"When this reverend fellow wakes," my father finally said, "let him have her. Let him remove her from my house. Let me never lay eyes on her again."

"Sir," Isaac said, his voice strained.

"Isaac, I'm sorry," my father said. "I have nothing to offer you now."

"That's not what I meant. She needs you, sir."

I cringed, feeling more wretched than if he had shouted at me. My father didn't answer but exited the room, leaving a carved-out feeling in my chest. Isaac scooted his chair back and attempted to speak but failed. Though he worked to stay composed, he managed only a nod before he left.

I stared at my hands, which were scraped from climbing the

hill last night and still dirty, even though I'd scrubbed them for ten minutes.

Forrester moved near me and said in a soft voice, "The worst is over. Go to your vicar. Sit with him. Your father will come around eventually. He'll like Edward once he learns his nature."

Too stunned to do anything else, I followed his advice.

Edward's room felt humid as I slipped inside and pulled a chair near his bed. His hair was damp and his breathing abrasive. I rested my head on his shoulder, then took his hand and intertwined my fingers in his, waiting.

∾

There was no end of surprises those next three days. Edward awoke that night to the news that he was to marry the richest heiress in England, and that Lord Pierson had paused dinner—something hitherto unheard of—as he wished to interview his future son-in-law.

Word that my father had granted me permission to marry the vicar from my school—and that a hasty but private wedding was planned—spread through the neighborhood. Maplecroft was besieged by curious busybodies and genuine well-wishers.

Lady Dalry presented me with her mother's tatted veil.

Kate picked my bridal bouquet, a handful of crocuses tied with ribbon.

My wedding dress, however, was the most unexpected and extravagant gift of them all. Evelyn Greenley arrived past gloaming the eve of my wedding. Her fingers trembled as she peeled back tissue paper, revealing a billowing ivory gown of silk from the House of Doucet in Paris. Agony scripted her face as she handed over what was to have been her wedding dress. Trembling, she fled back into the night.

The next morning, my veil fluttered against my face as I climbed the church steps and entered the chapel. In vain I searched for Isaac. His absence was palpable, but I had no chance to dwell on it. My father started me down the aisle.

Edward waited, bathed in the golden rays of the sun at the front of the small chapel. Honey-colored curls fell over his brow as he gave me a slight bow. Here was the one soul I could not endure separation from and, indeed, I think I was not meant to live without.

The warmth of his hand imbued mine as we knelt to be wed.

◡◠◡

I find it humorous that I spent both of my wedding nights in a carriage, travelling. Immediately following our wedding, Edward announced that Henry and Elizabeth's nuptials were forthcoming and we were leaving posthaste. My father, though he had declared he wished me removed from his life, did not approve of Edward's plans, but there was nothing he could do.

Thus, Edward and I presently disembarked from one of my father's unmarked carriages to the homey sight of warm, yellow light spilling from Am Meer's windows. The cottage looked so minuscule, compared to the great houses I'd lived in, that at first I laughed.

Through the open drapes, I spotted Henry, Elizabeth, and Mrs. Windham in animated discussion. Mrs. Windham was having some sort of a crying fit, and no amount of coaxing seemed to be helping.

"No wonder they didn't hear the carriage," Edward said, approaching.

I had to bury my face in his chest, I was so happy. The room was shabby but unplagued by the worries of society. I could almost smell the lilac of Mrs. Windham's powder and feel the lumpiness of the maroon chair.

I picked up my skirts, ready to pound on the door with its chipped blue paint and demand entrance, but Edward caught my arm. "If we go inside, we'll be trapped for hours. We're only here to tell them I'm back and can marry them, if they still wish. They must be wondering what happened to me."

"You mean you didn't tell them where you were going?" I asked.

"No. Henry was already insisting we barge into your father's house and kidnap you, so I did it my way." He grinned, then bent and scooped up a handful of pebbles, which he threw lightly at the window.

As the pebbles skidded off glass, Mrs. Windham ceased her tears and gave the window an angry glare. A second later, Henry stuck his head out the window, squinting.

"Stay here," Edward whispered, then stepped out from the shadow of the carriage.

Henry gave a whoop, and a moment later, he emerged from Am Meer, followed by Elizabeth and Mrs. Windham. "Have you any idea what you put us through! Elizabeth and I have spent days searching for someone to marry us. I have half a mind to box you. Don't just stand there with that daft smile. Explain yourself."

Edward gestured in my direction. "Henry, I'd like to present to you my wife."

Feeling suddenly shy, I stepped forward.

I had not realized how much I'd changed until I saw Elizabeth and Mrs. Windham gaping at me. Then, after taking a tentative step forward and studying me, Elizabeth screamed and flung herself into my arms. Our foursome talked all at once. I was passed from Elizabeth to Mrs. Windham, who thankfully remained too shocked to speak.

Henry received me last and lifted me in a bear hug. "I should have known Edward went after you." Setting me on my feet, he turned to Edward. "You should have told me!"

Edward reached out and pulled me back toward him as if he couldn't bear the distance either. "It's of no matter. It's done now, and I kept my promise to be back for your wedding."

"Oh, you must leave Julia with us for the night," Mrs. Windham said, finally recovering enough to speak and signalling with her handkerchief for me to come to her. "It will give you time to explain it to your parents. Besides, she and Elizabeth must have a lot to talk on."

"Not a chance." Edward wrapped his arms around me and pulled me closer.

Henry was the only one who chuckled, guessing the reason. "Where are you going now?"

"To my room in the church."

"Ed! You can't take her there!"

"Oh yes, I can! We'll see you all in the morning," Edward called over his shoulder as he pulled me into the night.

~~~

Edward fumbled with the key in dark shadows before the church door opened. Moonlight graced his smile as he tugged me inside. The simple wood pews and hymnals could be seen in the weak light.

"My room is in the back." Edward started us down the aisle.

It felt strange to think that we were going to sleep in a church. More than sleep! I felt my blush start to rise. Feeling timid, I allowed him to lead me to a door behind the pulpit. At first I couldn't see the room, but Edward lit a match and set it to the wick of a lumpy candle.

"It's not much," Edward said.

I pulled at the ribbon of my bonnet, smiling. It was awful and wonderful together. There was a bed meant for one. The space felt as barren as a monk's cell. He crouched over the hearth and added some tinder from a basket. "It's cold. I'm sorry."

I couldn't help but grin when I viewed the chamber. Of all the men in my life, Edward offered me the humblest circumstances, but I adored them.

In the dim light cast by the fledgling fire, he helped me from my cape. His kisses were different from Macy's. They weren't sophisticated, but inexperienced. Yet no shyness tinged his actions as his hands fumbled over the hooks and buttons on my dress.

I already knew we were better suited than any other couple I'd ever encountered, but that night, as he lowered me to his bed, his eyes held depths of emotion that would have unmade any soul. By the time my head was laid into his pillow, the fire blazed.

Later, in Edward's arms, I watched the dying embers. I wanted to lie awake with joy the entire night. I belonged. I had family again. I had married the man I'd dreamed about since my childhood. The boy I'd loved since the day we'd met. And he loved me too. Even in sleep, he secured me against him. Every time I stirred, he'd half wake and draw me closer, nestling kisses in my hair. His chest rasped, but he was on the mend. I knew.

Closing my eyes, I thanked God, my heart too full to bear more happiness. That night, I was too secure to fear Macy. The next day, Elizabeth, my friend, would become my sister. Henry was hours from becoming my brother. My life had been handed back to me. I squirmed, knowing it would stir Edward. He nuzzled my neck and mumbled something that could have been, "Can't sleep?"

No, Edward, I thought, *I'm too happy.*

DON'T MISS THE THRILLING CONCLUSION

— of the —

PRICE *of* PRIVILEGE

series

Available spring 2015

IN BOOKSTORES AND ONLINE

ACKNOWLEDGMENTS

I am so grateful for the lovely souls who participated in the making of this book.

A special thanks to Elizabeth Ludwig, Michelle Griep, Ane Mulligan, and Gina Holmes. I couldn't ask for a more special and faithful group of ladies to walk this journey with.

Thank you to the Tyndale team—Stephanie Broene, for her managing skills; Caleb Sjogren, for his thought-provoking edits and labor to capture the vision; and Julie Dumler and her incredible marketing and PR team. I am honored to have worked alongside you.

I am so blessed to call Wanda Wright, Kelli Reed, Star Marcum, Joy Shind, Laine Barley, and Annie Masters friends. Your encouragement, feedback, and help during deadlines were such an incredible blessing.

Thank you especially, Anna and Howard Vosburgh. Your help and friendship are invaluable, especially the way you helped me avoid slang in the editing process as we bibbled and xertzed coffee.

Lastly, to my beautiful, shining daughter—thank you for sharing those precious pieces of your childhood with me during this creative process. You bless me more than you'll ever know.

DISCUSSION
QUESTIONS

❦

1. Throughout the story, Julia longs to win her father's love
   and approval, to no avail. Can you think of an example of
   someone (perhaps yourself) pursuing love and affection
   from those who don't reciprocate? In Julia's situation,
   how would you advise her to proceed?

2. We often attribute suffering to sin and blessings to God's
   favor, but 1 Peter speaks of Christians being called to suffer. To what degree is Julia's suffering a result of her own
   choices versus the sovereign will of God? What does she
   learn about God's will through her suffering? How ought
   we to respond to suffering in our own lives? Can you
   think of an example from your life where good has come
   from a difficult situation?

3. Like most young adults, Julia has different goals for her
   life than her father does. In today's era, how would you
   advise teens who are strongly opposed to their parents'
   will? In chapter 22, Julia reads some Scripture passages
   about children obeying their parents, and these verses
   give her pause. How would you explain passages like
   these? (For instance, see Ephesians 6:1.) How would
   you advise wives when they are opposed to their husbands' leadership? Compare and contrast the differences between these scenarios.

4. How do we decide when to step in and cover someone else's mistakes? How might this book have been different had Julia, from the start, refused to go along with her father's lie about her family history? Do you think Julia is right or wrong in her choice? Are Lord Pierson and Isaac right or wrong to intervene in Julia's life?

5. Lord Pierson consistently treats Julia according to her faults, while Isaac seeks to treat people as if they have become what they are meant to be. How do these contrasting perspectives impact the individuals involved? Does the way we treat and view people affect how they behave and what they become? Can you think of an example from your own experience?

6. Discuss the differences between Lord Pierson's relationship with Isaac and his relationship with Julia. How much can be attributed to Victorian-era views of men and women, and how much is a reflection of Pierson's own personality and choices?

7. A theme that runs through the Price of Privilege trilogy is Julia's self-determination—discovering what choices and actions are truly available to her. At one point near the end of this book, after surrendering her life to God, Julia wrestles with whether partnering with Forrester indicates a lack of trust in God's sovereignty. How does surrendering to God's will differ from passively relinquishing all responsibility? When should we act, and when should we wait on God? How can we tell which is appropriate in a situation? What are some of the hardest things about surrendering to God?

8. What do you think the future holds for Julia, Edward, Lord Pierson, Isaac, and Macy in the final book of the trilogy? What do you hope will happen? What do you fear will happen?

ABOUT THE AUTHOR

JESSICA DOTTA has always been fascinated by the intricacies of society that existed in England during the Regency and Victorian eras. Her passion for British literature fueled her desire to write in a style that blends the humor of Jane Austen and the dark drama of a Brontë sister. She lives in the Nashville area with her family and works as a freelance media consultant and publicist.

Jessica is always happy to accept tea invitations from book clubs, especially when they serve Earl Grey and scones.

Visit Jessica's website at www.jessicadotta.com.